PRAISE FOR THE CALENDAR GIRL

*"January Calendar Girl was sexy, funny, entertaining
and just an overall great book."*
~Abibliophobia Anonymous Book Reviews Blog

*"Damn Audrey did it again! Made me smile, made me
laugh & made me cry with her beautiful words!
I am in love with these books."*
~Hooks & Books Book Blog

*"I have a new addiction. I count down the days until
the next Audrey Carlan's Calendar Girl book releases
as soon as I am finished with the current one. I am
loving the journey that Mia is on. It's seductive and
powerful - captivating."*
~Maine Book Mama Book Blog

CALENDAR GIRL
VOLUME ONE

Paperback ISBN: 978-1-943893-03-4
PRINTED IN THE UNITED STATES OF AMERICA

DEDICATIONS

January

Ginelle Blanch

You have been with me since the very beginning…
Your beta reads have saved me a hundred times over.
Thank you for believing in me, my stories,
and loving them as I love you and all your pieces.
Namaste my friend.

February

Jeananna Goodall

One year ago, I released my first novel.
Since the first one, you've been my cheerleader,
beta reader, and number one fan.
Now, I'm honored to call you my friend.
You love my characters as if they were your own,
and keep me connected to them emotionally.
You have many gifts and talents,
I'm so grateful you share them with me.
Love and light.

March

Heather White

Mia is in Chicago because of you.
You too left the familiar and went on a journey.
This month's book shows how amazing taking risks can be.
Sometimes they are life changing, life altering even.
More often than not, they are worth it.
You are beautiful and I adore your presence in my life.
BESOS my lovely.

TABLE OF CONTENTS

January

CALENDAR GIRL

AUDREY CARLAN

WATERHOUSE
PRESS

CHAPTER ONE

True love doesn't exist. For years I thought it did. As a matter of fact, I thought I'd found it. Four times to be exact. Let's see, there was:

Taylor. My high-school sweetheart. We were together all through high school. He was an all-star baseball player. Best the school had ever seen. Big, more muscles than brains, and a winky the size of a circus peanut. Probably because of all the steroids he was taking behind my back. He dumped me graduation night. Ran off with my virginity and the head cheerleader. I heard he was a college dropout working as a mechanic in some no-name town with two kids and a wife that no longer cheers for him.

Then there was the teacher's assistant from my first psychology class in the Las Vegas Community College. Maxwell was his name. I thought that young boy walked on water. Turns out, he walked all over my heart by screwing a girl from every class he TA'd for. In his case, the TA stood for Tits and Ass, and he made sure he had plenty of it. That's okay. He ended up getting two of the girls pregnant at the same time, then was kicked out of the college for misconduct. At nineteen, he already had two different baby mamas hounding him for child support. There was something ultimately poetic about that. Thank God I always required he wrap it before he stuck it in me.

In my twentieth year, I took a break. Spent all year

waiting tables at the MGM Grand on the Las Vegas Strip. That's where I met lucky number three, Benny. Only I wasn't lucky and neither was he. He was a card counter. At the time, he said he was in sales, worked the casinos, and loved to play poker. We had a whirlwind romance, which wasn't all that romantic. I think I spent most of the time drunk and underneath him, but alas, I believed he loved me. He told me all the time. For two months we drank; we swam in the hotel pool, and fucked all night in one of the rooms I was able to score from my buddy in housekeeping. I served him and his friends free drinks at the bar, and he'd give me a room key most nights. It worked. Until it didn't. Benny got caught counting cards and disappeared. For the first year of his disappearance, I was frantic. Then I found out he'd been beaten to within an inch of his life. He spent time in the hospital and skipped out of town, ditching me completely without even a word.

The last mistake was the one you could say was the straw that broke the camel's back. The same reason I was certain true love is something crafted by greeting card companies and people who write romance novels and romantic comedies. Blaine was his name, but it should have been Lucifer. He was a smooth-talking business man. I use the term businessman loosely. In actuality, he was a loan shark. The same loan shark that loaned my dad more money than he could possibly ever pay back. First he turned on me, then he turned on him. Back then I thought our love was the stuff of fairytales. Blaine promised me the world and delivered me hell on earth.

"That's why I think you should just take this job from your auntie and call it a day." My best friend, Ginelle, smacked her gum loudly into the receiver. I pulled the phone away from my ear. "It's really the only way, Mia. How else are you going to get your dad out of this bind with Blaine and his goons?"

I sucked down the crisp water as the California sun split the drops into shards of speckled light across the rippled bottle. "I don't know what to do, Gin. I don't have that kind of money lying around. I don't have any money lying around." I sighed, and it sounded loud and overly dramatic even to my own ears.

"Look, you've always been in love with love—"

"Not anymore!" I reminded my lifelong best friend.

Through the phone, I could hear the noise of Vegas. People thought the desert was a quiet place. Not on the Strip. Slot machines tinkled and bells rang in a monotonous drone no matter where you were. You really couldn't escape it. "I know, I know." She shuffled the phone making it crackle in my ear. "But you like sex, right?"

"I'm not like Barbie, Gin. Math isn't hard. Please don't ask me stupid questions. I'm dying here." Or rather, if I didn't find a way to come up with one million dollars, my father would be the one dying.

Ginelle groaned and smacked her gum. "I mean, if you take the job as an escort, all you have to do is look pretty and fuck a lot, right? You haven't been laid in months. Might as well enjoy the ride, eh?"

Leave it to Ginelle to find a way to make being a highly paid call girl sound like a dream job. "This is not *Pretty Woman*, and I am no Julia Roberts."

I made my way over to my bike, a Suzuki GSXR 600, which I simply referred to as Suzi. She was the only thing of value I owned. Slinging a leg over the seat, I situated my phone and put it on speaker. I pulled the heavy weight of my long black tresses into three chunks and deftly braided them into one thick rope. "Look, I know you mean well, and I honestly don't know what I'm going to do. I'm not a whore. At least, I don't want to be a whore." The mere thought sent rivers of dread barreling through my chest. "But I've got to figure something out. Make some serious cash and fast."

"Yeah, I hear ya. Let me know how the meeting with Exquisite Escorts goes. Call me tonight if you can. Shit, I'm going to be late for rehearsal, and I still have to get dressed." Her voice turned labored, and I could picture her running through the casino to beat-feet it to work, cell phone plastered to her ear, not giving a shit who watched her or thought she was a lunatic. That's what made her so special. She told it like it was…always. Just like me.

Ginelle worked for Dainty Dolls Burlesque Show in Vegas. Like the name, my best friend was short and sweet and knew exactly how to best shake her ass. Men from around the world came to watch the risqué show on the Strip. Still, she didn't make enough to bail me or my old man out, not that I'd ever ask.

"Okay, love ya, bitch," I said sweetly as I shoved my braid into the neck of my leather jacket so it fell down between my shoulder blades.

"Love ya more, skank."

I turned the key on my bike, revved it up, and pushed on my helmet. Slipping the phone into my inside coat pocket, I hit the gas and sped off towards a future I didn't want, but one I had no way to avoid.

★ ★ ★ ★

"Mia! My sweet baby girl," said my aunt as she wrapped her bone-thin arms around me, crushing me to her chest. She was strong for such a slight woman. Her black hair was pinned up into an elegant French twist. She had on a white blouse that was soft as silk, probably because it was silk. It was tucked into a fierce black leather pencil skirt, paired with sky-high stilettos that sported that red sole I'd heard so much about when randomly flipping through the latest Vogue. She looked beautiful. More than that, she looked *expensive*.

"Aunt Millie, it's so good to see you," I started to say when two fingers with long nails capped in blood red nail polish shushed me.

She tsked her tongue, "Ah ah, here you will call me Ms. Milan." I rolled my eyes for dramatic effect. She narrowed hers in return. "Doll-face, first off, don't roll your eyes. It's rude and unladylike." Her lips pinched into a tight line. "Second of all..." She walked around my form assessing me as if I was a piece of art, a statue. Something cold and impenetrable. Maybe I was. In her hand, she held a black lace fan that she opened and closed then flicked against her open palm during her perusal. "...never call me Millie. That woman is long gone, died when the first man I ever trusted fried up my heart and fed it to his dogs." Such a vile image, but Aunt Millie was nothing if not honest.

"Chin up." She smacked the underside of my chin forcing an immediate adjustment. Then she did the same to the bare patch of sensitive skin at the base of my spine where my tight concert t-shirt didn't quite meet the painted-on jeans I adored. Instantly, I straightened my spine, thrusting my chest out. Her red-lipped smile widened showing perfectly bleached, straight teeth. The teeth were the nicest money could buy and a regular expense for the rich girls here in Los Angeles. I couldn't spit five feet without hitting someone who sees their dentist more than is medically necessary, but just barely less than they see their dermatologist for their monthly Botox injections. Aunt Millie was obviously a regular paying customer at veneers-R-us. Still, as she kissed the edge of fifty, she definitely had it going on.

"Well, you're definitely gorgeous. More so once we get you into something presentable and take your test shots." Her face twitched into a grimace as she took in my very biker-on-the-go threads.

I stepped back and banged into a leather chair not far behind me. "I haven't agreed to anything."

Millie's eyes narrowed into a point. "Did you not say that you needed a lot of money and fast? Something about my no good brother-in-law being in the hospital? In trouble?" She sat down slowly, crossed her legs, and laid both arms delicately on the white leather arms of the chair. Aunt Millie never liked my father. Which was unfortunate because he did the best he could as a single dad, especially when her sister, my mother, abandoned her two daughters. I was ten years old at the time. Madison was five and, to this day, doesn't have even one tiny memory of our mother to hold onto to.

I bit my lip and looked into her pale green eyes. We looked so much alike. Aside from all the little nips and tucks she'd had, it was like looking into a mirror twenty-five years from now. Her eyes were the same light green, almost yellow, that I'd had people rave about my entire life. Green amethyst they'd say. Like looking into a rare green diamond. Our hair was exactly the same shade of jet black, so much so, that when the light hit it, you'd swear it was midnight blue.

Adjusting my shoulders against the uncomfortable chair, I took a breath. "Yeah, Dad's got himself in big this time with Blaine." Millie closed her eyes and shook her head. I bit my lip, the memory of my father pale and gaunt, bruises covering every inch of his body as he lay lifeless in the hospital. "He's in a coma right now. Four weeks ago they beat him pretty bad. He still hasn't woken up. The doctors think it could be the trauma in his brain, but we won't know for a while. A lot of his bones were broken. He's still in a body cast," I finished.

"Jesus Christ. Savages," she whispered and slid a hand up to her hair sweeping back a strand around her ear silently composing herself. I'd seen her do this before. Millie was a master manipulator and could control her emotions better than anyone I'd ever known. I coveted that talent. Needed it.

"Yeah. And last week when I was holding vigil at Dad's bed, one of Blaine's goons came to see me. Said, this was it for Dad. If they didn't get their money *with* interest, they were going to kill him. Then they'd come after me and Maddy for the money. They called it "survivor's debt." Whatever that is. Either way, I have to come up with a million dollars and fast."

Aunt Millie pinched her lips together and flicked her first nail against her thumb over and over again. The incessant ticking almost made me lose my shit. How could she be so calm, so callous? A man's life, my life, and the life of my baby sister hung in the balance. She didn't care for Dad, but she'd always had a soft spot for me and my sister.

Millie's eyes shot to mine, fierce and sparkling with an unknown excitement. "It can be done, in a year. Do you think they'd give you a year if you made payments?" Her eyebrow came into a point as she focused her full attention on me.

The hairs on my arms started to rise, and I jutted my shoulders back in defense. I shook my head. "I don't know. I'm sure Blaine wants his money, and since we had a thing a while ago, I could probably plead. That sick, sadistic fucker always liked me down on my knees begging."

"Keep your sexual escapades to yourself, doll-face," she grinned wickedly. "Looks like we'll just have to put you to work right away. Top dollar accounts only. We need to move up everything. I'm going to need you here first thing tomorrow morning for the photo shoot. It will be an all-day event. We'll shoot stills, some video, etc. I'll have my guys get them up on the secure site by the following day."

It was all happening so fast. The words *"It can be done"* rang through my ears like a life line, a raft out in open water surrounded by sharks, but still afloat.

"But do I have to sleep with them? I mean I know there's different kinds of escorts." I closed my eyes waiting until I felt something warm clasp my hand. She had covered both of mine with hers.

"Doll-face, you don't have to do anything you don't want to do. But in order to make that kind of money, you ought to consider it. My clients and I have an unwritten agreement, if you will. My girls sleep with them, and they add twenty percent to their fee. That twenty percent is left in cash, in an envelope in my girl's room. None of that is exchanged with me or my service, as prostitution is illegal in California." Millie touched her chin with her index finger. "But my girls should get more for the convenience, don't you think?" She winked. I nodded lamely, not knowing what to think but going along with it anyway.

"I'm going to book you by the month. It's the only way to make a six figure paycheck each month." Her pale green eyes looked bright. So much so that I almost believed this could be easy if I just had an open mind. "You'll be flown wherever the man is, and be whatever he needs for that month. However, I do not sell sex. If you sleep with them, it's because you want to, although when you see some of the men I have on a waiting list, you'll think twice about not hopping into the sack, not to mention the extra payout." She grinned and then stood. She walked around her glass desk, sat down, then turned to her computer silently dismissing me. I felt stuck to the leather seat incapable of moving. Thoughts of how the hell I'd make this work swirled like vicious vultures through my mind, hunting and pecking at my morals one by one as if they were living prey available for the taking.

"I'll do it," I heard myself whisper.

"Of course you will." She looked at me over her computer. Her lips turned into a crooked grin. "You haven't any other option if you want to save your father."

★ ★ ★ ★

The next day was a whirlwind of activity. I felt like Sandra Bullock's character in *Miss Congeniality*. I'd been prodded at, scrubbed, plucked, and waxed to within an inch of my life. I felt like a human pin cushion and almost ended up punching out the beauty consultant Millie hired to "fix" me. Her words, not mine. I couldn't deny the proof was in the pudding. When I looked in the mirror, I barely recognized the woman staring back. My long black hair was shinier than ever, falling into perfect waves down my back and over my shoulders. Everywhere the light touched my skin, a shimmer effect twinkled back. The normal sun-kissed tanned look that I'd worked on for weeks in the California sun now shone like a fine honey, really highlighting all of my best features. The dress she had me in was lavender, comfortable and slinky. Fitting perfectly along each rounded curve and toned edge giving it the desired effect. Sexy and sleek. I looked like a dark angel as the photographer set me on a cold white marble bench. He moved me this way and that, and before long, I actually got the hang of pouting prettily and staring blankly off into the distance devoid of emotion. That's what I had to be now. Emotionless.

Once we were finished, and I'd redressed into my street clothes, which always consisted of jeans and a tight tee, I made my way back to Millie, or *Ms. Milan's*, office.

"Doll-face, these shots are magnificent! I always knew you'd be perfect for modeling." She clicked at her computer as I walked around and glanced at what she was seeing. All the air left my lungs as I took in the image of myself the photographer had taken.

"Amazing." I lost my words for a moment. "I can't believe that's me." I shook my head as one image after another loaded up to the Exquisite Escorts website. If I didn't know for a fact that was me, I'd never believe it.

A slow smile slipped across my aunt's lips. "You're very

beautiful." Her light-eyed gaze caught mine. "You look so much like…"

"Whatever." I shook my head and leaned a hip on her glass desk not wanting to hear how much she thought I looked like mother. "What next?" I asked while crossing my arms over my chest feeling a strange desire to protect myself against whatever was going to happen next.

She leaned back into her black leather chair, her eyes twinkling. "Want to see your first assignment?"

A slow sense of dread crept up my spine, but I stiffened my shoulders and looked at her with a bland expression. "Game on."

Millie chuckled then clicked a few times into her internet browser bringing up an image of one of the most excruciatingly gorgeous men I'd ever seen. There was nothing that could take away from this man's stunning good looks. Even in the overtly corporate headshot his dirty blond hair, green eyes, and chiseled jaw were something to write home about. His hair was long, layered, and had that messy, yet perfectly styled, appearance that was all the rage right now. Something didn't add up. The man couldn't be more than thirty. Plus, he was not the type of guy who would need to hire a date. He looked like the type of man women fell all over themselves and became brainless husks of lust for.

"I don't get it. Why would he"—I pointed at the smiling good looking man in the picture—"need a date?"

My aunt leaned back, clasped her hands over her lap and smiled. "He chose you."

I know I must have looked confused because she hurriedly continued. "I personally sent the first few test shots over to him and his mother. I work a lot with his mother. Anyway, he agreed to the match. He'll send a car for you tomorrow morning. He's in the area, but you still have to stay at his residence for the next twenty-four days."

It's possible my head had been hit by an imaginary baseball bat it shot back so fast. "Twenty-four days! Are you insane? How the hell am I going to take jobs or show up for auditions?" My acting career wasn't much, but I did have a low-rent agent that sent me out on a few jobs here and there. And there was the restaurant I worked at in the evening.

Millie looked at me as if I had dared to grow a second head. Her lips compressed into a thin line, and her nose crunched up unattractively. "Mia, you will quit all your jobs for at least a year. You are now a paid employee of Exquisite Escorts. Your assignments will run from one to twenty-four days depending on the client's needs. Since *you* need to make a lot of cash in a short amount of time, you need to take the bigger jobs. After the twenty-four days, you will have the remaining days in the month at home to relax, recoup, and repair any beauty needs. At the turn of each month on the calendar, you will be reassigned a new date."

"I can't believe this!" I started pacing her office, suddenly feeling like a caged animal needing to break free. It just dawned on me that my life as I knew it was over. There was no more going out on normal dates—not that I'd had any recently. No more auditions, making my fledgling acting career a distant memory, and there would be little to no time to see Dad, Maddy, or Ginelle.

"Believe it little girl. This is not a joke. What your father, what your ex-boyfriend is doing has made this decision. You're lucky I'm even making room for you. Don't be an ingrate. Now sit down and shut up!" Her voice was completely devoid of its usual warmth having morphed into the cold, formal tone of a determined businesswoman.

"I'm sorry." She was trying to help me, but this was all so...sudden. Unbelievable. I slumped into the chair in front of her desk and let my head fall into my hands. Shaking it repeatedly did not change the outcome. I was now a girl for hire. Each month I'd be assigned a new man, and if I slept with them, I'd make twenty percent more in cash.

I shook my head and laughed. The kind that proved I was bat-shit crazy. I leaned my head back onto the cool leather and looked up at the white ceiling. After a moment, a creeping resolve calmed me. This is what I had to do. So I let a sexy guy take me to boring business dinners and whatever else he had in mind. I didn't have to sleep with them and, most importantly, there was no way I would fall in love. A new man each month wasn't enough time to fall head over heels like I had in the past. Who says I have to give up my acting career? What better way to perfect my acting skill than by being whatever these men wanted me to be? Then, after the month was up, I'd be someone else and my dad would be safe. As long as I could get Blaine to agree to monthly payments, this could work.

With a deep breath I stood and put out my hand to my aunt. Her smile was wicked, yet still sexy. She was very good at her job. "Alright, *Ms. Milan*," I emphasized her fake name so she'd understand my commitment. "Looks like I'm your new Calendar Girl."

CHAPTER TWO

Weston Charles Channing, III. I stared at the name wondering why anyone would want to have a Roman numeral behind their name. I'd just bet he was a pretentious rich boy whose mommy didn't want to be embarrassed by the Hollywood harlots he trotted to posh events. At least, in my head that's the only possible reason that worked as to why someone so devastatingly handsome would need to hire an escort. Shuffling through the pages, I finally found the list of *rules* "Ms. Milan" sent home with me last night.

1. *Always look your best.* *Never let the client see you unprepared. Makeup should be done, hair styled, nails polished, and clothes unwrinkled at all times. The client will provide you with a wardrobe of their choosing. Your sizes and preferences have been given to their personal stylist.*

I rolled my eyes and looked longingly at the fat stack of jeans I had in my closet organizer. A personal stylist? Jeez, these people had far too much money. How hard was it to pick out your own clothes? My sizes had been sent over? Awesome. Now the guy knows I had a few pounds to lose. Being five nine gave me the advantage of looking thinner than I was, but I knew my aunt preferred her girls around a size zero. Whereas, I was a curvy size eight, sometimes even a ten, if I was being honest. Probably considered plus size in the modeling world.

He picked you. I reminded myself while filling a small

backpack full of essentials. Lotion, makeup, perfume, my Kindle, a small bag of my favorite jewelry. There wasn't anything of value, but they were mine and, at the very least, I needed to be *me* in some small way. I also grabbed a brand new journal and my personalized stationary. Figured since this was a yearlong experience, might as well try to learn something from it. Hell, maybe I could even write it into my own movie one day.

Tossing the bag into my overstuffed chair in the studio apartment I rented for cheap, I looked at the rest of the list.

2. Smile constantly. *Never appear to be angry, sad, or emotional in any way. Men don't hire women so they can deal with your emotional problems. They hire a woman so they don't have to.*

Emotionless. Way ahead on that one. I'd given myself a strong talking to after meeting with Millie and agreeing to the job.

3. Don't speak unless spoken to. *You are there to be pretty and charming when called for. Discuss the needs with the client before any social or professional events so you are in agreement on your position.*

What are we? Five? Be a Barbie doll. Got it. That's easy enough.

4. Make yourself available at all times. *If the client wants to stay in, you will stay in with them. Be respectful, mind your manners, and follow the client's lead. If he is looking for companionship, offering to cuddle is acceptable. Sex is not required.*

She wants me to *cuddle* with the client when he wants to fuck? I laughed out loud. That's going to be an interesting transition. "Hey there fella, wanna cuddle with me?" A snicker left my lips as I continued to read.

5. Sex with clients is not included in the contract.

If you choose to offer sexual companionship, that is of your choosing and is not the responsibility of Exquisite Escorts. We do, however, require all of our escorts to be on some form of birth control that can be proven at any given time. A blood test may be requested.

Where does she come up with this shit? I mean, really? Who would want to get pregnant by a man they've just met and didn't love? Oh yeah, rich men, dumb women. A cocktail for disaster. Well, I'm not one of those women. Once my dad is safe and his debt paid off, it's back to my life. Whatever that is.

Glancing at the clock I realized it was time to go. Even though Millie wanted me to arrive in one of her limos, I assured her I'd meet the client. That was my one term. If this first go around worked out, then I'd be more willing to have her clients pick me up. For now, I was leery as hell and would take my bike, even though I promised her I'd take a cab. Like she'd find out anyway.

Donning my sexiest black jeans and a black tight mesh top, I added my cropped leather jacket and tall suede knee-high boots. I knew Millie would kill me if she saw this getup, but I needed the element of surprise to check out this Weston Charles Channing, the *third*, before I willingly agreed to be his companion for the next four weeks.

Finally the text arrived. It was from an unknown number.

To: Mia Saunders
From: Unknown Number
Looking forward to meeting you. El Matador Beach. Find the concrete stairway down to the beach. I'll see you soon.

Cryptic. He's having me meet him at the beach at eight in the morning? Quickly, I pick up my iPhone and ask Siri for directions, noting it's seven now. The computer-automated voice brought up the beach and showed it was six miles northwest of Malibu. Must be close to his home because it was a solid hour on my bike to the beach from my studio apartment in downtown Los Angeles. My apartment wasn't much, just a few hundred square feet of space where the futon I bought for fifty bucks in a yard sale doubled as my couch and bed, but it's what I could afford. Looking around, I noted that I'd made it as homey as I could. The walls were a soft beige, and though the furniture was hodgepodge and mismatched, it somehow worked.

It's the first place I could ever call my own. And I had to leave it. I grabbed the bottle of water on the counter and poured its remains into the one potted bamboo plant I had on the tiny kitchen counter. It was a sad attempt at being green, but it was supposed to be a lucky plant. Hopefully, the plant would survive. As I walked out the door, backpack slung over my shoulder and helmet in hand, I realized just how much the plant and I had in common. I sure hoped I survived this absence too.

★ ★ ★ ★

Loose gravel and rocks shot across the earth as Suzi, skidded to a stop before hitting the metal girder that ended just before a rocky cliff. The concrete staircase I'd been searching up and down the beach for was clearly visible from this parking area. This section of the beach was small and seemed secluded. Only one car sat in the parking lot on the chilly

Monday morning. Probably because normal people were at work at eight a.m. on a weekday. I didn't know what to think about meeting my date here, but I wasn't altogether upset about it. The view was incredible, the beach breathtaking. The blue waves rushed against the beach in white clouds that burst into nothing as the waves hit the sand. This was actually one of the few times I'd been to the beach since I moved here six months ago. Most of my time has been spent trying to break into the acting world. The location didn't matter. I just needed to get the hell out of the desert. The ocean reminded me of the opposite of the dry Vegas heat and was comforting in its own way because of the contrast.

A lone figure was out in the water surfing. I watched the person take on each wave like a professional, dipping the long yellow board to match the waves. I scanned the beach but didn't see anyone else. No other cars dotted the parking lot aside from the one Jeep and my bike. *Maybe he wasn't here yet?*

I watched the surfer for a few more moments as he rode a wave all the way to the edge of the sand. He hopped off as if the board delicately drove him to the shore. Must have been surfing for a long time with that level of balance and strength. Maybe he even instructed here at this beach, although I didn't see a building of any kind on the bare expanse of land. The man shook his hair and detached a strap connected to the board from his ankle. I couldn't see his features from this distance. As if in slow motion, the surfer looked over in my direction. He couldn't see me because I was still wearing my helmet. I flipped up the visor to get a better look and watched as he unzipped his wetsuit and revealed a massive amount of very wet, thick, tanned muscles. He pulled out each arm and let the wetsuit hang from his waist as he lifted his board in one arm and made his way up the beach at a trot.

In complete and utter fascination, I watched his body move up the landscape. The surfer was a feast for the eyes. Brought a whole new meaning to the phrase "eye candy." He continued to come closer, each square pec and toned ab more visible as he got closer. The sexy swath of skin that dipped in making a delectable V had dots of sand and ocean water mingling together. Made me wonder what it would taste like. Salty from the ocean with hints of his natural flavor.

Warmth filled my body as he made his way up the stairs to the landing. My ears started to pound and it felt as if the sound of the ocean was making a roaring, wobbling noise inside the confined space of my helmet. It was like when you have all the windows in a car closed and someone opens one. You are instantly flooded with that warped sound that permeates your ear like a physical thing, pounding against your eardrum.

Slowly, I tugged my helmet off, flung my neck back allowing my hair to whip and tumble out, free from the tight confines. I sucked in a deep breath as the man I'd been waiting for stopped at the top of the steps and stared. His stare was...intense, lustful. Fat drops of water from his hair dripped onto his broad shoulders and down over a chest that could have been chiseled by the gods.

He eyed me from my boots up my legs to my chest before finally meeting my gaze. "How pleasantly unexpected," he grinned.

"Yeah, unexpected." I licked suddenly dry lips and bit

down. He moved gracefully as he walked over to the grey 4 x 4 Jeep Wrangler. It wasn't an expensive car though it looked to be in good enough condition. It didn't have a top, which, I imagined, was why the owner could toss a giant surfboard in the back without any trouble. *Were those things light?* I didn't think so, but he made it look like it weighed nothing. The muscles in his arms tensed and tugged as he positioned the board just so, sending a flurry of excitement tingling along my pores.

"You're Mia?" he asked as I dismounted the bike and strode over, making sure to give an extra sway to my hips as I did. His eyes seemed to twinkle in appreciation as he caressed my form with his gaze.

"That's me. You Weston Charles Channing, the Third?" I held up three fingers and cocked a hand on one hip.

He chuckled and leaned against the side of his Jeep giving me an even better view of his bare chest. Damn, he was beautiful. His green eyes were dark when they met mine. "Third," he mimicked my gesture. "My friends call me Wes," he said causally.

"Am I your friend?" I said coyly.

"One can only hope, Ms. Mia." He winked then turned and rustled around in the back of his Jeep. He pulled out a white t-shirt and quickly pulled it over his head covering that beautiful body. I almost thanked him for the distraction. Immediately dumb Barbie left the building and intelligent Mia made her appearance once more. "You ready to go?"

"Your dollar, you say where and when," I offered.

Wes licked his lips, looked me over again, smiled and shook his head. "I'd offer you a ride, but it looks like you've got one."

"That I do. I'll follow you."

★ ★ ★ ★

By the time we made it back to his home in Malibu, my libido was back in check though I didn't think it would take much for me to get worked up again. The gates of his home opened, and I followed him up a small winding driveway until he stopped in front of a home that looked more like something you'd see in the mountains. It wasn't quite a log cabin, but the house was made from giant stones intermingled with wood. Lush greenery surrounded it in all directions making it feel like it was nestled into a secret garden hideaway.

I pulled my helmet off and held onto my backpack while following him up the stone steps. The door wasn't even locked when he opened it. I guess if you lived in Malibu and had high gates with fencing surrounding your property, you didn't worry too much about security. Perhaps he had security somewhere.

We walked into a giant cavernous room with dark wooden exposed beams meeting at the center. The floors were a rich cherry wood and spanned the entire palatial space. Area rugs in dark rustic colors dotted the floors alongside deep burgundy plush couches that look puffy enough to run and leap into. The room was bright and airy, surrounded by windows. The entertainment center was enormous and took up an entire fifty foot wall. Scattered in all the shelves and cubby holes were books and a wide array of DVDs. Tapestries in vibrant hues filled the walls. Plants and art were everywhere the eye could see. It's nothing like

I expected from a man in his late twenties or early thirties. I made a mental note to find out his age at some point along with what he did for a living. You had to be pretty smart or independently wealthy to own such digs.

"This place is incredible," I said and walked over to the open French doors stepping onto the wooden balcony with a wrought iron railing. The view was of the rolling mountains and open vistas that seemed to go on with no end until the horizon. Living in downtown Los Angeles didn't give me a lot of opportunity to appreciate Southern California the way one would looking out that view.

Wes smiled and clasped my hand. His was warm and soft. Comfortable. "Come here. I'll show you what drew me to this place." He tugged me along to follow the balcony around to the other side of the large home.

The sight stole my breath when we finally made it to the other side of the wraparound porch. "Oh, my God," I whispered in complete awe. His hand tightened on mine, sending a bolt of electricity to tingle at the back of my neck. In front of me was an unobstructed view of the Pacific Ocean. It spanned the entire half of the house. Wes leaned closer to me and whispered in my ear as he pointed over to a sandy area nestled against a rocky terrain.

"That's El Matador Beach," he said close enough for me to feel his breath kiss the skin of my cheek. I could almost see where he was surfing from here.

"It's..." I lost the words.

"Amazing. I know," he said, but not in a smug way. No, he seemed to take in the view with his own sense of wonder, which surprised me. A man who lives here, sees this every day and is still taken by the gift before him. I realized

AUDREY CARLAN

then that I might have been remiss in thinking he was a young, hotshot, rich kid. His eyes reflected something older, well beyond his years. He gripped my hand and pulled me toward the house. "Let me show you to your room."

I followed him through the several thousand square foot home. Room after room flew by before I could catch much of a glimpse. I thought it odd that he continued to hold my hand, but I didn't say anything for fear he'd stop. It was nice feeling the warm, large hand in mine. Made me feel safe and protected in a way I hadn't experienced in years.

Wes led me to a set of double doors. He finally dropped my hand and opened both doors at once. "This will be your home for the next twenty-four days," he smiled as I entered.

The room was white on white. Everything. The furniture, the bedding, even the artwork was varying shades of white with only the barest hints of color. It was such a dramatic contrast to the rich, thick colors of the living room. Without realizing it, I frowned.

"You don't like it?" His hands fell down to his sides. He moved over and opened another set of double doors. Within were enough clothes to choke a horse, all in wild arrays of colors, textures, and fabrics. Now this was more like it. I could move into the closet. It certainly looked big enough. I ran my fingers over the hanging clothes, all with the tags still dangling from them.

"It's beautiful, thank you. So why don't you tell me a little bit about why I'm here," I asked as I exited the closet and sat on the bed. Wes was a tall, large man but not beefy. He was over six feet and trim. Had the body of a strong swimmer who definitely spent some serious time in the gym lifting weights.

He took a breath and brought his hand up to his chin resting his elbow on the arm of the chair. "My mother," he said, as if that explained all the secrets of the universe. I crooked an eyebrow, and he shook his head. "I have these events I need to attend professionally and personally over the next few weeks. Having a woman on my arm would help ward off the socialites and gold-diggers that often vie for my attention, preventing me from getting the networking I need to do completed."

"So you need a buffer to ward off the vultures?" I chuckled, crossed my legs then pulled off one long boot, stretched out my other leg and repeated the process. Wes nodded then watched with rapt attention as I pointed and wiggled my socked toes. I looked down and realized why he was holding his hand over his mouth, a veiled attempt to hold back his laughter.

I had on my Christmas socks under my boots. Tall to the knee green and red stripped socks stared back at me proving I'd just committed fashion suicide. Not to mention, I was certain I'd just broken one of Millie's escort rules by wearing the hideously ugly socks. I bit my lip and chanced a glance at Wes, but he just continued to smile the cat-that-ate-the-canary type grin.

Rolling my eyes, I huffed, "I got ready in the dark."

"Obviously," he laughed. "I think it's cute."

"Cute? That's like the kiss of death." I narrowed my eyes at him. "You think I'm cute? Well, no refunds, buddy. You said yourself, I'm here for twenty-four days. No take-backs!" I stood and put my hands on my hips.

He leaned back and crossed his bare feet at the ankle. Oh, I hadn't noticed his feet before. They were long, lean and perfectly groomed. Tiny bits of sand stuck to the tops of the upper arch at the top of his foot. That libido I'd kicked to the curb and stuck in a hidey-hole peeked out and was paying close attention to the finer details of the man before me. It wasn't fair. Even his feet were sexy.

"Relax, Ms. Mia. I said your socks were cute, not you. You are quite possibly one of the most devastatingly beautiful women I've ever had the pleasure of laying my eyes on. I can't wait to see you naked." His lips twitched into a sultry grin, and his eyes smoldered.

I took a slow breath and stared as he stood up. Our gazes held, and it seemed like minutes passed by as we catalogued the others' nuances. "Um, well, I'm glad you think I'm pretty enough to be here. Like I said, you've got me for the month and…wait…" Something he said just clicked. "Excuse me? You can't wait to see me naked?" The words left my lips in a loose jumble. "That's not included in the contract…"

"Oh, I'm well aware of what's in the contract," Wes said as he came over to me, slid a hand around my waist and plastered me against his body. I gasped as the steely ridge of a very large erection pressed into my belly. His gaze scanned my face, and he leaned closer, so close I could feel his breath puff against my heated lips. "If I get you naked, it will not be because I'm paying for it." Wes's lips touched the skin just behind my ear where he placed a gentle, whisper-light kiss. I stayed perfectly still, pleasure rocketing through every limb, each nerve focused, waiting for his next touch. The rough edge of his stubbly chin slid along my smooth one sending shivers down my spine and a wave of heat to settle between my thighs. "You'll drop your clothes for me when you're ready. I won't even have to ask," he whispered before pressing a small kiss to just the edge of my lips.

He pulled back, his green eyes swirling with restrained lust. "I have work to do in my office. Feel free to look around, sunbathe, use the pool. I'll need you ready and wearing a cocktail dress at five sharp. We have a business dinner to attend," and with one last squeeze to my hip, he turned and left. The skin of my hip still felt the phantom imprint of his touch.

"Damn," I said, lightheaded after holding my breath for so long. Once his lips touched down behind my ear, I'd lost the ability to breathe. "He's going to be trouble."

CHAPTER THREE

The pool was heated and refreshing. I used the time I had to work on my tan and get some exercise by way of laps in the pool. Weston, or "Wes" as he likes to be called, had not made an appearance. I imagined him behind one of the many closed doors I passed on my way to the patio.

While I was drip-drying, a petite, though quite round woman, dressed in a pair of khakis and a sweater holding a tray, entered the patio. Instantly, I reached for a towel that was not there and looked around. She smiled wide and walked over to a basket in the corner by the door, lifted the lid and pulled out a huge, multicolored beach towel. "Here you are, love," she said in a British accent handing me the towel. Her salt-and-pepper-colored hair and soft brown eyes reminded me of an older Mary Poppins.

"Hi, I'm Mia." I pulled the towel completely around my body hiding the miniscule red bikini I'd found in the wardrobe. There were several others, but they were all tiny, so I chose one at random.

'Mary Poppins' smiled and held out her small hand. "Ms. Croft. I keep the house in order, provide Mr. Channing with his meals, tidy up, and the lot." I nodded and wrung the excess water out of my hair and pulled it up into a ponytail. "I wanted to bring you a little nosh, introduce myself, and let you know that if you need anything, you can buzz me by pressing the *Aid* button on the mounted intercom in each room." She pointed to the panel of buttons on the wall outside. "I'll be sure to provide you with a daily schedule of yours and Mr. Channing's activities so you are prepared. How about I push it under your door in the mornings?"

I shrugged. Like her, I was a hired hand, only I was meant to look pretty and scare off rich girls. We all had our crosses to bear. "Whatever works. I'm easy."

Ms. Croft looked me up and down and then tilted her head. A smirk adorned her thin lips. "I'm getting the feeling you're anything but easy, poppet," she winked. "This should be interesting," she said vaguely before she turned on her heel and re-entered the house.

Whatever *that* meant. Scanning the awesome view one more time I thought, *this is going to be easy money*. Hot guy, I'm *not* going to fall in love with, a killer pad with a view, and enough new clothes to choke a horse. So far, seemed like a pretty killer gig. Through the open patio doors, I saw the clock hanging over the stove in the kitchen and noted I had an hour and half before Hot Surfer Rich Guy needed his new "companion" for my first day on the job.

I decided as with everything, I was going to knock his socks off, even if they weren't Christmas red and green.

★ ★ ★ ★

Mr. Channing arrived at my door with a brisk knock then strutted right in without waiting for an invitation. *Note to self: Don't get dressed out in the open, or you're liable to give the Lord of the Manor a peep show.* Though something tells me he wouldn't mind at all, if the way his eyes were passing over my form from top to bottom—not once, but twice—was any indication The view on this side of the room wasn't bad either. He was de-lish-ious in a finely tailored black suit. He had on a crisp white shirt with the collar open showing a sexy slash of male throat. He held up three ties as he took in my attire.

I was wearing a deep eggplant purple cocktail dress. It had beading at the halter neck, which flowed into two swaths of fabric over my breasts leaving the center open for maximum cleavage, then crossed over at the ribs, again with the jewels, leaving enticing cutouts at the dips in my waist. I'd never worn anything so sexy, elegant, or expensive. I felt like Elizabeth Taylor in one of her diamond commercials. The rest of the dress fell into an A-line ending demurely at the knee. Even though I was on the busty side—this dress left no room for a bra with its open back—it held the girls up nicely with the inside shaping. I looked and, better yet, *felt* beautiful for the first time in a long time.

"Wow," was all Wes said as he stood with a look of awe over his handsomely rugged face. He held out the three ties and presented them to me. "Which one?" he said on a swallow before clearing his throat. I grinned, loving every second of taking this wild card by surprise. I might be a bad ass biker babe but I knew I cleaned up well.

The ties were nice, and one did go better with my dress than the rest, but instead of taking the ties from him, I placed both my hands at his collar, pulled it out and laid it over the collar and lapels of his suit. "I like it without. You look hot." No reason not to be honest. He did look hot.

His lips crooked up into a too-hot-to-handle grin and I bit my lip, feeling the lace of my panties go damp. Shit, if he didn't stop, I was going to jump him. Like Ginelle so crudely reminded me this morning, it had been months since I'd felt a man's touch. And honestly, it was more like a year. I'd had it with men after Blaine and spent the year telling myself I could live the life of a nun as long as I had a vibrator and plenty of cookie dough at the ready. Faced with the man in front of me, I wasn't so sure celibacy was the smart decision. For right now, I was primed to take down Hot Surfer guy.

"Mother won't like that," he whispered before clasping my wrist and tugging me to him. I wobbled on the sickeningly high stiletto heels his personal shopper bought and tumbled into him, chest-to-chest. My hands landed on the hard wall of muscle that could still be felt through his suit and shirt.

He looked down at me as I looked up. "You always do what your mama says?" I challenged.

He laughed and his eyes went a beautiful shamrock green. I found I could stare into those leafy eyes for days on end and feel like I'd won a prize. "No, but it is Mother's event. I do like to be a good boy when it suits." He leaned in close and inhaled at the base of my neck. "Christ, you smell like sunshine and a cool breeze in the summer," he said dragging his lips along my chin. Shivers of excitement ran through me from the roots of my curled hair to the soles of my feet. "And you look beyond beautiful." He kissed the side of my lip again. No full lip contact. I almost harrumphed, but I figured it was part of his game, and he was good at it. The art of seduction was obviously something he enjoyed. At this moment in time, I was all for it.

"We better go," I warned.

Wes smiled and tugged on my hand turning and leading me out of the room. I barely had a moment to grab the matching handbag that had my phone, lipstick, and ID in it. As we reached the door to leave, Ms. Croft was standing there. She had a handful of pocket squares. She looked at my dress, picked the matching one and made a fuss over putting it into the breast pocket of his suit jacket.

"There," she smoothed her hands over his suit coat. "You look perfect, Sonny." Her eyes were bright and glistened as if she was preparing her own son for his senior prom. Weird. I declined to mention it. He put the ties into her capable hands.

"Thanks, Judi," He leaned forward and kissed her wrinkled cheek. He looked over to me, sized me up again and turned back to his maid-slash-cook-slash-housekeeper. Not really sure what she was. "The dress is perfect." He thanked her and led me out to the limo waiting out front.

Judi bought the clothes? Any further thoughts were obliterated, and my mouth dropped open at the size of the limo. It was long, stretched beyond anything I'd ever seen. I'd never been in a limo, but as we approached, Wes tilted his head to the side and looked at me with a funny smile. "You ever been in a limo?" he asked, clearly amused.

I straightened my shoulders and walked up to the limo as if I'd been in one a million times. "Of course." I pulled open the door. He put a hand over his mouth, clasping one arm at the elbow and laughed. I cringed, apparently not in on the joke.

"Then why are you trying to get in on the passenger side?" He gestured to the door I held open. I looked inside and saw the driver's wheel. When I adjusted my stance, there was a gentleman in what had to be a black chauffeur's uniform holding open the back door.

"I knew that. I was just going to ask the driver where we were headed." I sauntered over to the door, cheeks burning hot.

"Of course you were." He placed a hand low on my back and ushered me inside with a chuckle.

Once we were settled, he offered me a glass of champagne, which I readily accepted.

"Thank you."

He smiled and poured one for himself as well. We clinked glasses.

"What are we toasting to?" I asked.

"How about to being friends?" He grinned then set a warm hand high on my thigh, much higher than a 'friend' would. It felt good there. "Good friends." His eyes dropped to my mouth as I bit my bottom lip.

"Friends with benefits?" I inquired, lifting an eyebrow for maximum effect and crossing my legs. That hand of his went a few inches higher until it brushed along bare thigh.

His gaze focused on mine and made me feel warm, positively hot, under his heated look. "God, I hope so," he whispered and leaned closer.

To foil his plans and keep my sanity in check, I immediately lifted my champagne flute and placed it against my lips and took a hearty sip of the bubbly concoction.

Wes leaned back and groaned, adjusting his crotch— less than subtle. I giggled, and he shot a few daggers my way but ended with a head shake and a grin. Yeah, I was going to enjoy this game of cat and mouse. Although at the moment, I wasn't sure who was the cat and who was the mouse. In the end, I was having far too much fun to care.

We arrived at a swank mansion in the Malibu Hills not

far from where Wes lived. As we walked up the steps, I could see people milling about through the windows. Everyone was dressed to the nines and holding a drink. Most of the women in attendance seemed to be my age, which I found strange since the men were not.

"What do you do anyway?" I whispered as he led me to the bar. I realized when we walked in that I had very little information about what I was to do, besides keep the Hollywood harlots at bay.

"I write scripts," he said casually as we waited for the bartender to approach us. It seemed odd to have a full length bar in someone's house, but the room was huge, the size of a ballroom, so maybe it wasn't so strange. Chandeliers dotted the ceiling and a wall of windows led out into an open view of the ocean just like at Wes's house, only on a much grander scale. This person was über rich. Unlike Wes, who was just beaucoup rich.

He handed me another glass of champagne. "Like for plays?" I asked while scanning the area. Instantly, I spotted a pack of girls dolled up and ready to strike in the corner. They were focused on Wes, and had lusty dollar signs in their eyes.

"More like movies."

"Huh. Would I know any?" I turned to him and he smiled.

"Probably," he snickered and took a sip of something amber-colored in a cocktail tumbler. I could smell whiskey a mile away, and it didn't bring fond memories. I cringed and turned back to the vultures.

Wes put a hand on my bare shoulder, eyes narrowed and uncertain. "What's the matter?"

I took a deep breath and pressed down the frustration I had with my father and his drinking and the gambling habit that had gotten me into this mess in the first place. I shook my head. "Nothing."

He tipped up my chin and looked into my eyes. "It's not nothing. I won't ask again," he warned.

Nonchalantly I shrugged. "I hate the smell of whiskey; no biggie." Curving outward I loosened his hold. He set down the drink and gestured to the bartender.

"Changed my mind. Gin and tonic," he said and the man nodded.

"You didn't have to do that," I started, but he cut me off by lifting a hand to my cheek. He cupped it and swiped just his thumb against my bottom lip tenderly.

He held my lip, and I wanted so badly to press my tongue to the digit and steal a small taste. I didn't though, fearing what he'd think or do.

"I wanted to. Now, let's go introduce you to Mother."

With mammoth effort, I followed him, wanting nothing more than to rush out those double doors, down to the beach until I reached the ocean, where I'd promptly drown myself. What the hell was I doing at a fancy-dancy party, on the arm of a man who wrote movies and had more money than I'd see in my lifetime? I was the daughter of a Vegas gambler, abandoned by my mother at a young age, worked mostly waitressing jobs, and only recently was trying to hack it as a small time actress.

Wes led me through the throngs of people. Snippets of conversations about exotic vacations, the latest new action movie, who was who in Hollywood, and what major corporation was doing what flooded my mind as we passed each small group. The men looked appreciatively at me as we passed, their women—not so much. Pouty lips and anorexia were obviously the latest trends, both of which I didn't have, and in this dress, *nothing* was left to the imagination.

We made our way through the crowd to the back of the room where a cropping of high back chairs and bookcases were. An older woman, perhaps in her fifties, stood near a man who looked suspiciously like Wes. He also was tall with blond hair, except this distinguished gentleman in a dark grey suit that complimented his wife's pale pink dress was built like a linebacker, unlike Wes who had the leaner build of a regular swimmer-slash-surfer.

"Mother, Father," Wes approached the couple. The older woman had pale blond hair, almost white, and startling blue eyes. Her lips were full like her son's and coated with a mauve lipstick that paired well with her skin tone and coloring. Her hair was pulled into a severe French twist and pearls hung from her neck and ears. Her look was classic elegance.

The elder Channing clapped his son on the back. "Son," he said with a note of pride. His mother promptly air kissed both cheeks, which normally would seem really pretentious, but then she held his cheeks in both hands and smiled warmly at her son.

"I see you went with my pick," I heard her whisper and turn towards me. The nerves I had prior to meeting up with Wes were back—with a vengeance. *The mother picked me out?* I mean, I knew that she and Aunt Millie were acquaintances, but that's kind of strange for a mother to pick out an escort for her son. It kind of gave me the heebie-jeebies.

Wes turned to me and brought a hand to my back. The

skin-on-skin contact sent a jolt through me. I'd forgotten the entire back of the dress was open aside from the crisscrossing two-inch beaded straps at my shoulder blades. The rest was completely open to the waist. His hand burned white-hot where his fingertips traced small circles. I shivered and stood closer to him without even being asked.

"Mother, Father, this is Mia Saunders, my date," he grinned and I held out my hand. "Mia, this is Weston Channing, the Second, and my mother, Claire."

"Lovely to meet you, Mr. and Mrs. Channing."

Wes's mother crossed her arms over her chest and put her hand up to her cheek. She was blushing prettily and smiling so wide I felt as though she was internally laughing at a private joke. His mom leaned into his father's side. "Isn't she breathtaking?" She winked at me and shook her head.

"Um, thank you?" I offered and his father laughed.

"It's good to meet you, Ms. Saunders."

"Oh, Mia's fine." He tipped his head and chin.

Apparently, the conversation was over because he turned away and grabbed Wes's arm. "Now Son, tell me about this latest project you've got going. I hear they want to offer you three percent of the budget. That would net you only three million when they're bringing in several hundred million on your last *Honor* series. You've got to up the ante," his voice boomed with a heavy timber.

The *Honor Series*. Weston Channing, the Third wrote the flipping *Honor Series*! Holy fuckballs! His movies have been the biggest hits—*huge*— since the first one, *Jeramiah's Honor*, released three years ago. There's been one each year. His inventive way of mixing a soldier pursuing the love of their life with copious amounts of blood, violence, explosions, patriotism, and some wicked hot love scenes have made for epic movies with record-breaking box office numbers.

"...they're going to give me ten percent of the overall budget and directing opportunities," Wes's deep rumbling voice broke through my haze. Right when I cleared the cobwebs after realizing I'd been contracted for the month with movie royalty, a couple of women came up behind Wes.

The two vultures were waiting patiently for him to notice them. One was twirling a lock of her bottle-blonde hair and wearing a god-awful gold, strapless dress with her plastic boobs pushed up to maximum capacity. I scanned her outfit and cringed. She was so skinny, every one of her ribs was visible. The brunette standing next to her wasn't much better. Fake boobs—one actually looked bigger than the other—because I could see almost every inch of them through the whisper thin fabric of her glued on dress. Her nipples had hardened, and I wanted to let her know that she needed to rub her tips and warm em' up before she embarrassed herself, but something told me that she wanted them that way.

Show time. Gotta earn that hundred thousand dollar payout. Even the thought of that much money going to Blaine every month made me want to hurl. Once my father was better, I was totally going to kick his ass for getting into a situation once again!

"Hey honey, I think there are some people over there," I pointed randomly to the other side of the room, but gestured with my eyes to look behind him. Wes caught my less-than-covert eye movement and looked over his shoulder. Bimbette one and bimbette two promptly pushed out their fake ta-tas in greeting then puckered their fat, collagen-infused lips.

Wes simply hooked an arm around my waist. "Always keeping me in line, thanks." He nuzzled my cheek, and I grinned.

"It's a tough job, but someone has to do it!" I practically bounced with glee, my tone so fake and put-on.

Wes leaned forward and placed a warm kiss on my neck, then inhaled. "Mmm, thank you," he whispered just under my ear. He was so close I could feel the warmth from his lips graze my neck before he pulled away.

"Mia and I will see you at the charity ball next week," he said.

His mother surprisingly got right into our space, as in, barely a foot away. "No, no, no, that just won't do. I want to spend more time getting to know Mia, dear." She smiled one of those mom-smiles that actually make you feel like there's nothing more precious in the world than you standing in front of them. Of course, I never really had that, but if I did, I'm sure it would look just like Claire Channing.

Wes stiffened next to me. "Mother…" he warned.

She smoothed her hand down his lapels and buttoned one of the buttons on his shirt. I giggled under my breath as she fretted over him. "Oh honey, relax. I know Mia's just a *friend*. So no harm in bringing her over for Sunday brunch, now is there?" she asked using a tone that I knew carried a whopping dose of guilt trip. Momentarily, I wondered if she was Catholic. My grandmother used to have that same tone and it was usually followed up by a phrase taken directly from the Bible.

Wes sighed and shook his head. "We'll be there. Same

time?" he queried.

"That's my good boy." She air kissed both of his cheeks then turned to me and did the same.

We walked toward the bar once more. "I need a drink," he said leading the way.

I couldn't help it. I started laughing.

"What's so funny?"

"You do always do what your mom says!" I laughed. Once we got to the bar, I moved over close. "Mama's boy!" I shot into his ear.

"Oh shut up. I'm seriously questioning the sanity of agreeing to this. I could have gone with a brainless Barbie doll, you know." One eyebrow rose sharply, his lips in a mock scowl, but his eyes gave him away. They were filled with humor and were sparkling green.

I moved to take another pot shot at him, but I wobbled on my spikey heels. He caught me against his body. I rested my hand on his shoulders as he placed his arm around my waist.

His eyes went from a normal Crayola green to a bright forest green in an instant. He licked his lips, and I couldn't help but lick mine in return. The warmth of his hands at my bare back seeped into my skin. It's as if the entire room melted away when I was in his arms. I could feel his heart beating against my chest.

Thump thump, **thump thump**, **thump thump**

"You're trouble," he pinched his lips together and leaned closer. We were less than six inches apart, right in the middle of a business cocktail party standing directly in front of the bar where everyone could see us.

"And you're a mama's boy!" I went with deflecting the

situation and backed up and out of his embrace as quickly as my new shoes would take me and shuffled onto a stool.

"So that's how you're going to play it, huh?" he grinned and brought a long-fingered hand up to his chin where he stroked his thumb and forefinger along his jaw. "Game on, Ms. Mia."

CHAPTER FOUR

When we got back to the house later that evening, I feigned being tired and practically ran to my room, shutting and locking the door. I'd waited by the door, straining to hear through the wood if he was going to follow me. As much as I wanted to be with him, as in between the sheets, I really should keep distance between us. I hadn't had enough time to talk myself out of becoming emotionally attached to Wes. He was so nice, down to Earth, made a point to include me in business related conversations even if they were pretty casual. It would be wise for me to remember my place. I was nothing more than the hired help.

Then again, why couldn't I have fun? I was an adult, he was an incredibly hot, willing man. We were young and had the better part of a month to be around one another. If tonight's sexual chemistry was anything to go by, I'd bet my bike that he was stellar in the bedroom. It would do me well to get a good rogering, loosen me up. It had been a year since I'd had sex and my vibrator wasn't cutting it anymore. I needed that physical connection. A warm, male body.

I stood in the center of the room looking around at all varying shades of white. The bed looked like a white fluffy cloud. I bet it was comfortable, too. Wes didn't seem like the type of guy to skimp on the luxury fabrics for his guests. No, he'd make sure everything was just so. Walking around the room I debated my next move. He was out there somewhere. According to the clock on the nightstand, it was very late. One o'clock in the morning. We'd had a great time. I made a game of counting how many times a gold digger approached him, and how many times I'd gotten the stink eye. *Twenty-four.* He had twenty-four admirers in one evening. It made complete sense why he needed to hire a buffer. If he actually spent any length of time talking to those women, he wouldn't have made contact with any of the producers, directors, or actors he had gone to the event to see.

And Wes was perfectly in his element. He moved around the room like oil swirling through water, slinky, liquid, and never co-mingling longer with one person than another. I was pretty sure there was a method to his madness, but I didn't ask. I just followed along and played buffer. When a stick with boobs approached, I'd turn, introduce myself and make it a point to touch and lean on Wes enough that the woman would scowl and slither away like the snake she was. They all were. Aside from Wes's mother, Claire, I did not meet one decent woman. And very few over the age of twenty-five. It seemed as though older men in the business liked to have a piece of eye candy attached to them. The women just stood by their side with vapid eyes staring out the windows as they teetered on spiked heels and sipped absurdly expensive champagne. Probably to the point where they spent the evening completely stoned off the booze but not so much that they were shitty.

I guess if you thought about it, I wasn't much different. Technically, I was by Wes's side for the same reason they all were. Money. I needed it, and whether or not they *needed it* or *wanted it,* it really didn't make a difference. Having put those thoughts together, I felt a sourness hit my gut, twitching uncomfortably. That high from the evening left me in a rush of disgust.

Before I knew what I was doing, I was walking through the darkened house. When I reached the living room, I moved to a hallway I hadn't seen before. There were a single set of double doors at the end. Pressing my ear to the door I could hear the sound of a television. Surprising even myself, I knocked.

"Come in," I heard Wes say.

On a deep inhale, I opened the door. He sat leaning against the headboard of a massive sleigh bed. The room was dark, cave-like with a lit fireplace on one side of the room and on the other a wall of glass windows with what I suspected was an ocean view, knowing which side of the house that window faced. The curtains were mostly closed. Manly, heavy looking wood furniture dotted the walls. I looked over at the TV, and it was paused on what looked like a soccer game.

Wes didn't say anything when my gaze finally made it to his. He hadn't moved an inch, either. The skin of his bare chest glowed a golden brown from the light of the fireplace as he reclined in only a pair of pajama bottoms. Christ, he was a work of art. The firelight flickered off the hills and valleys of his muscled abdomen, and defined pecs making me salivate. My heart started pumping so hard in my chest I was sure he could hear it, too. Instead of going back to my room, pretending I had to ask him something or feigning I was lost, I lifted my hand up to the halter clasp on my dress and tugged.

In one swift movement, the dress fell to the floor in a

heap of purple silk. Wes gasped as I moved the hair that had fallen down the front of my body and shifted it behind my back. I stood perfectly still in nothing but a black lace thong and the stilettoes.

"Come here," Wes's voice was deep and strained. The easygoing tone he'd had earlier when we met and throughout the evening was long gone. In its place was control, desire, and lust. My three favorite things.

With effort, I walked cat-like to the side of the bed stopping two feet in front of him. I could feel the heat of the fireplace lick across my skin, warming it. As Wes's gaze traced every inch of me, my nipples tightened painfully while the space between my legs softened. With every tiny flick of his eyes over a curve, a naked edge, my clit throbbed, ached, *begged* to be touched.

"Turn around," was only the second thing he'd said to me since I'd walked in. I said nothing. Still in my heels, I pivoted on the balls of my feet, presenting him my backside. He growled low in his throat at seeing my bare ass.

The fire's heat warmed my naked front and just when I thought I would die from anticipation, a feather-light caress started at the nape of my neck and moved slowly down my spine, touching each bump and ridge. I gasped when I felt the same heat from the front hit my back, only it wasn't the fireplace. The smell of ocean and man permeated the air around me, and I closed my eyes. Soon that light touch got harder. Wes's hand held my biceps and pressed me back into him. Skin-to-skin.

I could feel his breath on my neck as he pushed my hair to one side. His other arm wrapped around my body with one strong hand clasping over a bare breast just as his lips touched the sensitive column of my neck. I couldn't help it. I whimpered the moment his thumb and forefinger plucked at the erect tip, sending ribbons of excitement scuttling through every nerve ending.

"Sweetheart, we need to set some ground rules." His voice was a grumble against my skin. He swirled his tongue over the ball of one shoulder and bit down.

I moaned. "Ground rules?" I barely made out the words, while enjoying his talented fingers as they tugged and elongated each peak. My body was on hyperalert, his hands massaging and cupping each globe while those relentless fingers gave each nipple the most beautiful torture.

"Rule one: We're going to have an insane amount of sex this month." He pressed hard on each tip simultaneously. I cried out in bliss, the heat between my legs soaking the wisp of fabric I was wearing.

"And that's a rule?" I said breathlessly leaning further back into him, grinding my ass into his thick erection. Sounded like a damn good rule to me.

Wes groaned and then retaliated by twisting each nip, perfectly adding just the right amount of pleasure and pain.

"Rule two is when we're together like this, it's only me and you. The entire month we're monogamous."

I bit down on my lip and focused on swiveling my hips pressing against what I could feel to be a pretty impressive package. "Agreed."

Both hands moved off my breast for a moment then they were back, though somehow wetted. They slid smoothly around each areola and I melted, barely able to stay in a standing position.

He must have sensed the instability and moved to lock

an arm around my waist but kept up his sweet seduction of my breasts. Jesus, the man was my new hero. If he kept this up, I'd come without ever being penetrated. I leaned an arm back and clasped him behind the neck, arching into his hand, wanting so badly to kiss him, but his lock on my waist and the firm pressure of his front against my back prevented it.

"Rule three: We *never* sleep in the same bed. We do not want to confuse this with something it's not. I like you, Mia. A lot. I wouldn't want to hurt you by making you believe I was in a position for a relationship. Understand?"

The hand that was around my waist shifted and crept low, very low, until he was there, right *there* where I wanted him most.

"Oh, fuck yeah, I understand," I said and pushed my hips into his twirling finger. And I did understand. We wanted exactly the same thing. Friendship and physical release.

He chuckled against my neck, the puffs of air stirring my hair. Out of nowhere he flipped my body around, sank to his knees, and yanked down my panties. They were stuck at the ankles where I had neglected to remove my heels. As I locked eyes with his, he opened me with his thumbs, flattened his tongue, and went to town on my clit.

"Oh, oh, oh." I was relegated to monosyllables and nothing more.

Between licks I could swear he started talking. My brain was having a really hard time paying close attention, but finally he pulled away and I zeroed in, gripping his hair and trying to push him towards my aching cleft. "Rule four:"— his eyes twinkled and he inhaled my scent then licked his lips like he was enjoying the finest delicacy and was about to feast. "Never fall in love," he said with a grin then sucked the throbbing nub into his mouth and flicked his tongue against the tip.

I almost fell over. I leaned back, and he helped me into a position where I was lying on the bed, legs dangling over the edge, and opened wide, him in between them. "That might be impossible…" I whispered as his tongue drove into my sex. I was right on the edge when he stopped in the middle of a perfect combination of tongue and finger action. I groaned loudly.

"Excuse me," he said, voice tight with a razor's edge.

I gripped his hair and did an ab curl up to my elbows. "Relax, Wes. I'm in love with your fucking tongue. Now stick it in me and make me come so I can return the favor."

The sexiest grin I'd ever seen slipped across his face. "Best decision I ever made, hiring you." He licked his lips and leaned down to blow across the wet flesh.

I lifted my hips, "Prove it!" I taunted and he did, again and again.

★ ★ ★ ★

"So why are we having dinner with this guy again?" I asked while Wes led me into an elevator that would take us to a restaurant at the top of a skyscraper. I'd lived in Los Angeles half a year, and I didn't think I'd been to a 'dress up' dinner once. Reminded me how sad my dating life was. At least with this job, I'd get to experience the finer things…at least I hoped that was a pleasant side effect. Guess it would depend on the client. Right now though, I was holding the hand of what I'd definitely consider the sexiest man alive and thoroughly enjoying myself.

Last night after he took care of me multiple times with his mouth, I returned the favor by giving him what I would consider a top notch blow job. When he was done, we showered together and talked while we cleaned up. When I noticed him get hard, I promptly got on my knees and took care of it, to then have him finger me into another state of sated bliss. It was odd, but I realized this morning that we never had actual intercourse. On top of that, we'd never even kissed. It was by far the best sexual experience I'd had and yet, the emotional side was left to the wayside. Maybe that was in fact the trick? What my best friend, Ginelle, and all my other girlfriends had already figured out.

Fucking…with no strings attached.

It seemed to go against the grain for me. Even though I considered myself a badass, half attitude, eyes always-on-my-goals type of girl, I had still fallen in love with every man I'd ever slept with.

Every single last one of them.

But after last night, I felt better with Wes than I ever had with any of them, and it was all based on mutual respect, friendship, and a heaping dose of pleasurable orgasms. After I had finished showering, he stayed in, and I made my way down the hall, through the living room and face-planted into a cloud. I vaguely remember Wes covering me up and kissing me on my temple with a "Goodnight, sweetheart." Then I woke to my schedule slipped under the door and bacon and eggs at the breakfast bar. Ms. Croft served both Wes and me as I went over the schedule for the week. Wes explained the finer points, such as whether an event was casual or not, and I'd made notes about clothing, timelines, and the goal for each outing.

It actually seemed like a real job. As if I was a personal assistant to Weston Charles Channing, the Third, and not a hired hooker. Technically, I wasn't a hooker, even though I did have sexual relations with him on the first date. But, that was because I was horny, lonely, and he was hot, and I felt down about myself. Wes definitely fixed that problem and set the rules. I was perfectly happy with those rules and planned to stick to them. No screwing around with anyone else, no sleeping together, as in going to *sleep*, and no falling in love. Easy peasy.

Wes pressed the button for the top floor and leaned against the elevator wall. "It's a meeting with the primary director on *Honor* number four that I've named *Honor Code*. It's about a soldier who writes secret messages and codes to his officers while hiding undercover with the enemy. He sends messages to his girl with those same codes, but she doesn't know what they say until he leads her on a journey toward finding out how to decipher the letters."

I smiled at him, watching while his eyes lit up explaining his story. "Sounds really romantic."

He grinned and waggled his eyebrows. "That's the idea. It gets the women hooked on movies that are typically geared towards men. Blood, violence, things blowing up, the military, espionage, things a man's man can really wrap his head around."

I nodded and followed him as he led me to a quaint table for four. A man in a suit and a petite blonde were already sitting.

"Mr. Underwood, Mrs. Underwood," Wes held out a hand to shake each of their hands. "Good to see you. This is my date, Mia Saunders."

I shook both their hands, and Wes held out my chair. I beamed up at him and his eyes softened momentarily before turning back to his business persona. The pretty blonde to my left said her name was Jennifer, and complimented me on my dress. It was actually a pretty tame cocktail dress. Royal blue jersey with a deep V to offer a nice dose of cleavage, but other than that, it wrapped at the front, tied at the side, and didn't have any other embellishments. I wore my hair down and had flat ironed it leaving it a shiny black sheet of ebony down my back. The best part of the outfit was the shoes.

Ms. Croft might look like Mary Poppins, but she must have had a gold card membership at Prada, Gucci, and Louis Vuitton, and scoured over the latest trends because she was right on point with these LV ankle booties.

If I didn't make it a year with this gig, at the very least I'd have some serious cash in designer shoes and clothes I could hock if I had to. These shoes alone were listed as twelve hundred and fifty dollars online. It may sound gold-diggerish, but I had to check.

"The dress is nothing, check out the shoes!" I leaned out a foot and we instantly started gabbing about her outfit, the designer, and what she did all day. Basically, not a whole lot. She was official arm candy and spent her days making sure Mr. Underwood's needs were met. I figured that meant she did what she wanted all day, made sure his cook made what he wanted, his maid ironed his clothes and kept his house clean and kept herself, his sparkly piece of ass, waxed, buffed, and primed to go when he got home from work all day.

"It's true; I don't know what to do with myself," Jen whispered. Yep, in twenty minutes we were already on a first name basis, and she was telling me her problems. I had that kind of face. Turned out she originally met her husband, whom she married only a year ago at the tender age of twenty-three—he's thirty-eight—when she was cast as an extra in one of his movies. Apparently, it was love at first sight or lust at first sight. I laughed internally at my own joke.

Twisting my lips to the side, I leaned closer. "Why don't you volunteer or something. Got any hobbies?"

Her big blue doe eyes blinked happily. "I love to swim. I swim every day!" and it looked like it too. Her body was svelte but not in the anorexic way that seemed to be the theme in Hollywood. She definitely had the fake ta-tas, but they looked good on her size fourish frame.

"You could volunteer at a local 'Y'?" I offered, but she scrunched up her face and shook her head.

"I don't think Jay would be okay with that."

I mulled it over for a minute. "Do you like kids?"

Again, eyes lit up like the candles on a fifty year old's birthday cake. "I love children! Believe it or not, I used to teach preschool before I met Jay." She looked over at her husband, and her smile widened. I caught his gaze when it slid to her, and he winked then continued nonstop in his conversation with Wes. She turned to me happy as could be. It was almost infectious how cheerful she was.

"Why can't you work with kids, or better yet, have some of your own?"

Her head slammed back as if struck, then she looked at Jay and then back at me. "We've only been married a year, and we only dated a few months before that. Don't you think it's too soon?" she said, though I could tell her wheels were turning.

I shrugged and took a hefty sip of my wine. "Doesn't matter what I think. It only matters what the two of you think and want. If you want kids, you're young, have at it. Besides, he's fifteen years older than you. That's got to slow down some swimmers. Could take a while." I leaned back nonchalantly.

As Jen thought about it she became physically excited with her enthusiasm. Her back went straight, her knees started bouncing, and she couldn't stop fidgeting, or smiling for that matter. Her eyes were locked on her husband. Again he turned, looked at her, but this time he held up a finger to Wes to pause whatever they were talking about. I'd started tuning them out when I realized that Jennifer wasn't a soulless bimbo.

"What is it, darling?" Jay asked his wife.

She smiled wide and I swear, that smile could bring peace to the Middle East. "Just happy. And, I can't wait to talk to you when we get home," she leaned a hand over and placed it over his on the table. He leaned forward and pecked her lips then nuzzled her nose.

"Is it anything that can't wait?" he asked with concern, all eyes on her, his focus redirected completely.

She kissed him softly and shook her head. "Nope, it's good. Very good."

Wes leaned over and slid an arm around me. "Anything I should know about?" he asked conspiratorially.

"I'll totally give up the goods later," I whispered in his ear referring to the gossip.

"I'm counting on it," he nuzzled my neck. "And I want to know what was up with that, too," he gestured with a head tilt to the happy couple mooning over one another. I laughed at his blatant innuendo.

Dinner continued without a hitch. Apparently, I'd helped keep Jen busy which allowed Jay to feel at ease with discussing the upcoming movie. Turned out, he was going to let Wes direct a lot of the heavier dialogue scenes between the couple and possibly even the bedroom romantic scenes. I found that hysterical and laughed when he made his announcement.

Wes's eyes shot to mine and narrowed. "Sorry, I remembered something funny from earlier, don't mind me," I covered, but I could tell by the way Wes tucked me into his side when dessert was delivered that I was going to get an earful.

"What was so funny?" he asked when Jay went out for a cigarette and Jennifer went with him.

Twiddling with my napkin, I leaned closer to him. "I'm sorry. I just thought it was funny that Mr. I'm-Not-In-A-Position-To-Have-A-Relationship is going to be directing romantic scenes. It just seemed out of your wheelhouse is all," I giggled.

He looked as though I'd ruffled his feathers when he brought up a hand to cup my neck. "You weren't complaining last night." His voice lowered to that sultry timbre I recalled him having when he was issuing the rules. So much so it sent fire shooting through me to warm and soften the space between my legs.

I leaned very close, so close my lips were only an inch or two from his. Definitely close enough he could feel my breath against his lips as I spoke.

"Last night was fucking..." He inhaled and licked his lips. They looked good enough to eat, and I wanted a taste so bad. "...except," I added, "we didn't fuck." I let the word 'fuck' roll of my lips with a hard 'k' sound. "We had sex, not romance."

Wes's hand came up to clasp my neck while a thumb caressed my cheekbone as his lips came impossibly close but still didn't touch mine. I could practically taste the coffee on his breath from the after-dinner drink. "Is that what you want? Romance?" he asked, his lips barely hovering against mine.

"No, I wanna fuck..." I barely got the word out before a heavy hand landed on my shoulder.

"You two love birds!" Jay Underwood broke the moment, and we both slumped back into our chairs. I was beginning to think I'd never feel the lush taste of his mouth, the pressure of his lips against mine, and I wanted it... dammit! I was getting very impatient for it, but damned if I was going to make the first move.

Wes covered his mouth with his hand. I'm pretty sure it was to conceal silent laughter.

"Later sweetheart; we've got all night," he promised.

"Yeah, yeah, I've heard that before," I fake yawned and lifted my tea and took a sip. Lukewarm. Blech.

His mouth dropped open and he shook his head, green eyes dazzling in the candlelight. "Challenge accepted."

CHAPTER FIVE

We barely made it through the door when Wes twirled me around and used his body to press me into the wall. His lips went instantly to the sensitive skin of my neck. He licked a long trail from my clavicle up to behind my ear. The hair on the back of my neck stood up, goose bumps rising on my flesh as I closed my eyes. Wes's hands went under my skirt and over my bare ass, as he lifted one leg and then the other with no trouble at all, wrapping my legs around him. He hoisted my tall, curvy frame against his and pressed me harder into the wall at my back.

"I'm going to be so deep inside you, you'll feel me in your throat," he promised.

"Fuck," slipped from my lips as he carried me toward my room.

"Exactly." He bit down on my neck, trailing his teeth along the slender column.

Every nerve, every pore, every molecule was focused on merging with this man.

Without preamble, he dropped me onto the bed and stood staring down. "Take off your dress," he demanded. His eyes were black, filled to the brim with lust. I could tell he was taking a moment because he clenched and unclenched his hands into fists, the tendons in his neck bulged with his desire.

I whipped the dress over my head and stood up on my

knees in a matching deep midnight blue bra and thong. At seeing me exposed, he sucked in a harsh breath and let it out with a hiss.

"Your turn. Lose the suit," I said while trailing my hands down to cup each breast. His jaw clenched as he made quick work of dropping the jacket and tie, and opening the dress shirt to reveal that sun-kissed chest I love so much. I bit down on my lip. "All of it. I want it gone." My voice sounded raspy and needy.

Wes grinned and slowly removed his belt and loosened his pants. He took a condom out of his pocket, ripped it with his teeth, and placed it on his straining erection, all without ever losing eye contact. I lifted my hand behind my back and undid the clasp of my bra. Just as his pants fell to the floor, so did my bra.

"Christ, I can hardly look at you," his voice held awe. "So fucking gorgeous." He ground his teeth loud enough I could hear it.

My eyebrow rose and I gazed at all that was his naked glory. Tall, tan, muscles for days, and a thick hard cock ready to please. "You're not so bad yourself," I offered while enjoying the view.

"Prove it," he taunted with a grin. My words from last night coming back to me proved he paid very close attention to our interactions. That made me happy, giddy in a way I didn't want to think too much about.

Crawling to the edge of bed, I placed my hands on his hard chest. I leaned down and licked the flat disc of his nipple. He moaned, then hissed low in his throat when I bit down on the bit of flesh. His hands tunneled into my hair. I brought my face close to his and hovered around his lips, close enough he could feel my breath against his lips. He licked his own, preparing for that first touch. I didn't give it to him. Instead I kissed just the edge of his mouth.

"Are you toying with me?" he asked, a hint of playfulness in his tone.

I moved to the side of his cheek, running my chin along it, then licked and nibbled on his earlobe. "Whatever do you mean?" I whispered, making sure to blow enough air against the sensitive spot so he'd understand my intention.

His fingers gripped my hips and looped into my panties, tugging them down unceremoniously. I gasped when the air hit my wet center.

"I think you are," he countered then pushed me back onto the bed. I fell in a whoosh against the comfy cloud of blankets.

Just as I opened my eyes, his hands were on my knees. He opened me wide, saw my aching moist sex and groaned. He trailed one finger through the wetness. A whimper slipped past my lips when he twirled one finger against the tight, aching knot of nerves. "I'm going to devour you." His eyes flashed to mine. "But first, I need to be inside you."

He centered himself over my cleft and pushed just the tip inside. I arched wanting more, needing more. Using the strength of his upper body, he hovered over me. "Watch me take you the first time," he said, his voice a sexy, possessive growl. And I did. Watched, as he took me inch by torturous inch. The lips of my sex were stretched wide over his girth, his thickness making me feel full, stretched to capacity, more so than any lover before.

I groaned, my head tipping back, no longer able to watch while he pushed that last inch inside. He was already so deep. "Mia," he whispered, his voice tight. My eyes snapped open and stared at his lust-filled gaze. He braced himself on his elbows and his hands cupped my cheeks. He reared his hips back and slammed home as his lips took mine. United in that moment as one body, there was no Mia or Wes. There was just us.

The kiss was fiery hot, wet, and overwhelming. He plunged his tongue into my mouth the same way his cock rammed into my body. With precision, depth, and so much pleasure, everything that I was, quaked with the effort.

I wrapped my legs and arms around him, holding onto him as he drilled into me, his cock reaching places inside me I didn't even know I had. He'd triggered feelings so intense I cried out and clung to him as the first orgasm raced through my body.

"Fuck yeah, Mia. You squeeze me so good. Again, sweetheart." Wes rode me through the orgasm but still didn't find his own release. Shit, the man was a stallion in the sack. I swear I drew all the aces in the deck when my aunt lined me up with him.

Wes sucked on my lips then pulled himself out of me. Before I could protest, he turned me around and yanked my hips up. "Perfect fucking ass. Damn, Mia." He smacked one cheek then plowed back into the heat between my legs, even before the sting of his slap left my skin.

"Jesus, fuck, you know what you're doing," I moaned and let my upper body fall onto my forearms.

He gripped my hips and set up a punishing rhythm. I could hear the sounds of our flesh smacking against one another. "Need that squeeze on my dick," Wes growled as he leaned over my body and reached a hand between my legs. His fingers zeroed in on my 'O-trigger' and I was gone. Bucking wildly, the walls of my sex clamped down on his rock hard cock until he roared. Three swift plunges more and his entire body stilled, nestled flat against my ass as he pulsed inside me.

Wes collapsed over me, his breath coming in fast pants against the hair of my neck. We were both winded, lost in our combined pleasure. He rolled off then tugged me to his chest. We spent the next few minutes making out like teenagers. The room smelled of the ocean, sex, and the faint remnants of my perfume, Tresor. Pretty much, perfection. If you could bottle the scent, I'd wear it every day.

Lying together, I curved into his chest. "So, tell me something..."

Wes chuckled. "Could you be more specific?"

I shrugged. "Tell me anything, something about you." With one finger, I traced circles over his abdomen and pecs.

He sighed. "Huh, well, you know I love to write movies." I nodded. "And surf." He winked and I grinned. "You met my parents, and my nanny. Well, she was my nanny when I was a boy, now she runs the house."

"Ms. Croft?"

He nodded. "What else is there?"

I looked at him with narrowed eyes. "Uh, a lot. Do you have any siblings?"

"A sister. Older than me. Married, no kids yet. She's a grade school teacher. Husband's the principal at the school."

"That pretty much answers how they met." I waggled my eyebrows, and he winked. "What's her name?"

"Jeananna. How about you? Any sibs?"

I laughed at his slang term. "Yeah, Maddy, well, Madison.

Younger by five years. She's nineteen and attending school in Las Vegas."

"So why'd you move out here?"

I snuggled in closer to him. "Needed a change. And I thought acting was my calling. Still do, but…" I didn't want to go into my life story.

"But?" he prompted and I shook my head. "If you wanted to be an actress, how did you end up an escort?"

"Money." I shrugged. "You're my first, you know," I confided. He turned towards me so we were facing one another. His face filled with confusion. "My first client," I finished.

"Ah, and how's it going so far?" he smiled.

I feigned nonchalance. "Eh, 'bout a seven out of ten, I'd say."

He rolled over on top of me, pinning my arms to the side. "Hey!" I chided with a big smile plastered across my face.

"A seven! You give me a seven even though you have nothing to compare it to?" He laid a messy kiss against my lips. His hands stroked down my ribs and started wriggling. Instantly, I howled with laugher. Once he saw how ticklish I was, he went for gold, digging into my ribs, waist, and thighs until I was thrashing around, screaming for him to stop, laughter contorting my vision.

"Admit it? I'm a big, fat ten!" He slowed then stopped his torture.

"Okay, okay," I took deep breaths of blessed air into my lungs. "I'll say you're a solid eight." He wiggled his fingers again. "Okay a nine!" I screamed, and he continued his assault. "Nine point five!" He stopped.

"Nine point five, room for improvement…" His eyes sparkled with mirth. "I'll take it and turn it into a ten before the month is over!"

★ ★ ★ ★

For the next few days, I was left alone because Wes was working in his studio on *Honor Code*. He still came home each night. We'd share dinner together, watch a movie, or he'd read a book. Then later he'd ravish me before one of us had to get up and go to our own room. The routine worked better than I'd imagined it would. I had a lot of fun, and an even more phenomenal sex, without the risk of pesky emotions getting in the way. This escort business kicked ass.

I flopped over to the side of the bed after giving Wes one helluva ride.

"Now that, sweetheart, that was a fucking ten!" he praised. Laughing, I pinched his nipple playfully. "Ouch! Hellcat!"

"You're crazy, you know that?" He leaned over and kissed me, a hand sliding into my hair pulling me on top of him. "Again?"

"Can't help it, you make my dick harder than a surfboard," He licked into my mouth and squeezed the fleshy handle at my hip.

"Did you seriously just compare your dick to a surfboard?"

He stopped kissing me and looked at me, a serious set to his gaze. "I did, didn't I?"

I nod, my eyebrows rising toward my hairline.

"Your body makes me stupid. I forget how to string

two words together," he offered as an excuse.

"Whatever! I'm sore and need sleep. So get up, and mosey your sexy ass back to your bedroom." I slid off him once more and face planted into the pillow, snuggling into the comforter.

Wes's hand slid up and down my back. "Did you forget something, sweetheart?" he said, humor coating every word. I opened one eye as he stared down at me. "You're in my bed," he finished with a smirk.

"Damn it all to hell in a handbasket," I huffed, throwing the covers back and hopping out of bed as he got comfortable.

Stomping out of his room completely bare-ass naked, I heard him call out. "Tomorrow is brunch with my folks. Be ready at ten!"

"Bite me!" I yelled over my shoulder. Just as I turned the corner toward my room, I ran right into Judi.

Her eyes went wide as she took in my naked form. "Blimey, dearest me!" she gasped then covered her eyes. The surprise brought out her accent in spades.

I cringed then rushed around her. "Sorry Ms. Croft, didn't mean to scare you like that," I offered. Down the hall I could hear Wes, the rat bastard, laughing his ass off. He must have heard me get caught by Judi. Great. She already thinks I'm a hired whore, now I've proven it.

★ ★ ★ ★

"You're looking lovely this afternoon, Mia," Wes's mother praised, pulling me into a hug. It was an odd sensation having a motherly type hug me as if she genuinely wanted to give her affection.

"Thank you, Mrs. Channing. Your home is very beautiful." She smiled and I looked around the sunroom that was set up for Sunday brunch. A steward offered me a mimosa in a crystal champagne flute.

I took a look around at the room. It was decorated with elegance and luxury in mind. Rich golds and cream tones were paired with burgundy and navy throughout the décor. The table was set with pristine white china, a lace pattern crafted into the edge. More silverware than needed for three courses flanked each plate. A lush bouquet of roses sat in the center of the table giving it a summery feel even though it was January. I guess it didn't really matter, LA wasn't the Midwest. Like back home in Vegas, we didn't have crazy cold days where the temperature dropped below zero. I'm pretty sure it's never been below thirty degrees. At least it hasn't in my twenty-four years of life. Hell, I've only seen snow a couple of times myself.

"There you are!" A smiling blonde rushed in. A tall, very slim man with tortoiseshell glasses trailed behind her.

"Hey, sis," Wes greeted her, then pulled the pretty woman into his arms. She drew back and clasped his jaw.

"Lookin' good, Wes."

Wes smiled wide. Wider than I'd seen other than when he was tickling me. "Sis, I'd like you to meet my *friend*, Mia." He placed a hand low on my back.

I held out my hand. "Hi, Jeananna, right?"

She nodded and shook my hand. "So…" she drew out the word looking at her brother then at me. "Friend, eh?"

Wes chuckled. "Yes, Sis, *friend*." He emphasized the word 'friend'.

She rolled her eyes. "Whatever," she said as her blonde

hair bobbed and her green eyes sparkled with happiness.

After full introductions were done and we were at the table, that's where the fun really began.

"So Mia, what is it that you do?" Jeananna asked me. "Did you two meet on the job?"

I looked over at Wes and could see he was at a loss for words. "You could say that," I hedged shoveling in a bite of quiche.

Without preamble, Claire Channing butted in. "Oh please. Of course you met on the job. Mia's an escort. I picked her out myself. Don't I have the best taste, Wes?" Claire's tone was nonchalant, unbothered by the fact that in normal circumstances, it was unusual to pick out an escort for your son. Definitely high on the bizarre-meter. .

Jeananna's eyes widened in shock. "You're a call girl?"

Both Wes and I spoke at the same time. "What did you say?" I said as Wes scolded, "No she's not!"

I blanched. That quiche suddenly felt heavy in my gut. "So you're not sleeping with my brother?" she asked not a hint of malice to her tone. She could've been asking about the weather.

"Um…" I started to respond.

"That's none of your business." Wes stood and threw his napkin on the table. Redness colored his cheeks and neck. "I will not have you insinuate such hateful things about Mia."

Jeananna stood up and ran around the table. "I'm sorry, I'm sorry. It wasn't intentional! I just heard the word escort and you know, came to the wrong conclusion. I didn't mean anything by it." She worried her lip.

Claire stood up, "Now, now, Jeananna didn't mean any harm. It was a simple mistake," she placated but Wes wasn't having it.

"Not simple," he grated. "Mia is my friend, and she may have been hired to help me get through a month's worth of tedious lunches, dinners, and events, but she's not a lady of the night." His eyes snapped to mine. "Sorry, sweetheart," his eyes shone bright with remorse. I knew then I had to make it right.

I took a deep breath in. "Look, it was a simple mistake. I thought the same thing when my Aunt Millie broached the subject. But I decided to give it a shot, and I'm glad I did. Meeting Wes, and now you all has been quite the highlight of the experience for me." Claire's eyes warmed and she took her seat, as did Jeananna after she hugged her brother. "Besides, have you seen the shoes I scored?" Right then I turned in my seat and put my leg out to the sky like my dance teacher taught me to do back in high school. "Hot as hell!"

Claire's hand went over her mouth, covering her laughter. Jeananna looked at my heels with a hint of envy. Her husband didn't say anything but stared at my leg as if it held the answers to the universe, and Wes's dad clapped him on the shoulder with a "Well done, Son!"

"Anyway, I want to know more about you guys." I changed the subject and took a sip of my champagne and OJ. "Wes here tells me you're a teacher, and you're a principal. How does that work out?"

The rest of the afternoon went off without a hitch. Claire and Weston, *the Second,* along with Jeananna and her husband, Peter, shared story after story of Wes as a baby and growing up in the Channing family. I laughed more in that afternoon than I had in the last year. The lighthearted vibe was almost too much to bear for someone like me who never had a real family unit myself. It had always been my drunk father, and my baby sister, Maddy, who I spent most of my childhood and teen years raising. Even though I knew Daddy loved us more than anything, he could never stop his gambling or drinking away the memories of what our life had been when Mom was around.

When we left, Claire made Wes promise to bring me back next Sunday. He agreed. As we made our way to his Jeep, he hugged me to his side and planted a sweet kiss on my lips. "That was fun, you know?"

I smiled back, warmth filled my heart to bursting. "It was. One of the best days I've had in a long time. Thank you for bringing me."

He grinned and winked. "Anytime, sweetheart. They liked you."

I buckled up and looked out the window as he drove out the gates back down the winding road out of their posh neighborhood.

"I liked them. Very much. You have a cool family. You're lucky."

His lips turned down into a frown. "What's your family like?" he asked so softly I could barely hear him over the sound of the wind whipping my hair around.

Leaning back, I watched the beach in the distance and the waves crashing over the shore. "My sister Maddy is amazing. She's brilliant. Going to be a scientist. I spent most of my time growing up taking care of her."

"Where were your parents?"

"Parent," I corrected. His eyes shot to mine briefly. Within them I could see remorse and sadness. Not for himself, but for me. I turned away. "My mom was a showgirl in Vegas. Left my Dad and us girls when I was ten, Maddy only five."

Wes worried his thumb nail but kept his eyes on the road. "She never came back?"

"Nope," I shook my head. "And because of that, my dad started drinking. A lot. Gambling, even more."

He grabbed my hand and twined our fingers together before pulling it against his lips kissing the top of my hand. "Is that why you're doing what you're doing?"

I could've lied and told him some made up bullshit story, but that would've ruined what we had—the complete and perfect honesty we'd come to rely on in order to make this situation work for us both. Instead of responding, I just nodded.

"Want to tell me about it?" His tone was soft and pleading.

It was too soon. I wasn't ready to share my burden with someone. He was such a good guy he'd just want to fix it. Pay off the debt or something crazy. It's my problem. My father and my own constant desire to save him. I have to be the one to do this.

"Will you tell me someday?"

"Yes," and that was as much as I could promise for now.

CHAPTER SIX

"Wake up, sweetheart," I heard right before the tingling burn of Wes's hand met the bare skin of my ass.

"Jesus, Christ," I jumped up grabbing at the comforter to cover my unmentionables. "What the hell is wrong with you?" I yelled.

I was greeted with a grin instead of an apology. "Come on, get your suit on and some comfy clothes. We're hitting the beach!" Wes exclaimed, clearly thrilled with the prospect of a new day and visiting the coast.

He'd been working his ass off the past week. I only saw him late in the evening, excluding one unbearably boring business dinner. Though in the meantime, I've had lunch with Jennifer Underwood, the director's wife on his current movie, and Wes's mother, Claire. Everyone seems to be taking things in stride. Wes didn't have a problem with it either. Said it was great I was making new friends while he was busy. He seemed to be more concerned with me being bored all day rather than the potential blurring of any emotional lines by me hanging out with his family and getting close to his coworker's wife.

"What do you mean we're going to the beach? You realize it's January and cold as hell?" I pulled the comforter over my head and slouched back into the cozy hidey hole it offered.

I felt the mattress dip, caging me in. Wes pulled the

blankets off my head and did a ninja-like maneuver getting both of my hands locked over my head with one hand. He leaned down and kissed me, slow, wet, and so deep my toes curled. The space between my thighs started to heat and throb. Jesus, the man could kiss. He pulled the blanket further down and nudged at my nipples, first with his nose, then pulling one tip into his mouth, drawing from it.

"Now, this is how you wake a girl," I said through a low moan.

He rewarded me with deep, penetrating suction from his mouth against my breast. "I'll remember that next time. If I get you off, will you be in a better mood?" His tongue came out and flicked just the tip of my nipple while playing with it. The fingers of his other hand plucked and twisted my breast's twin.

I nodded dumbly, too lost in the sensation that was building, a slow burn that made me weak and incapable of speech.

He chuckled against my breast. "If I put my mouth on you, give you the relief you seek, will you do what I say?"

It was impossible to deny him. With his mouth and fingers worshipping my tits, I couldn't help but give him anything he asked. "Yes, God yes!" I moaned. His head moved from my breast down my ribs where he bit and nibbled, along the center of my abdomen, until he was *there*. Right there, giving me all that I wanted and more. Wes could have been a gold medalist in the art of cunnilingus. He knew exactly when to give, when to bite, nip, suck, lick. And he did it with finesse. .

Bite.

Nip.

Suck.

Lick.

Followed by a swirl and flattening his tongue as he rubbed around the center of my pleasure over and over until I broke. My body arched, hands flying into his hair to hold him against my wet flesh. He growled as he ate, lost in the moment as much as I was. Possibly even more by the way he plunged his cock into me.

We didn't make it to the beach for another hour.

When we arrived, we were met by another man, a surf instructor named Amil.

"You brought me here so I could watch you guys surf?" I asked immediately after shaking the hand of Mr. Surftastic. My tone was not pleasant.

Wes looked at Amil, then at me, and grinned. His smirk was mischievous, and I knew in that moment that I was in for it.

"No, as a matter of fact, I brought you here because *we* are going to surf. Amil is going to help me show you the ropes. He also has all the equipment and ladies' wetsuits. He runs the Surf Shack farther down the beach." He pointed to a spot far off on the horizon.

I looked at Wes, his blond hair blowing in the chilly morning air. A sparkle in his green eyes made them look almost emerald in the early light of day. He was as sweet on the eyes as the heavenly waves hitting the beach.

"You're serious then?"

He nodded and gestured to Amil. The instructor turned around, giving me an amazing view of his tanned muscled back, and pulled out a wetsuit that looked to be about my size. "Should fit. You're what, five ten, a hundred and forty pounds?"

"Five nine, and didn't your mother teach you that you don't ever discuss weight with a woman?"

Amil shook his head and laughed. "Can't say that she did."

"She fell down on her job," I said deadpan. "It's rude, and women hate it. You married?" He shook his head. "Girlfriend?" He shook his head again, still grinning. "Case in point." I clapped my hands together as if I'd just proven Einstein's theory of relativity.

Wes laughed out loud beside me. "She's right, dude," Wes said. I was a little taken aback by his use of the very Californian word. Not that Wes wasn't a cool guy, he was. Very much so. It's just, he's always had a bit of formality.

"Sorry Mia. My deepest apologies, but I wanted to make sure the suit would fit." He handed me a black wetsuit.

After repeated attempts at getting myself into the impossibly tight wetsuit, which I dubbed my Cat Woman suit, we finally got the sucker on and in place. My boobs were smashed against my chest and the neoprene fabric. I wanted nothing more than to unzip the top and let those babies loose! Looking down at myself, I couldn't help but snicker. The suit reminded me of catwoman from *Batman Returns*. I felt ridiculous even though Wes's heated gaze told me I did *not* 'in fact' look ridiculous. More like he was ready to rip the sucker right off me. Amil however didn't appreciate the lack of attention we were giving to his surf instruction. I just wanted to get out there and try this damn thing already!

Finally Amil was done with his "art of surfing" instruction and Wes led me down the beach. He held his surfboard and mine as we trudged through the sand. "I can carry my own board, you know?"

His eyes twinkled as the sun caught them. "I'm certain there's a lot of things you can do, sweetheart. But, I wouldn't feel like a man if I didn't help my girl. Besides, you're being a really good sport."

His girl?

Did he just say that?

"My girl?" I asked before the thought could turn into something wickedly emotional.

He grinned. "Yeah, you know what I mean." He shrugged.

Um, no, I fucking didn't know what he meant. Just as I was about to dig further into this landmine, Amil interrupted us.

"Okay, we're going to do some paddling and practical lessons out there on the calmer section of water."

"Come on, don't be a scairdy cat," he said, adding a mutilated meow sound for effect. Men just can't make kitty noises. They end up sounding more like an animal dying than a cute little furball.

As I was about to protest, Wes smacked my ass hard and pushed me forward towards the ocean. He was a perfect gentleman in the ocean, though. He helped lead me to the appropriate area in the water as well as worked with me on the positions, poses, and the balancing I was attempting. We decided I should attempt to get up on my knees first and get the hang of it before attempting to stand.

Once the newness and nerves wore off, I found I could actually ride small waves when on my belly. It took over an hour to get up on my knees, but I couldn't have been more proud of myself. As I was on my knees riding a wave, I could hear Wes hooting and hollering. I'd never felt more pride in myself than in that moment. Usually, I was cheering on my sister, Maddy, or my best friend, Ginelle, and her dancing. Even when I was in contemporary dance and had kickass performances I still didn't feel this sense of accomplishment. Maybe now it was because of the tall six-foot plus hunk waiting on the shore as I paddled in. His surfboard was sticking straight out of the ground. I shuffled towards him, dropping my board on the sand as I ran further up the shore.

"Did you see it?" I screamed with glee as I ran toward him.

"Of course I did! It was awesome! You're a natural, sweetheart," he said with open arms. I barreled into his chest knocking us both to the ground. Instantly, his lips were on mine, his hands in my wet hair holding me to him. He tasted of salt and the sea. Magical. We continued making out for a few minutes before we were interrupted by a deep, throat-clearing cough. Wes's hands had moved from my head and were firmly gripping my ass, his erection pressing right where I wanted it most. We pulled apart slowly, both of us panting and smiling like loons to see the laughing face of Amil.

Wes helped me up and pulled me close, our wetsuits mashed together. "You were great," he said with pride, sliding a thumb along my check before giving me a soft peck on the lips.

"Thank you for teaching me. Can we come back?" I asked, excited at the prospect of battling the waves again.

"For you, anything. My sweet Mia."

★ ★ ★ ★

Week three of my stay was filled with more boring business dinners and another swanky event. I didn't mind the events so much. It was nice moseying around, eating delectable treats and drinking expensive champagne and wine, but it wasn't exactly fun. Wes spent those evenings deep in conversation, working the room like the businessman he was.

He wasn't kidding when he said he didn't have time for a real relationship. The woman who commits to him is going to spend a lot of time alone. He'll need a woman who has a full life and career and is also happy to be his midnight girl—mostly available when he gets home, for a late night fuck and cuddle before falling into dreamland to then start all over again in the morning. A swift pang pierced my gut at the thought of Wes with another woman. Falling in love, getting married, having children, living happily ever after while I continued doing what? Being an escort?

I set down the puff pastry I picked up, and instead, chugged the entire rest of my glass of champagne.

"Wow, easy there, speed racer," Wes said as he hooked an arm around my waist and pulled me to his side. "You trying to get drunk?" His eyes narrowed but the hint of a smile at the corner of his mouth confirmed the playful intent.

"Why? You gonna take advantage of me if I am?" I asked with a saucy lilt and firm press of my tits into his chest.

He sucked in a breath, clasped me fully to his chest, then looked down. "Abso-fucking-lutely," he said with no humor whatsoever. Just the insinuation of him taking me dampened my panties.

"Don't turn me on. It's not fair when you have business to attend to." I pouted and kissed the side of his neck making sure to drag my lips along the column.

He groaned low in his throat and pressed his hips against me so that I could feel the heat and strength of his desire. "How the hell am I going to let you go in eight short days?" His eyes and the firm set of his jaw emphasized the serious nature of his statement.

I sucked in a sharp breath and looked intently into his eyes. The ones I had come to adore beyond all others. "It is what it is. What it has to be," I reminded him.

He leaned forward and touched our foreheads together. "But what if I don't want it to be?" He said the one thing that both of us agreed should remain unspoken. The thought, the mere suggesting of more, went against everything we'd negotiated when I signed the contract. It also had the potential for breaking the rules he'd set up that very first time we slept together over two weeks ago.

"Don't," I whispered, and he took in a slow breath then let it out. I could feel the moist warmth against the wetness of my lips.

"Okay, I won't," he said with a finality that spoke of his renewed commitment to keep this as it was meant to be. As it *had* to be.

There was no other option for me. Even if I wanted more, which I couldn't wrap my head around right now, it wasn't possible. I still needed a million dollars, and my dad still needed saving. There wasn't anyone else but me to make that happen. I wouldn't risk his life for the whisper of a chance at happiness. I'd never be able to forgive myself if I chose my own happiness over the life of my father.

Regardless of the fact that he's a drunk, that he spent too much of his time gambling and drinking away our financial stability, he was still one of the only people who truly loved me. And I'd never forsake it. Not even for Wes, as much as the thought filled my mind, heart, and soul with hope, it was not meant to be. I had a job to do, and I'd do it, or die trying.

"Come on, let's dance," Wes offered, letting the heavy moment slowly dissipate as he led me to the open floor. The event this evening was an introduction party for the future staff, crew, investors, and actors confirmed for the new movie Wes had been working his ass off on, *Honor Code*. This was the first night he could celebrate that achievement, and I was determined to make sure he did.

As he held me close, I thought about our time together. The last two plus weeks had been truly a dream come true. When my Aunt Millie offered me the job, I honestly believed I was selling a bit of my soul. Now that I'd had over two weeks to get used to the idea, and how I wanted things to go with future clients, I thought I'd be able to breeze through the next year. Possibly even make some contacts in the industry that I'd planned to break into once my year of servitude was up. Unless I loved it, then I'd just keep working, making the big bucks. Not that I'd see any of those dollars this year. I'd only kept a little to send off to Maddy for school necessities and enough in my bank account to keep my rent paid on my tiny apartment.

I figured if I got paid a hundred thousand over the next twelve months I would be ahead of the million dollar debt by two hundred thousand dollars. That meant I could pay Maddy's school tuition of a hundred thousand completely and have another hundred thousand to work with. That would give me enough to send my sister three thousand a month for living expenses for her and dad, pay my thousand dollar rent, and still have a few thousand in the bank each month to sit on.

Of course, my time would not be my own, which would eventually grate along every nerve I have, but I hoped the rest of my clients would be like Wes. Work a lot, need me very little. Then I could spend my time chilling in their swank homes.

Leaving Wes was going to be difficult though. I wondered if it would be that way with all my clients. I'd come to appreciate the time Wes and I had together, and the sex, which was off the charts hot. The thought of what he'd done to me just this morning made my cheeks heat. The way he took me up against the tiled wall of the shower… Jesus, that man could fuck.

"Hey, you look flushed; you feeling okay?" He stopped dancing, and I pulled away from his intense gaze before leaning my head on his chest. His heartbeat lulled me back into a contemplative state. I shimmied my hips telling him I wasn't done with our dance. I wanted to feel his arms around me. He made me feel like I was the only girl in the entire world who could hold his attention.

"I'm fine. It's warm. You make me warmer." I leaned my chin on his breastbone and looked up just as he looked down.

Wes's gaze locked on my face, his eyes taking in the features of my face. "You know, you're probably the most precious woman I've ever known besides my mom and sister?"

"Precious?" I giggled.

"Yeah. In other words..." He leaned down and slid his cheek alongside mine until his lips settled against my ear, "... you matter to me."

I hugged him tight, *so* tight. I wanted him to know just how much he mattered to me too, but, I couldn't find the words. They were clogged in my throat as I clung to his back, nails digging in through his suit jacket. He pulled back dislodging my extreme hold.

"Hey, hey. We don't have to go there, but Mia, you have to know." I shook my head not wanting to hear him profess any feelings that I couldn't reciprocate. Wes cupped both of my cheeks in his warm hands. "Mia, listen to me..." I sucked in a breath and waited for him to say what he needed to say. "Just because we won't be together as a couple when you leave here, doesn't mean we can't stay in touch. Continue to be friends." I could tell by the tone in his voice that he meant every word.

A sense of relief swirled in the air around me forcing a huge smile to spread across my face. "Really?"

He nodded. "Yes, really, sweetheart," he promised. "Now, let's get a drink and enjoy the rest of the evening. They're going to announce the cast assignments for *Honor Code* even though most of us already know. It's part of the fun," he winked, and I nodded.

Once we reached the bar, I ran smack dab into Jennifer Underwood. "Mia, oh my God, I've been looking all over for you," she said hurriedly then pulled me over to the side. Wes's eyes met mine, concern evident in his narrowed gaze. I shook my head with a 'don't worry' gesture.

"What's going on, Jen?"

Jennifer leaned forward conspiratorially then looked

around to make sure no one heard what she was about to tell me. "I'm late," she said then bit her lip.

"I'm sorry?" I offered not knowing what she was talking about.

She sucked in a resigned sigh, then leaned forward again to whisper. "No, I'm *late* late. As in my cycle," she finished.

Then it clicked. Oh shit! She's *late*! When we met for lunch a week after the dinner we'd had where we first met, she thanked me profusely for changing her life. Apparently, when she went home and told her husband, Jay, that she wanted to try for a baby, he was beyond thrilled. She said he'd wanted to start trying on their wedding night, but since they'd gotten married so quickly, he figured she wanted to wait. Now as far as I knew, they were going at it like bunny rabbits trying to make a baby.

I gripped Jen's hands tight and brought her close. "How many days? You just started trying."

"I know!" her voice rose over the sound of other conversations, and a few men in suits looked our way. I dragged her further over into a corner. "I'm five days late now, and I've never been even one day late before!"

"Holy shit!" I let out.

"I know!"

"Oh, my God!"

"I know!" she squealed and we both started jumping up and down like small children, our heels clacking against the tile floor. I hugged her close. I'd never really been affectionate with many women, just Ginelle and Maddy for the most part, but I felt a connection to Jennifer. She was good people, and I considered her very much a friend.

"You're going to have to keep me updated when I

leave." She nodded. That was one of the things I kept from Wes. I didn't tell him I'd told Jennifer what I was to him, but I swore her to secrecy; so far, she'd been trustworthy. "This is awesome. What did Jay say?"

"He wants to tell everyone I'm already pregnant, even though we don't know for sure." She rolled her eyes and shook her head.

"Men are stupid," I offered and she agreed. "So if you got prego right away, my guess is you're only two weeks, so a home test might not give accurate results for another couple weeks. Your best bet if you're dying to know is get bloodwork done and see the doctor. I'd imagine that's the most conclusive test."

"That's what I figured. I made an appointment for next Friday. Then I'll know a few days after that for sure. Unless, of course, my period comes." Her face fell into a frown.

I hugged her close and then started walking back over to the guys. "Well, let's just be positive and hope for the best, okay?" She nodded, instantly happy again.

We made it back to the men just as a horde of people were gathering around the small stage set up in the giant ballroom. The quartet stopped playing. Wes grabbed my bicep and handed me another glass of champagne. "Everything okay?"

"More than okay."

"Anything I should know about?" An eyebrow rose into his hairline.

I shook my head. "Nope. Stay tuned."

He chuckled then led me over to the stage as the emcee started announcing roles in Wes's movie. "Are you excited?" I asked.

"I already know who's been cast," he grinned.

"So what? Now everyone else will know, and everyone will talk about it for months! I'm excited, and I only know the premise of the story."

Wes's hand slid to my shoulder where he cupped it, easing me into his side as we watched people head up to the stage. Each took a bow when their name and assigned character were announced.

"I can't wait to find out who's going to be the soldier, Will, the one who sends his true love, Alison, the letters. Oh, who's going to play Allison?" I turned to look up as he looked down.

"No one's going to play Allison," he responded.

"Huh? But I thought that was the love of his life?" I'm certain my expression was confused as my eyes narrowed in on Wes's handsome face. He grinned and gestured to the stage.

"Watch." He lifted his chin just as a beautiful raven-haired vixen approached the stage. I knew that actress! Gina DeLuca. She was tall and thin yet still had some curves that wouldn't quit. Every man loved her, and every woman wanted to be her. What made her even better was that she had a heart of gold and represented herself to young women in a positive light.

Then I was shocked from my hardcore clapping when the emcee introduced the actress. "Gina DeLuca to play the female lead, Mia Culvers!"

My mouth dropped open. "No way!" I turned to Wes.

"Surprise!" His corresponding smile was absolutely stunning. Something I'd never forget, ever.

"You changed the main character's name to Mia?"

"I did," he said not adding anything else to make me understand why.

I blinked a few times, moisture filling my eyes as I looked at Wes. "Why?"

"Because you matter."

CHAPTER SEVEN

Holy fucking shit. I mattered. My heart filled with happiness as I thought back to a few nights ago when Wes admitted that he named the main character of his movie after me. He even changed what she looked like. She was supposed to be a slight pixie of a woman named Allison, who was blonde and blue-eyed. Most certainly not a busty, raven-haired Rubinesque beauty, like Gina DeLuca…or me.

I wasn't sure what to think or how to take that information. We agreed to not getting attached. Although if I was honest, I couldn't say I wasn't attached to Wes. I definitely was. Did I love him? I didn't think so. This whole time I'd been so focused on not falling in love that the option of opening my heart to him never presented itself.

The buzz of my phone broke me out of the constant loop of "what ifs" I'd been contemplating about Wes and me becoming a real couple. When it came right down to it that was not an option. He knew it, and so did I. That needed to be enough.

"Hello," I answered noting my Aunt Millie's name on the screen.

"Hi doll-face. How's life dipped in gold treating you?" My Aunt Millie's voice was filled with humor but only reminded me of my true station in life. I had been hired to do a job. That job bought me a life of luxury…for a one-month stay. It was not my own, nor would it ever be. I sighed loudly into the phone. "That good, huh?"

"No, it's fine. What's up?" I pulled a lock of hair and inspected the ends looking for splits. Time for a cut.

"I'm calling to tell you about your next client, dear." I could hear paper shuffling and the clacking of nails on a keyboard as she clucked her tongue.

"You will be heading to Seattle!" Never been there, could be fun, I thought, while she continued on. "This one is going to be interesting. "Alec Dubois is the client. Thirty-five, tall, dark, and handsome, fits the bill, but he's odd."

I refrained from commenting. I thought the whole process was strange until I met Wes. Then I realized it was possible for good, kind, normal men to need a companion for one reason or another, and in this particular circumstance, I was glad. Without it, I'd never have met Wes, and he was definitely someone I'd consider significant. He mattered to me too, though I hadn't mentioned it to him yet.

"...picked you off the website the day after I sent you to Mr. Channing. Made me promise he'd get the next month with you."

Cringing, I turned and grabbed a blanket off the chair and wrapped myself in it. "Is he a creeper?"

Millie laughed so loudly into the receiver, I had to pull it away from my ear. "No, baby girl, he's an artist! You're going to be his muse. One look at you and he said he must have you for his new series *"Love on Canvas."* I could hear her clicking, and then my phone beeped that I had a message.

I put her on speaker then looked at the email she'd sent. "Holy, Mother of God." All the air left my chest.

"He is a looker. Just like Mr. Channing, in reverse? Dark hair, dark eyes, average size." I nodded staring numbly at a picture of Mr. Alex Dubois, artist, on the screen. There was nothing average about this dude. He was a dead ringer for Ben Affleck. Only he had long hair that was pulled into a small bun at the top of his head and a mustache-beard combo. I couldn't wait to see just how long that hair was. The man in a word? *Fine*!

I sucked in a sharp breath and released it slowly to relieve some of the heat that filled my body. "So, uh, what does he want me to do as his muse?"

"Not sure. I know he makes unusual art pieces. All one of a kind. They go for hundreds of thousands a piece. However, if you take your clothes off, he's paying more. Period. If you have sex with him—and by God, what woman wouldn't want to—" She laughed. "—he is supposed to give you the additional twenty grand separately."

"Can he demand that I take my clothes off?" I asked, suddenly feeling dirty. Immediately, I racked my brain trying to remember what I signed off on in the contract.

"No, no, no, that is most certainly *not* part of it. However, he did mention it when he booked you. I explained that it would cost him another twenty-five percent on top of his fee, and that was only if you agreed to it, and technically, he's not to touch you sexually."

Twenty-five percent was twenty-five thousand dollars. "Seriously? I'll get another twenty-five thousand dollars if I let him paint nudes of me?"

"No doll-face, you'll get twenty thousand. Exquisite Escorts gets twenty percent on top of your fee. That means five thousand goes to us and twenty to you." I shrugged not really caring. I planned on taking my clothes off. That extra twenty thousand would help get me closer to my ultimate goal. At the very least, it would pay Maddy's unpaid school loans for her first year in school.

"Sign me up! As long as I don't have to sleep with him, I'll pose nude." Even saying it out loud lacked sincerity. Boy, was I in trouble. I hadn't even left Wes yet, and I was already drooling over the next guy in line. I'm a whore.

"You got it. Your flight will leave promptly on the first. Make sure you're on that plane. Your last day officially with Mr. Channing should be January twenty-sixth. That will give you a few days to get yourself to the beautician, get your hair done, your body parts waxed, and all your unmentionables seen to." That time I laughed out loud. "If that's it, I'll let you go…"

"Um, Aunt Millie?"

"Ms. Milan, remember?" she warned.

"Sorry. You realize I'm never going to call you that unless we're in front of clients, right?" I said dead serious.

"What is it, Mia?" her tone lacked the love of a doting family member that time.

"Is it possible for one of the escorts to see their clients again? Personally?"

"Oh please, no. Please don't tell me you've fallen for Mr. Channing?"

"No! No, that's not it." Not really, I told myself. It's not, it's really not. Probably. "It's just that we've become friends, and I'd like to be able to continue that friendship without breaking any rules."

Aunt Millie sighed loudly. "There are no rules per se, but you need to be careful, Mia. Men like that can promise a girl the world and never live up to that promise. Believe me, I've heard it all before. Too many times, in fact."

"So there isn't a rule?"

"No, just," she let out a long breath, "protect your heart. This business isn't for everyone, and you've had a hard road already. Take this time for yourself to have fun, let loose, and experience all that life has to offer. It's probably one of the only times in your life that you'll get the chance." I choked down the rising emotional tide sitting just underneath the surface of my strong façade. "Call me when you meet up with Mr. Dubois. I'll send everything via email." That was the last thing she said before hanging up.

My aunt was right. I couldn't let Wes convince me that this was something more than what it was. I had to go to Seattle. I would go to Seattle. I looked down at the phone. And Mr. Hot Artist Man was going to be my next experience.

★ ★ ★ ★

"Honey, I'm home!" Wes's voice boomed through the house and trickled outside where I was chilling in the heated pool. He entered the patio area in a suit and a smile. Christ, the guy was sexy. He was always good-looking, but there was something about the act of playing dress-up that I enjoyed. Maybe it was undressing him that I enjoyed more.

"You're home early." It was only two-thirty. I pulled myself up and out of the pool, and sat on the edge.

Wes stopped advancing toward me and stood still right at the edge of the pool. His gaze was on me but not on my eyes. He scanned my form with those emerald gems, the look so heated I could practically feel where they landed along my breasts, belly, thighs. I watched as he toed off his shoes then allowed his blazer to drop to the deck. As if cued, I leaned onto my hands arching my back suggestively, pressing my breasts out towards the sky and allowing my head to tip back. My legs opened a bit to balance me. The wisp of a bathing suit left nothing to the imagination, and when I lifted my head to see if my little show was working, I heard a heavy splash. Fully clothed, Wes's form sluiced through the water. He was like a dark shark swimming toward its prey.

He made it to the edge of the pool in one go. His body shot out of the water looking all kinds of water godish. I leaned forward and gripped his wet tie and tugged him between my legs. His hands went to my knees and slid them wide apart.

"That was impulsive," I said against his lips not yet kissing him, just allowing the water from the pool to drip between our mouths.

"Think so? Then you're going to love this." His mouth crashed over mine, his tongue seeking entrance. Wes kissed me as if he'd never get another chance, as though he was starving for the taste of my lips. I knew I was starving for a taste of him. "Been thinking of your taste all damned day," he growled before dragging his tongue down my torso and between my breasts. He slipped his fingers into the skimpy triangles of the bikini and pushed the fabric aside, baring my breasts. My nipples promptly puckered tight at the change in temperature. "I dream of these beauties," he said flicking the tip with his tongue before drawing it into the heat of his mouth. I cried out as my hands went to his head to hold him against me.

The sucking continued until I was squeezing his body against my form, trying to find some friction. When he had me on the edge of orgasm just from playing with my tits, something he loved doing, he pushed me back. I laid on the cold concrete, the chill reaching my bones until his clever fingers found the ties at the side of my bottoms and pulled. Oh, shit. He was going to do this right here, out in the open light of day.

"Wes," I warned, but the warning didn't carry much weight. I was too far gone in a haze of lust to put up much resistance. If Ms. Croft came upon us, she'd just keep on walking. She was pure class. Me, not so much. Wes nipped at the fleshy part of my thighs as he lifted each leg out of the water and set my feet on the pool's edge bending my legs at a ninety degree angle. Then he clasped each knee and spread me open just like a bird's wings opening to fly. And I did fly, the second his tongue touched down on that sensitive bundle of nerves. My hands flew to his head to hold him in place. He grabbed both of them and set them on the concrete and pushed them under my ass.

"Sit on 'em, no touching," he scolded. Ah, so that was how this was going to play out. He wanted full control. Shit, that meant he was going to take me beyond my limits and push me over the edge, over and over again. He'd done it once before. He'd given me so many orgasms that I passed out riding his cock. It was the most sensual, carnal experience of my life, until now.

With the tip of his fingers, he spread me open and used the flat of his tongue to send me into orbit. After one orgasm, he buckled down, holding my legs open, growling into my wet flesh. His next words were a dirty chant.

"Fucking you."

"Tasting you."

"Sucking you."

"More. More."

He growled low in his throat. "God, Mia, I could eat you all day," he gritted through his teeth before sucking my clit into his mouth, hard. I soared into a second orgasm. My body was shaking until Wes gripped my waist and lifted my limp body up and pulled me back into the water.

The shock jolted my system. Nerves were firing off everywhere as the tingles from my orgasm started to dissipate. Before I could fully come back, he had my legs around his waist with my back against the edge of the pool.

"Going to take you so good, baby. I'm going to make sure you feel me, even when you're gone." He thrust into me hard. I don't know when he did it, but his pants were floating somewhere in the pool, reminding me of a stingray on the ocean floor. Wes's upper body was still completely clothed in dress shirt and tie. I clung to the wet fabric as he pounded into me. The chanting started again. I don't think he even knew he was speaking. But I did, and I held onto every word, letting each clipped phrase singe into my memory so I could revisit this moment again and again when I needed him…missed him.

"I was here." thrust

"Together." thrust

"Fuck" thrust

"Love this" thrust

"Remember me." thrust

"Remember me," he said again, louder as he slammed into me, hitting that spot within that sent me reeling into the hardest, longest, release of my life. I screamed. My body no longer my own. My voice no longer my own. I came to with his mouth on mine and his tongue sweeping in and out. We were still connected as he walked me soaking wet into his room and laid me on the bed. He left me only long enough to remove his tie and shirt, and then crawled over me. He widened my legs and slipped into the oversensitive swollen tissue between my legs once more. Connected.

He didn't fuck me then. He made slow, agonizingly sweet love to me.

★ ★ ★ ★

"Hello, skank! Long time no talk," my best friend, Ginelle's, voice came through the phone not only harsh but with a hint of genuine upset.

"Hooker, I've been working," I tried but failed.

"Yeah, uh huh, riding Wes's cock could be called work, I suppose," she retorted, a tiny note of humor in her tone. My girl was forgiving me.

"Not all of us have talent and can dance like a goddess," I countered.

"True..." she drew out the word making it a few syllables longer.

"I miss you," my voice shook, and I wanted to bitch-slap myself for letting the emotion out.

A deep sigh came through the line. "I miss your ugly face too. I get hit on a lot more when you're around. You know, since I'm the pretty one." And...we're back to BFF status again.

"How's my dad?" I asked, scared to hear her reply.

"Better physically. Still hasn't woken up. They've moved him out of intensive care, so that's a good sign."

That was a good sign. It meant he'd live, but he wasn't out of the woods yet. "Did they say anything about why he hasn't come out of the coma?"

"They don't tell me much, Mia. I'm not technically family. You know that."

Now I sighed. Ginelle was more my family than the extended family I had on both sides. She was the only friend I trusted. "Thanks for keeping an eye on him for me. How about Maddy? I've only talked to her once, and that was for a few minutes when she was between classes. Seems like the full class load is kicking her ass."

"Yeah, it is. She's stressed about money, too. The bills are piling up. Need me to give her some cash?"

"No, no! I have money. Well I'm going to have a lot of money in a week. Enough to send her some to pay the bills and buy food. Soon though, I'm going to have a lot more! Just need to get on an airplane next week, and that hundred thousand goes into my account. Then I have an opportunity to get paid another twenty thousand, and that would be just mine."

"How you going to make an extra twenty thou?" I could hear her suck in a drag off her cigarette. Must be finishing up her lunch break with a smoke.

I chewed on my thumbnail and looked down at the ragged edge. "Next client is an artist. I'm going to be his muse or some shit. Wants me to pose nude. If I do it, it's an extra twenty large."

You could hear Gin blow out a breath into the phone. "Fuck! I take off my clothes every fucking day and don't get paid no twenty grand! Get me hooked up with Auntie Millie. I'm due some fat cash!" she harrumphed into the phone, and I laughed. She'd never leave Vegas. God, it's good to talk to my girl. She reminds me of everything I am, where my roots are laid, and that I'm still me. Even if I'm dressed up like a Barbie doll and playing the part of a trophy date, I'm still Mia Saunders. The girl who raised her sister from age five, took care of herself, and is going to save her dad's ass…again. Hopefully, for the last time. I could only hope that once he woke up and realized what he'd done, what had happened due to his choices, he might actually learn from it. Get some help with the drink. See a counselor. I'd given him information on tons of free programs along with the flyers and pamphlets for the local AA. Maybe, just maybe, this time he'd see the error in his ways.

"You coming home at all?" Gin asked as I pulled out the dress I was going to wear to this evening's social event. Wes was taking me to some movie shindig with the new cast. It looked like fun. I'd get to meet some famous people. Ones I hoped to work with someday. That career path was nowhere in sight for the time being. Funny how things had come around full circle. I finally knew someone in the industry, and there was no way I could even commit to anything or go on any auditions. That part of my life was on an indefinite hold until I got my dad out of hock.

"I wish. Heading straight to Seattle three days after I leave Malibu. Auntie has me set up on a horde of beauty appointments between that day and the day I head out. I'll try next month though," I offered weakly.

"Hey, I know you want to come home as much as I want to see your fat ass, but it's okay. Things are going to be fine here while you clean up your dad's mess. But shit, Mia, he's gotta learn from this go 'round. You can't keep upending your life for him."

"I have no choice," I whined. "If I don't, they'll kill him. And he's in a coma, Gin. It's not like he can defend himself."

This conversation was getting old. I loved Ginelle more than anything, but she spent an ungodly amount of time nailing me over my dad's bullshit and how I continued to save him. It's not like I wanted to. But I couldn't just let him be hurt or killed. Blaine and his goons are serious motherfuckers. Blaine is a coldhearted snake. He wouldn't think twice about killing Dad. Hell, he'd be more concerned about getting blood on his expensive suit than he would about taking my dad's life. People are collateral damage to him, and I had been one of his victims. Cheating, lying piece of trash!

Through the phone, I could hear rustling around then the ever present clinking and pinging of the slot machines as she made her way back through the casino. "Just promise me you'll find a way to have a life?"

"I will, I will. Besides, I've been having some fun here in Malibu. Wes taught me how to surf!"

"Okay, that is pretty cool. I've never even seen the ocean," she groaned. "When you become rich from escorting, will you take me to the ocean?"

I laughed. "And see your skanky ass in a bikini?" I pretended to gag and choke.

"You're messed up. I'm revoking best friend status."

"You can't revoke best friend status. It just is. Like the commandments written in stone. It just is," I said again lamely.

"Did you just compare our friendship to God's Ten Commandments? For real?"

"Um...yeah?"

"You're going to hell," she stated flatly.

"If I do, you're skanky ass better be there to pick me up!"

She giggled, and I smiled holding the phone tight. "You know I will."

"I love you, ho."

"I love you more, slut."

CHAPTER EIGHT

Nobu Restaurant in Malibu was swanky. Like entering into your own private posh world. The *Honor Code* actors, directors, and writers were all in attendance. There wasn't a huge crowd, maybe forty people. When we arrived, the hostess led us to a private outside area. The patio had a natural knotty wood flooring that spanned a huge veranda with wicker-cushioned furniture and hardwood tables. The entire expanse opened out onto a hundred and eighty degree view of the beach. The sun was just setting, and the colors of the sky bouncing off the water were breathtaking. Wes pulled me into his arms as I grabbed the rail. He hugged me against his front.

"Beautiful," he said into my ear before trailing his nose down the column of my neck.

"It is pretty," I agreed.

"Not the view, you." He bit down on that place where neck meets shoulder sending shivers of burgeoning excitement to swell and ache delightfully within me.

"Smooth talker." I pinched the side of his thigh where my hand rested.

"Ouch, see if I ever give the lady a compliment again," he said with mock agitation.

I turned around and clasped my hands around his neck, and kissed him. Nothing indecent, just a coming together of lips. I'd missed him throughout the day while he was at work, and this was the first chance I had to be close to him.

He groaned into my mouth and then pulled back and just stared. After a moment, he shook his head and smiled. I knew there was something he wanted to say to me, but right then, I knew it wasn't going to be something I could handle.

"Let's get a drink and a bite?"

His shoulders slumped, the moment broken. "Sure," he finished, grabbing my hand and leading me over to the bar. We got drinks and then a waiter came by and offered us some Asian style nibbles. While we were talking and snacking, the most beautiful woman I'd ever seen made her way through the crowd. She was wearing a deep crimson, strapless cocktail dress that accentuated her large breasts perfectly. The hemline came up just above the knee on her incredibly long legs. She had black, thick hair that looked a lot like mine, but hers was curled in perfect loose spirals that wisped along her pearly skin perfectly. Bright red lips and smoky eye makeup completed her look. The woman was every man's wet dream and every woman's nightmare. Except mine. I wanted to be her!

"Gina," Wes held out a hand towards the stunning woman. "I'd like you to meet my friend, Mia Saunders." Her eyes widened and her lips curved into a smirk at the way he said 'friend'.

She placed a small hand on Wes's shoulder, looked up at him, and batted her eyelashes prettily before turning to me. Wes was completely enchanted by her. Hell, I was too. True beauty like hers didn't come around too often.

"Gina DeLuca." She offered her hand and I shook it. "Any friend of Wes's is a friend of mine." Her voice sounded as if she was singing a melody, only with a sultry female crooner type vibe. Once she shook my hand, she stood in front of me and brazenly pressed her chest against Wes's. "I'm really looking forward to getting started on your story. It's a fascinating premise." Her hand came up and stroked his lapel. He stood there speechless staring down into the sexy woman's eyes.

I almost felt like I was intruding on a private moment. I most certainly was not needed for this conversation. And in spite of what I'd promised myself, I was getting jealous. No, I didn't have a claim on Wes officially, but I was his date for the next few days, dammit! I tried clearing my throat. It did nothing to break the spell she had over Wes.

"Maybe we could run some of the lines at my place sometime, you know, so I get a really good feel for the character." She licked her lips and the core of heat within my gut turned white hot with rage. Who did this chick think she was?!

"Um, sure, yeah, that sounds uh…" Wes tried and that was it. I shoved her out of the way, politely interrupting.

"Sweetie, I'm starving. You ready to sit and eat?" I batted my own lashes, but I was pretty sure they didn't have the same affect. Wes looked down at me, shook his head, and then a smile slipped across his lips. His eyes twinkled, and he pulled me to his side with a hand around my waist.

"Anything for Ms. Mia," he said kissing my forehead. "Sorry, Gina, will you excuse us?"

I looked over at the pretty, black-haired vixen. Her mouth was gaping open like she couldn't believe I'd butted in on her play when, really, she butted in on mine.

"Mia? Like in the movie?" she queried.

Wes looked over at me with that panty-dropping grin.

"Wanted something to remember my girl by," he said never looking at Gina. That gesture right there filled my heart with joy and sadness, knowing I would be leaving soon.

"Remember her? Where are you going?" she asked me directly, crossing her arms over her ample bosom.

I sucked in a breath and closed my eyes. "Seattle," I said and caught it when Wes winced.

"Oh yeah, for what?"

"Work." I had nothing better to say. It was the truth, but I wasn't about to tell this chick that I was the hired help or that Wes was technically a free agent who might appreciate her blatant come-ons.

Gina rolled her eyes. "What type of work are you in?"

"Well, for this job I'll be modeling for an artist over the next month while he paints me."

Gina plastered on a fake smile. "And will you be wearing any clothing during these paintings?" She hit the nail right on the head.

"I think that's enough, Gina. I'll see you on set in a week. Come on Mia, let's get some food and find a place to settle." He gripped my hip and turned me around walking in the opposite direction of the pretty actress.

We got to a table way in the corner that had an even better view of the ocean at night. A server brought us new drinks and laid a plate of noshes between us. Once I took a bite and let the puffy pastry bite melt in my mouth, Wes pounced.

"So, Seattle?" I nodded not wanting to really get into it with him. "And was Gina right in her assumption?"

I shoved another bite of fishy goodness in my mouth and had to cut off a moan. Damn, this place was amazing.

"Was she, Mia? Are you going to be naked in front of this artist while he paints you?" Instead of responding, I shrugged. "It's a simple question," he said through clenched teeth.

"Maybe. He does some nudes, so it's a possibility," I said thinking that might be better than the absolute truth or outright lying.

Wes shook his head and took a long pull of his beer. "I need a real fucking drink." He got up and stormed over to the bar. I sat back and thought about how this night was turning out. I was jealous of him, now he was jealous of some guy neither of us had even met. What the hell was happening?

When he came back, he had a tumbler full of amber colored liquid that made my stomach turn. Ever since that first night, he'd made an effort not to drink whiskey, and I appreciated him for it. Now though, he was drinking it like it was water.

"Why are you mad?"

He shook his head. "Not mad." he clenched his teeth, a muscle in his jaw ticking away. "I think I know when you're mad. We've been living together for the better part of a month."

"Do you even want to do this?" he asked finally.

"It's not a matter of whether I want to. I have to!" I whispered loudly leaning forward. He looked around.

"You don't have to do shit. Everyone has a choice. You could stay." And there it was. He definitely wanted me to stay even though he knew I couldn't.

"Don't..."

"Why not! Because it will make you feel something?"

he sneered.

I stood up and walked away. Wes didn't follow me.

★ ★ ★ ★

The sound of glass shattering woke me from a dead sleep. I got up and tiptoed along the hallway keeping myself dead silent until I found Wes laughing with half his jacket on, the other half twisted around his hand as if he'd been trying to get it off.

I walked over to him and tugged on the jacket. That was a bad idea. Once he was free, he steamrolled me into the opposite wall, lips on my neck. He bit down hard, and I cried out trying to push him off me. "Mia, Mia, Mia, I want you so bad. Don't want to lose you…please," he begged but I had no idea what his slurred, drunken words really meant.

"Come on. Let's get you to bed," I said trying to adjust him. He walked a few steps then stopped and grabbed me to him. My back hit another wall. This time his hand cupped my breast, and he tweaked the nipple with expert fingers. I moaned.

"Fuck yeah, I love those little noises you make. Almost between a moan and a whimper. Makes my dick so hard." And he wasn't kidding as evidenced by his rock hard erection thrusting against my hip. Before I could move, he had one of my legs slung up and over one hip. Even in a drunken state, he knew exactly what he was doing, only his movements were a little bit sloppier, less coordinated.

"Wes, not here., We need to get you in bed."

"You'll come with me?" he pleaded, licking and biting along the column of my neck. "Stay with me in my bed."

"Yeah sure, we'll fuck in your bed this time," I said leading him to his room. Once we got there, he turned around, gripped me by the hips and kissed me. Even tinged with whiskey, the one liquor I couldn't stand, he tasted great.

"No, I want you to sleep with me. All night long. I want to wake up to you one time," he begged leading me over to the bed. He sat, pulled down my panties, and I lifted up my camisole standing before him naked as the day I was born.

"I love this body." His hand traced down from my clavicle, over my breast where he gave a little squeeze, down the curve of my waist, over my hip bone, and down my thigh. I shivered when he completed the journey on the other side.

"Just this once, stay all night. Let me wake to you," he leaned forward and took a nipple into his mouth. Bolts of electricity roared through my limbs, pleasure being the first to light up, and quickly followed by lust and need.

"Just this once," I repeated.

That night we made love for the second time. Desperate, clawing love. Somewhere in the middle of the night, Wes woke up sober and took me again. He told me he wanted to reenact everything we did so he'd be certain to remember it. I knew I'd never forget it.

★ ★ ★ ★

I woke to Wes watching me sleep. His blond, shaggy hair fell over his eyes, and I pushed it to the side, wanting to see all of him in the beautiful morning light.

"Why are you an escort?" he asked. There was no judgment, no harshness to his words. Just the simple question as if it was something he'd been dying to know since day one. He probably had.

It was time. He deserved to know why I couldn't give him more. I know he wanted me to stay, possibly live with him to see how being together for *real* could turn out. He knew it didn't bother me that he was so busy, which was the reason he claimed he didn't do relationships. I could take care of myself and had proven it. I wasn't a clingy chick like most trophy bitches. But that was just it. I didn't want to be a trophy wife, or girlfriend, for that matter. It was important that I find my own way, be my own person. And right now, I couldn't do that because I had to help my dad.

Instead of skimming the truth or making up something plausible, I laid it out for him.

"My dad owes some really bad guys some money. A lot of money."

"I have a lot of money," he said quietly. Tears pricked at the corners of my eyes at his admission. I turned towards him, put my hands in prayer pose, and tucked them under my cheek. He mimicked my pose.

"Yes, you do, but it's your money. My dad got in bad with some loan sharks for gambling. I'm working to pay off that debt."

"How much?"

"A million."

He let out a slow breath. "I have a lot of expendable money, Mia. I could help you."

I shook my head. Knowing the type of man Wes Channing was, I knew once he found out that my family was in trouble, he'd want to help. Only this was my problem, not his.

"I know you could, but I haven't asked for your help."
It was imperative that I make it perfectly clear that this was
my decision. I wasn't a damsel in distress and he wasn't a
white knight, charging in to save the day. Fairytales don't
exist, especially for chicks from Vegas with a truckload of
baggage.

"But what if I wanted to help?"

"You're very kind, Wes."

He shook his head and leaned onto his back. "No Mia,
I'm not. I'm selfish. I don't want you to go. I don't want you
to go pose nude for some rich artist in Seattle. I want you
here with me, in my house, and in my bed. I'll pay whatever
price it takes to get that."

All of the air left my lungs in a whoosh. "Do you love
me, Wes?"

His gaze shot to mine. "Um," he licked his lips and bit
down on the plump flesh. Made me want to kiss it better. "I
know I like you. I like you a lot."

I smiled wide and traced his nose from the bridge
down to the tip with one finger. "I like you too, Wes. A lot.
But this is something I have to do. Not only for my dad,
though that is the driving force, but for me, too. And you
need no distractions. Your movie starts filming next week.
You're going to be directing for the first time…"

Wes ran a hand through his hair. "I know all those
things. That doesn't change that I want you here."

"I know it doesn't. And if I'm being honest, I don't
want to go, but I am going to leave. And you and me? We're
going to stay friends. Right?"

He sighed then pulled my body up and over his. I rested
my arms on his chest then leaned my chin on his sternum.

"Of course we are. If nothing else, you're the best girlfriend I've ever had."

My eyebrows shot up into my hairline. "I mean, you know. Best friend that's a girl."

"I understand," I pecked him on the lips.

"So you're leaving in two days, and there's nothing I can do or say to make you stay?"

I shook my head and rested against his heart, letting the heavy thump lull me into a place that was half awake, half asleep. I knew in my heart of hearts that the only reason I'd stay, could stay, even consider staying, would be if he loved me. There was no denying that I was falling for him, but I held a part of me back, knowing that love was never supposed to be on the table. Not after falling in love with every man I'd ever slept with. This time with Wes, I'd guarded my heart so fiercely that he'd only gotten small bits and pieces of it along the way. The whole enchilada was still safe with me in full control.

"Where does that leave us then?" He slid his hands down to cup my ass cheeks, and he gave them a tight squeeze. It reminded me of how much I was going to miss his bedroom skills. Going back to a battery-operated boyfriend was not high on my list of things I wanted to do in Seattle. Like see the phallic space needle. That was high on the list.

"How about we leave it as friends?"

He grimaced. "Best friends?" I tried.

He lifted me up by the waist, centered his hard cock between my thighs, and I sank down onto it, pierced by the steely girth and length of him. Jesus, the man was well hung, and even better, he knew exactly how to use it.

"Benefits," I whispered on a hard thrust, and he grinned.

"Best friends, with benefits," I said then tipped my head back, anchored my hands on his muscled pecs and squeezed from within.

Wes's body went tight. "Now you're talking." He pulled me up and slammed me down. We both cried out. "Now ride me."

CHAPTER NINE

"What do you want to do today?" Wes asked when I entered the breakfast area. To my surprise, he was cooking, flipping pancakes to be exact. I looked around scanning the area for Ms. Croft.

"Where's Judi?"

"Gave her the day off. Since it's your last day, I wanted the entire day alone with you." He grinned then winked.

I sat on the barstool in front of the island where he was finishing up our breakfast. The pancakes weren't burnt and smelled delicious. I stared in awe at the short stack. Butter dripped down the sides enticingly mixing in with the thick syrup. Then he squirted a can of whipped cream making some type of design on the top. With a flick of his wrist, he slid the plate in front of me. On the very top of the stack was a happy face.

"Happy cakes." He waggled his eyebrows, and I laughed. This man was such a dichotomy. Work-a-holic, surfer, escort-hiring, Jeep-driving, rich man, who made pancakes with smiley faces on them. "What?" He leaned his elbows on the counter and tilted his head. His face had the morning stubble I had gotten used to seeing, and adored. I used the tips of my fingers to skip across the prickly surface.

I shook my head and cut into the small stack of five perfectly round cakes. "You just surprise me. Every time I think I have you figured out, you sideswipe me with something else."

Wes shrugged and dug into his own breakfast. "What can I say? I like to keep you guessing." He smiled and I swore all those sappy chick flicks I tried to avoid were right. A good man could light up a room and make the world smaller, like something that could fit into the space where your entire focus lives.

"Back to your initial question," I said around a mouth full of the best pancakes I'd ever eaten—including my own—in my entire life. "I'd like to take a ride on my bike," I said, and he nodded.

"I'm game. Where we going?"

I grinned and flicked my unruly, morning bedhead hair over my shoulder. "Wherever the bike takes us. It's not where we go. It's the journey that counts."

Wes came around, sat down, and then turned toward me. I faced him, thinking he was going to kiss me. He usually did first thing in the morning, but today was different. Everything about my last day felt so heavy, weighed down by the finality of it. Instead of a kiss, I got a dollop of whipped cream on my nose. "That was deep," he said deadpan.

I shoved him. "Shut the fuck up!" He laughed.

"Come on, Mia. It's not the ride, it's the journey? Where did you come up with that shit? Tell me the truth. It was on the sticker when you bought the bike, right?"

"It's true though!" I shook my head, and we commenced eating breakfast. Every so often he'd tag my side with his elbow. Not enough to hurt, just enough to let me know he was there and messing with me. If I was being honest with myself, I was going to miss Wes. More than I wanted to admit. A lot more.

★ ★ ★ ★

"Jesus Christ," Wes said as I entered the garage where my bike had been stored. His gaze was all over me. From the black leather jacket I wore over my Radiohead concert tank top, down my ass-hugging skinny jeans to my knee-high biker boots.

"You like?" I cocked a hip to the side, knowing it accentuated my hourglass shape that he appreciated very much. He'd told me enough times how infatuated he was with my body. Wes liked a woman with a little meat on her. Stick-thin girls were not his gig. At least that's what he said. He could have fed me a line, but if the look on his face right at that moment was any indication, he liked what he saw.

He threw his leather jacket over the seat of the bike, made his way around his Jeep, and in two seconds flat, his mouth was on mine. Kissing for Wes was more than foreplay. It was a brand, something he seared into my skin and stayed with me all day. Hell, I'd never forget any of his kisses. They were that good. Light nips at times, simple swipes of his tongue at other moments, followed by full, deep, drugging movements the next. And his hands, oh, his hands were magnificent. He knew exactly where to caress, pinch, tickle, which is what he was doing to my ass and breast. One on each. No one could ever say Wes wasn't good with hands.

I sucked on Wes's tongue then bit his lip until he moaned. He pulled back and laid his head against my forehead. "I thought we were going to ride," I breathed against his lips then licked the rim.

"Yeah, until I saw you like that. Now my dick has other plans." He pressed his hips against mine. I could feel the hardness through his jeans.

With great effort, I pulled back, cupped his cheeks and stared into his beautiful green eyes. "Later. The wait makes the anticipation sweeter." I finished off by nipping his lips once more. He tried to chase after them, but I pulled away.

Giving him an extra sway of my hips so he got a nice hard look at my ass, I flung a leg over my bike. "Hey girl." I petted the tank and handle bars. "You ready to show Wes what you can do, sweet thing?" I spoke softly to Suzi.

"Um, I think you need to scoot back so I can get on." Wes gestured that I move back to ride bitch.

"I must not have heard you. Did you insinuate that I was going to ride bitch?" My eyebrows rose up into my hairline, and I narrowed my gaze.

Wes put one hand on the handlebar and one down by his side. "If that means your legs are squeezing me, and I can feel your heat all up my back, then yeah, that's exactly what I'm suggesting." He licked his lips and scanned my body with his gaze once more. Again, it was not lost on me that those eyes might as well have been hands because I could feel them running up and down me every time he looked my way.

"Well, I believe we have a predicament then. Suzi's my girl, and I'm the only one that drives her. You, my friend, need to wrap those thick thighs around me." I pushed forward and made room on the back. "Unless you're worried about your masculinity."

Wes surprised me. He put on his leather jacket and flung a long leg over the bike. Then before I could even turn Suzi on, Wes turned me on. He molded his form to my back, slid a hand up and under my tank in front, shoving my bra up and out of the way so his hand could get at naked skin. Then his fingers pulled and plucked at the hardening tip. I moaned as his mouth came down against my neck, sucking and nipping at the sensitive skin. I arched backward, leaning my head against his shoulder and pushing back into his hardness. Just as I craned my neck around toward him, the button on my jeans was opened and the zipper pulled down.

"Oh God," I whispered when his hands made contact going straight into my jeans. Those talented fingers zeroed in finding my heat. He pushed two deep inside while swirling his thumb around the tight knot of nerves throbbing for his touch. Wes didn't disappoint. With powerful arms, he arched my body back using my pussy and breast as his anchor. Those fingers of his going impossibly deep until I cried out, squeezing my eyes tight as the spasms signaling my release closed in.

Wes's teeth grated down my neck, and I thrust my hips up, using the heel spikes as my fulcrum. I knew he'd keep the bike up with his own powerful legs, so I pushed up hard, wrestling to reach that beautiful crest, the pinnacle of pleasure.

"Ride me, baby," Wes whispered against my hairline. That growly timber sent me even further into the bliss. I did what he said. Like a wanton hussy, I bent back over him, thrust my hips, forcing his fingers to fuck me harder. His hand was nothing but a blur between my legs as he worked me. Then he pinched my nipple with one hand, bit down on my neck, and drove deep with his other, hooking those fingers up and yanking down, crushing my clit with his palm.

Gone.

Sweet blessed oblivion.

"That's it, sweetheart, come back to me," Wes said into my ear, his thumb still twirling around my clit sending sweet tremors to scatter in every direction while I made my descent back to Earth. "I take it back," he whispered into my ear before turning my neck and kissing me.

"Take what back?" I asked still in my happy place.

"The ride was nice, but it was all about the journey. Watching you come apart in my arms, on this bike, that's something I'll never forget."

Me either.

★ ★ ★ ★

We rode up and down Highway One taking in the views between Malibu Canyon Road and Point Magu Rock. Wes pointed to a turn-off near a worn down sign for a public beach. The entrance was off the beaten path, but Wes knew where we were going. I stopped the bike at the tiny turnout with a dirt path that led down to a small cove. When we got there, Wes pulled off his backpack and pulled out a thin blanket. We spread it across the sand and settled looking out at the open expanse of ocean. The place was public yet completely deserted. There wasn't a house or person for miles. Wes dug into the pack again and brought out some sandwiches.

"You made lunch, too? A girl could get used to this. Amazing pancakes and now this? Let me guess, a gourmet turkey made with hummus and the freshest veggies?" I cocked a brow, and he covered his mouth while he snickered.

"Think again, princess." He handed me half a sandwich.

"Peanut butter and jelly?" I looked down and shook my head then took a bite of the creamy sandwich. It had the perfect ratio of peanut butter to berry jelly. He grinned and handed me a thermos. I expected water, but it ended up being ice cold milk. Perfection. "Milk?"

"Only the best for you, Ms. Mia." He took a big bite then grabbed for the milk.

"You know, PB & J is actually my favorite sandwich." His eyes widened. "It is. Seriously. I love it. And you know what, I love this. Sitting here with you after a long ride. It's…well, I'll remember this, Wes. Being here with you. This month has been the best of my life. And not just the sex." His eyebrows rose. "Okay, maybe the sex." We both laughed.

He took another swallow of milk then responded. "I know what you mean. Being with you is easy." I cocked my head to the side and he grinned. "Not *easy* easy. Just…it feels good. You don't make me work for it. Your needs are simple, and you're not a drama queen. I didn't think a relationship could be like that."

"Never was easy for me, either. Always something in the way," I admitted. Wes looked off into the distance as I stared at his profile. As far as beautiful men go, Weston Channing was tops. He didn't even have to try to look good. He was naturally good looking. Casual, professional, even when he'd just woken up and sleep crust was in his eyes, he was still heart-stoppingly gorgeous. But right now, sharing this private span of beach with me, sharing a bit of himself, that made him irresistible. "Have you ever been in love?"

His eyes shot to mine, a hint of a smile on his lips. He leaned back onto his elbows and shook his head. "No, I don't think so. A couple times I thought maybe, but like I said, it was never easy. I think when you love someone it should be easy. Things should just fall into place, you know?"

I nodded. "The planets, moons, and stars align and everything just works right?"

He laughed. "Something like that. You?"

"Me what?"

"Have you been in love?" I thought long and hard about his question. So much so, that his hand came up to my shoulder and gripped tenderly. "You don't have to tell me."

"No, it's not that. It's just it would be easier to ask me if I haven't fallen in love. In some way, I've fallen in love with every last man I've ever been with. Unfortunately, now, sitting here with you, I'm questioning whether I was actually in love, lust, or maybe just overwhelmed by them."

"Why do you think that is?"

I laughed, brought my legs up into my chest and tucked my chin onto my knees. "Not sure. It feels different with you."

"So you've been with me a month. Admitted that the sex has been the best of your entire life." I rolled my eyes at him but he kept on. "Agreed that it's different with me. Does that mean you love me?"

"Maybe," I said honestly not really knowing how else to respond.

"Well, fuck me."

"We're going to do that later, remember. Anticipation?" I reminded him.

Wes laughed and then turned on his side and propped his head on his hand. "What if I said I was falling in love with you?"

"Wes," I warned. He knew better than to go that route.

"No, let's just talk this out for a minute." He forced me to lean back and mimic his pose so we were lying on our sides looking into one another's eyes. "If you maybe love me and I'm falling in love with you, shouldn't we do something about it?"

I smiled. "We are. We're going to stay friends. You're going to go to work and direct your film. We'll stay in contact, and when my debt is paid…" I looked deeply into his eyes and stopped.

"When your debt is paid then what?"

"I come back home to LA where you are," I offered.

"But you're still going to leave tomorrow." The sadness in his green eyes stole my breath. It was long moments before I could respond.

"Yes. I'm leaving tomorrow."

He nodded and looked down. "So, then when you come back…" This time his words trailed off.

"I don't want you waiting for me, Wes. If you find something good with someone, you take advantage of it. Have fun. A man like you, who looks the way you do, is not going to have a hard time finding someone to warm your bed."

"Is that what you're going to do? Let your clients warm your bed?" His tone was hard, harsher than I expected, but I knew what we were talking about was dangerous territory. It had the power to ruin everything we'd come to have over the past month and could ever have in the future. It was time to tread lightly.

"I'm just saying that for this year, we're going to go our separate ways. We're going to do whatever we want."

He let out a long, slow breath and sat up. "That means you're not going to wait for me." A quick burst of air left his nose, like he was holding back a huff.

I shook my head. "No. I'm going to do what feels right at the time, for me. And I want you to do the same. But I don't want to lose you in my life."

He licked his lips then grabbed my hand, bringing it up to his mouth for a kiss. "I don't want to lose you either. It's just, I'm trying to find a place where letting you go is okay. Because it doesn't feel right."

I gripped his hand tight then brought it to my lips for a return kiss. "It doesn't for me either, but it's what's going to happen. Please respect that. Can you do that for me? And in the future, we'll just see where we're at. That has to be enough."

"It's nowhere near enough, Mia. If it's all I've got, it will have to do for now." He pulled me into his side and hugged me tight. I held on knowing that soon, I'd be letting go.

★ ★ ★ ★

All my stuff was loaded into the SUV, and I watched as it pulled out of Wes's driveway headed towards my apartment. The driver had the key to my tiny box and would put the clothing in and leave the key with the super.

Wes was expecting me to be here when he got home so we could have one last meal together. Unfortunately, I knew that doing so would break me. More than that, it would ruin me. After our time on the beach yesterday, we went back to his home and spent the entire afternoon into the evening making love. That's what it was. It wasn't fucking or having sex. We made love, over and over again until we were exhausted and passed out, snuggled together in his giant bed. Then he got a call that forced him to go into the studio this morning. He said he'd be home at six to take me out for our last dinner. Except I wouldn't be there. It would be too hard to say goodbye like that after everything we've been through.

Instead, I decided to share my thoughts with him on paper, writing him a cliché, but heartfelt, Dear John letter. Basically, I was a coward.

Weston Charles Channing, III,

Writing your name out like that cracks me up. Have you ever said your name out loud? Do it. For me. It's funny. You'll laugh. I did. ☺

In all seriousness, I want to thank you for this month. I was expecting to hate every second of this job and instead, it ended up being the most exciting thing I've ever done in my life. Meeting you has been a gift. You're a gift, Wes. I know that sounds cheesy and I almost scratched it out, but you need to hear it from someone who cares. And I do care. A lot. More than I should.

Being with you, spending time together, has changed me, for the better I think. I now feel as though I can get through this year and learn something from it, aside from just saving my dad. I think I'm going to be saving myself. It's time for me to live for me. If I stayed and let you take care of my problems, pay off my dad's debt, I would regret it every day of my life. It would always hang over my head and our relationship. Leaving this way, I'm leaving on my terms. And I'm leaving us still good friends. The best of friends. Friends with benefits? <wink>

Am I sad leaving? Yes. I don't want to leave, but you already knew that. I know what I'm doing sucks for the both of us, but I also know it's the only way I can truly be free. What's that saying? 'If you love someone set it free and if it doesn't come back it wasn't meant to be?'

I hope to come back one day. If it's meant to be, it will be, right? If it's not, we will always have a friend we can count on. I truly hope you understand that and where these words are coming from. I wish you the best. Your movie is going to blow everyone away because you wrote it, and your words are beautiful.

This morning when you thought I was asleep and you kissed me goodbye you said softly, "Remember me." Wes, I promise, I'll never forget our time together but most importantly, I'll never forget you.

With everything that I am,

~Mia

Then I kissed the letter right next to my name leaving a set of fat pink lips. One last kiss for Wes.

★ ★ ★ ★

The next couple of days were a nightmare of appointments my Aunt Millie scheduled for me prior to meeting hot artist guy, Alec Dubois. The hair and nail appointments were pleasant, if not boring as hell. I dig pretty things as much as the next girl, but spending four fucking hours getting your hair done, and another two for your feet and nails is ridiculous. After that, Millie had me with the aesthetician.

An aesthetician is another name for torture mistress. They start with a relaxing facial where they fill your senses with these beautiful scents, calming music, and a facial massage. Then they bust out the bright spotlight. Your choices at that point are close your eyes or lose a retina. The eye closing is designed to help you when they bring forth the excavator, I mean the "extractor." Otherwise known as a pimple popping, blackhead digging shovel that removes every pore on your face of the nasty gunk your daily makeup leaves behind. It's serious business, but I will say, my face never looked better. Bright, flawless skin that felt like a baby's ass. It was so smooth to the touch.

Then my day turned to complete and utter shit. I had to get waxed. Everywhere. The artist had very specific requirements. If I was going to drop my clothes, and he was going to drop an additional twenty -five thousand, I needed to be hairless everywhere but my head. The peach fuzz on my arms was okayed thankfully. My nether regions, not so much. If you've never had the pleasure of getting a Brazilian wax, consider yourself lucky. First, your assailant, I mean aesthetician, covers every inch of your lady bits with hot wax barely this side of scalding. Once that cools and hardens into a hard surface, the skin is held down while they proceed to rip a layer of skin and every single hair out leaving your bits hairless, smooth and looking less like a woman and more like a little girl.

It's demoralizing, and I can't imagine why women would willingly go through this if they weren't getting paid the big bucks. At least I know I'm getting a payout at the end of my suffering. What's their excuse?

★ ★ ★ ★

My phone beeped from my back pocket. I'd received a text. People were still getting settled before take-off, so I could check the message and maybe even have time for a reply.

From: Wes Channing
To: Mia Saunders
Got your letter. Sorry I didn't contact sooner. I thought it would be better if I gave it time. Want to wish you safe travels. There's something in your bag in the front pocket. I'll call you soon. Remember me.

I smiled and pulled the pack from under the seat in front of me. Inside the front pocket was a small black box about three inches wide by an inch tall. Once I opened it, the item inside made me smile so wide I thought my cheeks might burst. Inside the box was a brass key dangling from a small yellow and pink surfboard. It was the key I used while I lived with Wes. My key. Only this time, the keychain had a small addition. A sparkly red heart dangled alongside the surfboard.

A note sat jammed at the bottom of the box. I opened it.

Mia,
You forgot your key. It opens a lot more than a door. One day I hope you'll use it.
~Wes

With purpose, I pulled out my keys to Suzi and my apartment and attached the surfboard and key to Wes's house. His intention couldn't be any clearer. If I wanted to come back to him, I would need to be ready to give him my heart because I already had his.

February

CALENDAR GIRL

CHAPTER ONE

The twisted and rusted iron gates of the ancient elevator clanged loudly together as the driver pulled them down, locking them in place. He hadn't uttered a word other than, "You Mia?" when I came down the escalator at Seattle -Tacoma International Airport baggage claim. I figured it was safe to follow him since he had a sign with my full name on it, and Aunt Millie told me to expect a giant lumberjack of a man to drive me to my next client. The giant part was no joke, and it wasn't his height. The guy stood only a couple inches taller than me, but what he lacked in height, he made up for in width. Reminded me of a pro wrestler or one of those beefy body builders.

Once the elevator made it to the tenth floor, it came to a screeching, grinding halt, jolting me into Paul Bunion's baby brother. He was a solid wall, didn't even flinch when I bumped into him, just grunted like an animal. The giant doors opened and Bunion pulled open the gates and ushered me into what seemed to be an open warehouse. The rafters and piping were visible and no less than thirty feet above the concrete floor. People were milling around everywhere, half of them naked.

What the fuck did I get myself into?

Cameras were clicking, lighting units and reflectors were being moved around on wheeled carts as I stood in the entryway attempting to take it all in. Bunion set my bag off to a sidewall and pointed to a man crouched down, a camera glued to his face. "Mr. Dubois," he grumbled, then abruptly turned around and entered the elevator we'd just exited leaving me to fend for myself.

"Man of few words." I let a slow breath leave my too-full lungs. I didn't know what to do. Should I sit off to the side and wait for someone to approach me—hopefully not the naked men and women scattered around—or should I bug the guy busily taking pictures of something I couldn't quite see?

Instead of waiting, I decided to take better stock of my surroundings and walked around. The room was an open loft but not a home. Rickety windows lined the walls on the right, some opened from the bottom out, others were closed tight. It looked like it took a crank to open them, which I found incredibly cool and retro. Naked and half naked women passed by me, sizing me up as they moved in front of giant white canvases. They weren't really modeling, they were just standing next to the canvases, each model loosely holding a pose while attendants, dressed in black, were perfecting the poses with subtle shifts of an elbow here or moving a foot there. Then the attendant would back up and take a single photo and start over again. Tiny movements again, then another picture. It was downright weird.

I moved over to another area where there was a naked couple lying on a huge white canvas that had to be at least ten by ten feet in size. One of the attendants climbed up a small ladder that had a platform directly over their bodies and methodically poured what looked to be bright blue paint over every inch of them. "Don't move!" he screamed. "We'll have to start all over, and Mr. Dubois won't be pleased," he added tightly. The couple stayed in a naked clinch, the female model's hands wrapped around the male's head as if she was about to kiss him. His arms were around her, one on her ass holding a leg over his hip, the other cupping the back of her head.

Paint dripped down their legs and fell into globs on the canvas. "Still," the man warned. I was so fascinated by the inner workings of the odd scene in front of me that I didn't hear a person walk up behind me until my hair was swept off my neck.

"Perfection," I heard whispered against my ear before a soft kiss hit the bare skin at the curve where my shoulder and neck met.

I shuffled back, not looking where I was going, just trying to get away from the stranger touching me when I bumped into something behind me. Before I could turn, my boot caught the edge of the canvas, and I went toppling into the platform, which held the irritated guy with the paint. Then, utter chaos ensued. The man holding the bucket went tumbling forward, and blue, sticky paint flew out of the can into a fan of color before splashing down onto the canvas and tarp protecting the concrete.

The couple beneath must have seen the fall coming, because the man rolled the hot naked chick as if he'd been trained in combat services with the armed forces. He avoided the attendant, missed being doused with more paint, and narrowly escaped the platform that was about to fall on top of them.

I wasn't so lucky.

When I fell backward, my other heel went through

the thick canvas and stuck, and my body curved around in the opposite direction. I screamed out as my ankle twisted painfully, and I landed ass-over-tits into blue paint and torn canvas.

"Sweet Jesus!" The man I tried to get away from stepped into the mess and pulled me up by the armpits. His golden brown eyes were mesmerizing and worried. Small lines at the corners of each eye revealed he was probably a good decade older than I. Sandy brown hair with hints of russet gold and red streaked through in natural highlights was pulled tight into a small bun at the back of his head. A sculpted jaw and full lips were rimmed with perfectly trimmed facial hair. I'd never dated a man with a beard, but standing in front of this man, strong arms holding me close to a very tall and muscular frame, I couldn't fathom why I never had. He was drop dead gorgeous. Reminded me of Ben Affleck only way hotter.

"I didn't mean to frighten you. I saw you standing there, and your beauty was far beyond the likes of any mere model. I had to press my lips against your golden skin. You must be *My Mia*," he said with admiration. His caramel gaze scanning my features from the tips of my hair down to my spike-heeled boots. I would be tossing those boots the minute I could remove them from my rapidly swelling ankle.

A quick test by placing the ball of my injured foot to the ground sent pain ripping through my ankle and shooting up my leg. I cried out and gripped the man's forearms, digging my nails into his flesh. "Oh my, you're really hurt!"

"Ya think?" I rolled my eyes as he used his long arms to swoop me under the knees into a princess style carry and rushed me over to an arched loveseat. Only it wasn't a love seat, it had a curved back that started high on one end then came down low on the other. It was the type of furniture you'd see in old romantic movies where the damsel in distress would faint perfectly onto it; hand over her forehead slumping down with a pretty sigh. Me, I was gritting my teeth and ready to bite anyone that even so much as shifted my leg.

"I'll call a medic!" One of the ever-present men in black said to the stranger, who, by then, I'd surmised was my client.

"No, *ce n'est pas nécessaire,*" he said in rapid French. "Contact 3B. She's a doctor and a friend," he said his eyes boring into mine. "You'll be fine, Mia," he assured me, and when he spoke with that slight accent I may have actually swooned; a definite clench occurred between my thighs. Men with accents were deadly sexy. Then again, it could have been the pain raging through my limb that had me clenching. I was pretty sure it was the former.

Within moments, a tiny speck of a woman rushed in holding what looked to be an old-fashioned medical doctor's bag. She introduced herself and helped me slide off my boot without jarring the leg. She may have been a miracle worker. A snicker could be heard over my shoulder as the doctor was prodding my ankle. I looked over at my client whom I knew to be Alec Dubois, though we hadn't actually exchanged pleasantries yet.

"What?"

"Your socks. Positively enchanting, *ma jolie,*" he finished in French, which sounded sexy as hell but pissed me off even more, because I didn't know what it meant. Could be anything like klutz, or moron, but I'd never know. I looked down at my Christmas socks and then at the doctor. Her lips curved up, but she stayed completely professional as she checked my ankle. Her, I liked; the jury was still out on hunky French camera guy.

"Well, it's not broken. You've got a slight sprain. I'll wrap it, but keep off it as much as possible, and you'll be good as new in a couple weeks. You'll need to rest it, ice it, elevate above your heart and keep it wrapped. I suggest getting some crutches," she said and my shoulders sagged in defeat. I hated crutches. The entire world hated crutches. They sucked. Bad. I was not looking forward to the skin around my underarms being worn raw or feeling bruised, along with the bum ankle, especially on a new job. I wondered if he'd want a refund on his purchase. A moment of panic shredded through my heart thinking about my dad and how I'd get the next installment to Blaine if French guy didn't want me now that I was damaged.

"I'll take perfect care of you, *ma jolie*. You needn't worry for a thing," Alec sat down next to me placing an arm protectively around my waist sliding me close, so close it was as if he'd know me for years not moments. He definitely had some serious space invasion issues. Even so, it felt nice and helped relieve the fear that he was going to send me home.

"*Retournez au travail*," His obvious instruction was punctuated with some arm movements before he lifted me as if I weighed nothing.

"What does that mean? And what are you doing?" I clung to his shoulders so as not to fall while he walked towards the elevator.

"Taking you home so you can rest. You must be tired

after traveling. And now, with a sore ankle, you need to lie down." His eyes were kind as he looked at me. "And before, I told my crew to get back to work," his accent was stronger now, but it was obvious he'd been in the US a long time. His English was perfect.

I huffed but hung on. "This is so weird. I'm sorry about the painting and the mess, and now I've busted my ankle and I'm supposed to be this spectacular muse."

"Oh, you *are* most *spectaculaire*, the finest features, and your face in two is a perfect mirror image," he said as if this was the most astonishing news, though I didn't really understand.

I shook my head. "I don't know what you mean by a mirror image."

One of Alec's men in black followed us into the elevator carrying my single suitcase and pressed button twelve, which was the highest number on the panel. He didn't answer my question as we exited the elevator, and he carried me into another wide-open loft. It was the same size as the level we were on before, only this was complete with a kitchen, living space, and a set of stairs that I assumed led to a raised loft bedroom. There weren't any walls, other than in the corner with a door. If I was a betting woman, which I am— my dad taught me everything he knew about gambling—I'd bet that door led to a single bathroom.

He brought me to that door, and yep, it was a bathroom. I hopped on one foot to the sink when he let me go. Out of thin air, my bag appeared, and Alec rifled through it, pulling out a shirt and a pair of pajama shorts.

"Here, put these on. I'll get a bag for your clothes." Within moments he returned and handed me a garbage bag.

"You'll be okay?" he asked, a hand curled around the door knob.

"I'll be fine. Thank you." I could feel my cheeks heat as he shut the door.

Stupid, stupid, stupid klutz! As quickly as possible I trashed the jeans and shirt covered in paint and put on the shirt and shorts. Once done, I washed off as much paint as I could see. I'd need a full shower, but right now, I needed to settle things with my client, gauge his mood, see if he was angry with me.

When I opened the bathroom door he was there and swept me into his arms again.

"Ooophf!" I gasped as he carried me then sat me down on a plush velvet sectional in the deepest purple known to man. So dark it was almost black, though if you ran your hand over it, the fibers shifted and left a much lighter eggplant shade. Once I was situated comfortably, foot on the ottoman in front of me, Alec lifted his leg and straddled the ottoman, pulling my sore ankle into his lap. I leaned forward and held my leg at the sides not knowing how to respond to a man who touched with abandon.

"Now, your question, about mirror images?"

I nodded and bit my lip. He lifted a hand and with one finger traced the center of my face from the hairline at my forehead, over my nose, down between my lips and stopping at my chin. A shiver rippled through me at his heated touch, or was it the sultry way he looked at me as if I was the most beautiful woman in the world. Wes looked at me like that. Hell, Wes made me *feel* that way. A pang of guilt needled at me, but I shoved it away. Wes and me, we were not an item. Friends with benefits absolutely…with the hope of more.

One day. Maybe. Not today.

"If you cut your face down the middle here," he traced my face again with the pad of his finger, his eyes seemingly lost in his task, "each side would mirror the other."

I frowned. "So would anyone's."

His hand cupped my cheek, long fingers twining through the dark tresses to cup the back of my nape. "Yes, *ma jolie*, but they would not be symmetrical. Your face, it's *perfection*. Equal on both sides. Neither better nor worse than the other. It's unusual. Astonishing. You are unique," Alec's faced dipped close and he pressed a warm kiss to each cheek. "Tomorrow, we start work, *oui*? Today, you rest." He placed my swollen ankle onto the ottoman after setting a pillow under it. "I must work now," he said moving around as if he was already distracted by the tasks ahead.

Interesting guy, Alec Dubois.

★ ★ ★ ★

For the entire afternoon, not willing to brave the stairs up to the loft on one leg, I hobbled around, took a nap on the couch, called my best friend, Ginelle, and checked in with Aunt Millie. Both Gin and Aunt Millie found it hysterical that I'd twisted my ankle and was stuck at the mercy of a hot French artist guy. Gin called me a lucky bitch and Aunt Millie just ended her call with a "Have fun doll-face."

The door of the elevator dinged, and I could hear the metal scraping as the gates were opened. I couldn't see anything from my position on the couch, but I didn't have to wait long. Alec strode through the room carrying crutches and a white takeout bag that smelled deliciously like Chinese food. Without delay, Alec set the food on the coffee table, leaned the crutches on the side of the couch, then came to my side where he sat.

Before I could open my mouth he'd cupped both sides of my neck, his thumbs on the apples of my cheeks where he proceeded to kiss each cheek. His lips were warm and left an impression long after he'd moved back to stare into my eyes. "How are you, *ma jolie?*"

"Uh, fine, I guess," I blinked and he smiled. "What does *ma jolie* mean?"

Alec's lips curved at the edge as he cocked his head to the side. His hand reached out and pushed a lock of my hair away from my forehead, past my temple and behind my ear. The air around us was thick, filled with the promise of something I couldn't yet name. "It translates to 'my pretty' in English."

"Oh, okay," I whispered not capable of looking away from those tawny-colored eyes.

"Hungry?" he asked, his Rs rolling delectably.

I nodded. My throat felt dry as I watched him stand, enter the kitchen and bring back some plates and serving utensils before coming back to sit too close to me. One entire side of his body was plastered against mine. If I moved away, it would be obvious, and I didn't want to make another bad impression on my new client, so instead I endured his warmth. And his scent. That smell would be my demise. It was a mixture of fresh paint and Hugo Boss. The only reason I even knew that scent was because I'd once worked as a spray girl in the local shopping mall in Vegas. They had me spraying all kinds of crap. So much so you left working smelling like a bag of potpourri. Hugo Boss had a yummy male smell that seemed to arrow through my nostrils and land bullseyed between my legs.

With effort, I tried to scooch over a bit. Alec just looked at me and winked then finished plating the Chow Mein and Kung Pao. "I hope you like Chinese food," he offered the plate to me.

I gripped it greedily, brought it close my face, closed my eyes, and inhaled the heavenly mix of chicken, sauces and noodles steaming on the plate. The food smelled so good my mouth watered, and I moaned then dug in. When I looked up, Alec had stopped plating his own food and was staring at me. What I saw almost made me choke. Those eyes of his were blazing hot, his lust plainly visible. He wasn't even trying to hide it.

"You are startlingly beautiful." He touched the side of my cheek and cupped it. Inadvertently, I curved my face further into his palm, sealing the connection. It had only been a few days, but I missed a man's touch. Alec traced my bottom lip with his thumb then his voice turned husky. *"Tu est le cadeau de Dieu au monde."*

"What does that mean?"

"'God's gift to the world.' That's what you are. And I intend for everyone to glory in such a gift."

A gift. Alec thinks I'm a gift to the world. A beautiful one.

I wasn't able to respond. Not when he set aside the making of his dinner. Not when he took my plate and set it on the table. Not when he leaned into my space until we were a scant couple inches apart. But I did respond the moment my frazzled brain registered his kiss.

Warm, supple, and sweet. His lips brushed mine before he sucked in my bottom lip and ran his tongue along the sensitive tissue. That was as far as it got before I gripped his neck and pulled him further into me. My fingers tunneled into his hair. When I encountered a hair tie, that just wouldn't do. I pulled on that tie until it snapped and lemon-scented, thick hair tumbled in waves against my cheeks, shrouding our kiss in the haven of his luscious locks. Alec cupped my chin and turned my head to the side, sliding his tongue in and out, learning what made me tick, moan, and bite. And I did. Bite that is. I nipped at his lips like a starving animal would a steak. He didn't seem to mind. At one point, I was pretty certain he growled—yes, growled—into the kiss taking it impossibly deeper.

Excitement roared through my body, and I tensed, wanting to bring Alec closer, needing him to be. As I was trying to lean back on the couch so he could get on top of me, he pulled back. His forehead rested against mine. "*Très jolie fille,*" he whispered in the language that was quickly becoming a major turn-on. Not that it wasn't before, but after having his lips on mine, his tongue in my mouth, his words caressed along my senses as easily as I imagined his touch would. With purpose, with desire, with lust.

"Calm *chérie.*" His tone was a murmur and a balm over the heat burning inside. "There would be plenty of time for us to know each other physically. I want to enjoy you, anticipate your sweet taste on my tongue, your smooth skin along the pads of my fingers, your body on my canvas."

I pulled back and our gazes held. "Wow." I bit my lip and swallowed. He grinned.

"I do believe 'wow' is an understatement. Let's eat. Get to know one another on all levels. Only then will the physical manifestation of our joining be as sweet.

Alec Dubois was bizarre. Who the hell even talks like that? 'A physical manifestation of our joining?' He may have spent too much time reading *Ask Jeeves* online.

"You're a weird guy," I said before grabbing my plate, setting it on my lap and shoveling in a giant bite of noodles. Pure heaven! Almost as good as the kiss we'd shared moments ago.

Alec tipped his head back and burst into laughter. See, totally weird dude.

He grabbed his plate, loaded it up and leaned back, set his feet next to mine on the ottoman, turned his head to the side and looked at me. "Oh my sweet, you have no idea, but soon you will. Let's eat."

CHAPTER TWO

That evening, after being filled to the brim with the best Chinese food I'd ever had, Alex carried me up to the loft and settled me on his bed. He didn't have another room in the converted warehouse as far as I could tell. Regardless, he didn't assume we'd be sleeping together, even after our kiss. All of which I was grateful for. I needed the evening to find myself in this new world.

It was difficult for me no longer being in Wes's Malibu home hidden away in the hillside and snug as a bug in a rug in my bed of clouds. No, I was deposited onto a firm, but comfortable, king size bed and surrounded by cool tones and textures. Soft blue, Heather grey, and a few midnight tones interspersed. The bed sat on a small platform with a solid wood headboard no footboard but plenty of pillows to allow the user maximum relaxation. There were very few pieces of furniture in the space. A sleek, boxy five-drawer dresser, two minimalistic nightstands, one with a lamp, the other with a stack of books. I scanned the titles and noted several of them were in French. A few even had library seals with numbers that denoted an indexing system. I guess Frenchie liked to read and had a library card. Something about that made me smile on the inside as much as the outside.

So far, Alec had been mostly a gentleman. He'd not sent me packing when I twisted my ankle and had been very doting since dinner last night. Even though he had a distracted air about him, when he focused on me, really looked at me, he gave me everything. A girl could get used to being looked at as if the world around her had stopped moving. Then of course, there was that kiss. Shivers of excitement tingled down my spine remembering those warm lips. His tongue, knowing exactly how to tickle and taste, was a nice surprise. The fact that he kissed me at all was a surprise but not by much. I mean, the guy spent a lot of time in my space. He'd touched me more in one day than pretty much anyone ever did in a day, including Wes, and I know Wes *really* liked touching me.

Wes.

Nope, not gonna let myself go down that path. We agreed to be friends and move on from here. He knows I need to do what I need to do to save my dad, and I won't be doing it while abstaining. That's just not me. Once I'd gotten a taste of that heat, the passion like Wes gave to me—I craved it. Needed it. Felt bereft without it. My guess is it's like ripping off a Band-Aid, howl in pain for a few seconds and it's done. Ready to hop on a new cowboy and ride, so to speak. And that's exactly what I planned to do. There's chemistry between Alec and me, that's for certain. Based on that kiss alone, he'd be good in bed, and the way he spoke, it was a given in his mind as well. Time to have fun. Enjoy myself.

At some point in the night, Alec placed my crutches on the wall near the bed. I looked around then hopped to the clothes in the small closet. All men's clothes hung on the hangers. Nothing frilly, girly or pink in sight. Huh. Part of my contract was to provide me with the appropriate clothing needed for the month's stay. *Wonder where he put all my stuff?* I opened each dresser drawer methodically, scanning the contents. Men's boxer briefs, socks, pajama pants, t-shirts and jeans. Nothing for me.

My suitcase was also delivered sometime in the evening, so I pulled out a pair of clean jeans and a Radiohead concert tee. Thinking back, Ginelle and I had rocked out so hard and screamed so loud at that concert we couldn't speak the next day. We didn't care, Tom York was crazy talented and when a band like Radiohead comes to Vegas, I did whatever it took to get tickets.

Once I got dressed, I put on one sneaker and left the other foot wrapped and socked for the day. At the top of the stairs, I sat on my ass, let my crutches slide down the stairs and used the strength in my arms and my bum to get down the stairs without hurting my foot. I felt damned good about the process.

"Hey! I would have helped you down *ma jolie*." Alec came around the kitchen bar and over to me. My mouth dropped wide open. Alec was wearing loose plaid pajama bottoms and nothing else. His chest was golden, ripped, and on full display. A veritable feast for the eyes. His hair was long, wavy and came down to his shoulders. The colors were mesmerizing hues of brown, russet and gold. He walked over to me as if in slow motion. The muscles of his abdomen bunched as he leaned down to help get me settled with my crutches. I placed a hand around his waist and felt nothing but sinewy muscle.

Sweet Mother of God I was in so much trouble.

He helped me get settled with my crutches and led me to a barstool in the kitchen. Once I was seated, he turned around, and I couldn't contain the burst of air that left my lungs. Alec turned to the side and his eyes caught what I was staring at, positively drooling over. On the left side of his back from his shoulder blade and curling around his ribcage was a giant black tattoo. It was a swirl of words written in French.

"Your tattoo…it's…" I stared in awe at a loss for words. "It's…beautiful," I finally finished. Alec went to the stove, and in a cool trick move, cracked two eggs with one hand into a frying pan. For a moment, I wondered if I could get him to teach me how to do it before our month was up.

"*Merci,*" he answered cracking another couple eggs into the pan. Next to the eggs he plopped several strips of bacon into another frying pan. Instantly the bacon started popping and sizzling.

"What does it say?"

He pushed a stray lock of hair behind his ear and moved about his kitchen half naked very much at ease. I watched his body move as he reached for a ceramic, multicolored mug hanging from a hook then filled it with coffee. "It's a poem from Jacques Prévert a French writer. He wrote it in 1966." Alec pointed to the coffee in front of him. "Cream or sugar?"

"Both please," I responded. He finished up my cup, set it in front of me, then went back, flipped the eggs and turned the bacon.

"Do you mind me asking what the poem says?" I sipped my coffee trying to hide behind the large mug.

He licked his lips, leaned against the side of the counter and crossed his bare feet at the ankles. Jesus the man was fine. Wes was good looking but this man is no slouch. The two were polar opposites. Where Wes was light, Alec is dark and vice versa. They seemed to have the exact opposites in every aspect, right down to Alec's dark hair, mustache and beard to Wes's clean shaven yet sometimes scruffy chin.

"It's most of a poem about people viewing Witold's paintings. Roughly it translates to:

The mystery of everyday people
Painted with love in the furtive silence
And the obsessive noise of the street.
You follow their progress,
But you have only the back view of them, and like them,
You will give a back view to other visitors
Who will take your place in front of the paintings.

"It reminds me that many will look at my art, the images I capture or paint, and sometimes, part of the experience will be when another person captures that person viewing my art. It changes what they see. So now, the art is viewed in a way that the person standing in front of it, becomes part of it."

I thought on what he said for a moment. "That's deep."

Alec shook his head and smiled, then slid the eggs and bacon onto plates. He set one in front of me. "Eat up, *ma jolie*. We have a full day in the loft ahead of us."

"Speaking of full days, where are my clothes?" I asked around a mouth full of eggs.

He leaned over the opposite side of the island and bit into a slice of bacon. His eyebrows furrowed. "What clothes?"

"The clothes." I flailed a hand into the air. "You know, whatever you want me to wear while I'm here. That's supposed to be provided…" I let the rest just fall off. It made me uncomfortable talking about our contract.

Alec grinned a full cat-that-ate-the-canary grin, then set his hands wide on to the counter leaning closer to me. "*Ma jolie,* there aren't clothes for you to wear because I don't plan on having you wear anything while you're here. You are my muse, and I want to see your body, curves and angles as much as humanly possible."

I blinked, opened my mouth, closed it, then blinked again. He couldn't be serious. "You want me to walk around naked? All the time?"

"*Oui,*" he stated plainly as if the question didn't hold the entire weight of the world on it like it did for me.

"'*Oui?*' That's all you got for me?" I set down my fork and it clanged loudly against the plate. "You think I'm going to walk around here," again the arms went flying, "without so much as a stitch of clothing on?"

Alec's eyebrows narrowed once more. "Are you uncomfortable with your body, *ma jolie?*"

"Fuck. I cannot believe this!" I shook my head and crossed my arms over my chest. "No, I'm not uncomfortable with my body, well, not really. I could do to lose a few pounds, but I don't know one person who's comfortable walking around in their birthday suit all day long."

"Hmm, this poses a slight problem then. I am certain we'll work through this. Finish up your breakfast, we need to get to the loft. I need to do some stills of you before the light changes and then start with the paint." He shoved the last bite of his breakfast into his mouth while walking over to the sink. He rinsed his plate and set the dish in the dishwasher. "I shall get ready. We'll discuss more later, *oui?*"

"*Oui*," I said with a purpose-based sarcastic tone. He shook his head and rushed up the stairs. In a flash, he'd grabbed whatever clothing he intended to wear and headed to the bathroom. Seconds later, I could hear the shower going and the old pipes of the warehouse working overtime.

He wanted me naked all the time. Just like I thought, bizarre dude. I rolled my eyes and clenched my teeth. He didn't really answer me, just said we had a problem, effectively changed the subject, then bailed. Day two was not looking any better than day one. Well, I did get to see his beautiful body half-naked. That was pleasant and definitely edged day two over day one's falling and embarrassing episode. Even though last night's kiss could go to war against today's annoying I-want-you-naked-at-all-times load of crap, I did not plan to walk around naked. That was in no way part of my contract or anything else I'd agreed to. I'd read through that contract on the plane and nowhere in there did it say, 'Mia willfully agrees to run around stark naked for a month.' Lunatic!

★ ★ ★ ★

After breakfast, Alec led me back down to the lower level workspace. "So you own both floors then?" I asked while following him through the workspace. Surprisingly enough, there were only a couple people milling about and it was eight in the morning. Maybe they didn't work a standard eight to five job.

"Yes, this is my work space; the other, as you know, is my home. I like to be close to my home. Sometimes I work well into the night and morning. When I want to end my day, I don't want to have to drive across town to do it. This way I'm just a short elevator ride up."

I nodded. "Makes sense. Where is everyone?" I slumped into the chair he pushed out in front of me. Before us, about ten feet away, was a brightly lit area and two blank canvases hanging on the wall. One was about six feet wide by four feet tall. The other was a good six feet tall and four feet wide. So basically the same size only one was horizontal the other vertical.

"Creative day. I don't need much assistance today. Only you, my camera and paint, all of which I have in front of me."

"Cool," I looked around. "So, what do you want me to do?"

"We'll start with test shots. I'll need you to stand in front of the horizontal painting." He helped me to stand then scooped me up and walked me over to another chair that had been placed in front of the wall. On the floor under my twisted ankle was a pillow. He stood me next to the chair so I was using the back of it to bear weight on that side of my body. "The pillow is in case you need to place your foot down. I don't want you placing it on hard concrete and further injuring it. This should help, *oui*?"

I smiled wide. "Yes, thank you, Alec. Just do whatever you need to do. I'm fine, perfectly comfortable," I assured him.

He moved around the space and over to a tripod then adjusted the lights. "Okay, now remove your t-shirt. Leave the undergarment on, for now, I only need to see the angles and shapes of your shoulders, arms, neck, sides, of your upper body."

Taking a deep breath I bit down on my lip then lifted my shirt and flung it aside. "Okay, Frenchie, but it's gonna cost you," I warned.

"I'm well aware of the expense," he said behind his camera. The second I removed my shirt the camera started clicking.

I stood stock still in my black lace bra. It covered me completely, no more skin showing than a bikini top would, but still, I was nervous. Over the years I'd done a bit of acting and hoped to do more but never really spent any time modeling. Never thought I had the body for it.

"*Impressionnant*," Alec mumbled in French. That one sounded like a compliment, so I kept quiet and let him do his thing. "You're doing fine," he said.

A breath of air left me in a huff. "How is that possible? I'm not *doing* anything but standing here."

"With your beauty, it's enough. Besides, these are test shots for positioning, lighting, and such." After a few more clicks he came over to me. "Are you tired of standing?"

"A little," I said, because I was. It was harder than it looked to balance on one foot even if I had a chair to use.

We took a break, and he brought me some water and a blanket. I used the blanket to shield my nakedness. Then he had me back up, only this time, he had me throw my head over and ruffle my hair then bring it back up. I did this a couple times until he felt it was just so. I thought it was just messy and ratty, but he seemed to want the ratty, wild hair.

"Your colors are perfection, *ma jolie*." He walked over to a table, and brought over a paint brush and a small can of paint. The paint was cherry red. "This is going to feel strange but I'm going to apply this paint to your lips. It is not toxic."

"Sure, whatever you gotta do. It's your dime."

He shook his head and chuckled. I smiled but then made a poufy-lipped face while he delicately painted my lips. It glistened brightly and seemed to have a plastic-like quality to it. When he was done, he fluffed my hair a few more times and walked back to his camera."

"Now, Mia, think of something sad. Something that hurts your heart...very bad. Maybe even think of something you are missing, *oui*?"

I didn't want to mess up my lips so I just looked off into the distance and thought of Wes. What was he doing right now? Who was he with? Did he miss me? What if he was standing half naked in front of someone else? Those thoughts were too tortured, and I tried to change gears. Only God knows why, but I thought of my dad. I hadn't seen him in a month. He was still in a coma without his daughter sitting by his side. That thought hit me straight in the heart.

"Mia!" Alec said sharply and I turned my head so fast I blinked. A lone tear slipped down my cheek. The camera clicked. "Got it," he said softly. I whisked away the remaining tears that were on the cusp of falling.

"We done?" My voice cracked when he handed me a wet cloth.

"For this part of the project, yes, we are done. You may wash off the paint and have a rest. I'll get your shirt."

"Thank you," I whispered, feeling a little flustered and a lot emotional.

Once we finished and I was dressed, we sat side by side and looked out one of the rickety windows down to the Seattle street below. A light rain was pelting against the asphalt, and people rushed around to avoid getting soaked.

"What is this picture we're working on now?"

"You mean, what is the name of the piece?"

I nodded but stayed silent looking out over the wet street.

"No Love For Me."

Of course. It should be my fucking theme song. "I'm ready to get back to work."

Alec led me over to the canvas once more. No words were spoken when I removed my shirt, fluffed my hair and got into position.

Finally, I broke the silence.

"What's next?" I asked with a renewed focus.

"We find you love of course."

CHAPTER THREE

Day three of being with Alec brought me back into the loft. Last night, we returned from a long day of shooting stills in what felt like a million subtly different poses. We'd even skipped lunch; apparently, when the muse strikes, one takes advantage. Objectively, when a woman removes the top half of her clothes and you're a hetero male, it's not too far a leap to think the muse is going to go haywire. All men are pigs in one way or another. This one just happened to be masquerading as a hot artist guy Frenchman.

Gotta admit though, it was totally working for me. I was dying to get my hands on him. Anywhere. His hair, especially his hair. Long waves of russet and gold that fell perfectly to his shoulders. Tall, muscled frame with a narrow waist had me salivating for the second day in a row. Unfortunately for me, Alec was a workaholic to the extreme. After we finished in the loft and came back to his loft, we ate pizza for dinner, and he was off to the loft to work on the image he'd done that day. Didn't even come home before I went to bed alone…again. It irked me that he hadn't so much as tried anything other than that single kiss. I was primed and ready to take the next step. I needed to rip off the Band-Aid so to speak. To stop thinking about Wes and the surfboard keychain that held the key to his front door and his heart.

Today, Alec wasn't waiting for me in the kitchen. Once I'd butt-scooched down the stairs, I'd expected to find him up and making me breakfast like yesterday. Not so. What I did find was a note in his slanted male penmanship sitting by the coffee pot. It said:

Ma jolie,

Meet me at downstairs when you're ready. There is much to do.

~A

I ate a banana and had a cup of coffee before making my way on the crutches to the elevator and down to the loft. Today was far busier than the previous day. Again, there were several men in black scurrying around doing this or that, taking pictures, probably those boring test stills. I was glad that Alec personally did the test shots with me. At least that way I had someone I could talk to. The men in black had an issue with the models speaking. Every few minutes I'd hear a shush or "still" or "quiet" from one side of the room or another. Even though it was all very strange, it was quite interesting to see the inner workings of a world-renowned artist as he perfected his art and managed the minions doing the grunt work.

"Finally, you're here," one of his men in black approached on a huff. He gripped my arm and tried to pull me along faster than my crutches would allow.

As I struggled to keep up, my crutch's rubber end hit a wire trailing across the concrete floor. It hit it at a weird angle that caused me to tilt forward and nearly put all my weight onto my sprained ankle. I swayed precariously, but caught myself midair by balancing on the crutches. That was it! I'd had it. Thoroughly irritated, I yanked my arm out of his grasp. "Watch it, dude. You're about to get a crutch up your ass if you don't quit pulling on my arm. I'm not your dog on a leash." I pointed the crutch at his face and swung it around. "Back off!"

"*Que se passe-t-il?*" came an agitated voice behind us. Alec stood, hands on hips, a twisted, angry look marring his features. He looked lethal, like a lion ready to pounce on its prey. "What is the meaning of this?" he finally spoke in English.

"Mr. Dubois, your model was not being speedy and you were expecting her an hour ago," the minion replied. An hour ago? Screw that! If he wanted me to get up early, he should have set an alarm, maybe even have found interesting ways to wake me. Since he didn't, I was not taking the blame.

"*Imbécile,*" he murmured loud enough for the two of us to hear but not loud enough for the growing audience building around us. "Do you have poor sight?"

The man scrunched his nose and his head whipped back. "Sight? As in can I see?"

"Are you deaf too?"

This time the man took affront. "Look, Mr. Dubois, you said the models were to follow the rules and that included being on time. She was late, really late. A whole hour. I was just trying to move her along…"

"Enough. You," he pointed to the waif of a man, "are an idiot. Do you not see she is injured and cannot run with crutches?"

"I was just trying…"

"*Assez!.* No. Shut your mouth before you dig a hole so deep you'll never find your way to the surface," Alec grated. He looked around the room and held his arm out, scanning the space. "Now, to everyone listening, and I know you are…" A few people tried to look away as if that was going to hide the fact that everyone had been paying close attention.

"This woman is Mia," he pointed to me. "She is the entire muse for 'Love on Canvas'. As far as you are concerned, she is as precious and priceless as any of my paintings. Treat her as such. Now, back to work." He clapped his hands together twice before coming to my aide.

"Are you okay, *ma jolie*?"

"Fine, he just annoyed me. Tugged on me too hard and I almost fell. It's an honest mistake."

"One he will not make again," he bit out, then leaned forward and scooped me into a princess carry again. "How was your sleep?"

This was my chance so I took it. "Would have been better with a nice warm body lying next to me," I finished boldly. He stopped and stood still, his gaze on mine, tawny eyes turning a shade darker, pupils dilating.

"Is that so?"

"I never lie," which wasn't exactly true. I lied all the time when it suited me or I was stuck in a bind. Even though this suited me, this was not one of those times.

Alec grinned. "I find that hard to believe, *ma jolie*." He brought me over to the same place we were working yesterday and sat me in the chair I'd used.

Before he could let me go, I whispered, "Believe it Frenchie," into his ear then kissed his cheek sweetly. Nothing more than a reminder of our heated kiss a couple days ago.

"It seems we'll have to do something different with our sleeping accommodations posthaste. Don't want you to be uncared for."

"That would be a tragedy." I smiled wide.

His response was a wink before he turned around and got out the paint again and a small brush.

"Painted lips again?"

He came toward me and lifted his chin in a silent request that I look behind me. I turned sideways in my chair, staying mindful of my sore foot. That's when I saw it. Not it…me. Two of me. One was a black and white painted image of me. The other a combination photograph on one half of the canvas, the other half blank. Bright red lips were the only point of color on the second picture. The first painted image was so lifelike, even more so than the actual photographic image on the other canvas. I stood and hopped over to the painting. The brush strokes were miniscule and almost a perfect duplicate of the photographic image. You could even see the tear streaming down my face. The sadness in my eyes, the stance, slumped shoulders showed a tortured woman. Sad yet still…beautiful. A moment caught in time.

"It's…I can't believe…how?" I whispered and lifted a hand to touch the painting. Before I could, Alec gripped my wrist and pulled it back gently.

"No touching. It's still wet. I worked on it through the night."

My eyes went wide and I gasped. "I'm so sorry! I didn't realize. That's dumb. I mean, I should have known, it makes sense. Sorry," I frowned.

Alec's hand reached out and he caressed a lock of my hair, rubbing it together with his fingers before trailing one fingertip down from my temple, cheekbone and along the side of my chin. Goosebumps broke out against my arms and I shivered.

"Cold?" he asked with a hint of a smile. He knew what he was doing to me. How his touch ignited something inside.

"No," I licked my lips and stared brazenly at his, wishing he would lean forward and put his lips on me. Anywhere. Everywhere.

"Well then, let's get started." He combed his fingers through my hair, pushing it over my shoulder. Then repeated the movement on the other side. Not what I was expecting, but it felt good, so I went with it. "Sit, I'm going to paint your lips."

I groaned but hopped back over to the seat, plopped down and rolled my eyes before he came around and knelt in front of me. "Do you ever think about anything other than work?"

"Are you referring to the fact that I want to kiss you until I've stolen all your breath? Or the fact that if I could, I would shred your shirt, and suck on your pink tips until you begged for me to make love to you?"

"Make love?" I snickered even though his words made me hot and bothered; they were hot...and bothered me...a lot!

"Of course, *chérie*. the French make love. There are many forms of making love. Hard. Fast. Slow. Deliberate. I plan to do all those things to you, and for many, many hours. But not now. Now is the time for work. Later, we play."

I nodded not able to speak any further. I wanted to know what 'play' meant to him. I had a pretty good idea it was the kind of play I hoped it was. God willing. Slowly Alec painted my lips with the goopy cherry red paint. When he was done he lifted me from the chair and carried me over to the painting of me he'd done.

"This is where it gets tricky. I want you to place your lips over those on the painting exactly where they are painted. I will guide you as best I can. You will get close and then slowly press them against the painting so that the paint transfers."

I gave him a hard look, but, like yesterday, I didn't want to speak and mess up the paint on my lips. Now, more so than ever before. He gripped my head and I placed my hands on each side of the wall around the painting. First, I got really close.

"Be careful not to touch the painting anywhere else, or I'll have to redo it," he warned which sent a fissure of fear tumbling through me. I sucked in a long slow breath through my nose and let it out, then leaned super close to the painting. When I got to where I thought I should be, he centered me lightly by holding my head on each side before pushing ever so slightly so that I'd move forward.

I puckered my lips and kissed myself then pulled back. He helped me reverse so I wouldn't lose my balance and helped me to the chair. The black and white painted image now had a perfect set of red lips. It actually looked almost as though he'd painted them there, but you could tell it was a kiss. It wasn't perfect, but I thought it looked good.

"Exactly as I pictured it. You amaze me, Mia," he said in awe as he stared as his masterpiece. His arms were crossed over his chest, one arm supported by the other, one hand holding up his face at the chin where he stared and stared at his painting.

"Ever heard that saying, 'take a picture it will last longer'?" I giggled.

His head turned in slow motion and I caught his gaze. "This will last a lifetime in someone's home. Get passed down from generation to generation leaving a legacy for years to come."

Well, when he put it like that, I guess it was pretty flippin' fantastic.

★ ★ ★ ★

The rest of the day, he had me doing stills again. This time, I stood completely naked on top, facing the blank canvas that had half a picture of me printed on it.

"I don't understand why I have to be naked for this," I said, my hand covering my naked chest. The girls were covered in gooseflesh, and I didn't think that made for a very nice picture. My hair was down and wild once more, only this time he'd had someone come in and professionally mess it up. That had me laughing so hard he left the space on a turn of his heel to go check on his other work. Really, I knew I was annoying him. He probably wasn't used to his muses talking back or giving him a hard time. Made me wonder how many muses he'd had in the past. The thought that I was just one of many irked me.

"Have you ever hired a muse?" I really didn't want to know the answer but couldn't refrain from asking.

The camera clicked and he spoke to one of his attendants in French who adjusted the big lights a few inches. Another click. "No, *ma jolie*. You're the only one," he finally answered. And it was enough. I liked being his only muse for hire. Not sure that made me any better than the other models, but for my own mental stability, I pretended it did.

"What are we doing anyway?" I asked facing the blank section of canvas on the unfinished picture.

"I'm going to make you love your image. Which will

translate to the viewer as loving yourself."

I'm certain my eyes narrowed unattractively at his statement. "Come again?"

He let out a tired breath. "*Ma jolie*, I need to finish these stills so I can paint and have dinner with you, make love to you, then paint your image onto canvas. There is much to do," he said like a broken record.

That wasn't what slithered through my subconscious though. It was the way he made a laundry list of things he had to do and having dinner with me and "making love" to me where part of his chores this evening. "Don't do anything on my account," I responded angrily.

"Mia, your mood is affecting your image. Please stop thinking about being frustrated with me and focus on the job at hand."

I turned around beyond pissed, hands on hips, forgetting my tits were flailing in the wind for all to gawk at. "I can't do that," my voice rose several octaves, getting additional attention from his men in black working around the room. I thrust a hand over my bared breasts trying for a modicum of modesty. "I don't even know what you want me to do!" came out through my clenched teeth.

Alec came over to me and positioned me back at the wall. He leaned in close, pushing the hair off my shoulder and neck where he nuzzled in. "*Ma jolie*, I'm sorry, I don't mean to anger you. Tensions are high. Let's focus together, and we'll talk more later. *Oui*?" He said in that calm tone that, after only two days, seemed to work like a charm at calming me and centering my focus at the same time. With the barest of pressure, he kissed the top of my shoulder. It felt like a promise, one I'd be making sure he kept later this evening.

"Now, place your hand here," he lifted my right arm alongside the wall. The other, I want at the bottom of the canvas over your image's heart. I placed my hand delicately on the canvas. Even though it was a silkscreen image I didn't want to mess it up. Alec went back to his camera. "Okay Mia, please stare at your image. Think back to a time where you felt loved. Beautiful. At home in your own skin."

Instantly, I was catapulted to a memory of being a small child. It was before my Mom abandoned us. We were a happy family of four then. I had just won the lead part in our county's children's play. Mom was even happy for me, and she usually was primarily focused on her own desires and wins. But not that day. That day, she gave me a hug and a kiss, and told me she was proud of me and would always love me. Then my Dad scooped me into his arms and held me close. He whispered into my ear how he always knew I had something special. Something no other little girl had. And in that moment, secure in my dad's arms and my mother's love, I believed him. Best day of my life.

The camera clicked like wild. Then the memory continued, the next day, Mom left and never came back. I never did star in that play. For a long time I thought it was my fault that she left. Because I did something so well and got all Dad's attention, something I knew she craved a lot of, even when I was only ten years old. Now as an adult, I knew different. Well, mostly.

I looked up at twenty-five-year-old Mia's teary face in the image and pitied her. For just a second I allowed myself to feel pity for my upbringing, for the choices my family made, and how I later chose to live my life. How I was living my life now. What I saw wasn't a pretty picture anymore. It was of a sad girl who'd lost something precious. Something beautiful.

Without asking if we were done or if he'd gotten what he needed, I put on my bra and shirt, hopped over to my crutches and hobbled away. The wall around my heart was barely intact, crumbling at the seams. One more hit and I'd be on the floor in a puddle of rubble.

"Mia!" Alec called but I didn't stop, just waved goodbye over my head. It was late and the day had been long. He couldn't fault me for needing rest.

I made it up to the loft, went straight to the kitchen and found an open bottle of wine and a wine glass, poured a huge helping of the crimson liquid and took a huge gulp before allowing the tears to fall.

That was when Alec returned. He came to my side, grabbed another wine glass and poured his own. Then he leaned against the counter and looked at me while I tried to compose myself and pretend I hadn't just been bawling like a baby.

"Why don't you love yourself?" His words hit my wall like a sledgehammer and left a giant, gaping hole in their wake.

CHAPTER FOUR

"I love myself." The words spilled from my lips like acid hitting bare flesh.

Alec's gaze settled on mine. I was leaning against the kitchen island having just poured myself another glass of wine.

"Do you? Could have fooled me," he responded flippantly before tossing back a heavy slug of the red wine.

"You think you know me? After only a few days?" I ground my teeth together and narrowed my eyebrows.

Alec's lips pinched together and he turned his head and looked at me. That look said it all. Frustration, stubbornness and something else. "I think I know you better than you know yourself, or at least better than you will admit to yourself," he came close and cupped my cheek. I pushed it away and hopped back on one foot, protecting my ankle.

"What? You think because you're an 'artist' you have some type of special ability to read people? If that's the case, your magic is way off, Frenchie, because the last person I want to be near right now is you!" I slammed my glass down on the counter and the wine sloshed out both sides onto the counter. "Fuck!" I hobbled over to the paper towels and pulled frantically at the roll, grabbing far too much for the tiny spill.

"Let me," Alec tried to grab for the towels. Again, I shoved him away.

"I've got it. I've been cleaning up my messes and everyone else's most of my life. I can handle a tiny spill," I sniffed, holding back the damned emotions that were hanging just at the surface ready to break free. There was no way I was allowing myself to break down now. He'd see me as being weak, useless.

He pulled back and held up both hands, palms facing me. "Okay, okay, *Je suis désolé*. Sorry," he repeated in English.

I knew I was being a bitch. This wasn't his fault. He didn't do anything to warrant me treating him poorly. Once I'd wiped up the mess, he handed me a newly opened bottle of wine. I poured more in my glass.

"Talk to me, *ma jolie*. I am here. I want to be here for you," he said softly. I caught his gaze and could see he meant it. There was no pity in his tone or his eyes. Just concern.

"Alec, I'm sorry. It's just, doing the shoot today, when you asked me to think of a happy time, it brought back a great memory. Only that memory was smashed by another that was very painful. It was a time in my life I still haven't been able to work through. That's all. It's not you." I leaned forward and wound my arms around his body, and laid my head against his warm chest. I nuzzled there smelling his fresh woodsy scent. He held me close, wrapping both arms around me. One hand slid up and down my spine comforting me in a way only a man of his size could.

"I get the feeling you've spent a great deal of your life taking care of others, *oui*?"

Instead of responding, I just nodded against his chest not wanting to see his eyes. He took a deep breath and squeezed me tight. "So now, *ma jolie*, it's time you take care of yourself, *oui*?"

Again, I nodded from the safety of my hiding place.

"I shall help you. This project, Love on Canvas, will be an outlet. Together, and for the eye of the beholder, we will find you some peace, and I shall show you through art how perfect you are." He pulled me back by the shoulders. I took a hand and wiped away the tears. I didn't even realize I was crying before looking up into his beautiful eyes. They were so serene, yellow with warm brown flecks swirling happily. I couldn't look away, didn't want to. "This will be my best work yet and through it, you will find a piece of what you need to move forward." He smiled wide then leaned forward. And finally, Alec kissed me the way I'd wanted to be kissed since I first saw him in person.

Deep.

Wet.

Long.

His lips formed to mine. He leaned forward and pressed his frame against mine until I was caged by the counter and his arms on either side. I lifted both hands, and starting at his stomach, I felt him. Finely sculpted abs, each bump a road I wanted to travel with my tongue. His pecs were hard slabs of muscle under the thin fabric of his t-shirt. Once I reached his neck, I pushed up a few more inches and let my fingers glory in the silk of his hair. He'd pulled it down at some point, and right then, I couldn't be happier. He tilted my head to gain deeper access and his hands came into play. I was definitely enjoying his version of play.

Alec caressed my body like he was painting a canvas. Soft strokes here, harder ones there. All meant to seduce. I wanted his hands all over me—without the clothes. My foot was starting to throb painfully as I kept trying to put it down on the floor so I could pivot onto my toes to reach higher, press more of my body into his. Frustrated I jolted back, his lips leaving mine in an audible smack.

"What's the matter?" He asked taking heavy breaths I felt puffing against my face. His eyes held concern, but I cupped his cheek and caressed his moist lip with my thumb.

"My foot…it hurts. I need to…lie down. Bed?" I said as winded as he was from our kiss.

He grinned wide, placed his hands on my ass and lifted me up. Instantly, I wound my legs around his trim waist. "My pleasure, *ma jolie.*" He carried me to the stairs and slowly climbed them, treating me as precious cargo, planting soft kisses along my neck as he went. When we made it to the bed, he held me tight, placed a knee on the mattress and leaned down, never dropping me in the process. The thought of his strength and power hovering over me sent me into an upward spiral of want.

Once I was flat, I pushed my hands under his shirt to get at his skin. Fumbling, I yanked at it, and he leaned up and whipped it off his head, tossing it behind him. Then he unbuttoned the few buttons on his jeans and left them open. I could see nothing but bare skin, soft tuffs of russet hair and a bit of his hard dick. Frenchie wasn't wearing underwear. Fascinating.

"Commando?" I grinned.

His brows narrowed and he cringed. "*Quoi?*" he shook his head, "What?"

I placed my hands onto his waist then leaned up so I could slip them into the back of his pants to grip his bare ass. He groaned and flexed his hips when I did that. "You're not wearing any underwear."

Alec's tongue came out to moisten his bottom lip. I stared at that lip like it held all the answers in the universe. "*Oui*. I do not wear *le caleçon*. They are uncomfortable and unnecessary. Prevent me from getting to what I want faster. For instance, you."

Then his body straddled mine, his lips trailing down my neck. It felt good. Better than good. He gripped both breasts over my shirt before leaning back on his haunches and doing away with it. The front clasp of my bra was opened and gone in what seemed like a blink. With his fingers, Alec traced patterns all over my naked chest. I closed my eyes and allowed him to touch me this way. A way I'd not been touched before. Almost reverently, like I was special, my body precious.

"*Vous êtes de l'art,*" he whispered in French tracing the sides of my breasts and ribcage.

"*Vous êtes l'amour.*" His fingers skimmed the tops of each breast.

"*Vous êtes la beauté.*" His thumbs swirled in circles around my nipples.

I gasped and arched into his feather light touch. His words, along with those magical fingers, were setting me aflame. "What did you say?" I asked in a breathy whisper.

He leaned forward and kissed me above my heart. "I said that you are art." Then he moved to my breasts and kissed the fleshy tops of each. I sucked in a breath and held it. "You are love." His tongue came out and twirled around one peak, then the other, forcing a gasp out of me. "You are beauty." His mouth encircled my nipple and sucked hard in long drawn out pulls until the areola was prickling with sensation and tight as a knot.

My hands were not idle. I ran my nails up and down his long back then curled my fingers into his hair. The strands of his long tresses dangled along my body as he made his way down my chest to my belly. With ease, he pulled off my pants and underwear simultaneously. He situated himself between my legs and lifted one in the air. He kissed my instep, up my ankle all the way to the back of my knee where he licked and nipped. I had no idea the back of my knee was such an erogenous zone, but hell, my sex was weeping for attention, and he hadn't even touched me *there* yet. Alec repeated the same movement on the other side only taking extra special care not to tweak the dressing on my bad ankle. When he got to the back of my knee, I visibly shivered.

"Cold?" He asked on a grin. He knew I wasn't, but like before, he enjoyed toying with me. I had to admit the anticipation of what he'd do next had become part of the experience, and I relished it.

I shook my head as he put my leg down. He cupped both kneecaps and butterflied my legs out. "I want to taste your beauty on my tongue." His eyebrow quirked up almost as if he was asking permission. He waited long moments his gaze never leaving mine. He *was* asking permission. I licked my lips and tipped my chin. His eyes turned dark, heavy with intent. Like a jaguar, his shoulders moved into position and just as I looked down to see his beautiful body in between my legs, he struck, lightning fast. His mouth was on me and his tongue deep inside.

"Oh, God!" I roared before clinging to his head. He was not slow in his movements like I expected. Most men started off slow, tentative. Not Alec. No, he attacked my sex liked he'd never get another chance. Within, his tongue flicked delectably against every millimeter within his reach. Little bouts of electricity buzzed from my sex and outward. The scruff of his beard grated along the lips and sides of my center as he partook. The sounds he was making were animalistic, growling, groaning and humming with delight as my body bucked against his face.

Alec brought his fingers into the mix. A thumb twirled around my O-trigger while his tongue searched my heat. I slammed my hands on the bed and gripped the sheets in my fists as an orgasm coiled tight starting low at my spine and spreading out over my body like ivy crawling a fence. It coated me with its power, the very surface of my skin buzzing with the need for release.

"So divine. You are sweet, *ma jolie*." he lapped at his fingers before putting them inside me and hooking them up and yanking down. "Like the finest champagne." He lapped at *the spot,* and I groaned, the orgasm he'd built ready to burst. "I may never get enough. I'm going to gorge on your sweetness until I taste your cream, *chérie*." His words were positively filthy, but were the bit I needed to throw me over the edge. "Ah, yes." He tugged on my insides with fingers, lapped at my O-trigger, while my entire body tightened pleasurably into extreme nirvana.

At the height of my release, he pulled his fingers out, licked me around the tiny rosette at my backside which made me jerk and shake, then sucked at my cleft, literally drinking from me. When he was done and my orgasm had petered out, he held my legs open wider. I figured he'd climb up me and put his cock inside. At least that's what I was hoping for, about to beg for. He had other plans.

Moving slowly up my center with his tongue he placed

a finger at the tiny rosette below my slit and twirled the digit around it, gradually pressing a centimeter inside. I gasped and pulled my hips back not sure if I wanted an invasion in that dark place, but I couldn't help the tremors of excitement that jumped through me as he touched it. Alec was an observant man. He noticed my response and as I looked down he grinned, then sunk his teeth into the flesh of his beautiful bottom lip. I wanted to do that. Frustrated in every way, I plopped my head back down. "Fuck me, Alec," I begged and gripped at the sheets once more.

"*Non, pas encore,*" he murmured into my flesh.

I didn't know what that meant, but I did know what encore meant in English, and I was all for that.

This time when his tongue laved, it was slow, deliberate in its movement against my sex. It was as if he was soothing the flesh, possibly memorizing it. After a while, I got impatient. My hips gyrated side to side and around as he stroked with his tongue and fingers. Without further preparation, he slid two fingers inside me. I groaned. Finally! But before I could get into the joy of having his thick fingers exactly where I wanted them, he slid out. Not for long. His tongue replaced his fingers licking inside then moving up to my hot spot. Once he touched down there, I was back on my way to another incredible orgasm.

"Fuck yes," I lifted my hips and grabbed at his hair, forcing his face onto me. He didn't disappoint. He took that as the need to go faster, push harder, take more. I loved every second, so far gone in my search for the second peak, I didn't realize he had a moistened finger circling that secret place no man had ever touched until it was too late. That finger pushed down on the rosette, pressing in while he simultaneously sucked hard on my O-trigger. My hips tried to thrust into the air but Alec held them down, fucking my ass with his finger as I shook. It felt different, burning, and so insanely good I started to push into it, wanting it harder, faster.

"*Tres belle,*" he whispered and kissed my clit. He was soft with my sex but ravaging with my ass, plundering in, pushing me up the bed with each force of his hand into my body. I reveled in it, allowing him to take me in that dark way. A place no one's ever been before. A place I didn't even know I wanted to go until he took me there. My Frenchie.

Alec lifted up sitting on his shins but kept his hand working me over. He placed his other hand to manipulate me where I needed him most. I gasped and closed my eyes knowing he was watching me.

"*Ouvrez les yeux,*" he said, then in English he continued, "Open your eyes." I did as he bade. His eyes were black. No hint of the tawny brown they were normally. "I like to see you. Remember your face when you're inner beauty is brightest."

He pushed hard into me, and I gasped then jerked my hips. He fucked me hard with his fingers and when he pinched my clit between thumb and index finger with his other hand, I took flight. Literally left the plane I was in, my body opened up, free as a bird while Alec gave me my wings.

Somewhere in my subconscious, I heard a crackling noise and the scent of rubber wafted across my nose. Alec's hands cupped my shoulders and then he was there, pressing his length into me. The denim of his jeans scraped along my inner thighs as he thrust deep. It was like the pleasure was never going to end. I hadn't even come down fully when he'd plowed his thick length into me. He groaned into my hair, and I clasped my limbs around his body, holding him close, loving the warmth of skin as he pressed in and out.

"*Chaud, soyeux, et parfait,*" he said before kissing me fully. I opened my mouth and let him enter me in all ways, joining with him the way I wanted to from the moment I saw his picture. He was hard, long, and deep inside me. I never wanted him to stop, yet I wanted him to *get there* more. To feel what he'd given me two times already. So, with all my might, I shifted my weight and rolled over on top of him. That's when I worked him hard.

His hands immediately came to my hips and helped guide me up and down on his thick cock. He was magnificent like this. The muscles in his forearms tightened and strained with every thrust. A sheen of sweat built up over the bumpy highway of his abdominal muscles. I leaned down at one point and licked and sucked the flat disk of his nipple.

"*Putain oui*" he said through clenched teeth, his jaw working overtime. I nibbled and bit at his nipple until it was dark and erect then moved over to its mate and did the same. Alec's fingers dug into my hips signaling his need to be taken harder. I lifted back up, flung my hair back behind me, and rode him…hard. Every press down I ground into his pelvis sending sparks of excitement through my sex where I clamped down using my internal muscles, giving him as good as I'd gotten.

He spoke in rapid French. I couldn't understand any of it. He sat up, pushed with his feet until he was at the headboard. He leaned my body back and physically slid me on and off his cock. The French started back up again as he watched himself enter my body over and over. As much as I wanted this to be for him, I couldn't help that he was winding me up again. My body was coiled tight like a snake, and he knew it, too. He leaned his mouth forward and sucked hard on my nipples making them dark red raspberries until he couldn't take it anymore.

Finally, his head hit the headboard and I grasped the top of the headboard for leverage. That's when I took us both over the edge, barreling into a sea of sweet nothingness, the only sounds our strained breathing as we cried out in mutual release, my center putting a lockdown around his shaft the likes of which I'd never thought possible before. He held me close still pressing his hips up from beneath me, rubbing out the very last tremors of pleasure.

We stayed that way, me strung up on his cock, sitting in his lap, my hands still hanging onto the headboard. His hands moved up and down my back, arms, thighs as if he needed to touch me, to believe I was really there. I could understand it. When you leave yourself like that, and the pleasure is so extreme, you need something repetitive to bring you back.

Little by little our heartbeats calmed down, and I tucked my arms behind his back and held him close. He didn't let me go, either, preferring to touch and kiss me wherever he could reach. It was nice—really nice if I was being honest with myself.

For a moment, it reminded me of Wes. Sweet, beautiful, down to Earth, Wes. The one man, the only man I think I could ever truly fall in love with. I took a harsh breath and prevented the tears from coming. I wasn't cheating. I. Was. Not. Cheating. Even though I kept telling myself, there still was a hint of guilt hovering over me like a machete ready to lop of my head.

"What's the matter?" Alec asked pushing me back so he could see my eyes.

I shook my head. These were not thoughts I ever planned on sharing with Alec or anyone for that matter. "Just relaxing against you," I kissed his nose then nuzzled him there. "We should clean up, take care of the um…" I looked down and Alec's gaze followed.

"Ah, the condom, yes, I should do that." He lifted me off and then got up pulled off the condom and tied it at the end before setting it into a tissue and putting it in a wastebasket. I imagine the last thing he wanted to do was go down the stairs to the bathroom though that's exactly what I needed to do. I rolled to my back and groaned. "What is it?"

"I have to pee," I mumbled and he laughed. Before I could say anything, he lifted me up from the bed in his favorite princess hold and carried me down the stairs to the bathroom. Once in front of the toilet, he set me down and moved out the door.

"I'll make us a snack, *oui*?"

"*Oui*," I responded and he chuckled before shutting the door. I took care of my business quickly and then grabbed for the robe on the back of the door. It was a lush deep burgundy color that felt like squishy awesomeness over my bare skin. I didn't want to hop out there completely naked.

I hopped my way to the kitchen. He had a tray of items in one hand and a couple glasses of wine in the other. Still, he was bare-assed naked, and I greatly enjoyed the view. His tattoo slithered along his body and that reminded me how much I wanted to trace it…with my tongue.

"*Un moment*," he said as he jaunted up the stairs to the loft bedroom. Before I knew it, he was rushing down the stairs, his dick flapping in the wind. I giggled as he made his way over to me. "What?" he asked a lovely smile adorned his face. When he was happy, he was less intense artist and more friendly Frenchie. Though I thoroughly enjoyed both very much.

Once he reached me, he pulled me into his arms and carried me back up the stairs. "I see you found my robe," he said with a mock stern voice. Then he set me on my good foot, his hands going to the tie. "That is not acceptable. I told you, *ma jolie*, I like to see your naked body." I let him remove the robe then I crawled over the bed and got comfortable. He set the tray in front of us and handed me a glass of wine. The rich berry flavor drifted down my throat and settled nicely in my belly. The tray he brought had some salami, tiny blocks of cheddar cheese, green grapes and a bunch of strawberries.

My stomach growled while I scoured all my options then settled on a chunk of cheese. It paired well with my wine. "Thank you." I pulled the sheet up into my chest.

"For what?"

I picked up a strawberry and held it close. "For this, for tonight, painting me, sharing your work with me. I'm really honored to be here with you."

His hand came up and held my cheek. "You are my muse, Mia. You were meant to be here."

CHAPTER FIVE

Once we finished our meal, we messed around a bit more, kissing, caressing each other, getting to know one another better. After a deep kiss, I leaned on his chest and hugged him.

"Do you realize you barely say anything in English when you're fucking?"

Alec's body tightened before he responded. "I do not fuck, *chérie*. I told you, I make love to you, to your body." His tone was drop dead serious and I couldn't grasp why. "And I speak in French because you make me so far gone, I lose myself in you, in your sexy body."

I grinned saucily giving him my best smile. Then I thought about the fucking versus love making for a moment. "But doesn't that get tricky, the love making? Doesn't everyone fall in love with you when you do that?"

He held me tight and slid a hand up to my bicep and squeezed. "I would hope so."

"Wait a minute; you *want* me to fall in love with you?" I lifted off his chest and looked hard into his eyes. They were so pretty.

"Of course, don't you?" his face contorted into one of bafflement.

I shook my head hard letting my hair fly. "No, not even. I want to have *fun* with you. Then after, I'm going to be with another client who I may or may not have sexual relations with."

"As will I." He looked utterly confused, which said a lot, because I was pretty sure I was going off the deep end without a paddle.

I pushed my hair out of my face and behind me. "Okay, let me get this straight. You want me to fall in love with you, yet you know I'm going to leave and be with someone else. Do I have this right so far?" He nodded and smiled innocently. "And you are going to fall in love with me, yet when I leave, you're going to have this same awesome sex with another girl."

"Awesome sex?" he grinned. Fucking pig. All men think with their dicks I swear. This proved it. I smacked him on the chest.

"Pay attention."

"I cannot pay attention with you speaking of love and sex, two things I believe always go together beautifully, I might add. We should bring them together again right now." He pulled my body over his. He was already hard. For a moment I balked. Hard again? Holy shit, this man was virile. He gripped my ass and pressed his hips to mine. "Are we done talking, *ma jolie*. I want to make love to you again."

"No!" I sat up straddling his hips and crossed my hands over my chest. None of this made a lick of sense. "I don't understand you."

His eyes narrowed. "What is to understand? I make love to you. I fall in love with you a bit more each day."

I rolled my eyes. "Okay, let's continue with that. You fall in love with me more each day, yet you're okay with letting me go?"

"If you would like to stay, I would be amicable," he said

deadpan.

Arrrgggghh! "You would be amicable? I don't understand you." my hand flew into the air like a maniac swatting at flies that weren't there.

He pulled me down to his chest then rolled us over so he was on top. With one leg he kicked out the good one of mine and pressed into my hips. His large erection rubbed enticingly along my moistening flesh. I took a deep breath trying not to let it get to me. It didn't work.

He kissed me softly. "Let me make you understand, *oui*?"

"Please!"

"The French make love. I make love. I have to have some feeling for you in order to truly make love to you, *oui*?"

"*Oui*," I repeated. That made sense. The part of us full on falling in love then willy-nilly bailing on one another, did not make sense. As a matter of fact, it's what was so hard about me leaving Wes. As much as I didn't want to admit it, I had feelings for the guy, and now, Frenchie here wanted me to have feelings for him—love type feelings— which I didn't want to have.

He started talking again. "Therefore, I must love you a little to want to be with you in such a way. Yet, I can still love you and set you free. But you will always carry my love with you when you go, and forever. That piece of my love is yours for as long as you live."

Gotta admit, that was pretty beautiful. The way he thought of having sex and making love, how it tied to the woman and the relationship he had with each of them.

"So, we're going to love one another forever, only we're

not committing to one another in the way a married couple or even a boyfriend and girlfriend do," I confirmed.

"*Oui*. Exactly, *ma jolie*! You've got it. My commitment to you is to love you wholly for our time, and that will stay with you. And I will take your love with me. Then forever, we will both know that this time was built on trust, love, and friendship." He paused then kissed me softly. "Nothing more in life is needed."

My eyes misted over and a tear trickled down the side of my cheek at the truth of what he'd said. Alec wiped it away. "May I love you now?" His words were simple but struck deep.

"Yes, Alec. I'd very much like you to love me," I said through the lump that formed in my throat. And that's what he did, loved me, all through the night or at least until I passed out. It was exactly what I needed to get through what had happened earlier in the loft, as well as the guilt that was building about Wes.

Alec and I had a mutual agreement to love one another as friends, to treat each other with respect. We would enjoy one another's bodies and minds for the time I was there, and when it was done, it was done. We'd still care for one another and have a love that was exclusively ours that we could keep in a box inside our memories and revisit if we needed to. There was something achingly perfect about that. Right then, I vowed that I wouldn't try to prevent myself from caring for each client. I would allow myself to care in my own special way. Only it wouldn't be the "I'm in love with you forever way." Forever was sacred, something that would present itself when the time was right, with the right person.

I thought back to Wes and how much I missed him. This situation with Alec gave me new insight into my relationship with Wes. Showed me how I spent the entire month I was with Wes trying not to love him. Protecting myself and my heart from ever feeling those things. Except it didn't work, because I do love Wes. In my own way. And I think he loves me too. Only with him, I'm not sure it wouldn't be the forever kind of love. That thought cemented why it was important for me to leave when I did. I can safely say that we were both honest with one another, cared deeply, and if it's meant to be a forever kind of love, we have time to cultivate that. *If it's meant to be.* Until then, I would enjoy my Frenchman and all the experiences I was supposed to have while I was there and for the remainder of the year escorting.

★ ★ ★ ★

The next day when I made my way down to the loft, it was once again silent. I was beginning to see a pattern here. He took pictures one day, and the next day, when he did the painting, he released his staff so he could work alone. As I made my way further into the loft, I heard a hauntingly beautiful piece of music. The lilting voice and intense piano notes echoed off the walls as a woman's tentative lyrics weaved through the chords of the piano. She was almost speaking in a whisper yet still singing. It was utterly disturbing in its beauty. Then strings entered the mix. I closed my eyes taking it into my heart and soul. Remembering this moment for what it was. Graceful, vulnerable, everything I needed.

Click I was startled and opened my eyes to see Alec

standing in front of me a camera in his hand.

"I couldn't help myself. You were too precious, soaking in the light of grace. I had to capture it."

I tilted my head and grinned. "Did you get what you need?" I asked with a touch of sarcasm.

"Did you?" his eyebrow quirked. Always trying to teach me a lesson, my Frenchie.

I took a breath and scanned the floor choosing to leave it at that.

"Come, there is much to do." Alec turned on a heel and strode over to our space in the loft.

I hobbled over and took my seat. I gasped as I stared once more at my image. Only this time it was the wide canvas. One half had my picture silk screened, the other, he painted. He must have gotten up in the middle of the night after I passed out once round two of him "loving" me was finished.

"How...?" I was incapable of saying anything else as I looked at myself on the canvas. It was me facing the image he had photographed yesterday. My hand out, my forehead near the painting, only he painted my hand touching the heart on the photographed side. The way he mixed medias so uniquely was unlike anything I'd witnessed before. This is why he was a world-renowned artist and people paid obscene amounts of money for his art. And I was part of that, a big part. His muse.

"I don't need much sleep. Once I was inspired by your body, I had to paint it."

"Are you saying, we had sex and you were so taken by the experience you came down here and painted this?"

"*Oui*. Your naked body. Making love to you gave me all

the energy I needed to create this beautiful image for the world to see. Now you can see, *oui?*"

I stared at the black and white painting. Just a hint of my naked breasts showed in the painting. I could also see the happiness in my form as my image touched the sad heart of the picture he'd taken the day before. It was as if my happy self was consoling my sad self. Shivers rippled down my spine and out my arms.

Once more, he filled a saucer with sticky paint, then walked over to me, brush in hand. He proceeded to paint my lips as I quietly admired the painting in front of me. It held me captive like there was a gnarled hand clutching my heart. My heart pounded and tears fell from my eyes. The music in the room changed. The notes were loud and sweeping in their sorrow as they pitched high then low. Trombones and trumpets blared. Alec gripped my hand, swept me into his arms and carried me over to the painting. This time he didn't have me kiss my lips.

"Kiss here." He pointed to the hand over the heart in the second image. I leaned forward and kissed the painted canvas. A perfect lip print shone bright red on the painted hand. He applied more paint to my lips.

He pointed to my elbow and I kissed it. More paint. The shoulder, the middle of the back in the image. More paint. For a long time he reapplied the paint, had me kiss an exposed portion of my body on his painting. We did this until there were red lip kisses all over the painting he'd done. It was odd, it didn't take away from his art but added an entirely different element. The kiss marks were bright, stark against the black and white of the canvas and his drawing.

Once he was done, he helped me back into the seat.

Methodically he wiped my lips with baby wipes removing any paint residue. Then he handed me some water and a lip balm. I swear the man thought of everything.

He walked across the room and left me to the music and the painting. I stared and stared at myself. The one I'd done the first day was hanging to the left, the red lips and tear streaking down my face in the image was startling in its sadness. The picture on the right was the same image photographed but with the addition of me facing it, hand on the heart, only there were kiss marks over every couple inches.

The lighting above the artwork shone bright and seemed to start in the middle of the images and burst out, accentuating the depth of the dark and light along with the texture of the red paint making it pop out as if 3D.

"Have you figured out what it means yet?" Alec asked while looking at the painting. I looked at him for long moments. Watching him as he appreciated what he created. He was the one that should have been the subject of the artwork. He was so big, strong, and masculine. The hair he'd pulled into a tiny bun at the back of his head seemed to shine gold in the lighting. His beard and mustache made slight rustling noise as he rubbed his knuckles across it. "Have you, *ma jolie?*"

I shook my head and focused on the art. "I can see that it's beautiful, that it moves me in a way."

His gaze shot to mine. "It moves you?"

"Yeah," I whispered focusing on the first image. "This one, I look sad, but it's more than that. There's a quiet devastation there. The sorrow so deep in the eyes you've painted makes me think I'll never be happy. That she'll never be happy." I tried to take myself out of the image even though it was difficult. I had a feeling that was the last thing he intended.

He nodded. "Yes when I captured you, it hurt me. That's how I knew it was the right one. Art should make you feel something. Good, bad, happiness, sorrow, love, hate, cold, warmth. Everything we see correlates to a feeling within us. This particular one moved you the way it should."

"Why? Why would you want someone to feel sorrow and a sadness so deep they may never recover?"

His gaze held mine. "Because that is what I want the viewer to see. The painting is called, "No Love for Me."

Those words shot through my heart like an arrow. Tears spilled down both sides of my face "And the other?" I asked though afraid to hear the answer.

"What does it make you feel?"

I skimmed over the photographic image of my sad self and quickly looked away. "Shame." His jaw seemed to tighten and lock down, and he gave a slight nod. I focused again on the image where I held my hand over the heart of the sad Mia. "Hope." Again he stared and waited. I took in all the red lips everywhere all over the Mia reaching out to the sad image. "Love." I shrugged.

Alec turned and came over to me where he kneeled down. He moved forward, held my face in both hands and kissed me softly. I could taste the coffee he drank and something darker, something that was unique to him.

"You see what I want you to see. Shame, hope, and love." His eyes were wide, his features soft as he took in my face.

"But why? Those things are hard to grasp. Not only

that, they are often things that tear people apart."

"As sometimes art can do. It's all in the eye of the beholder. What you see, what I see, may feel different, as it should."

"Have you named it?"

He tipped his chin down in assent.

"What are you calling it?"

"Exactly what I want the viewer to feel."

I swallowed slowly waiting for him to finish. He didn't. "Which is?"

He traced my face from the indent at my temple down to my lips. He watched his finger with reverence as it slipped across my features.

"To Love Thyself."

CHAPTER SIX

Over the next week, Alec and I got into a regular routine. Stills, eating, sex. Painting, eating, sex. We hadn't left the building, and most days it rained. I longed for sunny Malibu and being free to swim, go for a walk, or surf. What I missed most, though, besides my family, was Wes. Don't get me wrong, Alec was amazing in more ways than one. Even though we had an easy camaraderie and had a blast in the bedroom, there really was nothing more to our relationship other than working and fucking. 'Making love' he called it; I called it fucking, and I loved to do it, though I didn't share that with him. It could have been worse, I guess. He could have been parading me around to boring museums to look at other people's art.

I wasn't due in the loft until the evening. That was a new request. Usually, he wanted me there first thing after I woke. The problem was when I was alone with my thoughts, I'd think of all the things in my real life I was missing. My dad, who hadn't woken from his coma but had been moved to a convalescent facility to be cared for by the State. Gin said it was an okay place, nothing special about it. She said she and Maddy visited every few days, read to him, try to keep him company. She sent me a picture of him lying in bed. The bruises around his face had healed. Most of his body was still in a cast of some sort.

Looking down at my phone, I saw my dad. It was as if

he was sleeping, not fighting for his life. The doctors don't know what his mental status will be if he wakes up. *When* he wakes up, I remind myself. No need to put out negative vibes into the universe. Even though I don't really believe in that shit, if it does happen to be real, I'm not going to be the one to mess with the higher power.

Scrolling through the list of contacts, I pressed the speed dial for Maddy. It had been a good week since I'd spoken to her, and I was missing my baby sis.

"Hey, Sis." Maddy's sing song voice rang through the phone. Instantly, the tight feeling around my heart lessened at her happy tone.

"Hi, Mads, how you doing?" I asked.

The shuffling of papers and a zipper could be heard through the line. "Eh, you know me, getting ready for class."

"What's this one?"

"Forensic Pathology," she answered.

I pushed a hand through my hair and tucked the blankets higher around my body. "Isn't that the study of dead people?"

More shuffling then she sighed. "Yeah, technically it focuses on determining the cause of death by examining a corpse. The autopsy is performed by a medical examiner, usually during the investigation of criminal law cases and civil law cases in some jurisdictions…" She went on, but I had blanked out after she said examining a corpse.

"You're going to cut up a dead person?" I couldn't contain the shock in my voice. Who would willingly want to do that? I mean, I know people did do that, and it was part of solving murders and such, but really, my sweet baby sister cutting up dead guys? The thought made the hair on my arms rise.

"It's called a cadaver, and it's part of my course work. Everyone has to do a variety of classes and I picked this one. It's really interesting. You'd never believe some of the sick stuff people do."

She'd be surprised. "I know what psychos do, and I don't want my baby sis anywhere near that shit. You're golden, baby. I don't want you tainted by what the scum of the Earth do."

"Momma Mia, you cannot protect me forever. I'm nineteen years old. Besides, you're only five years older than me."

"Didn't stop me from taking care of you to this point!" I shot back.

She sighed so long I could almost physically feel the weight of it pressing back down on my chest. "Mia, I don't know what type of scientist I'm going to be yet..."

"The kind that cures cancer or develops new pills that can keep me skinny forever! The kind that doesn't deal in death!" I sat up, my hackles rising. I did not want her surrounded by the ugly in life. We'd had enough of that growing up, and I had worked my damn ass off since she was five to make sure she'd see only light, as bright as I could give her.

"You know I love you," she said so softly, using that voice that she knew got to me. "I know you want everything for me, and I..." She paused, and that pause pressed the weight deeper, crushing my heart. "Mia, I have to be able to find my own way. Okay? Promise me you'll let me figure this out on my own."

Figure something out on her own? My baby sis doing

something all by herself. Without me to guide her, protect her, save her from getting shit on. I felt like a robot. *Does not compute. Does not compute.* I shushed my own ridiculous crazy voice aside and tried to be supportive. "I want you happy, Mads," I choked back the emotion. "Just promise me you're considering all options."

I could tell the moment she turned back into happy-go-lucky Mads. "Oh, I am! I'm also taking a botany class that's absolutely fascinating!"

"What's botany?" God, I felt stupid asking my baby sister what something meant. I'd heard the word before, but I couldn't place it.

"Plant science," she giggled.

Did she just say plant science? From the study of dead people to plants? "Plants?"

"Uh huh. It's actually really cool. We're studying the relationship of different plants and flowers to their environments. Next, we're going into horticulture which goes over the cultivation of plants and flowers for food and decoration."

Now that sounded really weird but also safe and pretty. Everyone loved plants and flowers and there weren't murders as part of something like that. "I like the sound of this course," I admitted.

"Figured you would. And Mia, there's this guy that I'm partnered with, and, oh my God, he's so hot!" she giggled again like the schoolgirl she was. It lifted that weight right off my chest and slammed it into next week.

Now this, this is the type of talk I could get into. "Oh yeah, tell me everything!"

And she did. Shared with me how they've been flirting

for a couple weeks, but he hasn't gotten up the nerve to ask her out. He was a year older and majoring in the plant sciences. Really liked that. Meant he was a nerdy guy. I suggested she ask him out. She freaked. No way was my sweet, innocent baby sister going to ask a guy out. I was proud of that. Even more proud that, at nineteen, she still had her virginity. A couple times she'd come close, but we talked through it and she decided the guys weren't worth it. I wanted her to have a special experience and told her so. Not like mine. Drunk off my ass in the back of my high-school sweetheart's truck. Shortly after, he'd ran off with a cheerleader with bigger boobs and a lower IQ.

I was honest with my sis and told her my experience. At the time, she was horrified that a guy would do that to me and promised that she'd never make the same mistakes. I figured sharing that shitty time in my life was worth it. If she learned something from it and protected herself, I'd done my job, and I took my job of raising her seriously. She was the best thing I'd ever contributed to in my life, and I was determined, even now, to make sure she succeeded. For the both of us.

After my call with Maddy, I felt a lot better. Knowing she was doing so well in school, had found a hot, nerdy guy to flirt with, and the bills were all paid at home gave me a real sense of peace. I knew then more than ever that taking this job with Millie's escort service was the right decision. Maddy had some extra cash in the bank, food in the fridge, and I was up-to-date on my payment to Blaine. I finished up my shower in a damn good mood then heard my phone ping while I was ringing out my wet hair. I hopped over to the toilet seat, sat my towel-clad fanny on it, then grabbed my phone and stared at the screen.

From: Wes Channing
To: Mia Saunders
How's Seattle?

Seeing Wes's name made my heart pound and butterflies take up flight in my stomach. I didn't know how this was going to play out with Wes. He'd said we'd stay friends through the year, so I imagined this was his attempt at following through. I thought for a few minutes about how I wanted to respond. Guilt that I'd been with Alec scratched at the surface of my subconscious, but I pushed it aside. I had to treat Wes like a friend and vice versa. Yes, there are some deep feelings there. Yes, I'd love to be sitting with him right now, but that's not the way my life is. It's not how my life is going to be for another ten and a half months.

From: Mia Saunders
To: Wes Channing
Wet. Did you know it rains just about every day here?

There, that should work. Something platonic. Friend-like. I read and re-read the simple reply then sent it. While I was blow drying my hair, I heard the phone ping again.

From: Wes Channing
To: Mia Saunders
Everybody knows that. On average it rains the same amount of days that it's sunny. Okay, checked weatherunderground. You'll get some sun in a few days. Of course, you could always come to

Malibu. Sun is high and the pool is warm.

Leave it to Wes to attempt to get me to come back. I wondered if it was always going to be like this between us. Easy, joking, yet with a level of serious desire hovering just under the surface.

From: Mia Saunders
To: Wes Channing
Excuse me, Mr. Weather Man. And thanks for the update. Malibu in January was nice. Maybe I'll plan a trip there next January. ;)

I added the smiling wink to help lighten the response. It was what we discussed, but I couldn't really make that promise. The better part of the year was still ahead of us and who knew where we'd end up.

From: Wes Channing
To: Mia Saunders
Then I'll look forward to your visit. Stay dry, sweetheart.

I didn't reply. Couldn't. Wes was everything I'd ever wanted in a man and more, but he wasn't mine. Maybe one day, but not now. It felt good texting with him. Reminded me of something to look forward to at year's end. I rarely had anything to look forward to. For now though, I had a sexy artist guy who was filling up my present with good times and something to remember. Of course, with Wes, I'd never forget.

★ ★ ★ ★

When six o'clock hit, I made my way down to the loft per Alec's instructions. I hadn't seen him all day, which was a first. It was good to have that time alone. For most of two weeks, I'd been on top of him, figuratively and literally. That last thought made me smile. Once I arrived at the loft, I could see Alec's form moving around at the opposite corner of the room from where we'd been working. He was behind his camera moving in a half moon shape taking pictures of a man standing ten feet away from him in front of a white background. A very naked, well-endowed man. Holy shit. I mean, it wasn't like I'd never seen a man before, but this guy was young, probably my age, largely muscled, with his cock standing straight up.

Attempting to make as little noise as possible on my crutches, I came up to the side. Every so often the man would close his eyes, place a hand around his erection and give it a few tugs. He licked his lips and leaned into it. The camera clicked like crazy and Alec called out soft encouragements.

"*Oui*, like that."

"Arch more; pretend you're putting on a show for your lady."

"That's it, release your hand and place both behind your head," was the last command.

I felt like a voyeur watching this man tend to himself while Alec captured the image. It felt racy and laced in sex. Two things that made the room sweltering hot and had wetness pooling between my thighs.

"*Fini,*" Alec declared with the last shot. He gripped a

robe near one of the lights and handed it to the model. The model put the robe on and looked at the images Alec showed lifting up his camera to him. "These will not be in the photograph. I will paint them, *oui*? You agree to them?"

The man nodded. "You do good work. At first I thought it was going to be like porn, but this is nothing like that."

"No it is not," he agreed softly then clapped the model on the shoulder. "You ready for the female?" he asked, and I looked around. My shoe scratched against the concrete and both men's gazes focused on me.

I lifted a hand and waved. "Hey," I offered lamely. Good thing it was dark in this corner or they'd see the blush I could feel creeping up my neck and cheeks.

"Mia, come here. Meet Aiden. He's going to pose with you, *ma jolie*," Alec's words hit me like a pail of ice-cold water.

"Um, what?"

Alec came over to me and led me to Aiden. We shook hands.

"Nice to meet you, Mia. I look forward to working with you tonight," he said sweetly. Okay, sweet, muscled, and hotter than hell? The universe is a sick, twisted bitch. Now I understood why they characterized it as a vindictive woman. Any god that could create Aiden, Alec, and Wes— three perfect incarnations of male forms, all coming into my life within weeks of each other—was an expert at cruel and unusual punishment.

I grumbled a greeting than turned to Alec. "What do you mean? I'm going to pose with him?"

"Forbidden Love, *chèrie*. I'm going to take stills of you both making love on the canvas."

The words *making love* crashed into me and my head jerked back. "Explain…fast," I warned speaking through a clenched jaw.

"Oh, *non*, you will not be *faire l'amour*," he rushed to say. "Making real love, *non*. It will be staged for the camera." He cupped my face in both hands. "*Maintenant, tu comprends*? You understand now?"

"No, not even a little bit. More details before I high-tail it out of here, Frenchie," I said using the tone he was now intimately familiar with after almost two weeks together.

Alec pinched his lips together and placed his hands on his hips. Aiden moved over into a chair and sat down away from us. I appreciated the gesture of trying to give us some space.

"*Mon amour*, I need to have the two of you, bare, holding onto one another like lovers. Then when I have enough, I shall paint it." He moved closer, "Of course, that is after I make love to you." His nose came close and he slid it alongside mine sending prickles of excitement to tingle and taunt my senses. "It will be my most inspiring piece yet. You and this man, who is very male, deep in the throes of passion." He leaned forward and kissed me briefly, licking just my bottom lip before pulling away. Frenchie used his kiss to talk me into something without *needing* to talk me into it. Bastard hot French guy.

I huffed and pushed my hair back from my eyes. "You said bare, as in naked, or did I miss that?"

"*Oui*, you know I need to see the body in order to paint it. Besides, no woman has a more beautiful body than yours." His eyes scanned my jeans and tight camisole. I hadn't bothered to wear a bra knowing I was going to be at least naked on top today, and with the way his gaze was running up and down my body, my nipples were beading tight, clearly visible. His hands stroked the side of my ribs, and his fingers brushed over the erect peaks. "I see you like this idea very much."

I pressed close into his body, thankful that my back was to Aiden. "I like the idea of being with you, but this guy, I don't know," I said honestly. It was hard enough baring my body to Alec for his art, but to be naked and rolling around with another naked guy pretending to make love to him? Seemed really forced, unlike the other pictures we'd done that were just Alec and me.

He watched me and waited for me to work through his request. His tawny eyes were kind, no pressure. And it wasn't like I had to have sex with the man. Just pretend to. I looked over at Aiden. His knees were bobbing up and down while he glanced at us then away quickly. "Fine, I'll try. For you." I wanted him to know this was not something I waited my entire life to do. It was outside my comfort zone, more so than being naked in front of him. I was doing it because I trusted his vision.

"Okay, Mia, you go over there and remove your clothes. Aiden, your robe." Alec was all business once more. Aiden stood and removed his robe. His gorgeous, naked body was on full display. Even soft, he was impressive. He'd make some woman very happy with what he was packing. I giggled looking at him but not seeing him.

Aiden frowned. "Something wrong?" He looked down his naked body and placed a hand tentatively over his dick.

I knew my eyes turned into giant saucers as it dawned on me what he thought I was giggling at. "Oh my goodness, no! You've got a great dick...I mean...um...I wasn't laughing at your size. Ugggh." I groaned and lifted my head to the ceiling. Fuck Mia. Now you've gone and made Adonis question his manhood. "Why can't I ever be normal?" I blew out a huge breath, my lips puffing out like a fish. Aiden chuckled.

"It's okay. I get you." His lips quirked and he walked over to the white sheet covering a padded surface and sat down in the center.

"Honestly, Aiden, I was thinking about how hot you are and how you'd make some woman very happy." I opened my jeans and pushed them down my legs.

He grinned. "No complaints from my girlfriend." Then he winked and all of a sudden it was okay. He had a girlfriend. Just knowing that he was here to pose and had a girlfriend at home made me feel so much better. It shouldn't, seeing as I was going to be rolling around naked with the guy, but it did.

"Completely naked, *ma jolie*," Alec said while climbing up the ladder above the space. I yanked my camisole over my head and my boobs bounced free, the nipples pulling into tight knots once more, only this time at the chill. "There's a heater there, so when you get on the padding with Aiden you will feel warm."

With a deep breath, I pushed down my panties and hopped over to the mat. My ankle was almost healed, but it smarted when I put too much pressure on it. I wanted to be careful with it to make sure it completely healed before I tried putting my full weight on it. Once I hit the mat, I crawled shyly over to Aiden.

"Don't worry. You've got a smokin' hot body yourself.

AUDREY CARLAN

You ready for me to touch you?"

I licked my lips and stared up into the bright lights above. I could barely see the outline of Alec's form. Fear crawled along my skin making gooseflesh bump at the surface.

"Um, I guess," I said not really meaning it at all.

"Lie back, Mia. Aiden, put your arm under her neck so she's resting her head on it. Place that right hand around her body and hold her back." Aiden got close and leaned onto his side. I looked down and could see his dick had hardened. I gulped and bit my lip trying to shake off the creepy crawly feelings I had seeing his excitement. I knew it was natural for a man to get hard when seeing a naked woman, but still, I didn't like it. At all.

Alec continued spouting orders. "Pull her thigh up and over yours to hide your manhood." Aiden followed direction and gripped me by the knee and pulled my leg over his. That's when his dick nestled against my pelvis, and I cringed.

"Mia," Alec snapped. "Pretend you're holding the man you love. Look into his eyes." I ground my teeth and looked up. Aiden's eyes were a chocolate brown. Kind, yet filled with the exact thing I didn't want to see. Lust. I bit my lip and held my hands loosely at his waist. His hand slid up my thigh then curved around the cheek of my ass. I stiffened. The camera clicked several times. Aiden's breath seemed incredibly loud in the space between our faces.

"Mia, you're not pretending," Alec warned. "Lift your neck. Now Aiden, kiss along the column slowly while I capture it. Dig your fingers into her flesh. He did, and I followed direction. As Aiden pressed his length harder

203

into me, I could feel a tiny bit of moisture touch my skin. Swallowing hard, I started counting in my head hoping to God Alec would get his shot and this would be over soon.

Alec clomped down the ladder. "This is not working. *Pas bon*. Not good." He brought a hand to his temples and paced. "Two beautiful bodies entwined should be *magnifique, oui?*" He was talking to himself. I pulled away and crossed my hands over my chest to wait it out. Alec's eyes came to mine. Aiden touched my shoulder, but, when he did, I flinched. Alec's gaze caught it. He saw everything.

"Aiden, you may go." He walked forward and handed him the robe.

"But what about the shoot? I need the money from this job," he said worrying his bottom lip with his teeth.

"You will be paid. You've done well. My vision is specific. The first piece will be painted." Aiden's eyes lit up.

"Really?"

Alec gave him a small smile and clapped him on the shoulder. "Really. Now go. I must work now with my muse."

Aiden headed to the bathroom to change. Alec handed me his personal robe, which made me smile wide. I pulled it on and sat cross-legged on the padding. He came and sat next to me.

"You did not like this shoot." *No shit Sherlock.* I sat there quietly waiting for him to come to whatever conclusions he wanted to.

"I need this shot. So I have an idea."

"Okay." My voice was small and timid, worried that he was upset with my performance.

He slid a hand to my face and looked intently into my eyes. "I will be your muse for the shoot."

CHAPTER SEVEN

"You? My muse? How does that work?"

I could hear Aiden move through the other side of the loft, open the elevator and slam the gate shut. That's when Alec stood and pulled off his long sleeved thermal shirt. His chest shone in the bright lights of the loft. Then he yanked on the wide brown leather belt. Once he'd unbuckled it, he unzipped his pants and shimmied them down. Again, commando. I licked my lips and gripped his hips then looked up his beautiful body.

"You will pose with me. I will use this." He held up a cordless remote control. It was cylindrical with a red button on top. It reminded me of an action movie where the bad guy had a bomb strapped to his chest with a cord and a button. Alec pressed the button and the camera flashed. "See, I will do the poses with you. Only with me, it will be *real* love on canvas."

Now this concept had definite possibilities. I grinned wickedly and lifted up both of my hands along his sides, leaned forward and placed a kiss on the crown of his cock. He cupped my cheek with one hand while I showed him my appreciation for this brilliant idea. Once I licked his entire length, I pulled back. "You didn't have to do that you know."

"Yes I did, *ma jolie*. You were not comfortable. One frown on your pretty face was too much. I knew the concept was hard to begin with, but seeing your face as he touched you, knowing that you were trying for me...*non, ce n'était pas bon*, not good. I should have known. You have committed to me for this time. That means you would not look to be in love with a stranger. Real love, the kind I want in my art must be *authentique*, real, and it must be given willingly."

I moved forward and took him into my mouth, sucking hard, showing how much his words meant to me. He valued my comfort above all and understood that I wasn't just a good-time girl. I was his completely for the month. We'd agreed upon it, and he'd taken that vow seriously, now more than ever before. Alec shifted and leaned back, his head tilting to the sky as I took him as far as I could down my throat. The camera clicked. Knowing he'd caught this private moment between us made me wetter, hotter for him. I wanted nothing more than to be taken, right here, right now.

He fucked my mouth for a time then abruptly pulled away. "Your mouth, it is too good. Alas, I need the image of us joined in the act of love." I nodded while he walked a few steps away, picked up his jeans and pulled out a condom. I wanted to tell him I was on birth control and that technically he didn't have to use one, but I refrained. Something about that didn't feel right. He suited up his erection and prowled over to me. He positioned me on my side the same way he did with Aiden. Only this time, I got as close as possible, smashing my breasts against his firm chest and willingly touched him...everywhere.

"I see you are no longer camera shy." His lips crooked into a smirk.

"Oh shut up and take your picture, Frenchie," I said

then put my mouth over his. I could hear the camera click every so often. His hands clung to my naked body as the lights flashed and blinked. At one point, he had the clicker in the same hand as my breast. I could feel the cold tip digging into my nipple adding a frisson of pleasure and pain against the aching peak.

"Now for the real love." He opened my leg, wedged his hips between mine and entered me, inch by delicious inch. My head tipped back and my hips arched forward. "*Oui, chèrie*, take my love," he whispered and pushed his way inside. He gripped my hip and pulled hard, slamming his thick cock home, pressing on that high spot within and crushing my O-trigger in the process.

Gone.

Instant gratification cut deep when the orgasm ricocheted through my body as if it played ping-pong up my spine. I held him close, never able to get close enough, my body bowed almost painfully as I held on to the high. Lights flashed behind my closed eyes, only it wasn't me, it was the camera. Capturing a most blissful moment in time.

Once he brought me down, I rolled him over and got on top. I stole the clicker from him. "Fair is fair," I grinned. Instead of stealing back the control he put those artists' hands over my breasts and played with my nipples, tugging and rubbing until they were white hot burning points of pure, raw, need. I leaned my head back sitting astride him. Then I lifted up and slammed down. His body tightened, and I clicked the camera. These may not be for his exhibit, but they were going to be hot as hell and to an artist, it's the gift that keeps on giving long after it's gone.

I rode my Frenchman so hard he was panting and

growling in his pleasure. I waited until he started speaking in non-stop French before I'd allow him a reprieve. That's when I knew he was closing in on the point of no return.

"*Votre sexe est si chaud.*"

"*Je pourrais vous aimer toute la nuit.*"

"*Encore plus, bébé.*" More, baby. I learned that one early on in our physical relationship.

Before I could take him *there*, he rolled me back over on my side. God, the man was a maniac in the sack. His stamina was unparalleled. His hips pounded into mine crushing my clit in the process. Before I knew it, I was back on the edge of heaven again. Both our bodies were slick with sweat. The set lamps only added to the heat.

"What did you say to me in French?" I asked before biting down on his lip and sucking it into mine.

"I said your sex is so hot and that I could love you all night. I think I will, *ma jolie.*" And that was all she wrote. He proceeded to pound into me. Words were no longer needed. The clicker was gone, somewhere near us, but I'd dropped it when my second orgasm spiked. Then my Frenchie pressed a hand in between our bodies and swirled a finger around the fiery knot between my thighs that throbbed for his attention. I clung to him as he played with me, fingers digging into his back, scratching down with the force of his thrusts. I wrapped my legs tightly around him and held on. He lifted up onto his forearms, pulled his dick almost completely out of me and rammed home. My teeth rattled and my toes curled as the orgasm tore through my body like a tornado did a house.

Violent.

Chaotic.

Destructive.

I cried out, my screams echoing and merging with his own as he found his release.

Bliss.

He had turned us back onto our sides mid-orgasm, and the last thing I remembered was a final click and a flash of light. Then I passed out.

★ ★ ★ ★

I woke alone, my naked body covered by a couple of robes. Classical music was playing through the speakers in the warehouse loft. Still sluggish, I propped myself up and looked around. Alec was on the other side of the room. He was wearing his jeans and nothing else. Yum. The muscles of his back flexed and rippled along with his paint strokes. I don't know how long I was out, but it must have been a long time because he'd finished most of a picture of Aiden. One of the ones where he'd had his hand wrapped around his cock, his body bowed forward, teeth clenched and head thrust back. I slipped on one of the robes and tested out my ankle. Not too bad. I slowly walked over to Alec but didn't make my presence known. He didn't hear me either, the music loud enough to cover my movements. He was lost in his own world anyway.

Quietly, I sat in a chair a good twenty feet away and just watched him paint. He was fastidious in his art. Perfect in his strokes. It was magical to watch. He painted the image quickly with precise movements. It seemed as if each stroke was paired with the sound of the piano keys touching down in the music. Musical art. Absolutely beautiful. The view, the man, the painting all coalesced into an ethereal experience, one I'd surely never forget nor see again in this lifetime.

After a long while, I couldn't wait any longer to touch him. On quiet feet, I took the robe off and left it hanging over the back of the chair. On quiet feet, I padded to where he stood, in a trance staring at his art. The image seemed complete to me, but I did not have an artist's eye. I didn't have an eye for anything but sexy men, concert tees, and motorcycles.

When I reached him I lightly wound my arms around his form placing my hands over his pecs and my lips to the space between his shoulder blades. He smelled divine. Like the woods, sex, sweat, and paint. Alec's chest moved with the force of his inhale at my touch. He was in a contemplative headspace, and I was breaking that, but he didn't seem to care.

I think Alec liked my hands on him. No, I *know* he did. "You're beauty and light." I kissed along his shoulder blades then slid my hands down along each ridge and valley of his abdomen. Christ, the man was cut. For an artist, he had the body of someone who spent countless hours in the gym staying fit, but I hadn't seen him work anything but me this week.

"*Non.* I am hidden in the dark, only lit when my art is on display. It is you who brings the light to surface. You are seeing your beauty reflected in me, the way my body calls to yours and yours to mine."

His words seduced me as simply as his art did, the way his body did. I was lost in both and in him. Slowly, I opened his jeans and grasped his hardening cock. In this position he was massive, over-filling my hands. I bit into the flesh on his back, unable to hold back the desire to have him sink deeply into me the way I've come to expect in our love making.

He dropped his palette and brushes, and pushed his pants down. They fell to his ankles, trapping him there. I swirled a thumb around the head of his cock and spread the wetness pooled there all over his length. Then I stroked. Up, down, hard fast, slow, and with purpose, just the way he liked. He clasped the palm of my hand and brought it up to his mouth where he licked and sucked each finger, pulling each one into his mouth, wetting it. Then his tongue tickled my palm, coating it. He guided my hand down to his length. He wrapped my hand around his shaft and showed me how tightly to hold him and then he moved me up, pausing at the tip and then pushing down hard, much harder than I would alone. I got the hang of his rhythm and then he let go.

The French started the moment his hands separated and rested along the wall, caging the painting in front of him. His native language never sounded so sweet until he was lost in the act. I enjoyed it more than I'd ever admit. In that moment, Alec gave me control, allowed me to love him with my hands. I held tight went up slow, came down fast, and repeated over and over. He moaned then kept himself aloft against the wall with one arm and reached back with his right. My breast smashed harder against his back when his fingers found me, slipping between my legs, wet and wanting, coating my thighs with my desire for him.

Two fingers twirled around my hot button then sank deep. I gasped and locked my left arm up his chest and hooked him at the shoulder. My right kept working him up and down, tight and soft, giving him the exact amount of pressure he needed. Together we worked one another over both losing ourselves in the joy of being one in this moment.

He spoke in French, I spoke in English. Both whispering our version of sweet nothings against the other, until I knew if he touched that aching bundle of nerves I'd go off. I clenched around his fingers, a signal of my impending orgasm. In response, his cock leaked more fluid out the tiny slit at the top. I tickled that spot and the bumpy patch under it then squeezed tight, jerked against his body and came. My pussy had a lock on his fingers, my hand a lock on his dick. We bucked and spasmed against one another, his essence coating my hand, and the concrete floor. My teeth sunk into his back and he howled as the last vestiges of our lovemaking worked their way out.

When we both calmed down, I softly kissed and licked the spot on his back where I'd marked him. Pulling back, I found two perfect crescents just above the skin where his tattoo was most prevalent. He handed me a towel on a table near his supplies. I wiped my hands but my concentration was locked on the marks I'd left on his skin.

"I'm sorry," I whispered against the bruise.

"*Tu ne devrais pas être désolé,*" he spoke in French shaking his head. "Don't be sorry," he repeated for me. "Never apologize for being swept away by passion. I'll wear your marks like badges of honor." He leaned forward pulled up his jeans but didn't button them before turning around and embracing me within the warmth of his arms. I held onto him still shaking from what we'd done. Tears fell down my cheeks as the emotions overcame me.

Alec soothed me the way he always did. Long strokes

up and down my bare back, whispered French mixed with English telling me I was beautiful. I was love. I was light. And for now, I was his.

Later, he had me posing for stills. It was three in the morning, and I didn't care one bit. I was freshly fucked, naked, and sated.

"Hold your hand out as if you are covering his manhood," he instructed. I did what he said. "Cover your breast with your hand and tip your head back and close your eyes, open your mouth." I followed his instructions to the letter.

The camera clicked, and I smiled. It clicked again. I opened my eyes and looked at my artist. My Frenchman. He was gorgeous behind the camera in his jeans, still open, showing me a peek at the goods I'd had twice that night already. I closed my eyes again, crossed my hand over my chest, and hid my center.

★★click★★

"Are you done?"

"I am now," he said with a sexy smirk. Then he came to me and lifted me into his favorite princess hold.

"You know, my ankle is doing better. I can walk."

"But I prefer to carry you." He tilted his head and carried me through the loft, into the elevator and up to his home where he tucked me into bed and curved an arm around my body as he settled himself in.

I could feel his breath against the skin of my neck. "Tonight, *ma jolie*, it was far more than anything I'd ever done before. Being with you is…it is like its own special place in the world. I shall never have this again. I want you to know I appreciate what you are giving me."

Even though I was tired, so ready to sleep, I rolled back over and held him close. He put his head on my chest and snuggled into my breasts. That's what he needed, where he wanted to be. I'd give him that, because he was giving me something too, the realization that I was more than just Mia the sister, the daughter, the friend. I am a woman. A woman with feelings, desires, aspirations, and I was not just the sum total of what my mother left me with all those years ago.

Being an escort was what I needed to do for now to save my dad once more. A means to an end. At least I'd enjoy myself in the process.

Cuddling close, I ran my fingers through Alec's long hair. He groaned and snuffed against my chest and slowly became dead weight. For the first time since meeting Alec, he fell asleep in my arms.

★ ★ ★ ★

Today Alec made me breakfast…in bed. Apparently he was pretty pleased with last evening's photo shoot. I couldn't wait to see the images. I encouraged him to view them in private in the event that I attempted to jump him. He said we would later, but again…we had much work to do. A quick morning orgasm with Alec's mouth between my legs, and I was rip roaring, and ready to go. Literally. He'd used it as a means to get me up and out of bed. Sneaky bastard. I'd made it too easy on him. All he had to do was please me, and I'd hop to it.

When we arrived at the loft, he hustled me into my chair. Only we were standing in front of the painting he'd done last night of Aiden. This time he had me remove all

AUDREY CARLAN

my clothes and stand side by side next to the painting. Then he had me turn to the side and place my left hand over the paintings erection covering some of it. My other arm was tucked into my hair. He leaned me on my elbow along the wall. So if I was lying down, it would look as if I was jerking Aiden off. Alec took a ton of still shots like this. That was it for the day.

The following day he had me once again in my chair and painted my lips. He led me over to the painting he'd finished last night only this one was simpler. It just had a silkscreen over the painting of my arm reaching out. Once he positioned me, he had me kiss the silkscreen image of my hand over Aiden's cock. It was interesting to say the least, though I didn't quite understand it.

"You will Mia, I promise," he said but didn't explain further. Another day passed, and this time when I arrived at the loft a giant painting of Alec and me deep into the throes of passion had been painted and hung alongside the image of Aiden. In between the one of Aiden, and the one of us held a silk screen of Aiden and me. Only this was not a picture I'd planned to see, nor did I think he'd taken it.

The picture was taken when Alec had stopped the photoshoot yesterday. This one was when we'd faced away from one another. Somehow though, our nakedness had been captured where a limb covered the important private parts. I had my knees up to my body, Aiden had turned and was reaching out to me. If the picture wasn't captured so honestly, I would hate it.

I pointed to the image in the center. "Why is that there?" I asked.

"You know why."

"Are you trying to be obtuse?"

He shook his head. "Not at all. Look at the three as a whole, not as one, and you will see it."

I stared at the first image. Aiden caught in the act of pleasing himself, finding gratification in his own hand. My hand coming over trying to hide his private moment from the world but not being able to. Then the image of him trying to touch me when I was uncomfortable and unsure of what we were doing. Then the painting of Alec and me intertwined. My leg was over his, he was inside me, but you couldn't see the actual penetration. My arm around him prevented my breasts from being exposed. The look on our faces was precious. We were both at the height of our love making tumbling over the abyss together.

When you viewed the three together, it told a story. A man pleasing himself. The man who was supposed to love and protect my character but didn't. His love was not being returned as shown in the second image. Then finding love in the arms of another.

"You see it now?" Alec whispered into my ear as his arm came around me from behind and pulled me into him.

I nodded. "Yeah, it's broken."

"Broken love?"

Again, I couldn't find the words so I just nodded and leaned back into him.

"Then that is what it shall be named. They will be hung together and labeled Broken Love."

Of course it would. Broken love. That's all I've ever had. It's all I know. How very fitting.

CHAPTER EIGHT

My time with Alec was going to end soon. Eight days to be exact. We had two more pieces to finish and I'd yet to leave this warehouse. I'd seen absolutely nothing of Seattle and even though the sun was shining now, I doubted Alec would want to leave. The last few days he'd been deep into adding finishing touches on each painting. He said he'd add something to them every day, almost to the point of no return when they'd need to be put up on the walls at the exhibit a week from today. The day after, I'd be leaving Seattle. Finally going home between clients.

Home.

Unfortunately, I wasn't referring to LA. I was headed to Vegas. I needed to see Dad and I was being forced to make my second payment in person. Give ole' Blaine a face-to-face meeting. Not my idea. Part of the deal. Son-of-a-bitch. I should have known all those years ago that getting involved with Blaine was bad news. Never failed. I always got myself into situations with men. At least now, I was being paid to and after the better part of a month it ended. Move on. No drama. Just a job. That's the way it's supposed to be.

Wes and Alec didn't feel like a job. They were nice men that I cared about…deeply. Men any woman would jump at the chance to commit to. Not me. Not even an option. Though I didn't believe that, even in different circumstances, my time with Alec would last longer than a few months.

Don't get me wrong. I enjoyed him, thoroughly, and he definitely appreciated having me around. Only it wasn't a relationship to build a foundation on. He needed me for his work. I needed him for the money. In the middle of that, we formed a bond that survived on physical attraction and friendship. Nothing more. Wes, however, was another story altogether. Wes was the kind of man you fawned over, bragged to your girlfriends about, dreamed of marrying one day. He was not the love em' and leave em' type, even though, at the beginning, he tried to go that route—until it no longer worked for him and he'd asked me to stay.

Wes asked me to stay. With him. For him. So *we* could be an *us*.

I sighed loudly looking around the empty room and out at the sunny day beyond the tall windows. Alec needed to take me out. Period. I'd been in this warehouse for over two full weeks. Stick a fork in me, I was done.

Just as I was heading to the elevator to shanghai Alec, my cell rang.

"Hello?" I asked the caller without looking at the display.

"Good afternoon doll-face. How's my best money maker doing?"

I rolled my eyes and slumped into the chair near the door. "Hey, Aunt Millie."

"What did I say about calling me Millie? It's Ms. Milan to you, baby girl," she reminded me and which I continued to ignore.

Even though she couldn't see me, I shook my head. "No dice. Never gonna happen. You changed my diapers, you know me better than my own mother—your *loser* sister—does. It will always be Millie, Auntie."

"Ugh. Don't remind me of what an old crone I really am. You might give me a complex. Which reminds me..." She paused and I heard a scratching noise, probably her making a note. "...to call my surgeon and get my Botox freshened up."

I groaned. "That's nasty, Auntie. Don't put shit in your face. You could stay that way."

"God willing!" she responded jovially. Millie chuckled then got down to business. "Anyway, the reason for my call is Mr. March. You're headed to Chicago!" Buttons over a keyboard rang through the receiver. I planted a hand to my forehead.

"Chicago." Never been there. Hell, I'd never been anywhere aside from Nevada and California. "Who's the lucky guy this time?" I responded sarcastically.

She clucked her tongue. "Anthony Fasano. Big restaurateur. Owns the largest chain of Italian Restaurants across the nation. You know, Fasano's?"

"Holy shit! I've eaten there like a million times. Gin and I love Fasano's. Best Italian in Vegas!"

"Yeah, well, Anthony Fasano inherited the twelve hundred store chain of restaurants throughout the US when his father passed away last year. Apparently, the family is big on him finding a wife and having an heir. He's the only male out of five children so you are coming in to be his on and off again long distance girlfriend, now fiancé from the West Coast. He's bringing you in so you can meet the family and get the heat off his tail."

"This sounds like all kinds of *Jerry Springer*."

"Look Mia, we only care that they pay the handsome

fee for your pretty hiney. What it entails doesn't really matter. Board meeting, social event, muse, pretending to be someone's fiancé to fool their family…" I could practically hear her shrug. "Doesn't matter to us. Just do your job. Besides, another fine male specimen. You could make your extra twenty percent. Speaking of, you received an additional twenty percent on your fees deposited into your account by Mr. Channing and just yesterday by Mr. Dubois. Seems like you're having a good time," she remarked.

"I'm sorry, what did you say?"

"Besides the fact that you're making a mint…"

"No! Yes. That. Wes and Alec paid me…for sex?"

I closed my eyes and felt my heart stop beating. "What the fuck?" I whispered, a deluge of tears formed in masses, ready for the dam to burst and set them free.

"Doll face, they're supposed to pay you. I'm surprised you didn't notice it earlier. Mr. Channing requested your bank routing information and transferred the money in before you left Malibu. Mr. Dubois had it posted by one of his assistants yesterday. What's the problem?"

I shook my head and clenched my hands into fists wanting nothing more than to pound both into the nearest wall. Heat flooded my body as if I was hot lava burning a path down a volcano. "I gotta go. Send me the info on the next client." Abruptly, I hung up pressed a few buttons and hit Send.

The phone rang a few times. Just enough for my rage to reach boiling.

"Hey you?" Wes's voice came through the line all salt and sand. "I was just thinking about you…"

"Save it. What the fuck do you think you are playing

at?" My voice was razor sharp and held no protection against the bloody sting.

"Excuse me, back up. What's the matter?" He sounded concerned, but it was all bullshit. Everything between us was a total fucking lie.

"The money, Wes! How could you do that?" My voice croaked trying to get the ugly words out.

"Didn't you get it? Oh my god. Is your dad okay? I can come out. I'll pay whatever you need. Tell me you're okay, Mia!" he roared through the line.

"My dad is fine. Still in a coma. I wasn't talking about what I owe the sharks. I was talking about how you could deposit the money for being with me. Intimately. Or was it just fucking to you?"

His voice was raw when he responded, filled with emotion. "It was never about the fucking money, Mia, and you know it as well as I do!" I could hear the fight in his voice, the attempt at holding back his own frustration.

"Then why? Why would you treat me like your whore!" The tears streamed down my cheeks faster than I could wipe them away.

"No. Christ, no! Don't you dare say that. Mia, it wasn't like that."

"Oh no? Then why is an extra twenty thousand dollars sitting in my account from you! Millie told me so!"

"Who the fuck is Millie?"

"My Aunt. *Ms. Milan.* It's her escort service. Ring any fucking bells? Ding, ding, ding!"

"You work for your aunt?"

I ground down on my teeth, anger filling the sadness and replacing it with white-hot rage. "Not the fucking point, Wes! I thought what we had meant something. That's why I didn't tell you about the fee! I would never have made you pay it. I'm not a call girl! I was with you like that because I wanted to be, not because you were paying me."

"Mia, sweetheart, listen to me. It's in my contract. Besides, I wanted you to have that money. You wouldn't let me pay off the sharks to help your dad. At the very least, I thought you could use that to help get you out of their debt faster. I'm so sorry. I never meant to hurt you." There was a long pause where I didn't hear anything but a deep sigh. "Fuck! I'm sorry. Mia, you gotta believe me. I would never think that about you. I care about you. So much..." he whispered the last part. "I miss you. More than I should. I'm...tell me what to say to make this better."

I sucked in a huge breath and stared out the window. Everything looked really green after so many days of rain and now sun. "Wes, it hurt. What you did. But..."

"But what?" He sounded like a man who was grasping at straws, at anything that would get him out of the hole he'd dug.

I closed my eyes and swallowed the lump in my throat. "I get why you did it. It's going back...the money."

"No, sweetheart, no. Please let it help you get out of this sooner. It's selfish, I know, but..." His breath was ragged coming through the line. "Maybe it will bring you back to LA sooner. Help your sister with college. Whatever you need. Mia, I just want to help you. Please just let me do this one thing."

"Wes..."

"Please."

"Fine."

"Thank you." Wes murmured softly, the way a lover does. "Are we gonna be okay? Are we still…"

"Friends," I offered.

He chuckled low in his throat. It was the most beautiful sound I'd heard in three weeks. "Yeah, friends," he finished.

"We are. I gotta go."

"Your client?" His words were flat, held no emotion.

I nodded even though he couldn't see. "I miss you too you know."

"You do?"

"I do. We're gonna be okay. Catch you later?"

"You know where I am, sweetheart. You've got the key."

"Bye, Wes." I hung up before I could hear his reply. Hearing it would make me want to jump through the phone and kiss him, soothe him, make him better. Make me better. At least he did what he did to help and truly didn't realize what message he'd sent to me.

I am no man's whore.

Time to deal with Alec.

★ ★ ★ ★

"*Ma jolie*! I am ready for you. We must do stills for "Selfish Love," Alec bustled the moment I entered the loft warehouse. He ushered me to the white sheet that had been spread over padding. "Clothes off, we mustn't waste any time."

Before I could express the rage simmering within me about the money, he'd whipped my top over my head and was undoing my pants. Instantly, the space between my thighs heated at his insistent caresses. Traitorous body.

"Frenchie, stop! I need to talk to you."

"*Non*. Remove your clothes, but leave your lingerie on." He moved from me to the ladder. His movements were quick, precise and not helping the situation. Alec was knee-deep into his creative headspace—that place where he'd stare blankly or paint incredibly fast, seemingly without seeing what he was doing. It was downright strange.

"Alec, I need to speak to you," I tried again as one of his attendants tugged at my feet trying to get me to remove my jeans. I did what they wanted, preferring to get this part over with. When I was left standing in a standard white t-shirt bra and matching simple bikini briefs, the attendant helped get me settled. The hair chick Alec hired to be on hand started fussing with my hair, making it sweep out as if I'd lain down, yet my hair was perfectly sprawled out.

Then one of them came forward with the red paint. "No!" I pushed a hand out. "I told you, Alec. I needed to speak to you. About the money that appeared in my account yesterday?" I gritted my teeth and waited for him to look at me. He didn't. Instead, he fussed with his camera, the lighting, yelled out commands until finally he answered me.

"*Oui*, I had it done yesterday," he said absently while looking through the lens of his camera.

"Why?"

"Place your hand into your panties, close your eyes and pretend you're having fun with yourself."

"Excuse me?"

Alec sighed and his jaw clenched tight, the muscle at the corner beating a rapid tempo. "Pay attention, Mia. We have…"

"We have much to do, yeah I know," I growled in

response. "I've heard that a time or two before."

His gaze flicked to mine like a bullet from a rifle, his eyes narrowing. "Then you know I am on a short deadline. The exhibit is in one week, there are two more paintings to be done. This one and one more I have yet to visualize. Now what is your problem? I sent the money, you received it, *oui*?"

"Yes, Alec, but…" I looked around. There were at least ten people hanging around, which was unusual for a racy photo day. He usually did those in private. "I want to talk to you alone."

"And we will, once these photos are done."

With a sigh of resignation I nodded and did what he said. Only the pictures weren't working, which made him a bear to deal with. Eventually, he kicked the staff out.

"Today has been a waste," he said, anger dripping from his lips. His long artist's fingers went into his hair and he tugged at the tie that held the massive mane of hair back, allowing it to fall forward. Alec paced and mumbled in French.

"Well what did you expect? You want me to finger myself in front of a room full of people, not to mention while I'm pissed at you?"

He stopped pacing, his head jutting back, his hands going to his hips. Almost reminded me of a chick. A hot, manly chick, but the hands-on-hips thing was a total girl move.

"And what have you got to be mad about?" His tone was laced with piss and vinegar. It ruffled my feathers just enough to rekindle the fire that I'd kept banked for the last couple hours.

I leaned up and crossed my legs. "You paid me for sex, that's the problem!"

He sucked in a deep breath and let it out slowly. "And you're upset with this? Why?"

"I'm not you're whore! That's twice today a man has treated me like I was their fucking whore. I didn't have sex with you because of the money! Jesus Christ, why are men so dense?!" I screamed into the open room. The sound echoed off the walls louder than I intended. He cringed.

"We had sex. Your contract states you are to receive twenty percent more for taking off your clothes, and/or having sex."

Groaning, I stood up and walked right up to him. "I thought you were making love to me?" I spat.

"I did. We were. Unfortunately, the eyes of the law might not see it that way."

"The eyes of the law see that as prostitution! The rule was one of those unwritten things you just do to skate the law with. Jeez."

"Then unwrite it from your contract. Ms. Milan has the item as an add-on note. No, it isn't written in the fine print, but your enforcer ensures you receive it. Plus, you did get naked many times for the art. The fee is owed to you for that alone. Now, you tell me how I should take that, *chèrie?* Hmm?

My shoulders slumped and my head fell down. Shit. It wasn't his fault. He wasn't doing anything wrong; he was following what he thought were the rules. It was official; I was an idiot.

At that point, he could have berated me, made me feel worse than I did, but he put his long, strong arms around me and held me while I wallowed in my own self-pity. It wasn't the men that had me believing I was a whore. It was me. My own insecurities had crept up and wreaked havoc on my psyche.

"I'm sorry."

"Shhh, it's okay. I can imagine this is hard on you."

Within the warmth of his arms I reasoned with myself. Told myself I knew what I was and what I wasn't. No dollar bill, or misunderstanding, or even Millie would change that about me. I was a lot of things, a daughter, a sister, a friend, an actress of sorts, I was this man's muse but I wasn't a streetwalker, call girl, or a whore. A slut maybe, but *not* whore.

Comfortable with how I'd worked it out in my head, I kissed Alec with everything I had left in me. Once done, I leaned back, walked over to my spot on the floor and sprawled out. With a wicked gleam in my eyes I stuffed one of my hands into the space between my bra and breast. His tawny eyes twinkled against the bright lights as he watched me. I slid my other hand ever so slowly down my body. Alec scrambled up the ladder and grabbed his camera.

"Show me how selfish you can be with your sexy body, *ma jolie.*"

And I did. Closing my eyes I played my body as if he was touching me. Every move was made by his hands. Every sigh was for him, every moan swallowed by his lips.

My imagination did not fail to secure him the perfect picture.

CHAPTER NINE

Hand-in-hand, Alec and I exited the warehouse. The sun shone bright, the wind blew against my hair, and the world opened up and greeted me. Hello world, I missed you.

"You realize this is the first time we've left the warehouse since I arrived, and I'm leaving in three days."

Alec lifted my hand and placed a kiss on the top. "I didn't, no, *ma jolie*. I'm sorry. I've been a terrible host."

I laughed and swung his arm while we walked. "You had…"

"Much work to do," we said in unison and then both chuckled.

"I am sorry *chèrie*. When I am focused, there is nothing but the work, food, sexual gratification and sleep."

"The last of which you don't get enough of," I chastised. He didn't. The man slept less than most insomniacs.

Holding his hand tighter, I turned to him. "So, where to?"

Alec had his hair back in his ever-present man bun. The sun made it look more red than brown and gold. Still incredible. He wore a thin, white, scooped necked thermal, and a pair of dark-wash jeans. A camera hung loosely around one shoulder. Alec Dubois was yummy. Manly, sexy, all that and a bag of the cheesiest potato chips. And I was the lucky girl that had his attention…for three more days.

"What do you want to do?" he asked.

I looked out over the Seattle streets and said the one thing any tourist would say. "Go to the Space Needle of course."

He grinned. "Well that's good. We have reservations there for dinner. For now, how about a surprise?"

"Sure."

Alec hailed a cab and we were off. He gave a set of directions that meant nothing to me and I people-watched until our ride stopped. Alec paid the driver, got out and held the door for me. I stepped out and came to a standstill.

About twenty feet in front of me was a wooden sign with giant letters in a startling white that said "Zoo." More specifically, "Woodland Park Zoo."

"You're taking me to the zoo?" I smiled wide.

"Why not? I haven't been, and I've lived here for years."

"No reason." I lifted my hand and took his once more. "Let's check out some animals." I didn't tell him that I'd never been to a zoo. Ever. That wasn't a hot spot in Vegas and once my mother left, dad stopped doing family trips of any kind.

Turned out, I really enjoyed zoos. There was so much to see, hear, touch and explore.

"So far, what's your favorite exhibit?" Alec asked while slinging an arm over my shoulder.

I shook my head. "So many to choose from. If I had to pick one I'd go with the Ocelots."

"The feline?"

Nodding I continued. "I can relate to the female cat. They live a solitary life, they mate when they need to, care for their young, teach them how to hunt and then set them free." Alec's eyebrows narrowed into points, marring his beautiful brow. "Plus, they are beautiful. If I had to be an animal I'd pick that. They're sexy as all get out!" I finished, trying to lighten the mood. "You?"

Alec twisted his lips. I'd hoped he wouldn't dig for information about my reply. Now was not the time to open wounds. Now was the time for experiences, making lifelong memories, especially since I was leaving so soon.

"If I had to choose one, I'd go with the arctic fox."

That seemed an odd choice. I would have taken him for a gazelle or something exotic sounding. "Okay, why?"

"Because they form lifetime monogamous relationships. I've always envied people who could do that. Now I see that a stunning creature like the fox does it and well…it just gives me hope."

"Aw, Frenchie. You're a softy underneath all that muscle," I tapped his chest, reached up on tiptoe and kissed him. He wound his arms around my back and kissed me hard. That's when I heard a click.

I looked over and noticed he'd pulled up his camera and took a selfie of us making out. "Cheesy. A selfie? You, an artist? Shocked!"

"How else was I going to capture this kiss forever in time?"

I thunked on his temple. "Use your noggin. Our time together, all there in your memory."

"And now I have it captured on film."

We spent the rest of the day roaming through the animal exhibits. I understood now what the attraction was. Families were everywhere roaming about. Made me miss Maddy. Had she ever been to a zoo? I made it a point right then to take her in the future. There were a lot of things that

Maddy and I didn't get to do growing up. I was going to rectify that. As soon as I got my dad off his loan shark "death row" and he was awake from his coma. Hell, maybe he'd want to go along. Doubtful, but it was possible.

★ ★ ★ ★

Later that evening, the cab dropped us off at the entrance to the Space Needle. First stop was the observation deck. A three hundred and sixty degree view of what the natives called Emerald City. Couples and families dotted the walk. We found a little outcropping where we could easily see the sun setting over the landscape. Breathtakingly beautiful. I stood with my hands on the rails in front and just stared out at the glorious sight. A wave of clicking broke my concentration on the visual eye candy.

"What?" I grinned over at Alec. He came close, swept his hands into my hair and kissed me. It was a kiss to remember. Slow, soft and so warm it sent a current of desire zipping through my nervous system. He pulled away and set his forehead along mine.

"You are too precious. Too beautiful. Too much for any man to keep for himself. The man that does secure your love…forever…he will be *un homme très chanceux*."

"What's that mean?" I whispered against his lips then caressed his nose with mine.

His fingers dug into the wild strands of my hair, and he held me at the nape. His eyes were the color of golden bricks, the kind that should only exist in fairy tales. "It means, he will be a very lucky man. To have your love for all eternity will make him very rich."

"Alec," I shook my head then leaned into his chest, the safest place I could be right then.

"Oh *ma jolie*, how I will miss your love in my life." He held me as tight as I was holding him. Possibly more. Even though I had a couple more days, this was the moment I'd remember through my entire life. The time where I realized that there were many different forms of love and it was okay to love those you give a piece of yourself to, even if they don't deserve it. Alec, he definitely deserved it, and we'd always have this time.

We made art together, and we loved together, in our own way. And that is what would matter when I looked back on my life and the decisions I made in the past. As well as any I would make in the future. My time with Alec was special and I anticipated that as I continued on this journey, each client would add to the pattern of my life.

"Come, let's eat so we can go back home and I can ravish you for dessert!" He waggled his eyebrows then led me back to the elevator.

The dinner at the Skycity Restaurant was impressive to say the least. I'd had the jidori chicken that was coated with a scrumptious smoky mozzarella and bread pudding. It was to die for! Alec on the other hand had the prime tenderloin. It had a bacon fondue type cheese that made my knees tremble. Over dinner we'd shared bites of our food, and finally a bit about our lives before "Love on Canvas." Alec was surprised I had been raised in the desert. He didn't ask me about being an escort or why I chose the profession, and for that, I was grateful. He focused more on my fledgling acting career and my interest in motorcycles. In return, I found out he'd moved to the States when he was in his early twenties but visited France after every major exhibition. He'd be leaving for his country a few days after I moved onto my next client.

Connecting with Alec on a level outside of our physical attraction was nice. I could see being friends with him after I left, though nowhere near the type of friend I considered myself with Wes. My surfer guy was in a class all his own.

★ ★ ★ ★

Today was the day. The Alec Dubois "Love on Canvas" exhibition. The warehouse loft had been completely transformed for a gallery event, at least that's what I was told. I was a bit nervous to see what people's impression of his art was going to be tonight, mostly because I was the ongoing theme in the pieces. Once finished, he had seven canvases in all on display. He said there was one past the six I knew about, but he wanted it to be a surprise. Working on the last one had taken up most of his attention the last couple days.

We needed that separation knowing that tomorrow I was getting on a plane headed for Vegas, a departure that would take me out of Alec's life…possibly forever. No one knew what the future would bring, just that there was no stopping it.

Millie had sent over my plane tickets to Vegas and the one-way ticket to Chicago where Anthony Fasano would be picking me up personally. My time in Seattle was running out. Less than twenty-four hours and I'd be on a plane home. Gin and Maddy were picking me up and taking me straight to Dad. I needed to see my old man.

The clock read six p.m. Time to get ready for tonight. I

shuffled through my suitcase and pulled out the one dress I'd brought. Being a Vegas girl, I always carried around a little black dress, one that didn't wrinkle and could be twisted up, yet still survive in the bottom of your purse. I was pretty sure I'd either need to go barefoot, rock some flip-flops, or commit fashion suicide by wearing my motorcycle boots with the dress. As I was pondering the very limited options, a giant white box with a bright red bow landed on the bed near where I was sifting through my stuff.

"For you," Alec's voice speared across my senses in a sultry greeting.

I turned around and my mouth dropped open. Alec was standing there ready for the evening. He wore a suit. The first time I'd seen him in something so formal. He looked dashing to say the least. My mouth watered at the sight of his beautiful body wrapped in fine silk threads. His suit was black on black. Everything. The jacket, the shirt underneath, to the slim satin tie. Definitely worked for me. My thighs were instantly moist, and tension sizzled in the air as I let the towel I'd been wearing while getting my clothes together drop from my body.

"*Douce mère de toutes les choses saintes,*" he said in hushed French. That wasn't helping my libido. Instead of bringing me down, he brought me higher. I bit down on my lip and swayed, watching him come to me. In a flash, Alec's mouth was on mine and my back was against the wall. His hands slid down to my ass and pulled me up. I groaned as the thick wedge behind his trousers pressed me harder into the wall right where I wanted him most.

"We can't do this now," I warned, not really believing the words myself. I sucked at his neck and lips, and dug my heels into his lower back. He groaned as his tongue entered my mouth. For long moments, there was nothing but deep, drugging sweeps of his tongue, nips from his teeth and the press of silk against flesh.

"We can. We are." I could feel his breath along my neck as he spoke. *"Nous allons nous dépêchez."*

"What does that mean?" I sucked on the spot he loved behind his ear and clutched the tight man bun at the back of his head pulling his face back.

His eyes were dark, and held nothing but the promise to please within their inky depths.

"It means we hurry," he flicked at his belt, undid his pants, pulled a condom out of his pocket, and in seconds, he was notched at the entrance to my sex.

"Fuck, don't stop now, Alec. Please, give me you." I said. He loved when I said those words and I knew it. He slid the wide crown of his cock against my center, rubbing it in the wetness there, moved his hands wide along my ass, and then impaled me.

"Sweet, Mother..." I called out, his steely shaft filled me deeper than ever before, so deep I lost my breath, then found it again when he breathed life into me with his kiss. "So good, it's always so good with you."

He moaned into my neck, slammed me into the wall and held me there, hung up on his cock, then dragged his hands over my sensitive skin to my breasts. Once there, he tweaked each peak hard. My nipples were two blazing hot points of need, and with every touch, twist, and pluck he sent me Nirvana-bound. "I'm gonna come," I announced, and he grinned against the erect tip then bit down into it.

That was it. Nothing more needed. The orgasm

shredded through me like a wood chipper destroys a tree trunk.

"Never forget the way you feel right now, *ma jolie. Je t'aime.* I love you," Alec said before taking my mouth. My pussy clamped down around his cock giving him what he needed while he thrust into me like a madman. When he was done, he pulled me off the wall and brought me to the bed where he sat, still imbedded in me. It took several minutes to settle the quaking in my limbs. Through it all, Alec held me and soothed me the way he always did. I often thought it soothed him as much as me.

"We're gonna be late to your own show," I giggled.

He smiled. "With good reason." he winked and indicated the large white box. "This is for you. To wear tonight."

Excitedly, I jumped off him and stood at the side of the bed. He took care of the condom while I opened my present.

Inside the box, I found a champagne-colored cocktail dress. It had tiny crystals that shimmered and sparkled in the light. The neckline was loose fabric that draped over my breasts enticingly. The slight wisp of fabric that held it at the edge of my shoulder did so in a way that made the drape of the fabric look perfectly natural. The hem was just to the knee and the dress fit like it was painted on. Alec held out another box as I was straightening the dress. The shoes were Gucci originals. They were a shiny gold with a four-inch spiked heel and a touch of a platform. Utter perfection.

"Never met a woman that didn't love shoes."

"All women love fuck-me pumps. Especially, sexy, hot as hell ones. It's written in our genetic code." I shrugged. "We're born that way."

Alec freshened up his suit as I finished getting ready, then he led me down to the party. It was in full swing when we arrived. The second we walked through the entryway camera bulbs flashed and applause filled the room. A blonde in a tight white suit immediately took Alec away. His publicist. I hadn't seen her since the first few days, but she had a lock on his arm that might have drawn blood if he attempted to escape. He looked over his shoulder at me. His downturned lips and narrowed brow proved he wasn't happy. I waved and blew him a kiss.

A man with a tray of champagne offered me a drink. I took a glass of the pink bubbly and made my way over to the first painting. It was me. Of course. Yet, Alec had added so much more depth to it than the first time I'd seen it. Now it was as if I could grasp the tear sliding down my image's cheek and smear the red lips pressed into the painting.

"No Love for Me," was written underneath the image. I walked over about twenty feet and saw the same image only this one included the silk-screened image and the painting of me touching the heart of the original. "Love Thyself." Reading the words was like sending a spear right through my heart to touch emotions not hidden far enough beneath the surface.

Incapable of looking at it any longer, I went over to the set of three paintings in a bundle where the most action was happening. The crowd was thick as the light shined down on the three giant canvas's hanging side by side. Above the trio it said "Broken Love" but under each one I noticed they had their own individual names.

The first of Aiden pleasuring himself with my hand over his erection was labeled. "Forbidden Love." Then the picture in the middle where Alec had caught a very harsh moment between Aiden and I was called "Love Hurts." Then the last. There was a much larger crowd around this painting. Alec and I together, entwined in our passion. It was definitely the most stunning of the three. He'd added red sweeping swirls of paint all around the couple on the canvas, highlighting the fiery passion the couple shared. Below it, the name simply said, "Our love."

And it was our love. Alec's and mine. Beautiful, passionate, wild, yet still a love that had to be nurtured, and cared for. It's purity captured perfectly on canvas.

I moved along the wall and watched people discuss the art. Not once did I hear any gasps, or see any scowls. That must have meant people were accepting of his vision.

This painting made me hot. Straight up wet between the thighs, and ready to jump Alec the moment I saw him again. "Selfish Love," he'd called it. Me, pleasuring myself for the world to see. Something about it was righteous and powerful. At least it made me feel that way.

Alec's arms wound around me as I stared at the painting. "You like it?"

"I liked doing it more," I said low, my words a veritable moan.

"Ah, I see. Later we shall revisit this scene, hmm?" I nodded quickly. "Let me show you the last. It is my best photograph to date."

That was saying a lot. Alec Dubois was a truly amazing artist and photographer. His pictures could be found on everything from calendars to signed lithographs. He led me over to the one painting that had a giant white drape over it.

I stood still as a crowd of people surrounded us awaiting

the reveal. "This portrait will be sold at twice the asking price. Half of that price will go to you, *ma jolie*."

That shocked me, and I shook my head no several times, but he just grinned and pulled the drape off. It was me. Only it really was me. *The real me.* Just Mia. I was standing at the space needle observation deck looking into the horizon. My hair was blowing like a black flag in the open breeze. I was serene, happy, elated, and taken with the beauty before me. I looked free in that moment. Not stuck in the confines of a job I didn't want but was getting used to. Not bailing out my dad or struggling to make it as an actress in LA. Raw beauty. And for the first time, I saw myself as beautiful. Alec made me see that in this image.

Tears formed in my eyes as I stared at what he'd captured. My body felt swathed in heat, the center of my vision being a bright spot of light, the rest a dark cave. I scanned the title below the painting. Tears slipped down my cheeks, falling onto the skin of my breasts and the concrete below my feet. I locked gazes with Alec, his eyes were glassy, wet, though he didn't let any tears fall.

Beneath the most beautiful picture of me I'd ever seen, said it all.

"Goodbye, Love."

CHAPTER TEN

Last evening was amazing. I had felt like Cinderella at the King's ball. Once the last picture was revealed, spectators starting connecting the dots. Newspapers, and other media professionals interviewed me, took pictures of Alec and me together, overall making a big fuss. It was fun. The glasses of champagne I'd consumed didn't hurt my mood, either. When it was all over, there were bids for all his paintings. They would spend the next six months touring galleries. Then the buyers would have their one of a kind Dubois original. First though, Alec wanted the general public to have the opportunity to view his work. I understood that. It was his life's passion and should be shared far and wide.

The window showed the sky was still dark, midnight in color. It had to be very close to sunrise. Before I'd gotten ready yesterday I'd packed everything up and had it hidden in a corner downstairs. My flight was early and I wanted to slip away unnoticed. As with Wes, I couldn't bear the thought of having to say goodbye to Alec face-to-face. I scanned his sculpted face and body. Stunning, and completely dead to the world. He'd had quite a bit more of the bubbly than I'd had and chased it with some fancy French drink I'd never heard of before. Then, he'd taken me to bed, fucked me to within an inch of my life and passed out while still inside me.

It was crazy, fun, emotional love-making that symbolized

the entire month. I wanted to leave with that as our last memory.

So, I slipped out of bed and tucked his t-shirt into my carryon. No reason I couldn't have it as a keepsake. Besides, it smelled wonderfully of Alec. I grabbed the entire bag and took a shower in the bathroom below. When I made my way into the kitchen it was just before five a.m. The cab would be here in twenty minutes. I had a seven a.m. flight to Vegas.

I pulled out my special stationary and a pen. It was that time.

Alec, my beloved Frenchman -

I'm sorry to leave you like this, but it's best if your last memory is of us making love. Because that's what it was, making love. I should have said it to you yesterday. I don't know why I didn't. I do, you know? Love you, Alec. In our way. The best way. As friends, as lovers, as two people who were destined to love one another for the time we had.

I'll always remember our time together. You taught me about all kinds of love, and the way you see it is special. It will stay with me all the days of my life. Through you and your art, I was able to see how a loving relationship could be if both partners are completely honest. You never lied, never led me on, you always told the truth. And for that, I am so grateful.

This experience, being your muse, it is something I never dreamed would change me. But it did. You did. For the better.

Thank you, Alec, for showing me that it is okay to love, to give love freely and accept the love given to me, even if it's for a short time.

Je t'aime. Au revoir.

~Mia

I kissed the page near my name and left the note by the coffee pot. Forcing myself to walk out the door and not rush up the stairs to have one last look. Instead, I pressed the button for the elevator and met my cab at the lobby door.

★ ★ ★ ★

The airport was packed. Once I'd gotten through the security rigmarole I found my gate and just barely made my plane. I sat down and hefted my purse in my lap. My phone buzzed in the front pocket. I pulled it out and felt an envelope. My heart started thumping, pounding deep in my chest, thinking maybe the call was from Alec. I read the cell display.

From: Ginelle Harper
To: Mia Saunders
Can't wait to see your ugly mug. Now Mads is yelling at me for calling you ugly. Sorry, skank. ;-)

I laughed, put the phone in airplane mode and then flipped over the envelope. Across the front was my name scrawled in an elegant slanted penmanship. Only it wasn't my name, it was what he called me. "*Ma jolie*." My pretty, in French. I miss it already. The phrase spilling from his bowed lips in the morning, his hair a messy tumble on the pillow.

Shaking my head took the pressure off the simmering emotions threatening to explode in a deluge of tears. I opened the envelope and pulled out a card. It was a replica of a painting, one of his actually. A town in France that he'd painted at some point and had been made into greeting cards. It was as funny as it was sweet. Egomaniac.

I opened the card and out spilled a handful of pictures. Photos of the paintings along with the one of us he'd taken himself. The selfie I'd made fun of him for. I was holding his face and kissing the daylights out of him. Strands of his hair had escaped the bun and mine were flowing wildly as we kissed. The sun shined down perfectly on us. I held the picture to my chest and let the tears fall. I would miss my Frenchie. Very much.

The last photo was a copy of me, the one he'd aptly named "Goodbye, love." It was the perfect ending to a beautiful month. He didn't write anything in the card. His pictures said all that needed to be said.

Like Wes, I'd never forget my time with Alec. I'd cherish those memories as a part of my life wherein I truly lived and loved.

I sifted through the emails about my new client sent from Aunt Millie. I clicked on the picture icon. Holy moly. Another hottie. This was one definitely Italian. As in, Italian stallion. Where does she come up with these guys, Hotties-R-Us? Anthony "Tony" Fasano was thirty-one, an ex-boxer, which was the picture I looked at. The man's body looked like it had been cut from tanned marble. His skin was olive-toned, hair jet black like mine, but his eyes where a steely blue. He wasn't as tall as I usually liked my men, only around five-foot eleven, but what he lacked in height he well made up for in raw male beauty.

Based on the picture of him standing and holding a boxing belt of some kind, he didn't have an ounce of fat on him. How is that possible? He owned a giant chain of Italian restaurants. That food is not known for being low cal.

Maybe it was an old picture? Like Millie said, it didn't really matter why he needed me. He just did. And I'd pretend to be his fiancée. God only knows why. A man like that, women would drop at his feet and worship for a chance to marry a rich good looking guy. Could be the same type of issue Wes had or maybe it's just too many hoochies, not enough girl next door types.

Oh well. A few days in Vegas and I'd be off to see Anthony Fasano of Chicago, Illinois.

Bring on the windy city.

March

CALENDAR GIRL

AUDREY CARLAN

CHAPTER ONE

The second my feet hit the ground level of the airport in Vegas, I was smashed between two bodies, one long and lengthy, the other petite and feisty. My nostrils were assaulted with the scent of mint gum and cherries as the two wiggly bodies bounced me up and down simultaneously screaming. The sound was an exact replica of the hyenas screeching in their cage at the zoo Alec and I had visited in Portland.

"God, I missed your face," Gin said before laying a wet one right on my lips. Ah, there's the mint gum. Then she was pushed out of the way, and my baby sister, Maddy, pulled me into her long arms. Cherries. Ever since she was a little girl, she's always smelled like cherries. I didn't want to know why. Like everything else, I accepted that it just was. That's all that mattered. Maddy held me close, her much taller frame making my five foot eight size seem small. Even though I was the big sister, she still held the record for height in our small family at five foot eleven. At nineteen, she was a definite beauty, but hadn't quite filled in like I had at her age. She seemed to have an unbeatable metabolism that kept her rail thin. Lucky girl.

Maddy's eyes filled with tears. I cupped both her cheeks. "Prettiest girl in all the world," I said watching the tears fall. "But only when you smile…"

"You always say that." Her lips tipped up, and I was graced with the smile I adored more than any other person's.

"Because it's true. And you are. Right Gin?"

Gin smacked her gum then locked her elbow with mine. "Yep. Now let's blow this popsicle joint."

I rolled my eyes. "It's popsicle *stand*, Gin."

Ginelle stopped in the middle of the airport arrivals. "Whatever, ho, you know what I meant. Who died and made you Mr. Webster?"

I laughed hard, and it felt good. Great rather. Tension seeped out of my pores as if it could manifest physically, drop to the floor, and pool out onto the linoleum. God, it was good to be home.

The girls led me to Gin's car. "Where's Dad's car, Mads?" I shoved my bag in the trunk then sat shotgun.

Maddy got into the backseat of Ginelle's Honda and twirled a lock of hair. "Um..." She looked out the window, her eyes moving from point to point like she was trying to think of something to say.

My shoulders slumped. "What's wrong with Dad's car?"

"Nothing really." She let out a long breath, kept twirling locks of her blonde hair, and curved her spine into the seat back. Whatever it was, she didn't want to tell me.

"Tell her, Mads," Gin pressed.

Maddy huffed and then sat up straight. She closed her eyes and opened them. Determination oozed in powerful bursts of color in those green depths. "The guys that messed up Dad, messed up his car, too."

Fire swirled in my gut. "Why the hell didn't you say anything?" Anger ripped down my spine and landed in my hands where I held them in two tight fists. If anyone came near me now they'd be toast.

"I just..."

"You just what? How are you getting to school?"

"The bus, mostly, and sometimes Ginelle." Her gaze drifted over to my best friend. Gin smiled briefly. "And also Matt, the guy I was telling you about. He's given me a ride a few times. Says he'll help me out any way he can." Her voice went tight.

"I'll just bet he would. Mads, that's not safe. You're not close to the school, and you're dead on your feet after all those classes. And what about when you stay late in the library?" I sucked in a giant breath and let it out angrily turning back in my chair. My fucking sister at risk. Doesn't have the use of Dad's car because Blaine and his fucking goons wrecked it. What else? What else could possibly happen?

Maddy's hand landed on my shoulder warmly. "It's fine, Mia. I'm okay. We make do with what we have, right?"

"Fuck no. We're getting you a car tomorrow. I can't believe all this time you haven't had wheels." With a pointed finger I poked Gin in the arm. "And you. You should have told me what was going on." With a deep sigh, I flicked the layers of hair off my face.

"You can't afford that, Mia…"

"Don't you dare tell me what I can and can't afford. You have been my responsibility for the last fifteen years. Just because you're nineteen doesn't mean I'm going to magically stop taking care of you." I ground my teeth trying to rein in my control. "Jesus. Just thinking about you walking from the bus stop to home in *our neighborhood* gives me hives, Mads! Don't do it again. Please, for me." I gentled my tone. "I'll get you a car tomorrow. I've made some extra cash on the last two clients."

"Is that right?" Gin gave me a sidelong glance knowing what it took to get the extra payoff. "And how did you do that, sweetness? On your back?" She snickered.

That time I punched her arm…hard.

"Ouch! Bitch! That was totally uncalled for."

"You calling me a whore, whore? Totally called for." I narrowed my eyes and stared her down. Even though she was driving I knew she could feel the heat of my gaze.

"Fine. It was called for, but I'm going to make you look at the ugly bruise every chance I get."

"Whatever. Can you take Mads and me to get her a car tomorrow?"

She nodded. "I took off the days you're here."

"Oh, that was sweet of you."

"I can be sweet." Her eyebrows furrowed.

"Didn't say you couldn't."

"But you implied that I wasn't usually sweet. I'll have you know that I was with this guy last night, and he went on and on how about sweet my vag—" I leaned over and clamped a hand around her mouth.

"Think you can share another time, hooker?" I gestured to Maddy in the back seat with my eyes.

"Oh whatever," Maddy butted in. "Like I don't know what she was talking about. You think I'm so innocent."

I let go of Gin and turned around in a flash. "You mean you're *not* innocent?" I'd have bet fifty whole dollars that my usually tanned skin went stark white in that moment.

Maddy crossed her arms over her chest then rolled her eyes. "I'm still a virgin. You know I'd tell you. Jeez. But I know what going down on a girl is. I'm not stupid."

"Has that happened to you?" I held my breath not sure

I wanted to know the truth.

She shook her head and bit her lip then looked out the window. "No, but sometimes it pisses me off that you act like I'm a child. I'm an adult, Sis. You need to accept that. And if I want to let a guy go down and kiss my hoo-hah, I totally will."

"Kiss your hoo-hah?" Gin repeated. "You mean your pus—" I pinched her leg before she could say something that would piss Maddy off further.

"Not a fuckin' word." I growled low for her benefit. Her eyes went wide, and she swatted my hand away.

"Mads, you know I'm here, right? If you want to talk about anything like that." I reached over the back of the seat, and she grabbed my hand. "Even if I'm not in Vegas, you can always call me. Day or night. Okay?"

She leaned forward and put her forehead on my hand. "I missed you," she whispered.

I squeezed her fingers back. "I missed you more."

That got me her patented perfect smile. Man, the Lord smiled on me when he gave me Maddy as my baby sister. I couldn't have picked a better one out myself.

"So, the convalescent home then?" Gin asked destroying the moment.

"Yeah. I need to see Pops."

★ ★ ★ ★

The convalescent home sat high on a hill overlooking a long stretch of dessert. It was weird. Like it was built to hold sick people and convalescing folks far away from Vegas proper so as to not taint the glimmer and glamour of the strip.

Unintentionally, my steps slowed as we walked the halls. The walls were painted a soft yellow. Desert mosaic art hung sporadically as we made our way down to the end of the corridor.

Maddy stopped at an open door. "He's in there. Do you want to go in alone?"

"If you don't mind?" She simply smiled softly. My sister was an old soul. The way she could read people emotionally had always been a gift. Not one I possessed, that's for sure. Maybe if I'd had more of her personality type and those kind eyes, I, too, would be able to stay away from men that were no good for me. Probably why she was still a virgin. She could spot a bastard a mile away.

"Come on, Gin, let's hit the cafeteria and see if Mrs. Hathaway has made any of her famous cookies."

Ginelle's eyes lit as if a sparkly diamond had just been presented to her. "We're out." She hooked Maddy's arm, and they strode off on the search for goodies.

I took a deep breath and balled my shaking hands into fists.

I can do this. It's Dad. Pops.

With measured steps, I entered the room, walked around the curtain that had been pulled for privacy, and found my dad. He looked like he was sleeping though I knew better. Tears blurred my vision as I got closer and took the chair next to his bed.

His hand lay by his side. I picked it up in both of mine, leaned forward and kissed the top of his hand. "Pops..." I said, though I could barely hear my own voice. Clearing my throat, I tried again. "Dad, it's me, Mia. I'm here," I whispered. Clutching his hand to my chest, I got as close to him as possible. He looked a million times better than he did when I found him after he'd been worked over by Blaine and his posse two months ago. The bruising around his face was gone. A couple of pencil thin pink lines slashed across his temple and the side of his face. Maybe they'd always be there; maybe they'd fade. Only time would tell.

The rest of him looked good. He'd lost a lot of weight. So much that he didn't seem like my big cuddly Pops anymore, just a lifeless husk that once held a great man. At least he used to be before Mom left. I choked back the sobs, but the tears came pouring down anyway.

"Why did you have to get in so bad with Blaine? Why?" I rubbed my chin against his hand then leaned my face into his chest and let it all out. My anger at him for getting hurt, for borrowing so much, for gambling, for being a drunkard, and leaving me to be the one to clean it all up. Again. Like always.

"Dad, you've really done it this time. The things I'm doing for you..." I let the words fall off, not wanting to admit that I was an escort. Regardless of whether or not I slept with my clients, it still sounded bad. The word *escort* alone held a serious negative connotation.

"I'm doing everything I can. Protecting Maddy. Making sure she's sticking with college. She's doing really well. Even met a boy...you might need to wake up to kick his ass." I stared at his face, hoping, praying he'd open his eyes. Nothing happened.

I grabbed a tissue from his bedside table, then blew and wiped my nose. "I've met some really great people over the last couple months. At first, I thought working for Aunt Millie was going to be a nightmare, but you know what, it's actually been pretty nice. My first client was Weston Channing the third. Yes, the third. I gave him shit about it all the time." I laughed and thought back to Wes and how we met. How the moment I saw him walk up those stairs on the beach that first day I knew I'd be swept away by his charm.

"Wes taught me how to surf. He also taught me that not all men are created equal." Chuckling I sat back, rested my feet up on the edge of Dad's bed and told him about my two favorite guys. How Wes made movies and came from a great family. Promised him if he woke up, I'd take him to see one of Wes's movies and buy him a big tub of popcorn.

"And then there was Alec. He was a Frenchman, Pops. A real, honest to God, French guy. He called me *Jolie*. It means 'pretty one' in French. Gotta admit, I did like that." I pushed a lock of hair back from my face and leaned my head back to stare at the ceiling. There were beach scenes printed in the tiles above Dad's bed. I liked that. Made it easier to think that when he woke up, the first thing he'd see was the beach and not a blank white slate.

"So, Alec painted me, Dad. Some of the paintings you wouldn't like so me much because I wasn't wearing any clothing, but he didn't take advantage. Not really. We had fun and he loved me. Only it was different than any love I'd experienced before or the very real and intense feelings I still have for Wes. I'd liken it to my love for Ginelle, only the boy version with a bit more physical contact." A lot more if I was being honest. I grinned and looked over at Dad. Nope, eyes still closed.

"Alec taught me that it was okay to love people beyond just you, Mads, and Gin. That you could care about another person, love them even, and not have to be with them forever. It was sweet. My time with Alec helped me see a few things about myself. It's sad to think I won't see them again. Though maybe not Wes. I'm still confused over him, Pops." I looked at his face, so serene and peaceful and knew this was the one moment that I could admit what's been plaguing me for over a month. Put actual words to the thoughts crawling around my subconscious.

Glancing at the door I couldn't see anyone. With the coast clear of prying ears, I laid it out. "Dad," my voice shook. I licked my lips and sighed. "I could fall for Wes, Dad. Really fall. And you know what?" I asked, even though I knew he couldn't answer. "That scares the shit out of me. My track record is garbage. Straight up foul. My heart wants to take the leap, but my brain reminds me of all the dickwads that came before. Aside from that, I have another ten months to work off before the debt to Blaine is paid." I huffed. "And of course, Wes offered to pay it. Asked me to stay. And I didn't. I left him in Malibu."

I rested my eyes and leaned back in the chair before pressing my hand into my heart. It ached. Hurt with the loss of a promise of more with Wes, one I couldn't accept. But I'd wanted to. More than I wanted anything. I wasn't the type of girl that had these grand ideas, where I believed life was going to be cash, cars, and endless youth. No, I grew up poor, worked hard, took care of my sister and helped my Dad survive. The life Wes had wasn't even close to the life I led which was a definite part of the appeal. The timing for Wes and me though wasn't right. That's why it was so easy to fall into Alec's embrace. Until it's meant to be, there's a lot of living to be had and experiences to partake of.

"I wish you'd wake up." I held his hand and kissed it once more. "Soon Dad, wake up. We need you. Maddy needs you. I need you."

My sister and Ginelle came back a few minutes later. I listened to Maddy update Dad about school, purposely not telling him about the guy, which I planned to needle her about later. Then Gin shared several jokes she'd learned recently. Through it all there were three pairs of eyes watching, waiting for any sign that my dad was still there. That he hadn't already left us.

Before I left, the doctor gave me the rundown of Dad's prognosis. He was doing well physically, almost perfectly healed from all his injuries. A physical therapist came in every day to work Dad's legs and arms. They were going to teach Maddy how to do it to give him more stimulation. I hated that she had to learn that. It killed me that I wasn't the one who'd be here to get the family through this.

By the time we left, I had a chip on my shoulder and an ax to grind. Home. I needed to go home. Eat a home cooked meal, throw back a couple of beers with my bestie, and sleep away the last two months. Tomorrow, I'd meet up with Blaine.

CHAPTER TWO

Ginelle and I walked through the casino dead set on our mission. Get to Blaine's office, give him the check for my second installment, and get the hell out of dodge. The next day I had a host of beauty appointments to tend to and then first thing the following morning I was on a plane to Chicago to meet my next client.

"Why do you think he has an office in a hotel anyway?" Gin asked as we stepped around some scantily clad women serving drinks.

It wasn't even ten in the morning and the booze was flowing. There's a reason the players can't see outside of hotels on the gambling levels. It makes them feel like it's still early. Pumps them full of artificial noises, music, all day buffets and drinks that they don't have to pay for as long as they're gambling. When you add all those things up, people become gambling, drunk zombies that are dying for a win. But they never do. The house always wins. It's the most well-known fact, probably in the world, yet people are still dumb enough to keep trying their luck and pissing away their kid's college money or their rent for that matter.

In my Dad's case, the hardcore gamblers, they *borrow* money. Lots of it. More than they could ever possibly pay back in their lifetime. All for the win, for Lady Luck. In my experience, Lady Luck was a cold hard bitch that smoked, had fake tits, and an STD.

"Blaine once told me that he didn't need to hide what he did. Said he was an "investor" and thought having an office and staff made him look less like the criminal he is, and more like the businessman he claimed he was."

Gin huffed and smacked her gum. "Pretty smart actually."

"Yeah, well, I never did say the man was stupid. Just a heartless bastard with a black soul."

We made our way to the elevators and then to his floor. When we arrived at the door I stopped, straightened my hair and adjusted my t-shirt to make sure it covered every speck of bare skin. I wore my leather jacket and paired it with black motorcycle boots with kick-ass studs on the heel. The cherry on top was the bright red 24-hour stay-red lip stain. The lipstick promised to keep my pout a bright, flaming red. I felt fierce and ready to handle a prick with a tiny dick. Really, he had an average sized dick but it made me feel better to emasculate him internally.

I turned to Gin and stopped with my hand on the handle. "Okay, this is as far as you go."

Ginelle's eyes flared white hot. She put a hand to her petite hip and presented me with the oh-no-she-didn't stance. "If you think for one minute…" Ninja-like I clasped a hand over her mouth and got close. Really close. So close I could smell the mint on her breath from her gum.

"Gin, Blaine already hurt one of my family members. Bad. Really bad. He's threatened to hurt me and Maddy. I cannot handle him threatening someone else I love. I need you to go and wait for me at the bar downstairs." I reached into my pocket and pulled out a twenty. "Please," I begged while pressing the twenty into her hand.

I let her go and her eyes watered. "But what if he hurts you?"

"He won't. I'm worth too much money to him. Trust me." I stared into her eyes letting her see the fierce love and protection there.

She took a long, slow breath. "O-kay. If you're not down in thirty minutes, I'm calling the cops."

"Fine. That's fair. Now go, before someone sees you." I turned her around and gently pushed her toward the elevator.

I waited until she got on. "I love your guts," she said.

"I love your guts, too. See ya soon, ho."

Her eyes widened, but before she could get in a jab, the elevator doors closed. I chuckled and then put on my brave face. Time to deal with a monster.

★ ★ ★ ★

Blaine's office was black, red, and white. Reminded me of a racer's checkered flag. Didn't seem all that inspired as far as decoration goes, but it did connote his desire for "winning" pretty nicely. A buxom blonde with big silicone tits, a small ass and even smaller IQ, with an anorexic-sized waistline led me to his office.

"Mr. Pintero, Mia Saunders is here to see you." She allowed me to walk past her. Blaine stood up. All six feet four of him towering over me. He was broad, with an additional solid forty pounds of pure muscle since I last saw him.

"Mia. Pretty, pretty, Mia," Blaine responded holding out a hand, reaching to pull me close.

I pressed my own out, hand up and palm facing him.

"Nope, I'm here for business not pleasure."

"Why can't we do a little of both?" His tone was sultry, his eyes like those of a snake, green and yellow. The pupil was black and beckoning, as if he could mesmerize me with one glance. I looked away and took a chair near his desk. I pulled an envelope out of my jacket pocket and slapped it on the glass surface of his desk.

"Here's what you were wanting."

"How could you possibly know what I want, pretty Mia? It's been far too long since we've seen each other. Long enough for time to heal some wounds, wouldn't you agree?" Instead of sitting across from me, he chose the chair next to mine.

"What do you want then, Blaine?"

"Time," he said simply.

"Okay sparky, I'll bite. Time for what?"

"I see you haven't lost that quick wit of yours."

"Blaine, the point? Get to it."

"I want you to have dinner with me tonight."

The man should be committed. "Are you insane?"

"Last time I checked, no," he said flatly.

Suddenly, it was too hot in the small room that overlooked the rest of the Vegas Strip. My skin felt like it was burning, covered with acid, or maybe it was the anger boiling, so fired up it was overflowing.

"You beat up my father so badly he's still in a coma."

"That's just business. You know that. He gave me no choice." He reached an arm out to clasp my hand. The second his skin touched mine I jerked it away.

"Don't fucking touch me. You lost that right years ago when you fucked me over. Now, you've screwed over my dad. You know he still hasn't woken from his coma?" My voice rose so loud the people in the next office could probably hear me. "They're not sure if the brain damage he sustained is going to affect his ability to speak or move his limbs!"

Blaine's serpent-like gaze locked on mine. "That was an unfortunate side effect of his punishment. I've taken care of the man that hurt your father. He is no longer a problem. The additional violence has been avenged, I assure you."

"You assure me. Do you hear yourself? Ever listen to what you're saying? You're talking about human life as if it's something that can be easily given or taken away."

"Life is fleeting."

"Yeah, when you have your goons pound it out of people. I can't even believe this." I stood up and pointed down at the envelope. "There's your money. Installment number two. In a month, I'll mail number three."

"You can bring it in person," he clenched his teeth and gripped the chair handles hard enough to turn his fingers white. "You *will* bring it in person." The tone brooked no argument, but I wasn't one of his minions.

"That was not part of the deal."

"Deals can be renegotiated."

"Not this one."

"What if I book your services for the month?" he threatened.

That's when I turned on a heel and got real close to his face. I could see my breath ruffling the lengths of his sandy brown hair. "I'd be very careful about allowing me anywhere near you when you're vulnerable."

"Ah, but I'm a risk taker." He smirked.

"Don't bet on me, buddy. It's the last bet you'll ever make. I can't be held responsible for what happens to you in your sleep. I can already hear my statement to the cops now." I stood up, twirled my hair and made a pouty face. "It was an accident officer, I swear. We were having sex, and he liked it rough. I didn't think he'd choke. One minute he was coming and the next going…" I clucked my tongue then looked down my nose at him. He visibly swallowed but didn't show any other outward sign that I'd hit home with the threat, but I knew him well enough to know he wasn't sure if I was bluffing or not. Didn't matter. Just the fact that he had to think about it made me a winner.

"Now, I'll be leaving. Thanks for the face-to-face. It's always good to see old friends. Especially when they haven't aged well. You should look into some eye cream and some face moisturizer. That desert heat is murder on the skin. Ta ta." I wiggled my fingers in a sexy wave and I was out of there.

★ ★ ★ ★

By the time I hit the bar Ginelle had two shot glasses lined up.

"Oh, thank God." She slumped into her chair. I picked up one of the glasses of Patron Silver and slammed it back. Then grabbed the second and did that one, too. "Hey! That was supposed to be celebratory!"

"Another two," I pointed to the glasses but looked at the bartender. He nodded, grabbed the tequila and poured another couple of shots.

After four shots to the head I finally stopped shaking.

"Are you okay?" Gin asked leaning close.

"Yeah, it's just, there is no human on Earth that can make me that angry.

She took a sip of her soda and set it back down. "Did he threaten you?"

"Yeah, threatened to be my next client if you can believe that."

Her eyes went as wide as ancient sundials. "What? That's crazy."

I pointed to her. "Right! That's what I said."

"Well, how did you get out of it? You're not really going to be his next client are you?" She squirmed in her seat, obviously as uncomfortable with this line of discussion as I was fifteen minutes ago.

"Hell no! Basically, I told him, if he did, I'd kill him in his sleep."

Her mouth dropped open and her eyes bugged out. Then she tipped her head back and burst out laughing. "Only you..." She giggled and continued to laugh until she started to hiccup. "Only you would threaten a loan shark—allegedly a guy who murders people as part of his job. You better watch your back."

I thought about what she said for a moment. Blaine could come after me, but that would be like killing the goose that lays the golden eggs. As long as I owed him money, or he perceived it as I owed him money, I was worth far more to him alive than dead. That line of thought worked for now. It would get me through the year at least. Long enough to pay him off and figure out my next move.

"So what beauty appointments do you have lined up for tomorrow. Part of my contract,"—I added air quotes around the word to emphasize my annoyance with it—"is to be perfectly presentable at all times."

"Well, with the budget you gave, you, me and Mads are going to a spa. I had a buy-two-get-one-free coupon. We're getting facials, waxing, manicures, pedicures, the works! Oh, and you're getting your hair trimmed. I had to pay extra for that, but you said you needed it so whatev's."

"And that was all within the budget?"

"I got people, who got people, who give me fat discounts. So yeah, it's in the budget." Gin rustled in her purse and pulled out a pack of gum. She opened it up and shoved a piece in her mouth, chewed a few times and groaned.

Staring at her, I tried to place my finger on what was different. Something was up with her. "What's with you and the gum?"

Her eyes brightened and a small smile slid across her face. "Trying to quit."

"Quit what?"

Her smile dropped and her face went slack. She twisted her lips pinching them between thumb and forefinger. "Smoking," she said quietly.

Oh man, and I didn't notice. Shit. Best friends notice when their friends all of a sudden no longer have a cancer stick poking out of their mouths. "Shit, Gin, that's amazing! How is it going? Why didn't you tell me?"

She signed. "Well, I *would* have but you've been all about Wes, and Alec and the job and you haven't asked me once how life back in Vegas has been for me aside from me checking on Maddy and Pops."

I closed my eyes and took a breath then opened them

and looked at my best friend in the whole wide world. "I'm sorry I haven't been a very good friend have I?"

She shook her head. "No, you've had a lot going on. I get that."

"It's not okay. You're important to me too. I want to know what's going on in your life. You're still my best friend and I fucked up. I won't let it happen again. Promise." And I meant it. Every last word. I'd been a sucky friend to Gin and she's done nothing but support and love me through all of this. Taking care of Maddy, checking on Dad, all while she has her own life and struggles.

"And if you do it again. What do I get?" Her tone was light and forgiving. It was our way. We'd never stayed mad at each other longer than a day in our entire lives.

I thought about it for a moment. "Naked pictures of one of my hotties?" I offered knowing Ginelle was nothing if not a sex-driven hoochie.

"Deal!" She put out her hand, and we locked pinkies, then she kissed our combined digits and then I did. No red stain on the flesh. Best. Lipstick. Ever. "You know though, you have been pretty bad…" She frowned and made a sad puppy dog face. "I'm thinking you should give me something to prove you've got the goods."

I licked my lips and stared at her. Then I grinned, kept my gaze locked on hers but pulled my phone out of my back pocket. With quick movements I brought up the section of photos I'd filed away. I scrolled to one and then turned it around.

Ginelle looked at it and her mouth dropped. "You fucking skanky assed whore," she whispered, mouth agape, eyes glued to the screen. I pulled the phone back and looked at the picture I'd taken of Alec lying in bed asleep. He was lying face down. His strong, muscled back and tight, bare ass were on full display. The long russet and gold hair fanned alongside the pillow highlighting his perfection. The light was shining just so that morning, and I had to capture it.

I found the next image. It was Wes on the beach after we'd surfed without the trainer. Over the month I'd gotten pretty adept at the art of surfing. That day I'd already come up on the beach and was checking my phone when he got out of the ocean, and started pushing down his wet suit. The fabric caught and so did my camera when that suit pushed almost past the point of no return. The picture showed his golden chest down to a supremely trim waist. A lovely happy trail led the way to a small tuft of curls where his cock lay hidden by the wet suit. I turned the camera around and Ginelle balked. She picked up her shot, slammed it back and swallowed. "I fucking hate you," she said while staring at the image.

"Yeah, I hate me too," I said looking down at my sweet Wes. The one who'd asked me to stay, and I still left something behind with that Californian movie-making surfer, but I'd never admit it. Not even for a moment.

CHAPTER THREE

The housekeeper who let me in brought me through the Penthouse apartment and beyond a set of double doors at the end of a spacious home on the fortieth floor. The elevator felt like an amusement park ride it took so long to get to the top. I'd bet good money the view was impressive.

Distracted, the man set my bag on a padded bench in front of a monster sized bed, turned around and disappeared. That's when I heard the sound of rushing water. Someone was taking a shower.

Shit. Shit. Shit.

That was the last thing I needed. To meet my new client when he was naked. I clenched a hand around the strap of my purse and planned to make a hasty exit when the door opened. A large form emerged from a wall of steam. The lighting around his silhouette created an ethereal picture that could feature very easily on the big screen. It stopped me dead in my tracks by the force of sheer wonder.

That's when my client entered the room, clad only in a small towel precariously dangling from his hips. Water droplets streamed down every scintillating inch of his muscular frame. My mouth went dry, and my heart might have actually stopped beating. It was okay because I decided right then and there it would have been a good way to go. Basically, in my twenty-four years, I'd finally seen perfection in all its naked glory.

"Holy mother of God." Drool may have slid over my lip and down my chin. Wes and Alec were something to write home about. And I did. Often. To Ginelle, who poured over every letter. Anthony Fasano, on the other hand, was beyond the realm of female comprehension. He was massive. A brick house. Based on what I could see of his thighs peeking from under the towel, they were the size of tree trunks. Square pecs and rectangular muscle cut like a graph along his chest and abdomen. And the arms...I couldn't even think straight for how much I wanted to touch those arms. Have them hold me close, wrap around me. Make all the hurt of the last two months go away.

Anthony's ebony hair was slicked back; water dripped from the longer layers, and fell onto the widest shoulders I'd ever seen. And I've seen my fair share of naked, hot guys. This guy was ripped, and not in that gross body builder way where the muscles bulged and veins stuck out of the skin like ropes. No, he was in a league of his own. I knew he was a boxer and had seen a picture of him in his boxing shorts but that paled in comparison to the real deal. Holy shit, was he the *real* deal. More like a handful of aces.

I licked my lips and stared, allowing my purse to drop to the bench near the foot of the bed. The body god's gaze traced my form from top to bottom. He leaned into the doorframe on one rounded, strong looking shoulder and draped the towel he was holding around his neck. Then he crossed those forearms over his chest. Oh man, I wished he hadn't done that. Instantly, my sexy feelers flared and I had to slow my breathing in order not to pass out at the sheer male perfection before me.

"*Papi*, Mia arrived," were the first words out of his

perfectly full mouth.

Wait...Papi?

Another man strode into the space and hooked an arm around body god's waist. A huge smile adorned his face. Where Anthony was massive, this man was smaller but still in shape with a washboard stomach and little to no fat that I could see. And I could see plenty. His body style reminded me of my Frenchman. Not quite slight, but then again the massive wall of muscles he leaned into could make any good sized hottie seem less than average.

Regardless, this man had a stunningly handsome face. Beautiful, almost androgynous. A face that made a person want to take pictures and hang them on the wall. Living in California, I was pretty certain he was Hispanic. Dark hair, dark eyes, dark skin, pointed features.

The way the two causally stood, practically naked, holding onto one another painted a very powerful picture. And that's when it hit me like a paperweight to the head. I'm pretty sure my mouth dropped open, and I held out a finger pointing to one and then the other. "Oh! Wow. Um, okay. So yeah. Now I know why you need me."

"Smart girl you picked out," the unnamed man said. Then his eyes did a loop from top to toe. "And ridiculously beautiful." His eyebrows narrowed. "Did you have to pick out the prettiest one?" He moved away from Anthony, crossed his arms over his chest and puffed out a breath of air dramatically. "Should I be worried?" He tapped a foot, actually tapped his foot like a chick about to nail her man.

Anthony's eyes seemed to tiptoe along my curves before he grinned wickedly. "May-be." He drew out the word. "And yeah, I had to pick the best girl. My family would want me to be with the perfect one." He extended his hand but looked at the man by his side. "She's pretty damned perfect, wouldn't you agree?"

The Hispanic man's lips pursed and then dropped into a scowl. "*Si.* You are very beautiful." He finally spoke directly to me.

"Uh, thanks, I think. And who are you?" That was the hundred thousand dollar question.

"I am Hector Chavez. Anthony's *partner.*"

"Not this month you're not," Anthony snickered.

Hector's face fell. "That is not even funny. We just need to get through this. I, for one, am not looking forward to it," his voice rose in volume as he pulled away, and then disappeared behind a door. Probably the closet.

"You guys are a couple?" I gestured to the door with a wave of my hand.

Anthony smiled wide and tipped his chin. My heart started beating again. Damn, I knew not all the good ones were gay, but this one was damned good and definitely gay.

"How about we get dressed and then discuss?"

"Oh sure. Yeah, of course." I turned around, and fumbled while grabbing my purse and bag.

"The room two doors down on the left is yours for the month. I believe you'll find everything you need for the next few days. Why don't you go get settled. Tomorrow, Hector will take you shopping for additional items." I cringed. Anthony tilted his head to the side, his ice-blue eyes focused solely on me. "I see that idea does not excite you. Most women would love an opportunity to buy ridiculous amounts of expensive clothing."

I huffed. "Well, I think you're going to find out rather

quickly, I'm not like most girls. Not to mention the fact that I am a woman, not a girl." I winked then looked down. "You may want to tighten that towel, I can see your dick." I glanced down once more where I could see way down his happy trail to the top inch of his cock.

He didn't move a muscle, just licked his bottom lip and assessed me with his steely gaze. "This is going to be interesting with you here, I can already tell."

I turned on a heel and opened the door. "What's the fun in life if everything's pre-*dick*-ta-ble," I shot over my back and walked into the hall.

He chuckled and shook his head then shut the door.

★ ★ ★ ★

I was sitting at the bar munching on a chicken salad sandwich when Hector and Anthony emerged a half hour later.

"By far, the best chicken salad I've ever had," I told Renaldo and swiveled my chair around to greet the men. Renaldo had given me the lowdown while he made lunch. Apparently, he was not only the housekeeper, he cleaned, cooked, and did whatever the guys needed. Turned out, he was also fluent in the art of gossip. It seems that because I was a hired employee, that gave me the right to be updated on the latest dealings with our hunky bosses.

Renaldo set two plates down on each side of me and continued about his task humming quietly. I liked the little fella. Definitely of Latin or Hispanic descent, he was plump, in his fifties, all of five foot five, discernably gay based on the way he gushed about the good looks of said bosses, and had a friendly, puppy-like quality about him.

"Mia Saunders," Hector approached with his arms out wide and pulled me into a tight hug. "Thank you for coming."

"No thanks necessary. You did pay for me to be here?"

Hector pulled back and brushed a lock of hair over my shoulder. "Yes, but you still have a choice. We're glad you chose us."

I shrugged. "Cool. It's good to meet you." I glanced over to the mammoth hunk and held out my hand. "Anthony Fasano, my new fiancé I presume."

Anthony chuckled and blew a fast breath out his nose before grasping my hand in a firm hold. "The one and only. It's good to meet my future bride."

Hector's head flung around so fast it could have been mistaken for a top. "Excuse me. You mean pretend bride. If anyone's walking down an aisle with *you*, big guy, it will be me!" He pursed his lips together and mumbled under his breath while taking the seat next to me.

"*Papi*, don't. You know I was joking. You don't have to be so literal." Anthony shook his head and rested his hands at his sides. "And you can call me Tony. If you're going to be my pretend fiancée we may as well get that one straight right off the bat." He moved forward and maneuvered his giant frame onto the small stool. Well, it only seemed small when he sat on it. I waited and watched the wooden legs to see if they were going to break under the pressure of all that male muscle.

Hector clinked his shoulder with mine breaking me from my stupor. "Hey, eyes on your sandwich, missy. All that hunky hotness,"—he tipped his chin at Tony and then back to me—"is mine and mine alone. You get that, we'll be just fine."

I opened my mouth to say something but instead let out a breath and nodded.

"So, what's my first assignment?" I bit into the sandwich and looked from one side to the other where the guys caged me in. In only three bites, Tony finished half of his sandwich. Damn, he was big.

He wiped his mouth with his napkin. "Tonight, the three of us get to know each other. Tomorrow morning, you meet Ma."

I'm pretty certain my entire face flattened like a pancake the way that information slapped me upside the head. "Tomorrow? After one night, you expect me to act like I'm in love with you and fool your mother. As in, the woman who gave birth to you?"

Both Hector and Tony nodded. Then Hector spoke. "Your description said you were an actress. We figured that was a plus for us. Besides, tomorrow's Friday night dinner and we always meet Ma and the family for dinner."

"The family?"

Tony smiled and took an alligator-sized bite of his sandwich pushing the remaining bit into his mouth. Renaldo set another sandwich on his plate and glass of milk in front of him. Tony sucked down half the milk in one go.

"Impressive," I said.

Hector bumped my shoulder again. "I know," he waggled his eyebrows and grinned.

I shook my head and focused on the matter at hand. Turning my chair so I was facing Hector, I laid it out. "You want me to not only pretend to be his fiancée but make his mother *and* extended family believe it too. All in one shot?"

Hector's brown eyes twinkled. "*Si*. I knew you were a smart one."

"Impossible."

"Nah," Tony clapped me on the shoulder and rung my body as if I was one of the guys. "You've got this. I can already tell. You're gorgeous, down to Earth, and you've got a bit of an edge. Italian's like that. Can you cook?"

"I do all right."

Tony licked his lips, leaned a forearm on the counter top and encroached on my personal space. "Like Italian food?"

"Is the Pope Catholic?"

He glanced at Hector next to me then back. "Are you easily intimidated…"

I pressed my chest forward, straightening my spine and got into his space. "Do I look the type that intimidates easily?"

"You didn't let me finish." Tony moved a bit closer and I tried not to flinch but couldn't help myself from pressing back. That pushed me into Hector who steadied me at the biceps. "Are you intimidated by strong women?"

"Look, I can handle myself against a bunch of tiny Italians."

Tony and Hector smiled so wide it was if they were mirror images of the other. "Fair enough. Then, let's get started on the specifics."

"Oh, snap. We're going to need a truck load of wine for this," Hector sighed and left the room, presumably to get a bottle of wine.

★ ★ ★ ★

"Oh my god! You did not do that!" I screeched almost sloshing wine onto the carpet. Instead just a few drops tagged the table. Hector face planted into my lap laughing so hard I could feel the heat of his breath against my knees.

Tony wiped up the spill and refreshed my glass.

"We did. Stark assed naked. Ran the entire length of the football field all wearing helmets and nothing else. We'd painted a different letter on our chests and when the last goal was made, we rushed onto the field. Most of our fraternity. We spelled out "L-O-S-E-R-S...S-U-C-K... I-T" standing long enough for the visiting team's side to get a good look before we ran like hell."

I patted Hector on the back. "You too?"

He nodded and then pushed up. "Shortly thereafter, Anthony and I became an item. Well, privately."

"So who knows you're a couple?" I asked the question I'd wanted to know all evening.

"Not many," Hector said sourly.

"*Papi* please," Tony begged.

Hector sighed then hugged me close. We flopped backwards to lean against the couch shoulder to shoulder, his side plastered against mine. It felt nice. Kind of like it would if I had a brother. "You see, My Anthony, does not want to deal with the press, his family, or business issues if he were to come clean about his sexual orientation."

"That's messed up." I was surprised at how strong my tone came across.

"You're telling me!" Hector clinked glasses with mine.

Tony set his glass on the table. "Look, it's hard enough being a young boxer turned businessman. Add being gay to that and I've got a disaster on my hands. The league might not let me box."

Instantly, I felt indignant. "They can't do that, can they? That's slander, defamation or something!" My alcohol addled brain couldn't quite come up with all the reasons that was awful at the moment, but the second I got the use of all my grey matter back I was going to come up with a humdinger of a reply.

"Sadly, they would find other reasons, but being gay would be the underlying cause. Then there's business. I'm an Italian man who owns a *family* restaurant. The face of Fasano's has always been my Pops, Ma, me and my four sisters." I liked that he called his dad the same nickname I did. Connected us in a way.

It was impossible to keep my mouth shut. "You have *four* sisters! Holy fucking shit. They are *so* going to know we're not a couple!" I shook my head and Hector nodded. "Women know when something's fishy. Are you sure they don't know about you already?"

Tony stood and started pacing. "They don't know. I've given them no reason to think otherwise. What you also don't know, Mia, and the biggest reason you're here is because of the family name."

"Fasano," I roared feeling like the kid in class that knew the answer and yelled it out without being called on.

He sat down on the arm of the couch. "Yes. I am the sole heir to my father's company, even though all of my sisters participate in some way. We make many of the decisions together." He shook his head then laid his head in his hands. "It's more than that. You see, I'm the only male Fasano left. If I don't have a child, our name dies with me. And with me being gay…" his words trailed off and his head hung again, seemingly carrying theT entire weight of the world.

"Do you want children?" I blurted out the question, as was my way when consuming copious amounts of alcohol.

Tony raked his fingers through the layers of his hair. His gaze went to Hector. "Um, well, we never really talked about it."

Hector seemed to get taller in his seat. He stood and walked over to Tony and cupped his cheeks. "Baby, do you want kids?"

I should have left. Snuck out. Just wasn't in my nature. No, I was the type to be quiet as a mouse and get all up in this business without getting caught.

Tony looked at Hector with love and sadness in his eyes. "I always did." His voice sounded hoarse, thick with emotion.

"We can find a way, adopt or you know, maybe a surrogate."

I smiled so wide then socked back the rest of my wine in one gulp allowing it to burn a trail down my throat. Standing up I flung out a hand to brace myself trying to get my legs back in working order.

"That's my cue. My work here is done." I bent over and bowed. The two men didn't even notice, too lost in each other. They just held one another, foreheads touching whispering words only they could hear. It was beautiful. More than that. It was special, and I was glad I got to experience it.

Without looking back, I hustled to my room where I promptly nose-dived into the bed fully clothed and passed out.

CHAPTER FOUR

Tony held open the large wooden door with the swirled metal handle so that Hector and I could enter the restaurant. It was six p.m. on a Friday night, and Fasano's was hopping with activity. Waiters in crisp, white dress shirts, black slacks and ties bustled around serving drinks and lavishing tables with the best smelling Italian food. My mouth watered as I got a whiff of sausage in the air.

One of the waiters turned around to pour wine, and I got an even better look at his attire. I laughed under my breath when I got a gander at the ties they wore. Pasta. The ties had pasta dishes printed on them.

"Something funny?" Hector leaned close as Tony led me to the back of the restaurant.

"Did you see the ties?"

Hector smiled and grinned. "My idea, actually."

"Really?"

He nodded and winked. Tony's hand went from the crook of my elbow, slid behind my back and cupped my hip. His breath was hot as he whispered into my ear. "Okay, everyone's already here. Just follow my lead and don't be surprised if I touch you…a lot."

Tingles rippled down my spine and landed in the small spot at my lower back. Tony was incredibly handsome. More than that, he was drop dead gorgeous…and taken. By Hector. Who I was fond of. Very much so. I sucked in a slow deep breath. We reached a thick red curtain that was nestled at the very back of the restaurant.

"This is our private room. Only our family eats in this space. It's equivalent to Ma's dining room at her house. Now that we're such a large group, we had to move our family dinners to the restaurant. I built this room on just for the Fasanos."

"Wow." I gasped as Tony pulled back the curtain and revealed a huge room filled with people who were laughing, drinking and eating. It was chaos. Everyone at the table yelled over one another, used hand gestures in the air as if they were swatting away flies, and pushed at one another when they spoke. Madness. Complete, utter, madness. That's the only way I could describe it.

When we entered, one person noticed and then another and so it went. Everyone in the room went completely silent. A small woman with olive skin, black hair, and familiar blue eyes stood up. She held herself with confidence. Her back was straight, chest pressed out, eyes zeroed in on me.

The petite woman walked up to us. First, she put a hand up toward her son who leaned forward and kissed his mother, on the mouth. It was nothing more than a mere pressing of lips but still, I can't say that I'd ever seen a grown man kiss his mother on the mouth. I certainly didn't kiss my father that way...or any way for that matter. We barely got by with an awkward hug most times.

"Mama," Tony said then stood tall and gestured to me. "This is Mia, my fiancée. Mia, this is my mother, Mona Fasano."

I smiled and said, "It's very nice to meet you, Mrs. Fasano."

Her lips barely twitched in reply. His mother moved closer to me, blatantly running her eyes over my entire body. "You are a very beautiful woman," she finally responded. I immediately melted more fully into Tony's side.

"Thank you." I gave her my patented wide smile.

She didn't stop at the compliment. Her head tilted and her lips pursed. "And curvy. Fasano men like their women with curves." She placed her hands on her own generous hips. If she'd been a thinner woman, I'd have taken offense.

"I like to eat, Italian food being my favorite," I lied. Didn't hurt to try and score points with the mother.

"Your hips are nice and wide, good for giving me grandchildren."

"Uh-um…" Now that came of nowhere.

"Ma," Tony attempted to interrupt. Again, didn't work. When the woman had something to say, she said it and people listened.

"Yes, you'll give me beautiful grandsons. We need to carry on the Fasano name you know?" Mona's eyes pierced mine. "You do want children?"

Tony came to the rescue then. "Ma, enough. I'm starved, and I want to introduce Mia to the rest of the family."

"Okay, okay." She clapped her hands then grabbed both my arms and pulled me into a tight hug. In my ear, she whispered the words that would crush any woman with half a heart. Her voice was raspy and thick with tears. "I wished for you. I prayed *every night* my Anthony would find his mate. I am so happy you are here." Mona pulled back, cupped both my cheeks and laid a big fat wet one on my mouth. Kissing a girl really isn't that big of a deal usually. Sometimes Gin or Maddy kissed me, but a woman I'd just met? One whose soul I would later destroy? Not cool.

Hector walked around us and hugged a bunch of the people in the room before finding one of the three open chairs at the front of the room.

"Come on sweetheart," Tony said leading me to the other side of the room. Sweetheart. That's what Wes called me. He would think this scenario was a hoot. Maybe even put it into one of his movies one day as a romantic comedy. A stunning business man, a boxer, hires an escort because he's gay and not ready to come out to his family.

I sat in the seat next to Hector. Pretty sure that move was strategic on Tony's part, but I could see the disappointment in Hector's eyes that Tony didn't sit next to his *true* mate. It was all so depressing. Two men, clearly in love, feeling as though they can't be together because of society, family, business and obligation. I grabbed Hector's hand under the table and squeezed it. He glanced sideways at me, just the corner of his lips curving up. "Don't worry. By now, missy, I'm used to it."

For the next hour, I was introduced to all four of Tony's sisters. There was Giavanna the eldest at thirty-nine. She must have gotten most of the mother's genes because she was short, around five foot two, thick, black hair, but her eyes were as dark brown as a roasted coffee bean. So much so that you couldn't really see the black of her pupil. It didn't take away from her beauty in the least. Though she had a few wrinkles, mostly laugh lines, at the corners of her eyes, it didn't change the fact that she was a looker. As were all the Fasano women. I couldn't keep track of her four children. They varied in age and ran around like chickens with their heads cut off. All I could get was a bunch of

Italian names that I wouldn't remember and the knowledge that there were two boys and two girls.

Isabella was next. A little taller than her sister. Maybe around five foot four and a couple years younger at thirty-seven. Same black hair and dark eyes. Only her mouth was the perfect bow shape like Tony's. She introduced me to her two young sons who looked to be school age. I couldn't really guess how old they were. I hadn't been around kids much in the past.

Sophia was third in line at thirty-five and another couple inches taller than the last, maybe around five foot six. It seemed the younger they were, the taller they got. Interesting fun fact I brought up later when joking around with Hector. Now this woman though was a class act. She was dressed in a pencil skirt, a silk blouse and her black hair was pulled back into a tight bun at the nape. A pair of tortoise rimmed glasses sat on her pert nose. Her eyes were also dark, but her skin was much paler than the rest of the family. Made me wonder how tan Mr. Fasano used to be. Maybe he was a pale Italian.

"So did you just get here from work?" I asked.

Sophia took a drink of wine. "Yeah, it's been a long day at the office. I'm the Chief Financial Officer for Fasano's Unlimited."

"The money gal." We tapped wine glasses in a mock toast.

"That's me. Someone has to keep all these hooligans in line. If it wasn't for me and my team, they'd be spending money left and right on ridiculous things. Tony and I keep the rest of the family grounded to what the Fasano name is all about. Great, authentic cuisine that families can afford."

AUDREY CARLAN

I nodded and looked around the room. Everyone seemed so happy. Genuine, smiles adorned every face. The family seemed comfortable and at peace with each other. Not something I'd ever experienced within my own family since my mother up and left us. Dad did his best but lacked the finesse of raising daughters a mother would have had.

"So, all of you work together at the company?"

"Yes, in different ways. No task is too small. For example, we have the kids stuffing envelopes sending out birthday announcements, coupons, etc. The siblings all have a role. Giavanna runs the daycare and afterschool program inside the building. I'm in Finance, Isabella runs Human Resources, and Angelina runs Marketing. Even Ma has an office, but she spends most of her time in the kitchen coming up with the recipes and planning out the menus. Tony, as you know, runs the company. Even Hector works as our lawyer. He's been around so long it's like he's another brother."

"I'll bet. He's a really great guy." Just as I was about to put out some subtle feelers on the relationship between the two, a hand on my shoulder stopped me. I turned around and was greeted by the grinning face of the most stunning woman I'd ever seen. Her hair was thick, and fell in long dark ebony waves down to her ass. Her eyes were the exact same steely blue of Tony's. Bow shaped lips tinged with pink, and a dress that flowed around her like a vortex of oranges, reds and yellows.

"I've been dying to meet you, Mia!" The woman leaned down and hugged me tight. "I'm Angelina or 'Angie' for short. The stud behind me is my husband Rocko." If there was ever the quintessential Italian man, it was Rocko. He

285

looked exactly like a young Sylvester Stallone. Honestly, it was uncanny the resemblance. And the name, so close to Rocky? Wild. I shook my head and held out my hand.

I opened and closed my eyes a few times to clear my vision. Nope, still the same look-alike. "You look exactly like…"

"Sylvester Stallone?" He waggled his eye brows, took my hand and pulled me into a rib squeezing hug that stole my breath.

Two pairs of hands pulled me back from Rocko's hold. "Easy with my girl there, brother," Tony responded protectively. I could practically feel the tension pumping off Hector as he watched the exchange.

"It's amazing how much you look like him. A doppelganger for sure!" I couldn't get over it.

He tipped his head back and laughed. "I get it all the time. Plus, I box with your man. It's how I met Angie. I trained him back in the day. We're phasing out of the league and spending more time in the gym training the next line of pro boxers. Well,"—he slapped a hand on Tony's bicep—"I'm in the gym training the newbies more so than Mr. Businessman here. Can't complain though. He keeps the family fed."

"Yeah, yeah. Whatever, Rocky Balboa. Go back to your seat will ya?" Tony said, his Italian Chicagoan accent more pronounced when he was kidding around.

Angelina gripped my hand. "Let's get together this week! Tomorrow maybe, for shopping? We have to get a dress for the release of the new Fasano's Frozen Food line next week. We're hosting a big party the day before with all the movers and shakers of the food industry. It's our biggest achievement yet!" she squealed.

"Tony has to be in the office, but I planned on taking Mia shopping for a dress. You can come along tomorrow. She needs a new wardrobe while she's here. It would be great to have a second opinion," Hector offered.

"Shopping with Hector is the best." Angelina's voice rose with her excitement. She couldn't have been more than a couple years older than Tony and the tallest of all the women. We both stood at the same height. I also hadn't noticed any children unaccounted for at the dinner. Looks like the boxer and the beauty hadn't yet procreated. Man, when they did, those kids were going to be model beautiful.

Then I realized what they were talking about. Shopping. Blech. I cringed thinking about having to shop for a new wardrobe. "That would be uh…cool, I guess. Thank you."

Angelina sat in the chair that Tony vacated to talk to another family member. "You guess? Look, Mia, let me lay it out for you. Hector is gay. He knows the best places to shop, exactly what will look good on every body type…"

Hector charged in. "That is true. You should listen to her. I've been dressing Angie since she was in her early twenties."

"And Hector has incredible taste in clothes." She added. "You have nothing to worry about. He'll suit you up just fine. And with a body like that, you're going to look amazing in everything."

"Says the prettiest chick I've ever met," I said sarcastically before applying my filter.

Instead of her catching onto my tone, her eyes lit up and a huge smile spread across her lovely face. "You think I'm the prettiest girl you've ever met?" I shrugged and took a swallow of wine. "That is the nicest thing ever. We're *so* going to be BFFs," she promised and pulled me into another hug. Man these people liked to touch. There was absolutely no personal space allotment with this crowd. I'm pretty sure every last one of them had hugged, shoved, kissed, me in one way or another that evening. Definitely something I'd need to get used to over the rest of the month.

We plowed through dinner, eating the most amazing Italian food, all served family style in big serving bowls and dishes. The wine flowed like water and, the family spoke so loudly over one another that my ears started to ring. Reminded me of the aftermath of being at a rock concert and the steady ringing in my ears in the quiet. It was like that only louder. These people really liked to talk…a lot… at a decibel level beyond what normal humans were used to hearing.

Overall though, I liked the Fasano's. They were boisterous, friendly, jovial, and gorgeous. It was like being in a room of Italian actors waiting to audition for a part. Back when I was in LA, my agent would send me on ethnic calls because of my curves and thick, black hair. He seemed to think I looked Italian, though I was pretty sure I was just a Heinz 57—a mix of everything.

The evening ended with batches of tiramisu, homemade by Mona of course, and the darkest coffee I'd ever had. Together they were a taste sensation on the tongue.

When Tony and Hector led me out of the restaurant later, Tony pulled me into a big hug. He looked over his shoulder with a panicked expression, then his lips landed on mine. They were soft, warm, and moist. His fingers tunneled into the back of my hair; he tilted my head, and his tongue dove in. I was not expecting to be kissed like that by Tony. A gay man. A gay man with a partner. Things were not adding up. Still, I couldn't help but respond. He was a damn good kisser. His tongue flicked against mine, then danced as we got the rhythm. I lifted both arms and wrapped them around his broad shoulders and hanging on to his neck. When I pressed the length of my body against his, he gripped my hips and pressed close. That's when I felt it. Well not *it* exactly. A lack of it. He was not hard. There was absolutely nothing happening down below. I pulled my head back, his lips leaving mine in an audible plop.

My eyes went to his, only he wasn't looking at me, he was looking over his shoulder. I turned and saw his mother Mona. She had her hands clasped together and a look of pure joy filling every wrinkle in her face making her look a decade younger. Guilt coiled around my heart as I became witness to the hope this woman had for her son. Her only son. Her gay only son. But she didn't know that. At that moment, I heard a clearing of someone's throat. My eyes slid to Hector whose face held the exact opposite of Mona's. Grief, sorrow, maybe even a twinge of anger filled his features. That snake around my heart squeezed so hard I could barely breathe. Mama Mona turned on a heel and went back into the restaurant.

"Hector…" I whispered. He shook his head and opened the car door.

"Get in Mia. I need a word with Tony."

"*Papi*, you know that was for show…it didn't mean anything," he swore, hands fisted at his sides.

Although I shouldn't have felt hurt, I did, because I did feel something. There was a definite twinge of the lady parts when he held me and kissed me the way a man kisses a woman he's lusting after. Only with Tony, I felt the proof that he really didn't get turned on from kissing me. It wasn't real. That reminded me that I needed to check any lustful feelings at the door. This man might be sex incarnate and have the most incredible body known to mankind, but he was playing for Team Hector.

I went over to the car. Hector didn't even look at me. I swallowed down the bitter pill of regret. Before I got in the car I put a hand to his shoulder and leaned close enough to whisper in his ear. "It meant nothing. Mona was watching. He wasn't even turned on. Only you could do that to him. Believe me, I know when a man wants me. That man wants one person. You." That was the most reassurance I could offer.

As I sat down, Hector leaned in. "Thank you for telling me that."

"Anytime. How about you guys take a cab back? Go to a bar and chat about how this is going to play out now that I'm here. I don't know that you two thought about what me being here was going to do to your relationship, but it's obvious you need some time alone." He nodded and looked down where he scuffed a toe along the concrete. "I have a key now. I'll see you guys in the morning. Yeah?"

"Mia, thanks," Tony said. He waved his arm toward the street, and a cab stopped in front of him. "Hector, please come with me." Tony's tone was soft yet demanding.

I watched as they got into the cab and drove away. The limo took me back to the penthouse, and I just made it into my room when my phone pinged with a text.

From: Wes Channing
To: Mia Saunders
Can you talk?

CHAPTER FIVE

I stared at the cell phone display. There were two ways to play this. One, ignore it until I wasn't feeling so emotionally drained. Two, call him and let Wes's voice remove the snake coiled around my heart after the shitstorm I'd just dealt with between Tony and Hector. I hoped they could work it out. The last thing I'd ever wanted to do was come between two people in love—which they were. Only it wasn't fair that they couldn't be free to be themselves. Or at the very least, Tony perceived it that way. Perhaps if I worked with Tony, made him see that coming out of the closet could be a good thing. That being with Hector, planning and building the family they obviously wanted was the way to happiness. What Tony was doing was eventually going to burn Hector so bad, he'd walk. I know the type. I'm excellent at walking away.

Decision made, I clicked a couple buttons on my phone. Within one ring the line was picked up. "Hey sweetheart, is it too late there? Well, wherever you are?" His voice was deep, throaty and reminded me of whispered promises in the dark, breathy moans, and nights filled with unbridled passion. I'd had an incredible time with Alec but Wes, he just did it for me. Everything about him screamed, deep, penetrating, hot monkey sex. After the night I'd just had, I'd love to lose myself in him.

"It's not too late, no. I'm in Chicago."

"Mmm, the Windy City. What's the guy do?"

I wasn't sure we were at that point in our *friendship* that we could comfortably discuss other conquests. However, since I didn't plan on ever bedding Tony, it probably wouldn't hurt to share. "Restauranteur."

"Ah, I know how much you love a home cooked meal." Instantly the image of him shirtless making me breakfast came to mind. His long body, muscled, tan chest so brown from the California sun it looked good enough to eat. And it was. Wes always had that surf and sand smell about him. Delicious.

I realized I hadn't said anything in awhile. "Um, yeah. Well, you know how much I like to eat."

"I do. Does he cook for you?"

"Not yet, though I'm hoping he will soon."

A long sigh came through the phone and long moments passed before anything was said. "Are you with him, like you were with me?" Wes asked and even though it hurt that he felt the need to ask, I didn't owe him anything.

"Does it matter?" I whispered softly and laid on the bed, the phone tucked close to my ear.

"Does to me."

"No, and I'm not going to be."

"Why's that? If I know you, and I think I do, you have a very healthy libido." That time I could hear the amusement in his voice.

Wes did have a month to get to know me. Too well really. He snuck by my defenses and dug a hole into my heart. A part that he'll forever own. Not that I was going to tell him.

"Because I don't think his partner, Hector, would be

too fond of me encroaching on his man."

A rumbling laugh came through the line. God, I missed that laugh. It was the kind of laugh that had the ability to heal war-torn nations. "So why did a gay guy hire the hottest escort in history?"

"Kiss ass," I shot back. He chuckled again and the sound reverberated through the line straight into my heart, lightening the evening's events. "No, it's pretty messed up. He's in a long-term relationship; I'm talking marriage-type relationship with this amazing guy. Only he feels obligated to his family and business to keep up the persona of cool businessman, Italian guy, badass boxer."

"Shit. Sounds like he's got some heavy burdens. Professionally, I can understand how he'd want to maintain his privacy. If he's the type of guy who can afford Exquisite Escorts, he's loaded and likely has the press on his ass." He blew a breath out that came across muffled when his lips must have gotten too close to the phone. "Seriously Mia, money's good and all, but it doesn't take the place of privacy and the ability to live a quiet life."

I thought about the gated community Wes lived in with 'round-the-clock security monitoring the neighborhood, the red carpets he hated walking, and the need to hire an escort to attend important events just so he could work the room in peace. Yeah, Wes knew exactly what Tony was going through only without the issue of sexual orientation being a factor.

"He also has some family stuff. He's the only male heir to the family's fortune, and if he doesn't procreate the name will die with him."

"Jesus *Christ*. Talk about pressure." I nodded even

though he couldn't see me.

"Anyway, enough about my client. What about you? How's your movie coming along?"

"Great actually. Gina is amazing in the role," his voice sounded wistful, and my jealousy meter spiked. "She just *gets* the character so perfectly. I'm glad I went a different direction with the character."

I bit down on my lip and held back the instant retort about how he replaced me with *her*, but knew it wouldn't be fair. What he did, naming a character after me was honorable. Sweet even. It was a gift, and I needed to remember it as such and not taint it with the green-eyed monster. Besides, I had no claim on him, other than friends…with benefits. "So, you and Gina are getting along great, eh?" I rolled my eyes and attempted to keep my tone light.

"Yeah, she's cool. Not as pretty as her namesake in the script though." His tone was suggestive.

"Is that right?"

"It is."

"But you're having fun playing with her…I mean directing her."

"Not as much as I'd like to *direct* you."

"Oh, yeah? And what would you have me do?" Right then, the conversation took a different turn. One I'd never tried but was eager to explore.

I heard his tongue cluck as if he'd held it against the roof of his mouth and then let it go the moment I finished speaking.

"Well, first, I'd place my hands on your knees and *direct* you to open them, baring yourself. Do you remember doing that, Mia? I can still feel how hot and wet you were on my fingers."

With my free hand I touched my kneecap and traced a small circle around it. "I remember. What next?"

He groaned through the line, and I set the phone down for a second, grabbed the hem of my dress and pulled it off in one quick sweep, tossing it across the room, and brought the phone back up to my ear.

I caught Wes mid-sentence. "…my hands would slide down your legs, holding you open, just so I could look at you. Watch you get wetter. Then I'd take a finger and touch the very tip of your pretty clit. Would you like that, sweetheart?"

I bit down on my lip and moaned softly. "God, yes."

"What are you wearing right now?" Wes asked.

"I took off my dress when you started talking, um, dirty to me. Now I'm lying on my bed, alone in the house, no one around, just you and me, in an emerald green bra and panties. What are you wearing?" I closed my eyes feeling dizzy and lightheaded. I couldn't believe we were doing this, but damned if it wasn't an incredible turn on.

Wes groaned through the line. "Just a pair of plaid pajama bottoms. You know the kind."

Boy did I ever. Wes's pajama bottoms were made of the softest cotton known to man. During my time with him, I loved pulling them on after sex or first thing in the morning. I even stole a pair. Not that I'd admit it.

"Are you hard, baby?" I tried out the endearment. It felt good on my tongue. Other things would feel better if he wasn't two thousand miles away.

"Fucking hell. I'm so hard for you Mia, I'm seeping at the top."

"Use your thumb, and rub it around the tip. You remember what it feels like to have my hand around your cock?"

"Fuck yeah, I do."

"Do it. Close your eyes and run your hand up and down, slowly at first. Imagine it's mine running up and down the long length. Use your thumb to rub the wetness around, along every groove, especially the part I'd swirl my tongue around. If I was there, I'd wet your entire dick licking all along the length before flicking the sensitive part under the crown with the tip of my tongue."

Wes moaned through the connection. I could hear his breath coming and going in faster bursts of air. "What would you *direct* me to do?"

"Remove your panties," he demanded. I shoved the green panties down and flung them aside with my foot. "You bare for me, sweetheart?"

"Yes," I lifted my hips as if a phantom Wes was above me and I was attempting to touch my body with his.

"Cup your pussy just like I would do if I was there right now. I'd grip it hard, you know how I like it."

"Possessive," I barely got out as I tilted my head back doing as he asked. The pleasure was extreme, running through my entire body like a jolt of lightening.

"That's right. I'd possess that sweet cunt. And while you rotated your hips around, trying to get relief, I'd press two fingers in at once. Follow my lead, Mia."

I did as he asked, pressing two fingers deep into my sex. Ribbons of heat rippled through my womb, and over my stomach, and up to my chest where my breasts were full and heavy. The twin points were erect and scratching against the satin. Delectable. So good.

"Now, remember when I took control of that pussy when we were on your bike?" I groaned in reply, nonsensical moans leaving my lips as I recalled his thick fingers pressing in and out of me, hooking just right, pulling me up his body from behind by his hold on my most sensitive place. "Hook those fingers deep, sweetheart. Just like I would."

I tried and failed. "Can't reach. Need you," I blew out a frustrated breath but continued working myself toward oblivion. In my mind we were back on that bike in Wes's garage, his hand down my pants fucking me hard and deep just like he always did.

"You close, sweetheart?"

"Oh yeah, want you, Wes. Want you inside…"

A litany of curse words came through the line as his breathing sped up. Mine matched his as we pleasured ourselves, lost to the passion of remembering each other.

"If I was there, I'd press my fingers into that spot deep inside you and tickle you there. I'd bring my tongue into the mix, swirling around that cherry clit of yours. It would be bulging and stiff when I wrapped my lips around it and sucked you until your tight pussy clenched around my fingers and you came all over me."

"Oh Wes, I'm gonna come, Baby. I'm gonna come so hard. I want you here…" I tilted my head back, every sense, neuron and pore concentrated on the pleasure between my thighs.

"I'm there, sweetheart. It's my fingers in you. Now take your thumb and rub that clit. Fuck, I'm gonna come too, right now, with you. So good with you, Mia. Never better. Christ!" He roared through the phone. I did what he said, using the wetness from my center and swirled around my clit.

It was the push I needed. In a rush of energy and light I came, my body tightening, a cry escaping my lungs as if possessed, and wave after wave of white-hot pleasure shook me straight through to the core of my being. Through the phone, I could hear Wes crying out in his own release.

After several moments, we both came down. The only sound the two of us breathing rapidly.

"Mia," Wes said in reverence. My name was a benediction on his tongue and I wanted to kiss it, soak in it, build my life around it.

"Damn Wes, you give good phone sex," I said. He laughed. "You know I've never done that before," I admitted.

"Really?" he sounded surprised or shocked. It made me sad that he was if the way he asked was any indication.

I sighed, pulled back the covers and crawled underneath them. It had been a long day, and after an orgasm like that, all I wanted to do was snuggle up to the man who'd given me said orgasm and fall asleep to the beat of his heart. "Yes, really," I yawned and closed my eyes.

"I look forward to a repeat performance."

Another yawn. "Me, too."

"I miss you, Mia."

I smiled and held the phone really close to my ear so I could hear every nuance of his breathing. It made me feel safe, as if he was right there next to me.

"I'll always miss you, Wes," I said sleepily already envisioning when I'd get to see him again.

"Sweet dreams…" was the last thing I heard before I fell asleep.

★ ★ ★ ★

When I woke the next morning I still held the phone clutched in my hand. It was completely dead. I rolled over and stared at the ceiling thinking about last night. The entire day, to dinner, to phone sex with Wes was a rollercoaster ride. At least the end was satisfying. I wondered what Tony and Hector did and if they worked out their situation. Those two were definitely in love. The forever kind. Not the hot artist Frenchman you bang for a month and likely never see one another again kind. I did miss my Frenchman, though. I was grateful for Alec and what he'd brought to my life in the month we'd been together. Not only did we make beautiful art together, he taught me so much about myself, about love, and about life. I'd forever be grateful to Alec and the time we'd had. Maybe I could use what I learned from that experience to help Tony and Hector. In the end, love was love, and a person really didn't get to choose who they fell in love with or how long that love would last. Since theirs was the forever kind, something had to give.

This is what I was pondering all through my shower, getting dressed and heading to the kitchen. I could already smell the eggs and bacon cooking. My stomach growled as I sat on the stool.

Renaldo looked over at me. "I believe your stomach is very happy to see me, *Si*?"

"*Si*! How are you this morning Renaldo?"

"Perfect as a peach, Ms. Mia. And you? You look as though you'd had a very good night's rest." His lips crooked at the edges, and he winked over his shoulder while turning the bacon.

"That I did," I grinned thinking back to the call with Wes. Damn that man knew how to talk dirty. He'd had me so hot, I'd gone from zero to a million in a few short minutes. I was so sated I'd literally crashed with the phone at my ear. When I applied my makeup this morning I could still see the faint outlines of the phone against the side of my face. As soon as it was charged I'd have to send him a thank you note. Tell him how much I enjoyed our chat, and not just the sex. I enjoyed talking to Wes. It felt remarkably normal, like we'd always been friends or star-crossed lovers. Wes just made things easy. I hoped that it would stay that way for the rest of the year. Only time would tell.

Renaldo set a steaming hot plate of eggs, bacon, and fruit in front of me, and my mouth was full of food when Tony and Hector came into the room. Tony had his arm slung over Hector's shoulders, a very satisfied look on his face. I pursed my lips and cocked my head. "Looks like I wasn't the only one who had a good night." Why the hell I said that, I didn't know. Something about these two men had me spilling my guts. So unlike me.

Tony's eyebrows went sky high as Hector pulled up a chair next to me. He put both elbows on the table and held his head in his hand. "Really? I'll tell you all about my evening." He grinned. "But you have to tell me why yours was so yippee Skippy seeing as we sent you off to come straight home from the restaurant?" I thought about it, shoveled in another bite of eggs, and then washed it down with a gulp of coffee.

"Deal."

And that is how Hector and Tony found out about Wes.

CHAPTER SIX

"And you just left? That was cold, girl." Hector snuffed indignantly, already 'Team Wes' before I ever even got a chance to explain the situation with my dad and the reason behind me being an escort in the first place. Men, I swear... sometimes they only hear what they want to hear. Doesn't matter if they're gay, they still have a missing gene that makes them lack an understanding of women and their motives.

I shook my head. "Hector, you don't get it. I had to leave. Staying wasn't an option."

"Then you better explain it to me fast, missy. If my Tony left me high and dry, I'd be a wreck."

"No, Wes and me, we're not like that."

"Oh yeah? What are you like?"

"We're friends."

"Friends who have phone sex? Friends who spend a month loving one another..."—I tried to interrupt but he threw up a hand cutting me off—"then begging the other one to stay with them...forever!"

Uggh. "He did not say that! Yes, he asked me to stay. Yes, I declined, even though I wanted to stay more than anything...but I just couldn't!"

"Why?" he asked. Before I could respond, a clacking of heels on tile floor interrupted us both. I sucked in a full breath attempting too cool my jets as best as possible. It wouldn't do to let the cat out of the bag to Tony's sister. One of the people I was meant to mislead during this assignment.

"Hey guys! I'm so excited about going shopping today!" Angelina, the youngest of the sisters, though still two years older than Tony, entered the room. She hugged Hector then me. "My brother at work already?"

"Yes, he left about an hour or so ago. Would you like anything to drink or eat?" Hector offered.

"Nope, just ready to hit the shops! Mia, are you excited or what?"

I groaned then reached across the table and grabbed my purse. "Yeah, sure."

"You don't sound excited." Angelina mumbled.

Hector chuckled and led Angelina by the elbow. "She doesn't like to shop." Angelina's mouth dropped open and her eyes bugged out.

"Are you a girl?"

"Of course I'm a girl. Just not a girlie-girl. I get by just fine."

Hector hummed. "Yes. The clothes she brought were all jeans, plain tank tops and concert t-shirts. Deplorable. Her pajamas are more stylish than her entire wardrobe."

He was so right. "That's because they were bought by Wes's stylist," I slipped and bit my lip.

"Wes? Who's Wes?" Angelina's eyes narrowed on me. She stopped and waited for my answer.

"Oh, just a friend. Gay BFF back home." The lies spilled from my lips like vomit on a rug. Acidic, vile, and tasting pretty damn nasty.

"Uh huh. Okay." She flipped her gorgeous long hair over one shoulder. "Well, let's get to it!" She led us out of the penthouse and to the elevator. Hector sent a disapproving glance my way, and I cringed and mouthed a "sorry" behind Angelina's back.

★ ★ ★ ★

Hector and Angelina had me locked in a dressing room at Gucci. They'd coerced me into trying on everything from dresses, to skirts, to jeans, and what I would call a mumu. Tasteful clothes with a style and flare I didn't share. After every outfit I had to come out of the dressing room and model the clothes for them. As in, get up on a pedestal in front of the mirror wall from hell, while they dissected everything from the way a hemline fell to something called empire waist. They poked and prodded at me as if I was an animal in a cage. Arguably, the clothes they decided were must-haves did look good on me, but the entire process felt degrading.

Throughout it all, Angelina kept up a dialogue about her brother and our relationship. It was starting to wear and not in the good way the pair of slacks I'd just taken off had.

"So have you and Tony set a date for the wedding yet?" Angelina asked.

I shook my head. "Not yet."

She pulled at the top I was wearing flattening it against my hips. "Really? I mean, you've been dating on and off forever right? At least, that's what Tony said."

"You could say that."

"I guess I don't understand what the holdup is. Mama said she's going to talk to you and Tony about a wedding this month while you're here. Just make it all official." Both Hector and I stopped and stared at Angelina, neither one of us moving a muscle. "What?"

Hector got back his breath far quicker than I did. "You aren't serious?" His dark eyes were wide on his face and his lips pulled into a deep scowl. He was not holding it together very well.

"Hector," I warned.

Angelina shrugged. "It's not like it's a big deal right? I mean you're in love, you're not getting any younger and Mama wants that male heir. She's having lunch with Tony now as a matter of fact."

My mouth dropped open and I'm pretty sure my eyes were bugging out of my head. Suddenly it got way too warm in the dressing room. I fanned at my face. "Um, Tony and I haven't really thought about the details."

"Doesn't matter. What Mama wants, Mama gets. Right, Hector?" she looked over at Hector who was walking backwards slowly until he'd hit the end of a chair and fell into it. "Right?"

Hector nodded, put his elbows on his knees and hung his head while running his hands through his hair. I'd not seen a man this defeated since I told Wes I couldn't stay. I jumped off the pedestal and knelt down in front of Hector. When he lifted his head, there were unshed tears in his eyes. I clasped his cheeks and shook my head trying to convey silently that it wouldn't happen. No way. No how. Tony loved him. He closed his eyes and breathed through his nose. One solitary tear slid down his cheek.

"It will never be me," he whispered.

"But it is you," I swore with as much finality as I could muster. I brought our foreheads close and repeated it. "It is you, *you* he loves."

Unfortunately, both of us forgot who was in attendance during our little bonding session.

"I knew it!" Angelina said and slumped into the chair next to Hector.

That's when Hector turned into a different person. His spine stiffened, his hands locked around his knees and he sat up. It was if he'd transformed back into cool, calm, all-together Hector everybody knew and loved. Not the love-stricken mess of a man battling some serious issues with his mate.

"Uh, Hector's just going through something, and I'm helping…"

"You're helping him and Tony pull the wool over the family's eyes about them being together."

I did not expect that. Hector's eyes turned a startling greenish brown color. "I don't know what you mean…" He tried and failed…miserably.

"Save it. You think I don't know that you and my brother have been in love since college? What do you take me for? I'm Tony's best friend. Well, besides you that is."

"He told you?" he whispered.

She shook her head. "No, but I know Tony. And I know you. Neither of you have had a partner all these years. Once and a great while Tony would bring a 'date' to dinner but it was always obvious he wasn't interested in her. Though I will say, when you popped up, I got a little concerned." She glanced at me and smirked. "If there was ever a woman that could make a gay man straight it would be you."

"What an oddly awkward compliment. Thanks…I think." I sat down on the floor in front of both of them. "So what now?"

Angelina shrugged. "Tony needs to tell Mama."

Hector shook his head so fast I thought it might disconnect from the spine. "Not an option. He does not want to disappoint Mona or the family. Plus, there's business issues involved, and the boxing league he still enjoys."

"Screw the league. He doesn't even box that much for them anymore since Pops died. Sides, Rocko has all that under control, and Tony can participate any time he wants. The league is a bullshit excuse."

"And the business?" Hector egged her on. "What of that? You think a family company like Fasano's can handle the tarnish to its image having a gay man running the helm?"

Angelina shrugged. "Work is work. I don't really care what the business thinks."

Hector sighed. "But Tony does. It's everything to him."

I placed my hand on Hector's knee. "No, I think you've got that wrong. You're everything to him."

Hector stood abruptly. "No offense Mia, but if that were true, you wouldn't be here." With those parting words he left the dressing room.

Getting up off the floor I slumped into the chair next to Angelina. "What a mess."

"Yeah it is. I'd suspected for a long time but this is the first time I ever felt like I had to stick my nose into it. Mia..." Her blue eyes, so like Tony's, were watery. "Mama really believes you're the one. She is convinced that she needs to marry the two of you off so you can get started on baby making." At the last part she bit down on her lip and looked away.

"Hey, it's okay. I'll talk with Hector and Tony. We'll figure something out. It will all be okay. I can stage a big breakup or something. No need to get so upset."

"It's not that, it's just, Rocko and I have been trying for some time to have a baby and nothing's happening. Mama doesn't even ask about it. It's all about Anthony having a son and carrying on the name."

I petted her on her back. "That's got to be difficult. Always feeling like second fiddle."

She huffed. "There's five of us, Mia." Her tone was tired, sounding drained of all life. "Someone is always second, third, fourth or fifth. It's just Tony's always number one."

I heard what she was saying and understood it. After dinner with the family and seeing the way Mona doted on her son and her grandchildren, the fact that Tony went so far as to hire an escort to pretend to be his fiancée to fool his mother showed the kind of power she held over the family.

"So what do you think we should do?"

Angelina stood and picked up the clothes we'd decided upon. I went over to the clothes I'd arrived in and started to put them back on.

"I don't know about Mama yet. The league will survive just fine. The business, well, we'll hire Tony an amazing publicist. Someone who can spin the fact that Tony's gay into something not warranting any news. I run Marketing, and I can brainstorm with my team, come up with some ideas. Either way, it's *our* family's company." She sounded more confident the more she spoke. "The news that the President is gay may be fodder for some talk for a while, but we have a good product. We won't go broke or lose the bulk of our business. People love Mama's recipes, and the prices are solid on a blue collar budget."

"It is damn good food. Best Italian I've ever had."

"Exactly! Tony needs to just get out of the habit of trying to please everyone. Trying to be everything to everyone. You know?"

Instead of responding, I nodded. It was true. I did know. More than I was willing to admit to someone who was virtually a stranger. Ever since my mom left, I tried to keep the family together. Do everything that needed to be done.

Take care of Dad when he was three sheets to the wind. No problem, Mia would handle it.

Help Maddy get through school. Yep, I'd work with her on her homework and stay up late into the evening hours trying to catch up on my own studies. But Maddy always came first.

I even made sure food was on the table and a roof over our heads. I worked my ass off at sixteen waiting tables in casinos to make a buck. Some nights I'd bring home the leftover buffet items before they changed it over the next day. Those were belly filling nights for sure. Even Dad would pat me on the back and tell me "good work" in one of his drunken slurs.

Of course, I'd done it all while under the age of eighteen. Hell, I'd worked enough jobs by the time I was eighteen to collect Social Security. Even now. I was an escort to bail my dad out of debt. Really, I had no business trying to tell someone else how to live their life since I'd sucked so horribly at living mine. However, all of that was changing. Things were slowly getting better. I now had resources. People who cared about my wellbeing. Maddy, Ginelle, Millie, Wes, even Alec would help me out of a jam. I couldn't put a price on that. And I liked Tony and Hector. Believed they were meant to be.

"I just want to help Tony and Hector in whatever way I can."

"How did they find you anyway?"

I wasn't sure what I should say. If I told her I was a hired escort would she think poorly of me? Usually when the term escort was used, people immediately thought hooker or call girl, but in my case, it wasn't true. Well, it mostly wasn't true. Technically, I did sleep with Wes and Alec. And admittedly, I drooled over Tony initially, but those feelings were long gone.

Angelina seemed to wait patiently for me to work through my response in my head, which I appreciated. There was a quiet calm about her. An admirable trait for sure. I stopped and glanced at her pretty face. Her eyes were kind, serene and so blue a person would want to swim in them.

"I'm an escort."

Her eyebrows rose to her hairline and she gasped. Then, instead of cursing or calling me out for my profession, she tipped her head back, her hair a wave of black satin down her back and laughed. A full belly, piggy-snorting guffaw that had her in stitches in mere seconds. Her laughter was infectious, and I couldn't help but join in.

When we met up with Hector at the register we both had tears streaming down our faces. "What in the world happened to you two?" Hector looked from me to Angelina. We both tried to stop laughing and failed. Finally, I caught my breath.

"She found out what I did for a living," I chuckled. That got his attention. He clasped Angelina's elbow and pulled her close.

"It's not what it looks like." Hector spoke through

clenched teeth.

"That you're paying for Mia's service for the month to get Mama off your back so you and Tony can go on living your life?"

"Okay, so it's exactly what it looks like."

That started both of us back on our laughing jag. Hector paid for the clothes then led us both outside. In the limo we got things back under control. Hector turned to Angelina and clasped her hand. "You can't tell Mona. She'll be devastated. I've promised Tony we'd get through this and I support his decision. He feels Mona is incapable of understanding what we are to one another. Knows that she believes real love is between a man and a woman."

"Even if it means he'll be hiding your love forever?"

Hector's shoulders slumped and he frowned. He closed his eyes as if he was thinking. We both waited. "If that's what it means to have your brother's love, that it has to be in private? Then that has to be enough for me. I love him. I'd do anything for him."

★ ★ ★ ★

Turned out Hector wasn't lying. He played the game well. Over the next week with the Fasanos we made appearances at business functions and family events. I spent most of my time with Hector and really just served as Tony's 'piece on the side' or trophy when he needed a pretty thing dangling from his arm. It annoyed me on so many levels. Not because I was being used for my looks but because I knew every time Tony introduced me as his fiancée and people gushed over our relationship it killed Hector a bit more every time.

Something had to be done. I just didn't know what.

CHAPTER SEVEN

"She'll be here any minute," Hector skidded into the kitchen in his dress socks. "Where the hell are my shoes?"

"*Papi*, why are you wearing shoes anyway?" Tony smirked while checking out Hector's feet.

"Ugh," Hector groaned. "He doesn't get it." While practically running past me he stopped cold. "Are you wearing that?" Those dark eyes of his assessed my tank and jeans. By the pinched, sour twist to his lips, he found the look lacking.

"I thought your mom coming over to make dinner with us was casual." I tugged on my tank, making sure it covered the slip of skin between my jeans and shirt. I'd left my hair down and wild. It was my best feature. Aside from my tits. Those were pretty awesome.

Tony glanced my way, gave me his own assessment and shrugged. "Hector's the style guy. You look fine to me."

I placed my hands on my hips. "See, I look fine to him," I said sticking my tongue out at Hector. "You're the one acting insane. What's the deal anyway?" Hector ignored my questions and stomped off. "Seriously. Why is he acting like he should be committed?"

"Oh he's committed all right, to making Mama believe he's the perfect man."

"He is," I said and Tony nodded. He stared off down the hall where Hector had stormed off. "You do think that, right?"

"Of course I do." His eyebrows pulled together as he cocked his head to the side. "I wouldn't have been with him for all these years if I didn't."

Honesty time. I'd been dancing around between Hector and Tony for the better part of two weeks. I felt as though I had a pretty good handle on the dynamic. Hector seemed to be the passive, less dominant of the two and Tony the alpha male. Maybe I could appeal to that side of him and get him to see what would lie beyond my time here, and if he doesn't come clean with his mother and family soon about his relationship with Hector, he stood to lose something he's always had…Hector's trust.

"Look Tony, it's been great being here and I love spending time with Hector and you."

"We've enjoyed having you, Mia. Truly. You're welcome back here any time. Helping us through this bind, it means a lot."

"Well, technically you're paying for it." I grinned and he smiled.

"It's just, I was wondering, have you thought about coming out?" Tony's smile turned into a frown. I held my hands out and stepped closer. "Just hear me out."

His shoulders slumped and he leaned against the counter and crossed his arms over his chest. Damn, those arms. Even gay they still made me drool. I shook my head and leaned on the opposite counter.

"Look, your sister Angelina knows the truth." Tony's eyes widened and his jaw clenched. "I didn't tell her! I swear. She figured it out last week when we shopped. Said she'd known since college."

Tony took in a breath and let it out, scraping his hand along his five o'clock shadow. Christ the man was handsome. "Jesus, so what did you say? Does Hector know?"

"He was there." I looked down at my bare feet. Hector had painted my toes a siren red along with my fingers. He did a great job. "Your sister basically wondered why you hadn't come out."

"And what did you say?"

"Me?" I held a hand to my heart and shook my head. "I didn't say jack shit!" I could hear the tone in my voice getting louder, but I couldn't help it. Irritation at the entire situation was like a fully loaded gun and the trigger was being squeezed. "Hector basically told her that you didn't want to disappoint your family, and the business and the boxing league could be issues. But mostly you were worried about how your mother would take it." Tony's shoulders slumped. He turned and braced both hands on the counter. It was as if the weight of the entire Fasano name hung like a heavy albatross around his neck.

"You know, Mia, it's so tiring. Always hiding, worrying about who might find out, what it would mean to Mama and the family. How the public might take it. I couldn't bear the thought of hurting my family and Hector in the process just for my own selfish desires."

I walked the couple steps and placed both hands on his back. "It's not selfish to want to be with the person you love, Tony."

"Isn't it?"

"No, it isn't. It's your basic human right. And Hector loves you. He wants nothing more than for you to be shouting it from the rooftops or at the very least allowing him to." I chuckled and rested my forehead on his back. He turned around and gathered me into his arms. Yep, they were wonderful. Warm, strong, and secure. Just as I'd expected. Tony was quite possibly the best hugger around.

"I don't know what to do." Tony whispered into the crown of my head.

"Yes you do. You've always known. You just have to do it."

He shook his head. "The timing hasn't been right."

I leaned back and looked into his eyes. His arms stayed loosely around my waist. "It's never going to be a good time to hurt someone." Tony winced, and I placed a hand over his heart. "But, once it's done, it's done forever. You don't have to worry about it anymore. You move on. Everyone moves on."

"And the league?"

"Angelina said that you weren't that involved anymore anyway, and it's no one's business." He tilted his head to the side, his eyes focused on mine. "Besides, as a huge sponsor, they wouldn't risk losing you. Plus, look at you? You're a giant among little people. And you're fucking hot. Everyone—and I mean *everyone*—will want to see all this," I waved a hand up and down his front, "slicked up and beating the shit out of another guy…gay or not." I winked and grinned.

Tony laughed then backed up. He swept a hand through his black hair. "And the business?"

"Again, Angelina says she's Marketing. She'll hire some fancy publicist PR guru to work their magic for a shit ton of money. Thinks it's something that will be big news for a short time, no more than a few months. Then it will blow over and business as usual. The food is too good and too affordable to go under for something like the President's sexual orientation."

He sighed, went over to the fridge and pulled out a beer and twisted off the top. In two huge slugs he finished it. Watching Tony eat and drink was like watching a professional eating competition. The man could just put things away as if his jaw was unhinged.

"And what of Mama, the family line? Everything is *not* so easy." His tone turned a smidge harsh.

I nodded and tilted my head to the side. "It will be hard and she may get mad, cry, or hell, she may even throw something. That is one fiery Italian!" And the smile was back. All white, even teeth. Too pretty for his own good. Then again, in my experience, most gay guys were too pretty or too good looking. "And you and Hector talked about having a family?" I asked dying to know, but being too afraid to stick my nose any further in their business.

Tony grabbed another beer and popped the top off tossing the cap on the counter where the other one was. "Yeah, he says he definitely wants to have kids and soon." Tony's smile got brighter, as if the sun was shining directly on him. Only thing, he wants us to be married or have some type of commitment ceremony first."

"I can see that. If you're going to bring a child into the world, the smart thing to do would be to get married first."

Tony's lips pursed together. "I guess I just never saw us getting married. It seems so old-fashioned and formal. Our relationship has always just been. There was never any pomp and circumstance. We just fit together you know? Like puzzle pieces."

"Is that how Hector feels about it? Because even only

knowing Hector for the past couple weeks, he definitely seems like the type of guy that would appreciate a little pomp and circumstance. A real big show of affection."

"You've been hanging out with Angie too much, Mia. You're turning into one of them."

I shook my head emphatically. "Nuh uh. No way. If I ever get married, which the odds are very, very slim, I'd just go to Vegas."

Tony's arm came out and he pointed at me. His smile now split from ear to ear. "See! I agree with that. A marriage in Vegas. Perfect!"

"Over my dead body," said the voice of none other than Mona Fasano from behind us.

"Mama! We didn't hear you come in." Tony went over to his mother and kissed both cheeks then hugged her. Hector was standing behind her with daggers in his eyes. I shook my head and tried with eye gestures to express that it wasn't what he thought.

Mona came over to me. She pulled me into a hug, kissed both cheeks then held me back at arm's length. Her steely eyes traced my form. "Yep, perfect for making my babies," she gushed before clapping her hands together. "Hector my boy," she called over her shoulder.

"Yes, Mama," Hector returned.

"What are we cooking, dear boy?" She turned and placed a hand on his cheek. The way she held his face was clearly affectionate. She loved him like a son. Hopefully, that would help when the truth came out. If Tony ever got his head out of his ass.

"Enchiladas!"

"Not Italian?" I asked surprised that the Italian mother

of all mothers, wouldn't be making one of her famous dishes.

Mona shook her head. "No. When I cook with my Hector, we make food from his heritage. Gives me the opportunity to broaden my skills. Someday I will make a dish that's Italian and Mexican fusion of cultures and sell it at the restaurant." Mona pushed on my hips edging me out of the kitchen to one of the bar stools. "Now, you go sit and we'll talk while Hector and I cook. *Capisce?*"

Sounded good to me. Tony handed me a beer then took the stool next to mine.

"So, what is this I hear about a Vegas wedding?" Mama Mona went right for the gut.

"Ma, we were just talking. It didn't mean anything." Tony said it to his mother's back while she worked over the stove, but his eyes were glued to Hector's. "I'd never run off and marry Mia. Never." His voice was breathy, as if he'd whispered it loud enough for all of us to hear on purpose. Hector's eyes closed slowly. When they opened they were back to being filled with love, lust, and hope. It was so clear how much Hector adored Tony and vice versa. The stigma attached to their love was creating a wedge that could eventually bring down the wall around their relationship. If that happened, everything would come out in a flood that could drown what they had. That thought alone drove nails into my soul.

"Good, because you are a good Catholic boy. You will get married in our church. St. Peter's. The same church your father and I were married in all those years ago," she said with triumph. "Admittedly, I was worried for some time that you would never marry. Now that we have Mia…" Her head turned and her smile in my direction was glorious. It literally shattered my heart into a thousand guilty shards. "…our family will be complete and you will carry on the Fasano name."

Mona put down the wooden spoon she was holding, turned around and hugged Tony. "You make me and your father so proud. If he was here today, he'd bless this union happily." She wiped a few tears from her eyes, cleared her throat and went back to work. Hector swallowed visibly, choking back the emotion I knew had to be tearing him apart.

"Speaking of Church, Father Donahue will be happy to perform the marriage. You'll need to sign up for counseling though. Perhaps this coming weekend?"

I'm pretty sure my eyes popped out of their sockets. Church? Counseling? I shook my head. "Um…I don't know about that," I started, but Tony cut me off.

"Ma, we're not decided on a date. We also haven't discussed our religion."

Mona's head flew back as if she'd been stricken. "What? That's one of the first things you discuss. Mia dear, are you Catholic?"

"I'm not anything. I uh…" Mona's eyes seared into mine like white hot points. "I wasn't raised in a religion."

She blew out a breath. "Have you been baptized Christian?" Her tone was accusatory. Instantly fear tingled against my spine which automatically triggered my defense mechanism.

"No." I clenched my jaw, my spine straightening.

"Have you been married before?" She placed a hand on her hip, the other still holding the spoon.

I shook my head, and she mimicked it. "Son, she's going

to have to start coming to our church immediately. In order to get married, she's going to need to be in good standing with St. Peters, and you will likely have to undergo the longer version of counseling in order for our priest to marry you to a non-Catholic. And, she'll need to be baptized. Soon. That is paramount. We need to get started immediately."

The weight of what she'd said flattened me like a steamroller. I had to get out of there. "Oh my god," I got up off the chair feeling freaked out. My lungs felt tight, and I could feel a bead of sweat building at my hairline. I couldn't breathe. Air. I needed air, right now. In a jumble of limbs I rushed to the balcony, flung open the door and sucked in the chilly March Chicago air. Thank God. No, not God. There would be no more talk of God that evening. I'd make sure of it.

Two strong arms came around me. Even though they were wonderful, they weren't the arms I wanted. Wes. I wished he was there. He'd get a kick out of this. From escort to mail-order bride. "Mia, it's okay. Don't let Ma get to you. We'll figure this out." Tony held me from behind. I took in long, slow breaths. The rapid beat of my heart started to go back to normal. When I felt I could stand on my own two feet I turned around and held a hand out to Tony pushing him back.

"You have got to tell your mother the truth. This is going too far."

He hung his head in shame. "I know. I just…it's so heavy. You know?"

"Yeah I do."

We both sat down in the lounge chairs facing one another. "But I'm not the only one that's getting slammed here. Hector is not handling this well."

Tony's head shot up and there were worry lines at the corner of his eyes. "What do you mean?"

I clasped his hands with both of mine and squeezed tight. "By not accepting who you are, you're not accepting him." Tony's eyes narrowed but he kept quiet. "This omission of the truth...I hate to say it Tony, but it needs to be said." He tipped his chin gesturing me to continue. "Look at it from Hector's perspective. You're basically saying that he's not good enough. That his love is not worth the risk."

He gasped and pulled back. "That is not true! I love him."

"Really? Then why are you hiding it?"

"You know why." Tony's voice was scathing, his jaw tight.

"Not good enough. Those are excuses, and after years, what? Close to fifteen years you've been using those excuses. It's time to set yourself free. Make him your priority. The same way he does you. All these years he could have outed you to your family, your friends, your business but he didn't. He has been content to stay in the background as long as he had you. Your happiness is what's important to him, but I swear, this plan of yours to fool your family to keep the charade going...it's killing him. I can see it in his eyes, why can't you!"

"Fuck! Why did this have to get so complicated?"

"It's life, Tony. Grow up. Choose Hector no matter the cost. That's what he's done for you. He put your happiness above his own because he chose *you*."

With that parting shot I left the balcony. Hector and his mother were waiting in the living room when I walked through heading to my room.

"Mia…" Hector's voice shook when he said my name, but I kept walking. Then I realized that in my anger I was being rude. To my clients, to Mona, to the people I'd come to care a great deal for.

I stopped before the hall and turned around. "I'm sorry. Suddenly I'm not feeling well. I'm going to bed for the night. Thank you Mona for coming. I'm sure your dinner would have been great."

Hector came over to me and stopped my progression down the hall. He pulled me into a hug and tears filled my eyes. "I'm sorry. We're sorry. Both of us." Hector spoke so quietly only I could hear. Jesus, this man was incredible.

"I know. I just need some space after tonight."

He let me go, and I went back to my room. I laid down on the bed, grabbed my phone and dialed the one person I shouldn't. It rang four times before the answering machine picked up.

"You've got Wes, leave a message after the beep and I'll get back to you soon as possible." Wes's voice was a strong rumble that came through the phone and powered straight into my heart.

Beep

"Hey, it's me, uh, Mia. I just…" I took a long breath and tried to think of what I wanted to say but came up with nothing that sounded less than desperate. "I needed to hear your voice." I closed my eyes. "We'll talk soon. Okay? Bye."

CHAPTER EIGHT

For the next week, things were strained between the trio we'd become. I was an outsider, and for the first time in three weeks, I felt like one. Tony was stressed, barely grunting hello's and goodbyes in the mornings. Hector was nicer, softer, still stressed, though it wasn't directed at me. Clearly, he was having issues with Tony and was reluctant to talk to me about them, which was understandable. I'd thrown a tizzy fit when dealing with the mother last weekend. I wasn't proud of my actions but still held fast to the fact that it needed to be said. The continued dance around this issue was ravaging the relationship and torturing both parties. Not to mention the strain of lying to one's family had to be hitting their consciences hard.

Then there was me, the chick stuck in the middle.

I stood in a bra and panties in front of the closet trying to decide what to wear. The March air in Chicago was chilly but mostly comfortable.

"Hey, get your hot pants on and your leather jacket," Hector said from the open doorway. I was so lost in my own thoughts that I didn't even hear him open the door. He entered and sat on the bed while I grabbed a pair of dark skinny jeans. He stood, pulled down a thin green sweater and a kick ass dark chocolate leather jacket. I went about putting on the clothes he chose for me while staying silent. When Hector wanted to talk, he did so in private, and usually encroached upon a person's personal space. I pulled up the jeans then he handed me the sweater, and I slipped it on.

"I know he loves me," he said while reaching into the closet to pull out a pair of knee high boots with killer straps of leather that had a crisscross pattern up the length. They were buttery soft and probably cost more than the car I bought for my sister Maddy. Instead of responding, I just sat on the bed quietly. Hector knelt down, lifted my foot and helped me slide into the boot. "It's just that he's so afraid of disappointing his mother. Before, it was his father I thought he was afraid to tell. Joseph Fasano was a man's man. Straight-up Italian and very old-fashioned. When he passed last year I thought maybe…just maybe he'd tell them. Mona loves me. Treats me like her own son." He looked up and there were tears in his kind, brown eyes.

I leaned forward and cupped both cheeks. "Yes she does."

"So I thought…" he shook his head. "It was too much to hope for. And now, I don't know. With you here, with all the talk of marriage and babies it just makes me wish for more. You know? The life that we should have had all these years."

A tear of my own slipped down my cheek. He brushed it away with his thumb. "Oh sweet Mia, none of this is your fault."

"Isn't it? I'm the one who's here."

"Because we brought you here." He frowned.

"True. You're right. This is *so* not my fault." I smirked and Hector laughed lightly breaking up the tension.

"Come, Tony and I are taking you out on a date. We

have something to show you." Hector reached into the closet and pulled out a bright green scarf. So bright I'd never willingly wear it.

"What's with all the green?"

Hector's eyes widened and he gasped. "Mia, its St. Patrick's Day. The entire city celebrates St. Paddy's in a big way, and we are too! It's our favorite holiday. No sadness, no worries, nothing but fun, friendship, and love today. You in?"

A huge sense of relief filled my lungs, chest, and heart. "I'm so in!"

"Come on, *señorita*, let's go!"

★ ★ ★ ★

A swift gust of wind blew my hair behind me as we exited the car. "Holy smokes it is windy!" I said to the two guys as each took one of my elbows.

"That's why they call it the windy city. Don't worry; wait a half hour and the weather will change." I looked up at Tony giving him the you're-blowing-smoke-up-my-ass look. "Seriously, it's a phenomenon. Lived here all my life. Never had a day where the weather stayed exactly the same."

"You should move to California. The weather is perfect every day there." I grinned and he shook his head.

"Oh, I see a spot at the railing over there." Hector pointed across a large patch of grass over to where a metal railing was in the distance. A crowd of people were hoarded all down the line of railing overseeing a large body of water.

We headed over and stopped at the rail. "Where are we?" I asked looking into the waves. The water was choppy and splashing up against the sides of the concrete below. We were at least a good ten feet or so from the actual water but you could still feel the shift in temperature the closer we were to the water.

"Chicago River,"Tony said with pride, his chest puffing out. I looked at Hector, and he rolled his eyes.

"Don't look at me. This is Tony's thing. I'm originally from San Diego." With a gloved hand, he pointed up and down his body.

I shoved his shoulder. "I didn't know you were from California."

He tilted his head and looked out at the water. "Yeah, went away for college, met Tony at Columbia then moved here with him after graduation."

"Columbia? Wow." I knew these guys were smart but had no idea they were Ivy League smart. Me, I was a college dropout. However, I was currently making a hundred thousand a month. Not too shabby for a former casino waitress from Vegas.

Tony moved around and got in between both of us then put an arm around our shoulders. "It's gonna happen right now. Mia, look at that boat!" His voice was tinged with excitement. It was the happiest I'd seen Tony all week. He had a beautiful smile and I missed it. His big arms hugged Hector and me close. Out of nowhere, Tony looked over his shoulder, scanned the area and then said, "What the hell!" He turned to me and kissed me very briefly on the lips, the way a brother would his sister. Then he turned to Hector and laid a big, fat, lusty kiss on him. It went on for a long time. So long even I was blushing when it ended.

Hector's eyes were the size of baby cats. "Happy St. Paddy's, *Papi*," Tony said and kissed him lightly on the mouth again. Hector's corresponding smile revealed shock, awe, and love.

Joy. Pure joy. Hector's, mine, and Tony's filled our little huddle as a boat shot down the Chicago River spraying green stuff into the water.

"What the hell is he doing polluting the water with that gunk?" I pointed, horrified at the display before us. .

Tony shook his head. "They are dyeing the river green!" He was practically bouncing out of his shoes. "It's tradition and non-toxic." I narrowed my eyes and waited for him to continue. "As part of a more than fifty-year tradition, the Chicago River is dyed green in observance of St. Patrick's Day. It will take days to dissipate. They use vegetable dye that won't hurt the fish or pollute the water. It's even sponsored by the local Plumbers Union."

I had to admit, it was really cool. The boat sprayed the concoction all along the river jetting back and forth down the stretch of space. Bright fluorescent green swirls comingled with the waves and spread the color out. Reminded me of Van Gogh's Starry Night the way the green made spirals in the water. I'd never seen anything like it. A city actually dyed a body of water green for a holiday, one that wasn't even a national holiday.

I shook my head repeatedly not able to comprehend how unique and utterly random the sight was. "What's the deal with St. Patrick's Day anyway?"

Tony pulled us both close, eyes glued to the water while he spoke. "It's a celebration of the bringing of Christianity to Ireland. For this day, the Catholic Church lifts the ban on alcohol and fasting for Lent to celebrate."

For a moment, I thought hard about what he'd said.

"Are you Irish?" I looked up at Hector and he shook his head grinning. I turned and focused on Tony.

"Nope," Tony responded.

"Then what's the big deal?" The importance of this event made absolutely no sense.

Tony pointed out to the water as if he was Vanna White. "An entire river was painted green in observance of a Saint from my faith. Anything related to the church is a big deal," he said deadpan. A tiny quirk curved the edge of his lips. I could feel the grip of his fingers around my bicep as he tried to hold back what was most certainly laughter.

"You just like to party. Admit it!" I jabbed him in the ribs with my elbow.

"Ouch!" He laughed out loud and Hector joined in. "Come on Mia, we've got a pub with our name on it."

My eyes widened as the cool air flapped my hair into Hector's face. "Sorry." He winked and continued forward. "You guys own a pub, too?"

Tony chuckled. "Have you always been so literal?"

"Not especially, but I don't usually hang out with rich dudes. I figure anything is possible when you guys are playing with your monopoly money."

"Come on, it's time to make friends with an Irish lad named Jamison." Tony's large form helped deflect the wind that was pummeling me.

"You know, that Jamison, he's an old friend of mine. It will be nice to get reacquainted," I grinned.

"Now you're talking!" Tony beamed and led us to the car.

★ ★ ★ ★

The guys brought me to a place called Declan's Irish Pub. We entered through a huge red door with black wooden trim. The sign outside was black with the words "Declan's" in gold cursive script. It was dark inside. A humming noise could be heard all around as we navigated through the patrons and found our way up to the bar. Three seats right up front were empty. A shot glass with a paper napkin on top that had the word "Reserved" written in black sharpie sat in front of the empty seats. Tony held out my stool and I sat down.

"Reserved seats at a bar?" I laughed shaking my head.

"Every year, *chica.*" Hector said.

"I know a guy," Tony said in that thick Chicago Italian drawl I've gotten used to over the past three weeks.

"You think you know a guy you fucking dago!" The bartender held out his hand. Tony leaned over the wooden bar and brought the ginger-haired man to his chest for a man hug. "Dec, how the hell are you, you fucking mick!" Tony spat out his own derogatory remark. For women, those would be fighting words. The red-head just took it in stride.

"Eh, business is good." He held his arms out gesturing to the full bar.

"It's St. Paddy's ya jagoff. Of course it's going to be packed." Tony continued to mess with the man who he'd called Dec.

"Who's the *Stella*? I know she isn't yours." The man's green eyes went to Hector's knowingly. Hector put out a hand and shook Dec's hand.

"This here is Mia. She's a friend from out of town and we're showing her around."

"And of course you had to bring her to my pub, because

it has the best food and whiskey in Chicagoland."

"Fuckin' A," Tony responded, his accent thick as wool.

"Well Mia, it's a pleasure. I'm Dec, or Declan." He held out his hand, I placed mine in his, but instead of shaking it he brought it to his mouth and kissed my knuckles. A little flurry of excitement tingled from my hand through my arm and over my body. His green eyes dazzled as he waggled his eyebrows.

Tony knocked my hand out of his. "Knock it off asshole. Now where's our drinks? And some menus."

Dec laughed, threw a bar towel over his shoulder and slid us three menus. Then he promptly poured us each a shot of Jamison Irish Whiskey and one for himself.

We all held out our shots, clinked glasses as Dec said, "Bottoms up!"

My phone pinged in my back pocket at the same time I slammed the shot glass back down on the table.

From: Wes Channing
To: Mia Saunders
Happy St. Patrick's Day. You know what they say about green eyes?

Hector's eyebrow rose toward his hairline when he saw the smile on my face. I held the phone close to my chest and read the message. Hector blatantly read over my shoulder, so I gave up and put it in front of both of us as I typed back.

From: Mia Saunders
To: Wes Channing
No, I don't. What do they say?

Instantly he responded.

From: Wes Channing
To: Mia Saunders
Where are you?

From: Mia Saunders
To: Wes Channing
An Irish Pub in Downtown Chicago called Declan's. Are you going to tell me what they say about green eyed girls?

From: Wes Channing
To: Mia Saunders
They're always up to something. Are you up to something?

From: Mia Saunders
To: Wes Channing
As a matter of fact, yes. Getting my drink on. Happy St. Paddy's Day!

I waited a few minutes but no response came. Strange. He must have been called away. Hector and I shared a glance then he shrugged, lifted up a hand and pointed at the two empty shot glasses. Declan promptly filled our glasses. "Want a beer, too?" he asked.

"Hell yes!" I slugged back the whiskey and breathed fire. The burn was nothing to the thoughts that were spinning around and around about Wes. Thinking of him too much and too often was foolish, and I was no fool. "And more shots!"

For the next hour, Hector and Tony told me stories of their youth, how they met Declan at Columbia and crazy enough, they all ended up in Chicago. Been friends ever since. Stood to reason why Declan surreptitiously insinuated he knew of their true relationship. He must be one of the few. Turned out he was also one of the guys that did the naked run across the football field.

All three guys had me in stitches until the laughter took its toll on my overfull bladder. I got up from my chair and swiveled around.

"Where you going?" Tony put a hand to my bicep.

"Breaking the seal." I shimmied in my jeans a little from foot to foot.

Tony's face scrunched up in disgust. "Nah, don't do that. You'll fuck yourself. You'll have to piss every twenty minutes now."

"Can't help it! And shut up!" I punched his arm and he acted affronted.

"Lightweight." He rubbed at his arm smiling. I knew for a fact I'd hit him pretty hard. Hopefully, he would have a nice purple bruise to show for it. Doubtful though. Those cannons were pretty tight. Probably felt more like a pinch than a punch. I snickered to myself about his caveman-like size as I made my way to the bathroom.

I did my business, washed my hands. In one of my more girlie moments, I bent over, flung my hair forward, and tussled my fingers through it and swung back up giving it some body. I had to throw out a hand to hold myself up. Time to eat. The whiskey was doing a number on me, and without food, I knew I'd be on the floor soon. Fucking lightweight my ass. Men think they have it all up over women. They don't know shit. Excuse me if I'm half the size of the giant who can drink a bottle to his head and probably not feel a thing. He should be happy I was a cheap date. Humphf. Indignant, I walked back out and pushed my way into the crowd.

It had picked up quite a bit since we first arrived. The after dinner crowd was fully in place and the pub was hopping with bodies everywhere. Celtic music played loudly keeping the Irish vibe going. I started wiggling to the beat when I ran face first into a hard body.

"Ouch," I rubbed at my nose and lifted my head. Even with all the colored lights providing a halo around his form my eyes were riveted to his green ones. I gasped not really believing he was standing there, right in front of me.

"Aren't you going to say anything, sweetheart?" The long dirty blond layers of his hair fell into his eyes.

"I can't believe you're here…"

His green eyes scanned my body. "Christ, you're a sight for sore eyes. Come here." And then I was there and he was there. My Wes. His lips were warm as they met mine. He tasted of mint and smelled of the ocean. God, I missed the ocean, the salty breeze…*him*. One of Wes's hands held my head in place while his other pulled me close. Our bodies were smashed together. Nothing existed but him and the electric pull of my body to his. I licked the seam of his lips and he opened, allowing me entrance.

Flawless.

Kissing Wes was flawless. Energy spiked in a ball around us as the crowd pushed us this way and that. A bunch of 'excuse me' came from somewhere, but we didn't stop. Couldn't. The magnetic connection spiraled through us both. He kissed me the way it's done in the movies when a man comes back from war and finally sees the woman he loves. Basically, like I was his whole world, and right now, he was mine.

"Holy fuck, get off her!" Tony's voice broke through the crowd only moments before I was ripped away. My arms held out like a marionette's needing its puppet master.

"No, Tony no!" Hector said and pushed himself between Wes and Tony.

"What the hell do you think you're doing?" Wes stepped forward crushing Hector and me in the process.

"No, no, Wes, no! That's Tony!" I pressed hard into Wes's chest trying to hold him back.

"Yeah, and he needs to get his hands off you or we're going to have problems." Wes growled, eyes burning, intent on Tony.

"Is that so?" Tony pushed into us, his frame forcing us into a sandwich.

"Guys, stop. Wes, that's my client. Tony, that's my uh, Wes!" I screamed trying desperately to be heard over the loud music.

Tony's eyes narrowed and Hector pushed him back. "Baby, that's her guy. You know the one I told you about, the surfing movie maker?" I closed my eyes and held my arms out to keep Wes away.

"Your guy? Your surfer movie maker?" Wes chuckled and pulled me to his side. "Is that what you call me?" He whispered into the side of my neck, sending all kinds of happy tingles pinging along my nerves.

By then, the whiskey had caught up with me, perfectly ruining any filter mechanism I had in place and I blurted,

"I could have said, Mr. Fucks Like a God? Would you have preferred that?" I put my arms loosely around his neck and got close, really close. He rubbed his forehead against mine.

"Hell yeah, I'd prefer that. As a matter of fact, tell that to all your clients and any prospective dates and boyfriends from here on out."

I snorted in a very unladylike fashion. "You'd like that wouldn't you?"

"Very much so. Can I meet your friends now that the big one isn't going to pummel me into next week?"

"Oh yeah!" I turned around and Wes put his hands on my hips. Both men watched the action. Hector grinned, Tony scowled. "Guys, this is my friend, Wes. Wes, this is Tony and his er…Hector." I ended with.

"Hector's my *partner*," Tony admitted loud enough for some of the folks around to hear, not that anyone was paying attention or knew him. Still, it was a massive step in the right direction. First the kiss at the river and now a public proclamation? My eyes shot to Hector's. His face detailed his surprise along with a hint of excitement, maybe even love. Then again, Hector always looked at Tony with love in his eyes. It was part of why I enjoyed him so much. He was easy to read and always said what he was thinking and feeling. Honesty like that was unheard of in the circles I'd frequented.

"Wes, sorry about that. But you know, drunk men, a beautiful woman, people can get handsy. I was just looking out for her," Tony slapped Wes on the back and shook his hand with the other.

"Appreciate it. It's good to know my girl is being protected," Wes offered.

My girl. He'd said it when I was with him and he'd said it again. Boy, was I in trouble.

"Well now that you're here, come on over and have some drinks with us." Tony said.

"Don't mind if I do. Lead the way." Wes held out a hand for Tony and Hector to go in front of us.

We all sat down and Wes pushed his chair close enough that he could put his arm around me. It was a clear sign of possession, and I didn't know what to do with that or how to take it. The whiskey pumping through my system wasn't helping because I'd allowed the gesture without saying a thing.

"How long are you staying in Chicago?" Hector asked.

"Just tonight. I've got a flight back to Los Angeles first thing in the morning. Since I was here though, I thought I might meet up with Mia. Hope that was okay?"

I looked up into his sea green eyes and got lost. His lips shined against the lights of the bar and his hair fell onto his forehead. I reached up and pushed it back. He lifted a hand and cupped my cheek. Without realizing it, I leaned into the touch. Not having his affection the last two months was like surviving a drought and only now was I getting a small sip. I needed more. So much more.

"More than okay."

CHAPTER NINE

My back hit the wall as the door slammed shut. Wes's lips, and hands were all over me. Just where I wanted them. The four of us, now drunk, took the limo back to the penthouse. Hector gave me the thumbs up as Tony ushered him to their room. I took that as the okay to have a man here in their home. Though there wasn't much that could have prevented me from staking my claim over Wes that evening. The whiskey combined with the ache to have him, was far too strong to deny. And that's how I came to be flush against the wall with Wes's hard body pinning me in place.

"Christ, I missed you. Missed this body." His hands curled around my breasts. "I need you naked. Now." He squeezed both breasts at the same time earning a low moan from me.

Without hesitation I lifted my shirt over my head and flung it to the floor. His hands pulled at the button of my jeans. Before I could shimmy out of them his hand was *there*. Right *there* feeling me, playing in the wetness he'd coaxed.

Wes's tongue licked from between my breasts up my neck where he stopped at my ear, biting down. "I love the way you feel. How your body responds to me. Proves that regardless of what you might say, you want me."

One long finger went deep, another followed it. So good. My head tipped back and hit the wall. "I never denied wanting you." I admitted breathless.

"But you try to." He pressed his hand deeper, his fingers hooking just the right spot, his talented thumb twirling around the center of my arousal, sending me into a pleasant oblivion. He was right. I did try to deny how much he affected me. Had to. It helped keep distance between us, but not now. In that moment, I was all in.

"I need you," I whispered as the pleasure spiked.

"Have you been with anyone since me?"

"Wes," I warned. This was not the conversation I wanted to be having when his hand was knuckles deep and his palm was being coated with my desire for him.

He kissed me, tongue delving deep before pulling back. "Have you been with anyone bare?"

"Only you," and I meant it. Alec and I had always had sex with condoms. Wes and I hadn't ,but I trusted him, still trusted him. His eyes were dark as they searched mine. Then he removed his hand from inside me, and pushed my pants and panties down. I kicked them off while unbuttoning his pants. He pushed them down just far enough to release his thick cock. Jesus I'd missed that part of him. So long, thick and ready for me.

In one swift move Wes had his hands on my ass and my legs around his waist. "Hold on to my shoulders, sweetheart." I did what he said. When he got the right leverage, he pushed me up the wall, my back grated along the rigid surface, burning the skin. The spike of pain added to the pleasure of the spontaneous moment. Wes pressed the wide knob of his cock at my cleft and pushed in. One of his hands held me at the shoulder the other at the hip. He yanked me down hard, impaling me.

"Oh God." Filled to the brim with his giant cock was

sheer bliss.

"Shhh sweetheart, they'll hear you." He reminded me of where we were. In my room at Hector and Tony's penthouse, fucking my first client while still working for my third. I'm certain there was something psychologically twisted about that but I didn't care. Wes felt so good deep inside me, filling me with everything I missed over the last two months since I'd last seen him.

He pulled out and then pressed back home. His lips came down over mine and I sucked on his tongue, ravaging his mouth, his kiss, like food to a starved woman.

"You remember this." He pulled out then rammed back to the hilt. I gasped and nodded, so far into my lust-induced haze I could only focus on the feeling between my thighs; the intense pleasure building deep in my womb as he moved in and out.

"I won't let you forget how good it is," he said moving out, followed by a sharp twist of his hips in again.

"When I'm gone, I want you to feel me." Out and then with both hands at my hips, he slammed in. I bit down on my lip as lightening shot through me, my body heated, tingled from every pore. One more thrust and I was going to lose it. Give it all up to him just like he wanted.

"Remember me," he said between clenched teeth. Those were the same words he'd said to me the last time we made love. This time they were tinged with pain and pleasure, and everything in between. He slid out, held me high and wrapped his arms completely around my back. I tightened my thighs around his waist and dug the heels of my bare feet into his back. Strung up on his cock, he tipped his hips back pressed me hard against the wall and rammed home.

The orgasm exploded through me, splintering pleasure out in all directions. Wes's lips came down on mine hard, holding me in his kiss as he jerked violently, pumping his release deep within me, bathing my insides with his essence. His mouth prevented my keening cry from spilling past my lips. I bit down hard on his lips as the last vestige of our combined passion slowed and petered out.

Our skin was slick with sweat and coated in our joy for one another. We shared the air panting in each other's faces as we rubbed our foreheads together, sealing the connection we'd had since the very beginning.

"You gonna forget me?" His tone was kind but laced with worry.

"Never," I promised.

"Let's get you cleaned up. I'm nowhere near done with you." He held me close and walked us over to the bathroom across the room.

"Thank God, because I want you again," I announced while peppering kisses all over his face, licking the salty taste of him off his neck, and enjoying the one man that I'd never lose a taste for.

He set me on the vanity and withdrew. Fluid from his release slid onto the tile counter. He stared at the space between my legs watching his essence leave me.

"Now that, I'll be thinking about later," he admitted, a boyish grin firmly in place.

I smacked his shoulder. "Get the shower going, pervert." I reached over and wet the washrag on the counter, cleaned between my thighs and got another to wipe down the counter. I tossed the two cloths into the hamper.

Wes must have used that time well for he was now gloriously naked. Jeans and shoes in a heap on the bathroom floor. His sun-kissed skin and sleek surfer's muscles never looked better. I walked the couple steps to him and placed both hands on his square pecs. I pressed my forehead into his chest and kissed the center. He was warm, familiar, and everything I missed about a life I wanted, but couldn't yet have. Tears started to form as I kissed the skin over his heart.

His hand cupped my cheek and his thumb wiped away a single tear. "I know. Me, too," he said softly. "Let's just enjoy the time we have, yeah?"

I nodded and followed him into the shower. He spent long minutes washing my hair. "It's grown a couple inches."

"Yeah, it grows fast," I said.

"So beautiful," his eyes followed the suds that slipped down my hair, to the tile floor around our feet and down the drain.

While I finished rinsing he soaped up his hands. He never used the buff puff when we showered together back in Malibu. "Hands-on type of guy?" I waggled my eyebrows at him.

"Don't you know it?" He placed his hands on my shoulders and massaged the soap into the tight tissue. It was heavenly. Strong fingers rubbed out every knot I had before moving seductively down my chest and over my breasts. He flipped me around and pressed my back to his front. Then he held both globes in his hands, running his thumbs and forefingers over the erect tips. My nipples twitched and tingled at every pass of his delightful fingers until they were tight and mimicked the tops of pencil erasers. Hard, high and round.

I moaned and leaned back into him, shutting my eyes. "I love your tits. They're large, full, and perfect for my hands. They tighten just so when I slide my fingers over them." His words filled the room as thick as the steam around us, adding to the heady feeling, making it feel dreamlike. Wes played with my breasts until I was gasping, moaning, pressing my hips into the air restlessly.

"What do you want?" He licked a line down my neck as he continued the sweet torture of my now oversensitive breasts.

"I want you inside me. Please." I begged shamelessly.

"Lean forward, sweetheart. Grab onto that towel bar. Tilt that sweet ass for me."

I clutched at the towel bar above my head at the back of the shower. Reminded me of the kind you see in fancy hotel rooms where the towels were away from the spray of water, yet conveniently placed so the guest wouldn't have to leave the warmth of the shower without covering up. In this case, it made a perfect bar for me to hold onto.

Wes lined up his feet alongside me, pressing mine father out. He gripped my hips, tipping them up the way he wanted. I waited, my breath caught in my throat. Excitement buzzed around me like a swarm of angry bees, the anticipation, the knowledge that I'd be struck with his erection tantalizing and forbidden.

Wes rubbed the cheeks of my ass. Expertly he widened my flesh, opening me from behind, then the crown of his cock was at my entrance. The barest hint of his manhood teasing against swollen flesh.

"You want it, sweetheart? You want me to fuck you hard?"

"God yes, please Wes. Love me like you do."

"Love?" He questioned pressing an inch inside. I tried to squeeze my thighs together, to force him further in. He held me back, only allowing movement when he permitted it.

"Yes, show me."

With a twist of his hips, his fingers dug into my sides before he thrust forward...teeth-chattering hard. I held onto the rack, jarred by his movement, my feet lifted up off the ground, hung up on his cock just the way he liked. He set me back down. I couldn't breathe, couldn't move. I'd never been more complete with a man. When he pulled back I almost cried, emotionally needing him to stay within me, stay close.

"Don't leave..." I choked out.

"Right here." One of his hands came over mine on the bar and held. Then he shifted back and pushed in. "Feel me, sweetheart. I'm right here. With you. In you. Part of you."

A fluttering sensation spread out from where we were joined, like butterfly wings flapping all over my body. Teasing, tickling, layering mouthwatering pleasure all over me. It was unusual, different, unlike any sexual experience before it.

"I'm going to come," I told him losing the ability to speak. The pleasure taking my body, mind, and subconscious on a journey I never wanted to come back from.

"Yes," he swirled his hips, stirring his hardness within forcing me to gasp. "You're going to come until I'm done. You're going to squeeze me sweet Mia, proving I control this body. When I'm inside you, it's only us. Me and you. The way it should be." He pulled out and jabbed high and hard. I squealed, lost in a sexual daze once more. Burning, hot electricity zipped through every orifice, searching for a way out, a way to expel the pent up excitement.

That's when the babbling started. He fucked my body in long, consistent strokes. I lost it. Chanting, saying useless, nonsensical things.

"Please…"

"In me…"

"Burning…"

"Now…"

"Love…"

"Hot…"

"Wes…"

That's when Wes slid one of his hands around my waist, the other gripping the bar above as if he was going to do a pull-up. He lifted his muscular body up on his toes and pressed me down on his dick. His rock hard cock reached so high, splitting the tissue inside me wide, forcing his entrance to a place high within that no man had ever been. I lost control. The orgasm shook me. Physically shook me, convulsing around him as if electrocuted. My pussy locked down over him and he roared through his release, his teeth biting down at the juncture where my neck and shoulder met. Spikes of pain shredded through me, adding kerosene to a fire already burning out of control.

He pulled one orgasm after another out of me, until I lost count of how many times he took me over the edge. All I knew is that when he finally stopped fucking me, the water was stone cold and we were both shivering. Wes rinsed my languid body off with the cold water. He covered me with a towel as I stood and leaned against him. There wasn't much more I could do. He'd fucked me dumb. My brain was no longer sending signals to my limbs. Everything just stopped working.

Wes hefted me up and out of the shower once he had me mostly dry. Then he pulled back the covers, put me in bed and snuggled up behind me. His body was plastered against mine, the moisture from the shower gluing us together in a way I adored more than I'd ever admit.

He sighed warmly against my neck. "I don't want to leave you tomorrow." I closed my eyes and pulled his arm around me between my naked breasts. His hands were near my lips. I kissed his fingers.

"You have to go," I whispered knowing that I needed him to leave as much as I wanted him to stay.

"I know." His tone was forlorn but strong.

"But it means a lot that you don't want to." I wanted him to know that this time was important. That any time with him was special.

"Oh Mia, I'm not going to let you take this away from us."

"I don't want you to. For the next nine months, I hope you'll remind me of what could be." I pressed his hand against my cheek and tried to remember how he felt. Lock it into my memory so I could revisit it always.

"I'll never let you forget what you could have. What's waiting for you."

On those words, cocooned within the warmth of his embrace, I slipped into dreamland.

★ ★ ★ ★

The sun streaking through the opened blinds hit me directly in the eyes, tearing me from the most blissful dream of Wes and me surfing. Of course in my dream I was an expert at surfing, even though I could only hold my own as a beginner in the real world. I needed to get back to the ocean to practice if I was ever going to be anywhere near the way dream Mia surfed.

Slowly I snaked a foot out behind me and felt nothing but cold sheets. Startled, I sat up and looked to my right. He was gone. Nothing but an indentation in the pillow next to me and a piece of paper where Wes had been.

The paper must have been pulled from my own stationery that was lying on the desk.

Mia,

Last night was one in a million. Scratch that, it was priceless. Being with you is like hitting the perfect crest, gliding through the ocean on an endless wave. It's exhilarating, frightening, and life altering.

You've changed me, Mia. I no longer believe that the perfect woman doesn't exist, for I've met her, made love to her, and worshipped her the only way I know how.

Since you've given me no other choice, I will stay your friend and continue to remind you of what could be. Nine months and counting. Until the next time, I'll be thinking about you and will call and check on you soon.

When you're ready, you have the key.

Remember me.

Your movie-making surfer dude,

~Wes

I clutched the letter to my bare chest and cried. Cried

for Wes, for me, for what could be. For what I hope to one day have. If he doesn't get stolen away by some other beautiful woman first. Regardless, I had to let him live while I continued this journey. Knowing Wes cared, that he wanted me to remember him, hoped that I would come back to him, was all I'd need to get through the next nine months. But like I'd encouraged Wes, I was going to live. I could not allow my feelings for him to get in the way of what I was doing, or the experiences I'd promised myself.

I had no idea where my life was going to lead me over the next nine months. As much as I'd have liked to thrown caution to the wind and leave it all, let Wes pay off the loan shark and run to him, I had to do this on my own. This year was going to be the year where I decided what I wanted for the rest of my life. Maybe it was Wes, maybe not. Maybe it was California, maybe Timbuktu. No matter how much my heart wanted to run to him, my mind was set. I'd made my decision. For the next nine months, I was going to live whatever life I wanted while I saved my dad from himself.

And I would remember Wes. Our time together, our friendship, what we have when we're together. Alec taught me that lesson, and like him, I loved Wes. In my way. And maybe, if it's meant to be, nine months from now, it will be the forever kind of love.

Just not today.

CHAPTER TEN

Tonight was the celebration of the big Fasano expansion into frozen foods. Celebrity chefs, media, restaurateurs, prospective investors, the entire Fasano clan, and then some would be celebrating at the local Fasano restaurant. I'd heard several cookbook publishers and some TV executives were going to be on location and wanted to talk to Tony about a TV opportunity, and Mama Mona about a Fasano cookbook containing the Fasano original recipes. It was all so very exciting and frightening at the same time. This event was supposed to be the coming out of my relationship with Tony as his fiancée. I warned him that the media would spin something nefarious having seen me with two other celebrities in the past couple months. He assured me it would be okay and that everything was under control. Translation in my head: Everything was not okay, shit was going to hit the fan, and I'd be stuck in the middle of it.

Angelina told me the entire restaurant had been transformed into a swank open plan. All the tables had been moved into the warehouse adjacent to the restaurant and replaced with hi-boy tables. The signs said the restaurant was closed to the public but would be open the next day. Regardless of what happened tonight, this was my last full evening with the guys and I wanted to enjoy it. I just hoped we could. Tony had been acting incredibly strange all week. When I would enter a room he acted jumpy, would lose his thoughts mid-conversation, and was spending far too much time in the office. It was doing a number on Hector, too. The man seemed utterly lost over the last week. We'd had a wonderful time on St. Patrick's Day, and of course, the guys grilled me the next day about Wes, but after that, things became strained. Tony was coming and going more often, spending less time with Hector and me, and acting like a guy holding a giant secret.

The secret part is what frightened Hector the most. He'd said in all the years they'd been together they never kept secrets from one another. Angie assured Hector that everything was okay at work, and that Tony was more on top of things than ever before. He came in early, left late, and Angie confirmed all that. There wasn't someone else; Tony just seemed preoccupied with this new business change. Arguably, it would take the Fasano name from a good place to eat to a household name. When a product goes from being in twelve hundred locations to being in every grocery store across the nation, that came with a bit of pressure.

Hector agreed to give Tony some space and spent the week with me. He worked his normal eight to five, but didn't go in early or come home late like Tony did. We spent time at night going to movies, playing games, and drinking far too much wine to be healthy. Their story was fascinating, and Hector and I had become fast friends. He was going to be someone I knew for the rest of my life. Someone like Gin, Maddy, Alec and Wes. Someone I could count on. My group of friends was growing, and I was thrilled that I'd added Hector to that eclectic mix. Tony and his sister Angelina, too. Even with Tony being overworked since my arrival, we had our moments, and I appreciated him. He was a thirty-year-old man with a lot on his plate professionally and personally. I admired his drive, and his need to make everyone happy—everyone but himself and the one person who mattered most, Hector.

Hector was still there for him. "Sacrificing during this time," he'd said, "is what you do when you love someone. You put their needs in front of your own, and one day, he'll do the same for me." And seeing them together, even when strained, there was no lack for love, compassion, or trust there. They were just stuck in a weird situation and trying to do the best they could to get through it and find their common ground again. I hoped for their sakes they could find it. I didn't want to see them lose what was so beautiful to an outsider looking in.

As I was packing my phone rang.

"Hello?"

"Good morning, doll-face. You ready to leave the windy city?" My Aunt Millie's smooth voice came through the line.

"Not particularly. I've enjoyed it here. Tony and Hector are great guys."

"Tony and…what? Who's Hector?" she asked.

"Hector is Tony's partner."

"Anthony Fasano is gay? The hunky boxer with the god-like body?"

"That would be the one." I grinned and shook my head. She was like the fairy godmother of hot guys.

Auntie tsked in my ear. "Too good to be true. I knew it when I laid eyes on his portfolio there was something off. So, it looks like you won't be receiving that extra payout this time."

I laughed. "Are you always worried about money?"

"Cash is king, doll-face. You know that better than anyone right now. Speaking of cash, I've just emailed your next client. You're going to love this. So up your alley."

"Yeah, why's that?"

"Well, you're going to Boston, Massachusetts."

"Never been. What's in Boston and why will I love it?" Aside from the best baseball team in the known universe that is.

"Boys, baseballs, and beer," she laughed.

"Three of my very favorite things!" I exclaimed actually bouncing up and down a little. I did love a good baseball game. It's one of the few things that Pops and I did together growing up. Even if he was three sheets to the wind, he would always watch the game. The Red Sox were our favorite. Initially, it was because I liked that they had socks as their logo, but mostly it was because my dad liked them and it brought us together. Something that bonded us. As a ten-year-old kid with no mother, I pretty much tried anything to connect with the one parent I had. Even Maddy loved the games and the team. She'd love hearing that I was going to Boston.

"Yep, and it gets better!"

"No. Really?"

"Are you sitting down?"

I turned around and sat on the bed. "I am now."

"You're going to be the escort for the newest it boy on the Boston Red Sox, Mason Murphy."

"No way! I've heard of him. He currently holds the highest batting average and most runs for the year!"

Millie giggled. "Doesn't hurt that he's a looker. Young

Irish lad is your age, tall, and built to please a woman."

Thinking back to the last game I watched him in, I couldn't agree more. Even then I might have spent some extra time rewinding the DVR to view his backside in those tight, white pants more than once.

"This is amazing. But why would he need an escort?"

"Something about having a woman on his arm makes him seem more committed to the team and his image. His publicist thinks having a girlfriend for the first month of the season will take the pressure off, show advertisers he's a loyal type guy."

I cringed and pursed my lips. "Whatever. I'm thrilled. This is going to be fantastic! Send over the details for my flight and such. I should arrive early. I need to get all the beauty stuff done in advance."

"I'll book you in a hotel for the three days you're there prior to being with Mr. Murphy. One that has a fully loaded salon and spa. You deserve some downtime, to help you get your head in the game."

"Ha-ha, very funny. Sounds good. Thanks, Aunt Millie."

"Anything for my girl. Talk soon, doll-face."

"Bye."

★ ★ ★ ★

"You look stunning, Mia." Tony hugged me close when both Hector and I arrived. Hector tensed next to me, a nervous energy pouring off him in waves.

"Thank you. We missed you today." I said trying to express just how much.

Tony licked his lips and looked at Hector. Not so much looked as traced every inch of the Latino, his eyes filled with the intensity one has only for the person they love. Hector looked down and shook his head, a wide grin splitting across his face. "Hector," Tony said softly. "Perfection, *Papi*," he whispered close enough for only the two of us to hear.

"You look so good it hurts me," Hector said to Tony, clapping him on the back and bringing him into a manly hug. They held on for a touch longer than hetero men would, stood closer too, but not long enough to cause suspicion amongst the rest of the patrons milling about.

Mona Fasano spied us from across the room. Something was different about the way she approached me. Colder in a way I'd not felt from her since we'd met. She hugged me, but it wasn't genuine. She did the same to Hector. His eyebrows narrowed over her shoulder at mine. I shrugged. With Mona Fasano, a person never knew what was cooking. She was a mystery to me.

"Son, there are people you must schmooze. I have decided we should do the cookbook. Let's connect with the powers that be."

Tony laughed and both Hector and I took joy in it. The man had been so stressed all week that this was the first time since we'd all gone out together that he seemed more like himself. Somehow at ease in his skin.

"Okay Ma, I'll be there momentarily." Again, Mona looked at me then at Hector and shook her head sighing. Then she was off, grumbling something under her breath.

"What's with her?" I asked.

"She's unhappy."

"That's obvious. Care to share with the rest of class?"

"Not particularly. All will be revealed soon. How about you both get a drink and mingle. There is a place up front I'd like you both when we do opening announcements. Okay? Promise me you'll be up front with the family."

Hector's voice went low and he leaned forward so only the two of them were in earshot aside from me. "Baby, whatever you need tonight. You know that. I'm here for you."

"Forever?" Tony asked conspiratorially. It was really starting to wig me out. Tonight was off, though Tony was acting more at ease than he'd ever been. Was it because he was going to announce that he was getting married to the public? Was it the food line expanding? The cookbook and TV deals under negotiations? All of that sounded like more work and more stress, not less. And Tony was acting like everything this evening was peaches and cream. Then there was his mother who was clearly grumpy for an unknown reason and directing it at Hector and me.

"Always, you know that." Hector promised. "We'll be up front. Now, go do your thing and know...I am so proud of you."

Tony's arm came out and caressed Hector's hand. A couple people caught the movement, but he moved away before I could say anything.

"Tony's acting strange, right?" I asked Hector as his guy made it to a group of people in fancy dresses and suits.

"Yeah, something is up for sure, but he hasn't shared with me. That's not surprising though. Tony usually works through his demons and then lays them out for me. Usually, right before he's going to make his move. So whatever it is, he seems to be feeling better about it. Must have come to some decision about the business that's making him more like his old self."

"Touching you in front of others is more like his old self? His mother shooting daggers at us?"

"Yeah, neither of those things is normal. Not much we can do about it. Let's get a drink, find Angie, and see what's cooking."

We spent the next thirty minutes getting champagne, chatting it up with the rest of Tony's family and overall enjoying ourselves. A loud voice came over the speaker. "Can I have the crowd gather around?" said Tony standing at the podium.

"That's our cue." Hector led me to the front of the mini platform area to a table where family stood.

Tony stood on the stage in a pristine light grey suit. His frame was wider than the podium and his hands engulfed the microphone. The crowd went quiet and everyone gathered around and focused on Tony.

"I wanted to start by thanking you all for being here. The expansion of the Fasano name into the frozen foods sector was a dream of my father's, Joseph Anthony Fasano. He ran his company with fairness, pride, and loyalty to the brand. With my mother and my sisters, we, too, will continue that legacy through this new venture by ensuring our product is good quality, family-friendly, and affordable. Something we have always committed to."

The crowd clapped and a few whistles could be heard. "Thank you. Now the brand is considering a few additional ventures. One, Ma Fasano's cookbook." A roar of applause rang out. "Another is the TV show on the home cooking channel." Crowd went crazy. "The cooking show will be a

Fasano Family adventure. My mother, my sisters and my life partner will be a part of the new show."

Whoops, hollers, and applause drowned out the gasps from Hector and me. What the hell did he mean his mate? There was no way he was going to get me to stay on with him and help him snow over the American public.

"And that's what brings me to my biggest announcement. You've heard it all professionally and, now, personally. I want to introduce the public to the person I love most in this world. The one who has been with me through everything life has thrown at me and never once left my side. My partner. My one true love. My fiancé…if he'll have me."

He'll have me? Oh shit. Holy mother of God.

Beside me Hector's eyes were huge and filled to the brim with tears. They spilled over the moment Tony's hand came out, reaching for him. "Hector Chavez. I love you, I'll always love you. I want to spend the rest of my life loving you. This business, my family name is nothing if you don't share it with me."

And that was when Tony got down on one knee and opened a red velvet box. A slim gold band was inside. "Be mine forever. Marry me. Legally. Take my name. Build a family with me."

The entire room was dead silent. Not even a whisper could be heard.

"Get off the ground," Hector pulled Tony up from his knees. "My man kneels for no one. He stands proud as I do for him. I'd be honored to marry you, to take the Fasano name."

Tony smiled huge, pulled Hector to his side and turned to the audience. Pictures were flashing like crazy. The noise level reached a dull roar as the finality of what was taking place hit home. Anthony Fasano, boxer, businessman, family man, had just come out of the closet and asked his longtime boyfriend to marry him, take his name, and have babies with him.

Holy shitballs! This was an epic moment. I stood there and scanned every member of Tony's family. Starting from the left side with Giavanna and her husband.

"Giavanna, do you accept Hector as my fiancé and as your future brother-in-law?"

She smiled wide and nodded. "Yes," her voice sounded horse, but I could hear the emotion within it.

"Isabella, do you accept Hector as part of your family?"

"I do, always have. And I'm so happy for you," she turned and sobbed into her husband's neck.

"Sophia..."

He didn't even have to finish. "Finally, you came clean," she said and the crowd laughed. Tony held Hector close as tears streamed down his caramel-colored skin.

"Angie, Do you take Hector as an addition to your family?"

Instead of responding she jumped onto the stage and hugged them both. "I love you, I love you," she said and kissed each of them on the mouth. Crazy Italian's and their mouth kissing. Then she whispered something to each of them. Two pairs of eyes widened and Tony pulled back. He dropped to his knees pulled his sister in front of him and kissed her belly then placed his large hand over her stomach. The smile he held told everyone around what was happening.

I looked at Mona Fasano as she watched her children.

Tears were leaking from her eyes so fast it was as if a faucet had been turned on.

"My sister's going to have a baby. My sister has been trying for years and is going to have a baby!" Tony screamed to the crowd. Everyone clapped and whistled.

Angie got off the stage, ran over to her husband Rocko and flew into his arms. He caught her and spun her around.

"Ma," Tony said into the microphone. "Do we have your blessing to make Hector an official part of the family? I know you wanted me to settle down with a good Catholic girl and have grandchildren, but that is not what will make me happy. Hector and I will have those babies, Ma, with a surrogate. We've already discussed it." Hector nodded frantically. "I know this is hard for you to accept. Even when I told you early this week you knew this was coming. It's always been Hector, Ma."

Mona nodded and placed her hands over her mouth. The sobs shook her small frame. Tony came down from the platform, Hector close at his heels.

"I love you, Ma. But I love Hector, too. He's my future and I can't pretend anymore. I can't live my life by someone else's rules and sacrifice mine or Hector's happiness. It's not right."

Mona pulled her son into her arms. "Oh you stupid, stupid boy. I would have understood with time. I understand *love*. I understand when someone is your whole world. That's what your father was for me. If that's what Hector is for you, then nothing anyone thinks or says should stop you from being together. I love you. She pulled back. Both of you." She cupped Hector's cheek.

"Now you really will be my boy even though you

always have been, haven't you?"

Hector's tears fell once more and she wiped them away. "I want my boys to be happy." Mona said pulling them both into a tight hug.

And that was that. The rest of the night was a celebration. Of Hector and Tony, and Angelina and Rocko finally getting the baby they so wanted. Talking to Angelina later in the evening, I found out that Tony went to each sister's house this past week and told them individually that he was gay, that he was in love with Hector and was going to ask him to marry him. Apparently, the sisters had suspected all along, but had respected his privacy all these years and kept their opinions to themselves. Then when I came along none of them knew what to think.

Angelina had spent the week with Tony working around the clock to spin this new information into something that wouldn't tarnish the Fasano name. The PR guru was spreading a "Love comes in all forms" campaign to deflect any naysayers about the restaurant, and the TV show was thrilled with the news. Said their target demographic just expanded. They'd have a different day of the week devoted to each of the five siblings and the mother alone. They were beyond excited about the concept and loved having a day where Tony and Hector cooked together to offer something new to the gay community.

Overall, love had won out against all odds and the family would end up being stronger for it.

★ ★ ★ ★

The next morning bright and early, I dragged my stuff out

to the elevator. I thought back to the night before. The evening had been beautiful, ending with everyone excited about the possibilities, the company doing better than ever, the Fasano family growing exponentially and the talk of new adventures aplenty. Tony had even come clean about my involvement but left out the part about me being an escort. Instead, he used the term friend. After a month of sharing life with these guys, that's exactly what they were. My friends.

I set the note next to a fresh bottle of Jamison Irish Whiskey I'd picked up at the liquor store yesterday during my walk. I leaned forward and kissed the spot near my name and reread it once more.

Tony & Hector,

I leave you today with happiness in my heart and tears in my eyes. Knowing the two of you has opened my eyes to the fullness life has to offer if you only allow yourself to take the risks. You did, Tony, and now your life will forever be full. Maybe in the future I'll be able to do the same. Thank you for showing me what bravery looks like.

Hector, I will miss our talks, movie dates, and having you dress me. I always look better when you pick out my clothes <wink>. Seriously though, you have a lot of love in you, and I'm thankful that you shared it with me...as a friend.

Thank you both for sharing your lives with me. I couldn't be happier for the both of you. Keep me posted, and I expect a wedding invitation.

Your friend in all things,
~Mia

It was true. I learned a lot from Tony and Hector. To

not be afraid, to never let another person choose what my happiness looks like. I would take that knowledge with me through the rest of my journey, and let it guide me to the right path. For now, the path was taking me on a jet airplane to one Mason Murphy of Boston, Massachusetts.

THE END

Mia's journey continues in

April: Calendar Girl
(Available Now in eBook)

Calendar Girl: Volume Two
(Coming Soon)

ALSO BY AUDREY CARLAN

ACKNOWLEDGMENTS

Sarah Saunders, for giving Mia her name and helping me make her a bad ass! There's a lot of you in our girl and I love it!

To my editor **Ekatarina Sayanova** with Red Quill Editing, LLC, you 'get me" and my stories in a way I've never had before with an editor. You make me a better writer with every new edit. Thank you.

Heather White - Also known as my PA Goddess, sometimes I wonder what I did in this life to deserve such a selfless person in my life. I'm so happy I have you to tread this journey with. Trust the journey baby!

Ginelle Blanch - You've been with me since the beginning, never complained, always shared your support and busted out your betas efficiently and blown my mind every time with the crazy screw ups you find. You have an incredible eye for detail. Thank you for sharing your gift with me.

Jeananna Goodall - The woman who reads everything I write before I've even given it a second read through. I adore you. You make me want to write and believe in every story, sometimes more than I do. Thank you for always giving me hope.

Anita Shofner - My present and past-tense QUEEN... you prevent my characters from traveling in time and my manuscripts looking sparkly. We Expect Satisfaction...is your slogan. I guess we'll just have to see where the year takes our Mia.

Christine Benoit – Thank you reading and verifying that my French was accurate. Your language is beautiful. I very much enjoyed adding it into my book.

To **Audrey's Angels**, together we change the world. One book at a time. BESOS-4-LIFE lovely ladies.

To all the **Audrey Carlan Wicked Hot Readers**... you make me smile every day. Thank you for your support.

And last, but most definitely not least, my publisher **Waterhouse Press** – You're the extra in extraordinary. I couldn't be happier you found me and gave me a home to call my very own. Mad love.

ABOUT AUDREY CARLAN

Audrey Carlan lives in the sunny California Valley two hours away from the city, the beach, the mountains and the precious…the vineyards. She has been married to the love of her life for over a decade and has two young children that live up to their title of "Monster Madness" on a daily basis. When she's not writing wickedly hot romances, doing yoga, or sipping wine with her "soul sisters," three incredibly different and unique voices in her life, she can be found with her nose stuck in book or her Kindle. A hot, smutty, romantic book to be exact!

Any and all feedback is greatly appreciated and feeds the soul. You can contact Audrey below:

E-mail: carlan.audrey@gmail.com
Facebook: facebook.com/AudreyCarlan
Website: www.audreycarlan.com